D1519885

THE HOOVER PRINT

Robert Bitterli

Devin Lane Publishing

To and for my wife and best friend Judy

Whose encouragement and support is the catalyst for the completion of this and all those novels yet to come.

Thank You, Judy!

Devin Lane books may be purchased for educational, business, or sales promotional use. For information please write: Special Markets Department, Devin Lane Publishing, 603 West 13th St. building 1A, suite #293 Austin, TX 78701-1796.

First Edition: October, 1999

Cover designed by: Tamara Dever, TLC Graphics

Library of Congress Cataloging-in-Publication Data

Bitterli, Robert
        The Hoover Print / Robert L. Bitterli. — 1st ed.

        ISBN 1-893980-00-6

        LCCN 99-90133

Acknowledgments

The Hoover Print is a work of fiction. Any portrayals of J. Edgar Hoover participating in immoral or illegal activities in this novel, were in the sole interest of enhancing the fictional aspects of this story.

"At the end of his reign, a king shall be judged, not by the vastness of his kingdom, or the power he held over his people. But by whether his subject's lives were made better."

His Royal Highness Amuela Boinya
King of Cameroon

Yaounde, Cameroon, Africa
The Presidential Palace
September 1, 1969, 11:15 p.m.

Furandi Bello, the son of President Mafany Boinya's closest friend, burst into the president's night chambers. The men with him were dragging two dead children by their feet, smearing wide streaks of blood across the floor. They tossed the children at the foot of the president's bed. It took a moment for the shock to register with the president's wife, and when it did, her screams echoed throughout the palace. Without hesitation, Furandi Bello shot the president's wife between the eyes. He then faced President Boinya, smiled, and shot him dead.

Washington, D.C.
1135 Eastman Avenue
September 1, 1969, 10:00 p.m.

Winston Barber, his wife, and their seven-year-old daughter had just returned from a civil rights rally at which Winston was a keynote speaker. As they entered their home, two men sitting in their living room stood up and startled them. Winston was pushing his family back out the front door when one of the men yelled after them.

"Stop! Get back here, boy! We're FBI!"

Winston stopped at the threshold of the door, shielding his family with his body. He checked out the men; their FBI badges were draped over the breast pockets of their dark blue suits. Satisfied that they were indeed the FBI, Winston brought his family back in to the house.

His daughter was peering around his body to get a better look, when Winston sent her to her room. As she was leaving, one of the FBI agents grabbed her by the arm and violently jerked her next to him. When her mother leaped forward to grab her daughter the agent shoved her across the room into the brick fireplace. A stunned Winston grabbed the agent's arm, forcing him to release his daughter. Without warning, the second agent shot Winston in the back. Both mother and daughter let out blood-curdling screams. The agent who had grabbed the little girl reached inside his suit jacket, for his gun and shot the mother in the head.

The little girl was up and out the front door, disappearing into the night, before either agent could react. The agents searched the area for hours, finally having to abandon their search for fear of being spotted.

Agent Ballard stopped to place a call. A stoic monotone voice answered.

"Yeah."

"Sir, it's Ballard. The situation with the African has been handled."

"Good, I want to see the two of you in my office in the morning."

"Mr. Hoover, sir, there is one minor problem."

"What's that, Ballard?"

"The girl—she got away."

"What do you mean she got away? Find her!"

"Yes sir." The phone went dead.

Hoover hesitated a moment and then dialed another number.

"Sir, the FBI completed its part of the operation. Have you heard from Cedes?"

"Yes, he just called. The CIA was successful on their end as well. We should be totally in control within the month.

"Cedes thinks we may have bought ourselves more trouble than we intended in tying our future to the Bellos."

"He may be right, John. You'll want to be careful, remember in six years they'll officially be your headache. I don't think Bello senior will be a problem, but his kid Furandi seems a bit unbalanced. Let's just pray his old man stays around a long time."

"I hope you're right about the six-year part. This should lock up Brook's support."

"I hope so, because the Boinyas were well-liked in Cameroon. The Bello regime is going to be much more brutal."

"Maybe so, but they will be much more receptive to U.S. business. We also got them to agree to give us military access to the port of Duoala. If Ackerman would just get his head out of his butt, he would see how important Cameroon is, as a launching point into the rest of Africa."

"I think he understands the strategic importance of Cameroon, John, he just wasn't prepared to pay the price for its cooperation."

"That's why I'm not sure I should wait six years."

"Even with Brook's support, unseating a popular incumbent president would be difficult and may leave you extremely bloody. It's best to bide our time. As long as Cameroon is still open, you'll have Brook's support."

"It's just frustrating watching someone that weak leading our country. What about your people who did the job— are you sure we can count on their discretion?"

"Of course; their loyalty is to me. They're part of an elite group of men that take care of special assignments for me at the agency."

"I hope you're right, Edgar, because if Ackerman finds out about this, we're both finished. I don't just mean in politics either."

"Don't worry, John, everything is under control."

"OK then, I'll see you for lunch on Wednesday."

Hoover hung up and dialed another number. A young woman answered.

"Venture Oil, may I help you?"

"I thought this was Walter's private line."

"It is, one moment please."

Hoover could hear the young lady giggle and then a man's voice came on the line.

"This is Walter."

"Walter, it's Hoover. I just talked to John; he says that you should be able to turn on the pumps in Cameroon by the end of the month."

"It's about time. I assume that we're dealing with the Bellos now?"

"As of about a half hour ago."

"What about the brother you were telling me about? What's the chance of him returning to Cameroon and taking over?"

"He won't be returning to Cameroon."

"Good, will I see you at lunch on Wednesday?"

"Of course; I wouldn't miss this one."

J. Edgar Hoover hung up the phone and called his office. When the recorded voice of his secretary answered, he left her a message. "Marge, please schedule lunch with the vice president and Walter Brooks for this Wednesday at the vice-president's residence." He hung up the phone and turned off the tape recorder. Hoover had been taping his conversations since he first started working at the Department of Justice.

Washington, D.C.
Federal Courthouse
September 1, 1999

The door between the private chambers and the private bathroom of Federal Judge Phillip Walker opened. A janitor entered, African American, with short salt-and-pepper hair, heavy eyebrows, and a thin black mustache. He wore faded coveralls, heavy work boots, kitchen gloves, and walked slightly stooped over. He pushed a mop bucket containing dirty water and an old mop, but did not turn on the light. The judge's bathroom provided privacy, and a small mirrored window had an excellent view of both the street and the steps below.

By 5:55, there was enough dawning light in the room for the janitor to work. He pulled the mop out of the bucket, unscrewed the handle from the mop-head, and withdrew a long tube from the hollow handle. He turned the bucket upside down and dumped the soapy water on the floor. He removed the false bottom of the bucket, pulled out a trigger housing and two rounds of ammunition: one approximately three inches long with a gold tip, and the other an inch shorter with a silver tip. He assembled the trigger housing and the tube, and inserted the silver-tipped cartridge.

He withdrew a cigar tin from his pocket, unscrewed both ends, and snapped it into place on top of the tube. Without opening the bathroom window, he looked through the scope and fixed the crosshairs on the back of one of the agents standing on the courthouse steps. He made some adjustments, opened the window, pressed a button on his sight and initiated the targeting laser. He peered through the scope and saw a red dot appear on the bald spot of the agent's head.

He then looked to the building across the street, found a window and sighted on it. Once he was satisfied that the red dot had found the right window, he set the weapon down and closed the window.

The janitor again reached into his overall pocket, pulling out a small jewelry box about 1-inch long, °-inch wide and °-inch high. From the box he extracted a flexible plastic thimble, placed it on his right thumb over the kitchen glove, and pressed his thumb down on the windowsill. He removed the thimble, replaced it in the box, and returned it to his overalls. The janitor sat down next to the window and waited.

At exactly 6:05 a.m., a black Chevy Suburban pulled up in front of the courthouse. Two FBI agents appeared from inside the courthouse, propped the doors open, and started down the courthouse steps. As they were moving down the steps, they scanned the buildings across the street for any unusual activity. As the Suburban stopped, the agents checked the streets for anyone that may have been following. Once they declared the area clear, two Secret Service agents emerged from inside the Suburban and joined their associates to form a V. The agents knew the height of the Suburban would protect their subject until the back of the V was formed. Eighty-five-year old former President John Canfield stepped out of the Suburban and into the middle of the V. Two additional agents followed and closed the V behind him. Six agents in a tight V formation making its way up the courthouse steps now surrounded former President Canfield, including those helping him up the steps.

In the judge's bathroom, with the window still closed, the janitor was watching the procession make its way up the steps. He had picked his spot and would wait for them to get there before he risked exposure. He was preparing mentally as the procession approached the second landing of the courthouse steps. That was when he would act. While moving up the steps, the height of the agents would obscure the former president— on the landing, however, he would be momentarily exposed to the janitor, especially from his angle and position.

As the front of the party reached the landing, the janitor opened the window, aimed at the group, and as President Canfield was helped up onto the landing, his head and shoulders came into clear view and without hesitation the janitor fired the silver-tipped round. Not waiting to see if the bullet found its mark, the janitor chambered the second round, aimed at the window across the street, and fired the gold-tipped round. He closed the window, disassembled the mop and its handle, replaced the trigger-housing and sight into the false bottom of the mop bucket, added water from the washbasin, mopped up the spilled water, and headed out of the judge's private bath and chambers into the courthouse hallway.

On the steps of the courthouse, Special Agent Richard Nolan thought he saw a flash, but before he could respond, the head of President John Canfield literally exploded and covered the agents in blood and skull fragments.

At almost the same time, the other agents heard a loud bang from across the street and as they instinctively turned their heads in that direction, they saw the last fragments from a broken window fall to the ground.

No more than one minute passed from the time the janitor fired the first round to the time FBI agents were entering the building across from the Federal Courthouse, and in another three minutes they had the building totally surrounded.

All FBI and Secret Service agents and other law enforcement officers were pulled from the courthouse to help secure the building across the street, leaving only the security guards at the metal detectors.

The janitor left the elevator in the basement and pushed his mop bucket through the metal detector as he went to exit the building. As expected, the mop bucket set off the metal detector, the guard got up, walked around the desk, and looked into the bucket. He kicked the bucket, watched the water swish back and forth for a couple of seconds, and then waved the janitor on. Once outside, the janitor threw out the water, picked up the bucket, and slowly walked to an old van parked behind the courthouse.

As the janitor drove away, he glanced into the rearview mirror and couldn't help but smile at the activity surrounding the wrong building.

Chapter 1

Scott Peterson, Assistant Director in Charge (ADIC) of the FBI's Washington D.C. field office, had just stepped out of the shower and was drying himself when his wife, not yet fully awake, entered the bathroom and gave him a look that said "it's too damned early for this," and handed him the phone. Scott smiled and tried to kiss his wife on the cheek but all he got was the back of her head as she turned and walked out. Scott knew this was much too early for a social call so he put on his professional voice.

"This is Peterson."

"Sir, this is Special Agent Nolan. We have a situation at the Federal Courthouse."

"At this time of day? Court's not even in session yet."

"I'm sorry sir, but it's President Canfield."

"Oh yes, today is the swearing in of his grandson. I guess he's going to be a judge. Please don't tell me that Canfield had a heart attack at the swearing in?"

"No sir; President Canfield was assassinated on the way into the courthouse."

"What! What the hell do you mean assassinated? The man is in his late eighties for God's sake—who the hell would want to kill him?"

"We don't know sir, but he was shot from long range with some kind of explosive bullet."

"Jesus Christ, I hope you guys have the shooter."

"We believe we have him trapped inside the Cooper building directly across from the courthouse."

"What do you mean you believe? Do you or don't you?"

"The shooting occurred less than five minutes ago and we had the building sealed off within seconds after the shot was fired. No one had time to get out of that building since President Canfield was shot."

"Good—who's in charge down there?"

"Special Agent Gibson, sir. He's now directing the search of the building."

"Good; what about the Secret Service and the locals—I assume the Secret Service is in total chaos?"

"They did want to take over the investigation, but Agent Gibson wouldn't hear of it."

"He should have let them have it. This one is going to be a headache. Is the area locked down?"

"Sir, the police are putting up the roadblocks and since the gun shot seemed to come from the Cooper building and most of us witnessed activity there, Agent Gibson didn't find it necessary to divert any of our resources to securing the Federal Building."

"What the hell are you talking about? A former president just got shot! I want the whole damned town shut down! I'll be there as quickly as I can. Meanwhile, have Gibson lock down the Federal Building. I want this guy, so make sure the locals don't let anyone through their web."

"Will do, sir."

Scott Peterson didn't wait for Special Agent Nolan to sign off. He hung up the phone and called his boss, Martin Flynn, the Director of the FBI.

"Mr. Director, it's Scott."

"Scott, what's going on? It's a bit early?"

"It looks like somebody assassinated former President Canfield."

"Shit? Canfield! Who did it? Why the hell would anyone kill Canfield?"

"We don't know, sir. The guys at the scene think they have him trapped."

"Well, thank God for that. Who is in charge down there?"

"Special Agent Gibson assumed responsibility."

"Where the hell is the Secret Service?"

"Gibson was well within his right to assume responsibility. Based on the Violent Crimes program, once Canfield was shot, he became our responsibility."

"Damn it, Scott, I know the rules; but if they don't have this killer cornered then we're going to be the ones catching hell. Does this Gibson have much experience?"

"I don't think so, sir. He's mainly been working protective details."

"Scott, I want you to get down there and take over until the response team gets there. I'm sure you won't be offended if I tell you that we're going to run this case from HQ instead of your field office."

"No sir, not at all."

"You'd better get going."

"Yes sir."

Scott Peterson was about to put the phone back in its cradle on the nightstand, when he changed his mind and dialed another number.

"Tom, it's Scott."

"Scott, it's a bit early, isn't it?"

"Well, you know what they say, "The early bird gets to be the next director.""

"So what does the next director want at this time of morning?"

"President Canfield was just shot, right in front of the Federal Building."

"What do you mean shot? He's damn near a hundred years old. Why would some sick SOB bother shooting him?"

"I don't know yet."

"You'd better find out or you'll never make director."

"Right now I'm not so worried about that. I'm more concerned about getting this guy. He doesn't sound like a wacko. From what I gather, he was shot with a sniper rifle."

"Have they got him?"

"Gibson thinks he has him trapped in the Cooper building."

"Good—so why are you calling me?"

"It just doesn't feel right. Everyone apparently saw something at the Cooper building and I guess there was even some debris. That sounds pretty clumsy for a professional hit man."

"Let's face it, Scott, some of those nuts aren't known for being the brightest people in the world."

"It just feels funny. Why would anyone kill an eighty five-year-old ex-president? This assassin goes through all of the trouble to set himself up across the street, yet he's dumb enough to shatter a window when he fires the shot. It's just too convenient; it's too easy. That idiot Gibson didn't even seal off the Federal Courthouse. I think our guy is long gone and I'm pretty sure the hit took place from the courthouse."

"OK, Scott—Gibson may have made a mistake by not locking down the courthouse, but that still doesn't answer why you're calling me. You know I'm on special assignment."

"That's why I'm calling you, Tom. I have a real bad feeling, call it intuition, call it psychic, or just call it a gut feeling, but I think this could be your assignment."

"That's a pretty big leap, Scott. Are you trying to tell me they found the print?"

"No I'm not; I just think they will. If it's him, I want to know and I want him caught."

"Is there some kind of link between President Canfield and Hoover's last two targets; the ADIC of the New York City office or Canon?"

"None that I know of. I don't even know if ADIC Ballard and President Canfield knew each other. I would just like you on the scene."

"OK Scott, I'll check it out. Just make sure Gibson knows I'm coming—I don't want any territorial attitude when I get there."

"Don't worry, Tom. I'm headed there myself and I'll by the there by the time you show up."

"OK, I'll see you in about thirty minutes."

Special Agent Tom West had just finished his eighteenth year with the FBI. He had enjoyed a very successful career. He was the youngest agent on the short list to head the FBI's Special Crimes division.

Shortly after missing out on the position of Deputy Director for Special Crimes, he was asked to head up a special task force. A security expert for one of the largest oil companies in the world was found slumped over in his recliner, dead. He had been shot in the middle of his forehead with his own revolver. A FBI badge was pinned to his sweater. William Canon turned out to be an ex-FBI agent turned security specialist, joining Venture Global in 1972, when the company was still known as Venture Oil.

Tom West was brought in when the National Center for the Analysis of Violent Crime (NCAVC) connected this case with the unsolved murder of an FBI agent ten years earlier. Michael Ballard, Assistant Director in Charge, of the New York City field office, had been shot in the back, in his own home, with his own gun.

ADIC Ballard was found face down; his 45 automatic was next to his right hand. His FBI badge had been placed on his back next to an entrance wound the size of a quarter.

The case took an unexpected turn when the only clue found at the scene was J. Edgar Hoover's right thumbprint on the grip of Ballard's service revolver. The NCAVC matched the cases when that same unusual thumbprint appeared at the scene of William Canon's murder, and by the obvious focus on the FBI badges. Although Tom had been passed over as director of the Special Crimes division, he was still considered the top investigator in the bureau, and as such was assigned to head the task force by the director himself.

West's investigation discovered that both Ballard and William Canon had served together under Hoover in 1969. William Canon left the FBI and joined Venture Oil after Hoover's death in 1972. They worked in what at the time was called the "special projects unit." Few senior agents, especially the ones around at the time, would discuss the special projects unit, except to say that it reported directly to J. Edgar Hoover.

Tom's investigation failed to uncover anything about the special projects unit or any specific cases that could link J. Edgar Hoover, Mark Ballard, and William Cannon in any way that would explain the two deaths and the fingerprints. Tom, of course, had no evidence or clues other than the badges and the thumbprints.

What he did have were lots of suspects. Ballard had been involved in hundreds of cases that resulted in sending many people to jail for a good portion of their lives. Any one of those would have had a motive to shoot him. None, however, would have, had access to Hoover's thumbprint, nor would that provide a motive for the murder of Canon.

His team was in the process of reviewing all cases on which Ballard and Canon worked together. This was made difficult by the lack of computerization of Hoover's private files and by the lack of access to any files of the special projects unit's cases. He was no closer to catching the "Hoover" killer than he was the first day he was assigned the case.

Now here he was, heading to another crime scene and hoping that either the assassin was caught and it was the "Hoover Killer," or if he wasn't caught that there would be no clues or fingerprints of any kind.

Chapter 2

As Scott promised, when Tom arrived at the scene, he and Gibson were waiting for him, neither looking too happy. Tom had known Scott a long time and they had worked together on many cases. They respected each other's work and even liked each other. On the other hand, Tom had only seen Gibson in the halls of the FBI building and was familiar with his work only through what he read in summaries and after-action reports. From what he had read, Special Agent Gibson was adequate but was probably working beyond his abilities.

Tom hated to step on any other agent's case, even if it were Gibson's, and particularly one this sensitive. In his own way, Tom let Gibson know that he was there at the request of Gibson's boss.

"OK Scott, you called me out here, so what do you have?"

While he was talking, Tom shook Scott's hand and walked over and extended his hand to Gibson.

"Gibson, it looks like your morning started with a roar." Special Agent Gibson shook Tom's hand with a sour look on his face as Scott began to bring Tom up to speed.

"Here's what we have so far. At approximately 6:10 a.m., President Canfield was being escorted in a standard protective wedge up the courthouse steps when he was shot as the wedge reached the first landing. The bullet exploded on impact and as a result, President Canfield's brains were splattered over several Secret Service and FBI agents. At the same time several of our agents saw a flicker of light, heard a rifle shot, and saw some glass debris fall from one of the windows of the Cooper building.

Agent Gibson immediately secured the Cooper building and began a systematic search of the building. He'd secured the office from which he believed the shot was fired and closed off the surrounding streets, as well as the Federal Building."

Tom nodded his approval. "Good work, Gibson. How long was it before you locked down the Federal Courthouse?" Gibson was a little surprised at the question. He was expecting questions about the Cooper building, not the courthouse. "I guess it was about twenty to twenty-five minutes after the shooting."

Tom glanced at Scott and could see the same thought running through his mind "they're wasting their time in the Cooper building". Before he said anything, however, Tom wanted to be sure.

"Scott said your people heard a shot at the same time that the president's head exploded. Now did they hear it at the same time or a split second later?"

"I'm not sure but I think they were saying that they heard the sound at the same time."

"OK, how about the office with the broken window—what did you find in it?"

"Nothing yet; it looks like it's a conference room and I'm waiting for our lab boys to get here and go over it."

"Would you mind if we took a look at it while we're waiting?"

Agent Gibson was getting a little uncomfortable. This was his investigation, his case, yet this guy comes in like it's his and Agent Peterson doesn't seem to be stopping him. Gibson looked at Peterson, who nodded his head in confirmation; Gibson had no choice but to agree.

"OK, as long as we don't mess things up. The lab boys still need to go through it."

Both Scott and Tom let a hint of a smile show, knowing that each had gone through this many more times than Gibson and for that matter more times than Gibson ever would. Both also knew that they were putting him in an embarrassing situation; so they just nodded and let the comment pass.

The Cooper building was a twenty-four-story building, and as such would take all day to do a floor-by-floor search for the assassin. As they made their way to the elevator, Scott and Tom could see that the search was still on the first two floors. Although they didn't say anything, they hoped that Gibson had enough sense to start a simultaneous search on the roof and the floor from where they thought the killer fired.

They reached the eighth floor and were relieved to see that Gibson had at least started a search on that floor. As they passed an FBI agent guarding the conference room Tom could see fragments of glass on the carpet below the window and some smaller pieces on the carpet further away from the window. His suspicions were confirmed but he needed one more piece of evidence before he had Scott call off this circus.

He walked to the window, looked out across the street at the Federal Courthouse for a minute and then did an about face. He looked at the opposite wall of the conference room, walked over to the large map hanging there, and studied it for a moment before calling Scott over.

"Scott, do you see what I see just south of Dallas?"

"Damn! Is that what I think it is?"

"I'm afraid so, Scott. I suggest you shut down this circus and open it back up across the street at the Courthouse."

Agent Gibson's irritation was now beginning to show. "Would someone tell me what's going on here?"

Scott was about to jump on Agent Gibson for his incompetence when he caught himself. "It's pretty simple. Our assassin is no longer here; in fact he never was here. If you look at the spot on the map under Dallas near Waxahachie, you'll find a bullet. That bullet was probably fired from the Courthouse across the street into this building to draw your attention this way. It probably had some kind of explosive head on it so that it would make the noise that your men heard. Take a look at the glass pattern on the floor, it's from the window into the room. There's glass five feet from the window. That wouldn't have happened if the glass had been broken from the inside out."

Scott laid out the rest of the probable scenario to Agent Gibson. "There were two shots fired from the Courthouse, the first was very professional, very clean, and very quiet. No one saw it, heard it, or felt it until the president's head was on everyone's suit. The second was fired within a split second of the first and was fired directly into this room from one of those offices across the street. It was noisy and messy, yet every bit as professional as the first bullet, because this one was designed to be noisy and messy.

"This guy is good. He was able to trick the eyes and ears of trained agents to think that the second shot was the first. Ordinarily our agents would have been able to pick up the timing difference between impact and the time they heard the shots. However, since this was the only shot they heard, and they saw the glass fall, along with the shock of finding the president's head exploded, that was enough for them to assume that the shot that killed the president came from this building. This guy is very good and certainly very long gone!"

Agent Gibson's face turned white as he slumped into a chair. "Oh my God, that means I let the killer get away. I let him walk right out the door while we were chasing ghosts over here."

Scott was watching Gibson and could see that he was beginning to lose perspective. This was something they couldn't afford right now.

"You're right, Agent Gibson, we did let the killer get away. It's too late to worry about that now. We need to get over to the courthouse and see if we can salvage anything. We need to find where the shot came from and see if we can pick up any clues or evidence. Move your people across the street to the courthouse. I want to talk to all of them on the steps in front of the courthouse in about fifteen minutes. Tell the local police they can open the streets up and have them investigate and report all abandoned or stolen cars in the city for the next twenty-four hours. Our guy is long gone but maybe he left something behind."

Tom was watching Gibson while Scott spoke and could tell Gibson was still feeling sorry for himself. Although the more time Tom spent with Gibson the more he found him to be incompetent, they still needed him to act quickly and with some degree of confidence. So Tom decided to bring a sense of urgency back to Gibson. "OK, it's 7:15; people are going to want to get into their offices and the night crew and night shift are going to want to leave. We need to make sure everyone is accounted for and that no one leaves the building until they are interviewed by one of us. So you need to get over there and secure all of the surveillance tapes for this morning and keep all the guards and other personnel in place until we get there."

Gibson didn't wait for Tom and Scott—he pulled his radio out of his belt and they could hear him shouting instructions as he was running down the hall.

Scott and Tom sat down at the conference table, looked at each other and shook their heads. Tom was the first to speak. "My friend, you do have a problem. Gibson is worse than his after-action reports make him sound. If you want this investigation handled properly and you don't want to be crucified in the press, you're going to have to take it over. I think he's just a little incompetent."

Scott grinned as he answered. "He does seem a bit slow, doesn't he? I have this funny feeling though, that this isn't going to be my problem for very long. I think we're going to find Hoover's thumbprint in that courthouse."

"Think so? Take a good look at all those windows over there. Your boy has probably already let half of the occupants back in that building. If there ever were any prints, they're all gone by now. Besides that, it will take Gibson a year to dust and print all of those offices."

"That's true, but Gibson doesn't have the experience that you and I have. We could probably narrow his search down to four or five floors."

"Oh, I understand; you want me to help you, find evidence that will allow you to pawn this case off on me, so that you can continue your quest for the director's chair."

"Tom, I do believe you understand. Just remember, though, you'll always have a friend in the director's chair." Tom got up walked to the window and looked out at the Courthouse. In a more serious and somber tone he replied to Scott's last comment.

"I'm going to need a friend in the director's chair. Because this Hoover Killer is good and if he doesn't make a mistake we may never catch him. This has to be one of the most perplexing cases the FBI has ever handled. Who in the hell would want to kill a hundred-year-old ex-president?"

"I don't know," Scott said "but he was only eighty-five."

"Do you remember when he was president?" Tom asked.

"He was president for eight years. I think in the `seventies and early `eighties."

"There goes any connection with Hoover and those two FBI guys. As you know, Hoover died in 1972," Tom said, with a hint of satisfaction.

"True, but Canfield was vice-president for eight years before he was president—that would put him right in the middle of Hoover's tenure as director," Scott shot back at Tom.

"Maybe so, but don't get too excited, we still haven't found the print."

Scott couldn't help but smile. "With Gibson on the job, we're only minutes away."

Tom turned from the window, gave Scott one of those "screw you" looks and walked back to the map. He looked between the spot on the map and the window several times. "OK Scott, five through ten."

"What are you talking about, Tom? What's five through ten?"

"Floors five through ten. Have Gibson concentrate his search on floors five through ten. That should give him more realistic search parameters. When we get over there we may be able to tighten them even more."

Scott got up looked at the map, brought his eyes level with the bullet, looked across to the window and nodded in agreement. "Five through ten it is. Let's go give Gibson the good news and meet with his men. We need to get those interviews started so that those poor people can go home. Plus, the press is probably all over the director. That means he'll be all over us if we don't give him something soon."

When they got to the courthouse steps they were impressed. Gibson had been able to commandeer about fifty FBI and Secret Service agents, some in suits, some in riot gear, and a few in shorts. Gibson was talking to two men when Tom and Scott walked up.

"Gentlemen, this is Special Agent Kirkland; he's in charge of security for this building, and this is Mr. Jenkins; he's in charge of the maintenance crews. Agent Kirkland was about to replace the night shift with the day shift, so a lot of these agents out here are his."

Now Tom and Scott understood how Gibson was able to get so many agents here so quickly. Before Scott could address the agents he needed some answers.

"Agent Kirkland, how many agents do you have on the night shift?" Scott asked.

"There are a total of eight at night. Each entrance on the main floor has one stationary agent and there are four entrances on the main floor. The basement has two exits and there is an agent at each of those. The other two agents are positioned in the security room, monitoring the security cameras."

"Are there metal detectors at all of the exits?"

"Yes, on both the main floor and the basement exits."

"Agent Kirkland, why didn't you put on extra agents for this crucial detail?"

"Don't try to lay this fiasco on my doorstep. We were told that you would be bringing the president at 8:00. I typically run two people at every exit during the day, four in the security room, and four rovers—that's twenty people. For today I added four on the roof, two on the stairs between the first and second floors, and two more in the second floor hallway outside of the courtroom where President Canfield was to swear in his grandson. That, in addition to the agents coming with him, should have been enough. Unfortunately, my additional people weren't due here until 7:00. We had adequate security laid on. You guys just forgot to tell us that you changed your arrival time."

Scott's face turned red. "I sure as hell hope you're kidding me, Kirkland."

Special Agent Kirkland handed Scott a copy of the briefing document, which specified an 8 a.m. arrival.

"You know damned well I'm not kidding. We usually make shift changes at 7:30. Today I had an 8:30 shift change scheduled, with the day shift reporting for duty at 7:00. That gave us an hour and a half of overlapping security with 38 of my people and whatever you brought in."

Scott turned to Gibson, ready to explode when Tom stepped between them.

"This is obviously something that we'll have to get into in the after-action report. Right now though, we need to get into that building and see what we can find." Tom turned to Mr. Jenkins. "Mr. Jenkins, how many people on your night cleaning crew?"

"Twenty-five, one on each floor except for the first two which have two people each and one supervisor," Mr. Jenkins answered.

Tom continued to press, giving Scott a chance to cool off. "Are all of your people accounted for?"

"No, not yet."

"Why not? Where are they?"

"My crew gets off at 6:00 and they must vacate the building by 6:30. They all have to leave by the basement exit. Those are the rules in our contract. I doubt that most of them have even made their way home yet."

Scott had heard enough. He could no longer be contained. He pushed Tom aside and stared at Gibson. "Wait, don't tell me—you let twenty-five people dressed as janitors walk out of the building within minutes of a presidential assassination."

Gibson's jaw tightened and his fists clenched as if he was trying to keep himself from exploding. As far as he was concerned this was not his fault.

"We weren't focused on the courthouse plus, the Secret Service didn't tell me that we were going to have twenty-five janitors leave the building through the basement between six and six-thirty," Agent Gibson insisted.

Scott took a deep breath, and put his right index finger into Gibson's chest to make sure that he got the message. "Don't you think that as head of the FBI's presidential security team, it was your responsibility to find that out? Don't make any long term plans—you and I are going to have a long talk about your career when this is over."

Tom didn't want this to escalate on the steps of the courthouse. "Scott, right now we need all the help we can get and we better begin searching."

Scott regained his composure, nodded at Tom and took the investigation to its next stage. "I want to see everyone in the security room. We'll be reviewing a lot of tapes while Mr. Jenkins tracks down his crew."

Scott talked to all of the agents assembled. He broke them down into six groups and assigned each group a floor. He instructed them to work the side of the courthouse facing the Cooper building.

Once in the security room, no one really knew what they were looking for. They had plenty of tape to look at. Each floor had a camera monitoring the hall, and there was a camera in each stairwell and a camera at each exit over the metal detector. Tom and Scott thought it best to start with floors 5,6,7,8,9, and 10 and to start at 5:30. with the hall cameras. Their hope was to find some inconsistency, someone or something that didn't belong. Mr. Jenkins focused on contacting his people, especially those working on floors 5 through 10. He also reviewed the videotapes from the exit cameras for the time period between 5:45 and 6:30.

By 8:30 they had reviewed the appropriate tapes at least once and found no anomalies. Janitors on each floor could be seen going into and coming out of offices the same way, showing no apparent signs of impatience or nervousness.

Mr. Jenkins had been able to contact all of his people except those on floors seven and nine. The exit videos showed that all twenty-five of the janitors were out of the building by 6:23, although they did have to back up the videos to 5:30 to find a couple that had left early.

Without better clues to follow, Scott and Tom reassigned the teams from floors eight and ten to assist the team on floor nine and to have the teams from five and six assist on seven. One of Jenkins' people brought in photos of all of the janitors scheduled to work the night shift. Jenkins and Agent Gibson compared those photos to the videos of the janitors leaving the building. The janitor working floor nine definitely matched his photo; the janitors on floors 5 and 7 matched at first glance, but didn't hold up under closer scrutiny.

It was now 9 o'clock and Scott had to make a decision. He would have to brief the director and the president very soon. The media had to be going nuts by now. He and Tom took one last look at the tapes of floors 5,7, and 9. Tom's face lit up as he was watching all three monitors—he had found the incongruity.

"Freeze floor five, now run floor nine until the janitor goes into the next office. Freeze it there. Now run floor seven to the same spot and freeze it." When they were all aligned he slapped both hands on his head and exclaimed.

"There it is!"

Scott couldn't see whatever it was that Tom saw. "OK buddy, I give, I don't see it. What did you find?"

"What time do you see on each of the tapes?"

"5:45 on the fifth floor, 5:51 on the seventh floor and 5:48 on the ninth floor."

"Good, so based on the fact that they all get off at six, we can assume that they're going in to clean their last office before they get off."

"OK Tom, I'm with you so far."

"Then take a look at where the janitors on five and nine are, and then look at the janitor on seven."

All at once it hit Scott. He could hardly believe they'd missed it earlier. "Damn it Tom, you're right! Five and nine are at the end of the hall where you would normally expect them to finish and the guy on seven is in the middle of the hall."

"I bet if we check every janitor in the building we'll find that they all finish at one end or the other. I bet this will be the only one that finishes in the middle."

"I sure as hell wouldn't bet against you. Good catch, Tom. This, along with a questionable match on the photo and the fact that we haven't been able to contact him does it for me. Go ahead and release the rest of the building. Let everyone in except those on the seventh floor. Let's find out whose office that is and take a look."

On his way to the seventh floor Tom was getting excited. If this was the "Hoover Killer," they may actually have him on video. They had never been this close. This could be the killer's first mistake.

21

On the seventh floor, they were directed to Judge Philip Walker's office. They were also radioed that Judge Walker was on his way up and they were not to enter his office until he was present.

Gibson, feeling the frustrations of the morning, finally had someone to strike out at. "We're conducting an investigation of a presidential assassination—who the hell does he think he is?"

Scott was a little more practical. "The killer's already gone and we could use a judge on our side. Two more minutes won't hurt us."

Judge Walker looked like he belonged to his name. He was about 6'2" and about 220 pounds. His erect posture made him appear even taller. As he approached, he took a handkerchief out of his pocket and placed it on the doorknob before he inserted the key and entered his office. "Come on in gentleman, let me take a look around and see if anything is out of place before you bring your boys in."

Scott instantly liked this guy. He had a no nonsense approach and he seemed to know what he was doing. "Thank you judge; I'm Assistant Director Peterson, this is Special Agent West, and Special Agent Gibson."

"Peterson, I know both you and West by reputation; I'm glad you guys are on this. There doesn't seem to be anything out of place. Gibson, did this happen on your watch?"

"I'm afraid so, sir."

"Well, don't worry about it. If these two hotshots live up to their reputations they'll have this wrapped up before lunch."

Scott and Tom put on their gloves as they wandered around the judge's office. The window that gave access to the courthouse steps was blocked by a credenza filled with books and papers. Tom was about to ask the judge what the side door led to when Gibson opened it and walked into a private bathroom. Tom caught the judge's surprise at Gibson's actions and tried to cover for him.

"We had already noticed that the assassin was wearing gloves; that's why agent Gibson didn't bother putting his on."

The judge gave Tom and Scott a look that said, "Don't try to blow smoke up my ass! This guy is stupid."

Gibson's face turned bright red as he turned and saw both Tom and Scott had their gloves on and even the judge was still holding his handkerchief. He felt like a rookie. He forgot to notify the security team of the time change, he let his escort get killed, he let the killer get away, and now he is walking around the crime scene without gloves. Not a good day and it was barely nine o'clock.

As they continued their search they found nothing unusual. The bathroom window had an excellent view of the steps leading to the courthouse as well as an excellent view of the Cooper Building across the street. Tom checked the window and found that it opened and closed easily. The lab team arrived and started their tests. They found several smudged prints in the bathroom and office, which the judge was sure were his. They also found a good set of prints on the bathroom door, which everyone knew were agent Gibson's, and a right thumbprint, which they would have to check. Scott and Tom were certain that the test results would confirm it as the "Hoover Print." By 11:00 they were able to release the judge's office and open up the rest of the floor.

Scott had to do two things: First he had to turn this case over to Tom; and second, he had to relieve Special Agent Gibson of his duties until a hearing could be scheduled.

The assassin had actually been in the building and Agent Gibson had let him walk out with the janitors.

Chapter 3

The janitor removed the mop and bucket from the van and placed them in a garbage dumpster just minutes before the city truck would pick it up. He then drove in the opposite direction another fifteen minutes before ditching the truck with the real janitor still drugged in the back. He grabbed a grocery bag, walked to the nearest subway stop, made two line changes, got off and went into the restroom. There, in a private stall, he removed his bushy eyebrows and a one-inch scar that ran along the left side of his face. He changed his wig for one with no gray and less coarse hair, then he took out his brown contacts and removed a prosthetic piece from his jaw that had given his face a fuller look. He removed the nosepiece, which made his nose appear wider, and the fake ears that slipped on over his own. The janitor was now ready to reenter the world, this time as one of the thousands of young professionals working in the nations capital.

He took a gym bag from inside the grocery bag, stuffed everything, including the overalls, into it and put the grocery bag inside the gym bag. He removed one glove and, after opening the door with his gloved hand, he removed the other and put both into the gym bag. Now dressed in Dockers slacks and a white Polo golf shirt and, except for the heavy work boots (which were mostly hidden by his pants legs), he had no resemblance whatsoever to the janitor who entered the bathroom only moments earlier. He looked like a young professional on the way to his club for a morning workout.

The janitor got back on the subway, rode two stops, got out, walked up to the street, got into his car and drove away. His final destination before heading home was the incinerator at the sheet metal plant, where the fires get so hot they actually melt steel. There he removed his size -9- ° work-boots, put on the size seven tennis shoes from the rear seat of his car, walked to the incinerator and threw in both the workout bag and the work-boots. In a matter of seconds everything was gone. It was a tough decision to get rid of the boots—with two inches on the sole and two additional inches inside the boot at the heel, the janitor was able to look between four or five inches taller. However, he knew it would be too dangerous to keep anything around that could later become evidence.

The janitor pulled into the underground garage of his building and took the elevator directly to his condo. He went straight to the bathroom, removed all of his clothes, and began removing a wide layer of tape from his upper chest. It was much easier this time than the first time. The first time, the janitor's chest was raw and painful for days after. This time, however, he'd rubbed his chest down with lotion, wrapped it in surgical cloth and then taped it. Once the tape was removed, the janitor reached up to the side of his throat and pulled back a rubber throat mask that included an extended Adam's apple.

The five-foot-eleven-inch janitor then stepped into the shower. Fifteen minutes later she emerged as a five-foot-six-inch African American beauty with baby soft mocha skin, short black hair, and an exotic look that could adorn the cover of any glamour magazine in the world. As the last remnant of the janitor, she cut the rubber throat into a hundred little pieces and placed them and the tape that had bound her breasts, into the trash compactor that she would empty on her way out.

She decided since she had worked all night cleaning offices, she deserved a nap. It was, after all, her day off.

Chapter 4

Christine was awakened by the telephone next to her bed. It seemed like she had just fallen asleep. It was noon, though, and the mid-day news was coming on as she answered the phone.

"Hello?"

"Hello, Christy, where the hell are you? All hell is breaking loose here."

"I don't want to hear that voice on my day off! If my apartment isn't burning down you're in serious trouble! It's my day off and I'm not coming in no matter what!"

"Christy, you have to come in, we need you. You and I have to brief the director!"

"On what? I don't have him on my schedule for another two days."

"Here I am trying to save your career by making sure you don't miss this meeting and you're giving me static."

"It's my day off and the director knows it. Tell him I'll brief him on anything he wants when I get back tomorrow."

"I don't think he's going to accept that in this situation. You obviously haven't heard the news."

"Okay, you've got me. What is so important that I would be called back from my first day off in over eight months?"

"President Canfield got killed this morning."

"Canfield?"

"Yes, former President Canfield."

"What happened?"

"He was assassinated."

"You're kidding, he has to be ninety years old."

"I'm not kidding, and I'm told he was only eighty-five. I'm recalling the entire team."

"Your team? Have you guys found another Hoover print?"

"We think so—we'll know for sure in a couple of hours. If it is Hoover, this time we have him on film."

"Good, so why am I being called in on this? This sounds like a job for you and Scott!"

"The director wants to hear the organized crime view on this."

"Organized crime? What's to know? The mob doesn't kill eighty-five year old ex-presidents. This has to be the work of a wacko."

"If we find Hoover's print on the scene, we can pretty much count out the wacko angle."

"I have no idea why anyone in organized crime would want to kill this old man. That's exactly what I would tell the director, besides—shouldn't Martinez go? He is the head of the organized crime division."

"You know the director doesn't want him. As soon as he can he's going to let him go. He's just worried about minority law suits."

"What am I, chopped liver? I'm a woman and I'm African American, how much more minority can you get? Tell him to replace Martinez with me and he won't have to worry about minority law suits."

"Come on Christy, you know the organized crime angle better than anybody. I promise I'll go to bat for you with the director."

"Ok, Tom, I'll be there in about an hour and a half to pull your fat out of the fire one more time. I just need to run to the bank and talk to my broker."

"I don't know why you're still with the FBI with all the money you have."

"I do it so that I can hang around people like you. I'll see you in a little bit."

Christine got off the phone and went to her study to retrieve her palm computer. She never liked using the landlines to check her accounts. The wireless modem on her hand held computer usually served her best. She could scramble the signal and fake its place of origin with ease and it was almost impossible to locate, especially while on the move. Today

Christy would be on line just long enough to check her accounts in Switzerland and Costa Rica. She decided the risk was minimal and checked her accounts from her condo.

Christine's Costa Rican account was now worth just over $40,000,000. With what she had in Switzerland, she now had more than $100 million in off-shore accounts.

She smiled as she closed her computer and knew that someday soon she would have to use those funds for whatever her parents had intended. Every time she thought about the accounts, she thought about the mysterious way she'd found out about them.

An envelope in her mail box with no return address. The only thing inside was a key to a locker at Dulles Airport. There she found an old gym bag with a cassette recorder in it with two thin envelopes and one overstuffed envelope.

She remembered not being able to play the tape because the batteries in the recorder had died. In each of the thin envelopes there were two sheets of paper with nothing but numbers on them. The overstuffed envelope had fifteen pieces of paper in it. It looked like an itemized list of expenses. By the time Christine got batteries, her heart was ready to burst with excitement and curiosity. The tape was obviously very old, but even now all she had to do is close her eyes and concentrate and she can hear every word.

"Ms. Peal, please do not attempt to trace this tape. We are only the solicitors your family hired many years ago to oversee the family's estate.

"Our instructions were precise. If something were to happen to both sets of parents then the first surviving child to reach the age of thirty was to receive these envelopes. Each envelope contains two sheets of paper with numbers. One number is a telephone number to an overseas bank; the other is the nine-digit account number and seven-digit code for that account. As you are the only surviving family member, and you have recently turned thirty, these accounts are now yours.

"You will find the larger account, as of July 10, 1991, has a balance of $71 million. The smaller account as of the same date has a balance of $3,567,893.54.

"It was your family's wish that the smaller account be used to provide the best schools and a comfortable life for all surviving family members. These funds are now yours to do with as you see fit.

28

"It was your family's wish that the larger account be managed until such time that the oldest surviving family member reaches the age of thirty. At which time further instructions will be forthcoming as to the preferred disposition of the funds.

"The third envelope contains an itemized accounting of all the withdrawals from the smaller account. Please note that all withdrawals were conducted for the expressed intent to provide you with the best of everything. Unfortunately we were unable to locate you after your family's tragic death's until after you had already been taken in by the Peals. That's why we had to pay for your education by providing you with grants and scholarships."

Christine had spent many nights since then staring at the ceiling, wondering where the money came from and what she was supposed to do with it. It did clear up one thing for her—how the Peals, who were at best a middle-class family, could afford to send their adopted daughter to the best schools in the country and how they could afford private tutors and pay for her summers in Europe. One thing she was sure of; she never felt unfortunate being raised by the Peals. They may not have had seventy million dollars, but they loved her and cared for her very much and she for them.

Christine had long since moved both accounts. The larger one she split between two different continents, while she gradually moved the smaller one into several different brokerage accounts under her own name. She made no secret of these accounts implying only that she had inherited some money and had been extremely successful in her trades. The agency and most of her peers are fully aware that she's worth several million dollars. After giving her brokers their instructions for the day, she hung up the phone and began to get ready to go to "work."

Christine felt like removing herself as far as possible from her janitor night. She put on her favorite push-up bra, a white V-neck silk blouse, a white jacket with a white skirt worn three inches above the knee, clear pantyhose, and white high heels. After makeup and perfume, she looked in the mirror and liked what she saw. She grabbed her briefcase, the trash from the compactor, and headed to the garage.

Christy felt good—she felt like having some fun. Instead of taking her Volvo (which she usually did for work) she decided to take her Viper Convertible. She wrapped a silk scarf around her hair and pulled out of the garage with a smile on her face and that "everything is all right with the world" feeling.

When Special Agent Christy Peal entered the FBI building in downtown Washington D.C., she felt the energy of the thousands of agents working there. For the entire building there were only about fifty reserved parking spaces; hers was right next to Assistant Special Agent in Charge (ASAC) Fredricko "Freddie" Martinez. ASAC Martinez was the current head of the Organized Crime Division. The entire division and just about everyone at the Bureau knew who the real brain behind the organized crime division really was. If there was any serious work to be done or questions to be asked everyone bypassed Martinez and went directly to her. As she pulled into her space, she noticed that her boss was there as was the director, whose' agency car was parked in his space. As she made her way to the building, she reflected on her very first organized crime case.

She had been a rookie agent in the FBI field office in Dallas, Texas. A friend of hers was one of the first Black (as they were known then) mid-level managers in a medium-sized manufacturing company, came complaining to her that he was being extorted. He was being pressured to unionize all of the Black workers under a new union label and to deduct fifty dollars per month from each employee. He was told that if he didn't unionize his 120 employees, they might not have a place to come to work and he might just find his black ass in a ditch. A cross had already been burned on his front yard and his family had been threatened. Christine was his last hope—he would either have to move his family or give into their demands.

The FBI wanted to pursue it as a civil rights violation case, but Christine knew that it would receive more attention and manpower as a organized crime investigation. After weeks of discussions, she was temporarily transferred to the organized crime division and set herself up as the employees' representative.

She refused the offer and set herself up in a local apartment. Two evenings after she turned down the final offer, two men attempted to burn down the company's manufacturing plant. FBI Organized Crime Unit personnel caught them in the act. Two additional men attempted to rough up or kill agent Christine Peal. No one will ever know which, because Christine attacked them both as they entered her apartment and killed one with his own gun; the other one died from a broken neck as he hit the corner of a marble coffee table. By the time the agents sent to protect her came out of the bedroom it was all over.

Christine had felt an adrenaline rush that gave her a high like never before. She felt in tune with every living thing in the universe. All of her senses were on full alert, a feeling that she liked very much and would experience again in the future.

Those caught attempting arson, identified their bosses, who in turn gave up their bosses. Christine had killed the hoods that attacked her, therefore all those involved in the extortion attempt could be charged with two counts of homicide in addition to racketeering, civil rights violations and attempted arson. The Organized crime unit was so impressed with Christine's work that they requested her temporary assignment be made permanent. Christine liked the work, especially the undercover situations. The constant danger of being in the enemy's camp provided her with a similar feeling of her first encounter with organized crime. She knew this was where she could find the kind of action she craved. She quickly agreed to the transfer and immediately established her own goals. First on the list was to totally eliminate this group singling out blacks for extortion.

Christine and the rest of her team tried for months without success to get to the top man of this organization. Once it was clear that they had gone as far as possible up the chain and they were not going to get any more assistance from the underbosses currently under arrest, the team was reassigned to another operation. Christy, however, was not satisfied. She pleaded with her superiors to give her thirty more days and she would guarantee that they would never hear from this particular crime family again. Her superiors finally and reluctantly agreed. She would have thirty days, but if she had made no significant progress by then, she would have to abandon the case and rejoin the rest of her team.

Having exhausted all other avenues and feeling the pressure, Christine decided it was time to escalate her efforts if she was going to meet her goal of driving this family out of Dallas. It was time to visit the head of the family.

She had put on her black stretch ski pants, a black turtle neck sweater, black tennis shoes, black gloves, and a black ski hat and set out to infiltrate the private compound of the head of this Dallas crime syndicate. From the time she started to get ready her heart was racing and a feeling of total exhilaration swept through her body. She knew that what she was about to do went against all FBI rules and regulations. She just didn't seem to care; in fact, that made it even more exhilarating. To her surprise she found herself extremely calm with her mind clear and focused as she entered the compound.

She caught a ride on the first truck that went through the gate. In the darkness, she jumped from the truck once she was through the gate and rolled into the bushes. Priding herself on learning from every situation, from this one she learned that next time she is going to have to come up with some suction cups with grips for her hands to make it easier to hold on to the back of trucks.

She worked her way through the bushes to the main house. There she had to overcome one exterior guard and two rotating cameras. She knew that the rotating cameras were just a matter of timing—it was the guard that would be the problem. She could count on the element of surprise and hoped her FBI hand-to-hand combat training and her desire to live would do the rest, just like it had in her apartment that night. Once she had identified the camera's patterns she moved quickly. She had to disable the guard, pull his body into the bushes and get inside the house, all before the camera panned back into the area.

The element of surprise did help her with the guard. She was able to administer a blow to the back of his head with the butt of her pistol which didn't knock him out but stunned him long enough for her to administer a second blow to his temple when he turned to attack her. She grabbed him by the feet and dragged him under the bushes and hid on top of him as the camera made another pass, and then jumped up and began to neutralize the alarm system. This took longer than she had expected due to a backup alarm system that she couldn't bypass with foam and had to do manually.

Once inside, there was no shrieking alarm or siren, no rushing footsteps or hurried voices. Christy found a security room with two guards just off of the kitchen. Two additional guards were watching TV in the living room.

That meant her target was upstairs in either his bedroom or his study just off of his bedroom. Christine made her way past the guards and up the stairs on to the second floor, where she found Tommy "The Smack" Viron sitting at his desk in the study, doing paperwork like any ordinary businessman. Staying in the shadows of the study so the security cameras would not pick her up, Christy quietly called out to Tommy Viron.

"Tommy Smack, don't make a sound and don't make any sudden

moves! You have a silenced forty-five pointed at your head. If you do anything to alert the cameras, I'll blow you away."

Tommy hated the nickname "Smack"; he'd gotten it by being the largest smack dealer in the southeast while he was making a name for himself. He was so much more now. He didn't think it was fair that people would always remember him as a dealer and not much else. Now here was this broad in his house, showing him no more respect than you would an ordinary dealer. It just wasn't right.

"What do you want bitch, and how the hell did you get into my house?"

"Watch your mouth Tommy, or I'll close it for good. All I want you to do is listen. After I'm done talking, I'll leave. Is that clear so far?"

"Yes."

"Good—the way I see it, the majority of your operation has been shut down by the FBI. What I want you to do is close down the rest of it and get out of my town. You have exactly twenty-one days."

"You crazy bitch! What makes you think you can run me out of town when the Feds couldn't?"

"That's simple, Tommy! I don't have to play by the same rules that they do. I can get to you anytime I want. If I have to come back, I'll shoot you full of an advanced AIDS virus and you'll live one more year in extreme agony and all of your compadres will think you were a fag."

"Jesus Christ, bitch—what did I ever do to you?"

"That doesn't really matter now does it? Let's just say I can't stand wops. If you're not out of town in three weeks I'll be back. I expect all of your goons to go with you. When you wake up in about three hours you'll be okay, but if you're not out of here in three weeks, next time you won't be as lucky."

Before Tommy "The Smack" could turn around, Christy had delivered a tranquilizer dart from her forty-five to the back of the "Smack's" neck. As he reached back to grab the dart, his eyes closed and he was out. To the guards watching the monitors it looked like Tommy was swatting at a fly on his neck.

That was the last that the FBI or anyone else in Dallas heard anything from Tommy "The Smack" or any of his goons. They just disappeared.

As she arrived at her office Christine smiled to herself as she reflected on the twists and turns her career had taken and how fate had put her in a position where she could finally avenge her family.

She walked through the reception room and into her office, her secretary right behind her with a stack of papers and several messages.

"Good morning, Doris, what are you doing here? I thought I gave you the day off?"

"You did, but Agent West's secretary called me at home and said, you may need me today and that I should come in."

"She did, did she? Next time she does that, remind her that you work for me and not for her or Tom West."

"Yes, ma'am."

"Since you're here, what do you have for me, Doris?"

"You have three messages from ASAC Martinez and one from Director Flynn. They both want to see you. I also have copies of two handwritten preliminary reports on this morning's activities. You should probably review them before you see the director."

"Does the ASAC have these reports?"

"Not to my knowledge."

"How do you do that, Doris? On second thought, I'm probably better off not knowing. Ok, give me ten minutes to review these, then call the director's office and tell him I'm in and after I'm done with the director get me Martinez on the phone."

Christine reviewed both reports; the one submitted by Special Agent Gibson was sloppy and full of holes. The one submitted by ADIC Peterson was more complete and more critical of the FBI's performance (especially Agent Gibson's handling of the situation). Both reports confirmed what Christine suspected—the FBI had no clue as to the identity of the hit man.

Good to her word, Doris gave Christy ten minutes before she interrupted. "Ms Peal, Director Flynn wants to meet with you right away, but his assistant said that he preferred to come to your office."

"Good, thanks. When the director gets here go ahead and call ASAC Martinez and let him know that I'm in."

Christine was wondering why the director of the FBI would come to her office instead of having her come to his. She knew that Martinez would never come to her office but instead always summon her to his. She was sure he wanted to be briefed so he in turn could brief the director. Making himself appear as the expert. This time however she would have already briefed the director.

Director Martin Flynn was not a typical political appointee. He had a long and distinguished career protecting and serving his country. He started his career as a naval officer, then served twenty years in the FBI, rising to the position of deputy director and then as a senator from Ohio where he served on several committees dealing with Intelligence and Security.

When Director Flynn was appointed, his confirmation hearing was one of the quickest of any previously appointed director. The rank-and-file saw him as one of their own and as someone who could help the agency through his Washington relationships.

Christine respected this director and knew he could be a powerful ally. It was not uncommon for him to go directly to people who could help him. The department heads who were comfortable in their positions had no problem with this style and, in fact, began to employ it themselves. Those deputies and department heads like Martinez, who knew they were on a short leash, were extremely uncomfortable with this and often made life for their subordinates more difficult.

Doris showed the director in. As he passed through the door, his 6', 200- pound frame partially blocked the doorway. Christy started to get out of her chair to greet him, but he motioned for her to stay seated as he slumped into the chair in front of her.

"Hello, Christine—sorry to bring you in on your day off. I know how rare those are, but I really need your brains today."

"No problem, sir. I was just preparing to come to your office."

"I decided to stretch my legs, I hope you don't mind that I came down to your office?"

"Of course not sir. I just don't know how much help I can be in this situation."

"I need some history on the organized crime angle. I'm going to have to meet with Congress and the president's staff in the morning and I need more than the Hoover Killer got away again."

"So you've confirmed that this was a Hoover hit?"

"Not yet, but West and Peterson give it a 90% probability. How much do you know about what happened this morning?"

"I only know the basics. President Canfield was shot through the head as he was being escorted into the courthouse. The killer misdirected the FBI agents and got out dressed as a janitor. The agents found a print that evidently will confirm this as a Hoover hit. We've also recovered a tape with the janitor on it, but lost all trace of him after he left the building. That's about the extent of my knowledge."

"Realistically speaking, that's all we have. We did find the real janitor. He was unharmed although he did have a slight headache. Evidently he was overpowered by, as he put it, "this huge black man," who then drugged him and stuck him in the back of his own van, which is where he woke up about 10 this morning. So you can see, I really need you and your mind on this. I need to be able to tie someone or some group to this by the time I talk to Congress in the morning.

"I need to know if there was any mob involvement, or if this was a terrorist act or just some nut trying to rub our nose in it. I need some names or at least some educated guesses. Scott and Tom will work on Hoover. If someone hired him, I need to know who. That's where you come in. I want you on Tom's team. Your job will be to oversee the mob and terrorist angle on this."

"Mr. Director, I'm sure that you're aware the FBI has a very good terrorism department. They know a lot more about it than I do. Plus, any terrorist activities would likely be generated from outside the United States and that puts it out of my expertise and our jurisdiction."

"You let me worry about jurisdiction. As far as terrorist expertise, I've already assigned our top man to the team. You guys will be working together on this."

I appreciate your confidence sir, but what does the ASAC have to say about all of this? This will obviously take up all of my time."

"Don't worry about Martinez. I'll tell him about it this afternoon. Who knows, when this is all over you may have his job. Then again with all of the exposure you'll be getting on this, I'll probably lose you to one of those more exciting agencies."

"I don't think so, Mr. Director: I've found my home. In any case, I'd better get busy. How much time do I have before our next briefing?"

"I need you to bring me up to speed at 7 this evening. I'll come back down here; I want top security on this."

"Of course, Mr. Director. I'm not sure how much I'll be able to give you by this evening, though."

"Just give me what you have. I'll need something to say in the morning."

As the director stood up to leave, he turned before walking out the door with one final comment to Christine. "Don't worry about Martinez—

I'll keep him out of your hair."

As the director left Doris entered. "ASAC Martinez called and wants to see you in his office right away."

"Thanks Doris. Would you please get him on the phone for me?"

"Certainly Ms. Peal."

After talking to Christine, Martinez was furious. The idea that his top agent would be working directly for the director didn't sit well with him at all. Who the hell was she, to tell him that if he wanted to know more about the case he should talk to the director? Even as these thoughts were going through Martinez's head, he was dialing the director's line.

Christine allowed herself only a moment to bask in her small victory. She needed to develop a plan that took advantage of the opportunity the director had just provided her. The first thing she had to do was to see what they had on Hoover. She would have to view the video and then talk to all of those involved.

Twenty minutes after asking Doris to locate the tape, Christine was sitting in a projection room at the other end of the FBI building, staring up at a 12-foot screen which contained a life-sized image of a janitor exiting the Federal Building. In the room with her were Scott Peterson, Tom West, four technicians, and the guard from the metal detector through which the janitor exited. When Christine first spotted the guard, her heart skipped a couple of beats and she could feel that familiar adrenaline rush. After greeting Scott and Tom, she made a deliberate trip over to the guard to introduce herself. It was immediately obvious to her that she had nothing to worry about from this man. He was far more interested in her cleavage than he was in the film of the janitor.

After running the tape back and forth several times, the identification technicians (ID Techs) came up with a description and a digitized image of "Hoover." They decided that he was between 5'10" and 6' tall, an African American male weighing about 200-pounds, with short black hair and probably no facial hair, and he may or may not have a one-inch scar on the left side of his face. Several versions of computer-enhanced photos would be sent to every law enforcement agency in the world immediately.

Christine was pleased with herself. Looking at the life-sized janitor on the wall in front of her, she couldn't recognize herself. She stayed a few more minutes talking to Scott and the others, making sure they had no additional leads that could possibly point them in her direction. She then excused herself in order to prepare her briefing for the director later that evening.

Christine knew that she had the opportunity of a lifetime. She would be on the team investigating the assassination of President Canfield. This would also provide her access to all of the Hoover files. She now had a legitimate reason for searching the archives.

Christine spent the rest of the afternoon preparing for her meeting with the director. She pulled together some file photos and some of her notes on the various drug cartels, as well as flow charts of U.S. crime families and their possible ties to politics.

Chapter 5

The director called around 6:30 to let Christine know that he and the others would be down at seven. The group had grown and he recommended they conduct the meeting in the conference room adjoining her office.

It didn't take Christine long to figure out why the meeting had to be moved out of her office. Scott, Thomas, and another agent (who she assumed to be Agent Gibson) arrived just before seven. They were followed by two agents, one of whom, the taller, she recognized as ASAC Kevin Young, the current head of the agency's anti-terrorist unit.

Director Flynn arrived at seven, flanked by two agents that Christine didn't recognize and trailed by her boss, Assistant Special Agent in Charge Martinez.

"Sorry to keep everybody so late but it couldn't be avoided. I think most of you know each other, but just in case let's make some introductions. Christine, for the most part, this is the Hoover task force. You know Tom and Scott of course, with them today is Special Agent Gibson. Agent Gibson is not a permanent member of this task force, but he was the agent in charge this morning, so his input will be vital. I believe you also know ASAC Young, who heads up the Counterterrorism Program, and this is Special Agent Hector Quantara, who's in charge of Domestic

Terrorism.

"I think all of us understand the priority assigned to this case. The president has been calling my office about every thirty minutes to check on our progress. Needless to say the press is all over him. Canfield has become kind of a sentimental favorite since he's been out of office. The White House is flooded with calls expressing their sympathy and their outrage that we could let this happen. Everybody wants to know why, and that includes me. That's why we're here and why this task force has been created. We have strong reasons to believe that the assassin who shot President Canfield is also responsible for the recent murders of ADIC Ballard and ex-FBI Special Agent Canon. I expect this task force to find out if this guy is an assassin for hire and if so who's hiring him? If not, I want to know what his problem is. Does he have some kind of grudge against these people or is he just a nut? But most of all, I want this guy caught.

"Each of you brings a specialty to this task force. You're going to have to dig deep into your treasure chests, because we have to close this one out in a hurry. The whole world as well as many of our own government agencies are going to be keeping a very close eye on us.

"The scope of this project is going to take us across international borders and agency boundaries. As you guys know, contrary to popular beliefs, we are authorized to operate beyond our borders. However, if our investigation takes us across international borders, I expect to be notified and I expect the appropriate agencies to be involved.

"Due to the nature and high profile of this investigation, Tom is going to serve double duty as ADIC Washington DC and as head of this task force." All in the room nodded their approval of Tom's selection.

"Before we get into the individual briefings, let me lay out everyone's responsibilities. Special Agent Quantara is obviously going to ramrod the domestic terrorism elements of this investigation. Most of you know Counterterrorism ASAC Young, he has assured me that Agent Quantara will be provided with all the resources and support that he needs.

"Christine is, of course, our organized crime expert. Agent Quantara and Agent Peal will be working closely together in hopes of either identifying or eliminating terrorism and the mob as being behind these murders.

"Tom currently heads the Hoover task force. His focus will continue to be on the Hoover killer and bringing him in.

"Special Agent Jim Brodrick is here from NCAVC (National Center for the Analysis of Violent Crime). They're the ones that picked up that second Hoover print and alerted us to it. Jim, through NCAVC, will be keeping an eye out for any other similarities to our crimes.

"Jim also has some other skills. He's been around the agency a long time and knows where most of the bodies are buried. Just about everybody owes him at least one favor. He can get things done in a day that would take the rest of us a week. We don't have time for a lot of red tape on this one. His skills don't end at our agency's borders; he can help you with any government agency including Congress and the White House.

"Special Agent English—stand up, Francine. Special Agent English runs the Office of Public and Congressional Affairs. What Francine does, basically is keep you guys out of trouble. If you need to talk to anyone high up in government or a highly influential private citizen, you need to talk to Francine first. If you're not sure they're a "VIP" then check with Francine. I have a feeling that this investigation could get extremely sensitive and I would like to avoid having complaints about our lack of tact land on the president's desk. Don't underestimate the value that Francine and her people can add. We've worked together on several sensitive cases and she has managed to keep everyone focused on the issues instead of the egos and titles. We try to use her whenever we have multiple agency involvement, so she'll be an executive member of this task force.

"Everyone of course knows Freddie Martinez. He's the ASAC for Organized Crime. Freddie has come to me with an interesting proposal. He wants to create a second task force working independently of our main task force and out of the publics' eye."

A sudden tension filled the room, and then everyone started to fire questions at the director all at once. Tom finally took control.

"Excuse me, Mr. Director, I'm sure you realize this poses several questions, not to mention some major concerns. It's going to be tough enough coordinating this case and getting the resources that we need without stumbling over one another investigating many of the same leads. How are we going to share our resources, especially those overseas or the deep-cover agents that are in place in some of these terrorist groups and in some of the organized crime families? We can't ask them to be responsive to multiple contacts. Exactly what is the point or mission of this second team? Who has priority if there is a conflict over resources, information, or sources?"

"There is no reason for everyone to get all excited about this. I've given this some thought since he first proposed it to me. I think this could work, I don't think it could hurt. Freddie guarantees that if there is any kind of resource conflict or a priority issue, he will bow to the primary team. Freddie's focus will be on catching Hoover."

This time it was Tom who couldn't keep himself contained. "No disrespect to the ASAC, but we already have a whole task force on this; how does he expect to swoop in here and find Hoover overnight?"

"That's a good question Tom, in fact I asked that myself. So I'll just let him explain it to you himself. Go ahead, Freddie."

"It's not the way it sounds, Tom. I don't mean to cast aspersions on your group, they're doing a fine job. The problem is they're FBI agents and as such, they're doing it the FBI way. I believe that Hoover knows FBI procedures inside and out. I think he's using those procedures against us. He always seems to be one step ahead of us; hell, he even has Hoover's thumbprint! You can't exactly get those in the Yellow Pages. So I'll say what everybody is afraid to say—Hoover has access to our computers or he has an accomplice in the FBI or he is a former FBI agent himself, or all of the above. I'm not sure which, but however we look at it, if we're going to catch Hoover we're going to have to throw away the procedure manual. We have to keep the team small for security and manage it the old-fashioned way before we had computers. I alone will maintain all meeting notes and files. Not a single progress report will be put on the computer or shared with anyone except, of course, the director."

Tom just about came out of his skin. "Are you trying to tell me that one of my people is on the take or that you don't trust the people in this room?"

"I'm not saying that at all, Tom. I'm just saying that if something were to go wrong or be leaked, the fewer people that know what's going on the fewer people we will have to investigate."

"So, I assume that the current Hoover task force will be reassigned?"

"No, it will continue its job with the same diligence as ever. The whole idea is for this task force to operate in the shadows and keep the attention focused on your team."

Tom couldn't believe it. Martinez had put himself in a no-lose situation. If he accomplished nothing, no one would ever know and he and his team would get the blame. If Hoover was caught, Martinez and his team would emerge and take the credit.

He would have access to all of their intelligence but they wouldn't have access to any of his. While Tom was contemplating the situation he was in, Christine interrupted his thoughts.

"Mr. Director, if we're not privy to the data the ASAC has and he's not privy to the data that we've gathered, how will we keep from butting heads in the field?"

Before the director could answer, Martinez leaned forward on the conference room table to make sure he was heard. "I will still be part of your task force and sit in on your briefings, so I'll know if we're about to butt heads."

Christine couldn't let that happen. She had to act quickly. "Wouldn't that defeat the entire purpose of your task force? You may be swayed or influenced by the direction our investigation is heading and hence contaminate your own out of the box independent approach."

"Christine does have a point, Freddie. Let's just make your group totally independent and since both of you are going to be reporting to me, I'll keep you from unnecessary collisions. Okay? Oh by the way, Gibson will be working with Martinez."

Freddie Martinez was obviously not pleased; he had counted on a lot of the legwork being done for him by the main task force. By now though he knew Director Flynn well enough to know better than to argue this point, so he just nodded his head in agreement.

Christine also nodded in agreement and sat back in her chair, relieved by this small victory.

"Okay, now that that is out of the way, I have to brief Congress and the President's staff in the morning, so I hope you guys have something for me!"

All eyes shifted to Martinez, expecting him to get up and leave. As soon as Director Flynn realized what was happening he cut it off. "Let's get one thing straight here people, this is not a competition, no one is getting an upper hand, we have one mission and that is to get this case solved. We're taking two different strategies to get there but we're all still FBI agents and you're all still working for me. Right now I want to hear from everybody that has any input. I also want everybody to hear the basics of this case. So let's get on with it. Scott bring us up to speed on this morning."

"I'll let Agent Gibson fill you in on the early hours and then I'll bring you the rest of the way." After Scott and Agent Gibson brought everyone up to date from their perspective, the director looked Gibson straight in his eyes and without changing his facial expression said, "you kind of screwed up here, didn't you?"

Gibson was about to defend himself but thought better of it and simply replied, "yes, sir".

The only new information that their canvassing and interviews had uncovered was that someone in overalls was spotted walking from the general direction of the abandoned van and headed in the general direction of the subway. The description roughly matched that of the janitor in the video and he was carrying a bag of groceries. It wasn't much to go on but Scott had assigned some people to be at the subway the next morning in hopes that one of the regulars had spotted him.

Tom had no significant updates from the Hoover team, except for the confirmation of the Hoover print.

Agent Quantara had been monitoring the major hate groups, militias, and known terrorists currently in the country. His intelligence group uncovered a gathering, at which the heads of several militia groups were present, ten days earlier. Present at that meeting also were two men that didn't look like they belonged and had not yet been identified.

Quantara was convinced that it would be impossible to bring in everyone that was at that meeting without causing a major national incident. It would probably be just as difficult to bring in or even implicate any single individual attending the meeting, without causing an uprising in the entire militia movement.

The director's curiosity piqued when he heard about the two that didn't belong. "Quantara, was one of those men African American?"

"Yes sir, both men were in what looked like expensive suits and one of them was African American and the other looked Asian. That's what made them stand out. You just wouldn't expect a black man or an Asian at a white supremacist or militia meeting unless they were being hung."

"What's the chance of one of those guys being our hit man?"

"I don't know—we haven't been able to identify them. We even ran them through the NSA computers and I sent the photo of the Asian over to Christine's people to see if we can match him with one of the Asian crime families."

"Christine, why don't you follow up on that photo and see what we can come up with. Tom, why don't you let Quantara look at the video you got from the courthouse this morning; maybe he can identify the janitor."

Christine nodded her agreement at both Quantara and the director and slipped Quantara a note to come with her after the meeting. Thomas also nodded his agreement, but was not too encouraging. "We'll certainly compare notes on this, but don't get your hopes up. No one has ever seen Hoover."

"I know it's a long shot, but we really have little else to go on. Christine—ok what do you have?"

Christine reviewed the possible U.S. connection with a very general and scattered approach, until the director interrupted. "Christine, I need more than this. So far I've got some drug people from South America may have ordered it and some U.S. families may have done it. That's not going to make me very popular tomorrow morning and we all know how I like to be popular."

"Yes sir, I do have an additional scenario, but it is extremely sensitive and I would not want to present anything unsubstantiated at this time."

"Christine, don't do this to me—if you have an idea or have heard something, I want to know about it."

"Mr. Director, I really would like to get more confirmation before I give life to these rumors. This could be extremely prejudicial."

Flynn realized that she really didn't want to disclose what ever it was with Martinez still in the room. Against his better judgment he decided to give her some latitude. "Ok, let's put this off for now. Freddie, do you have anything to add?"

"No sir, not at this time."

"Scott, what about the videos, surely we can get something off of those?"

"We're running them against our complete video and still data base, but so far nothing."

"Okay, stay after it. From now until this thing is resolved, Scott will be briefing me daily and the NSA, CIA, and State weekly or as needed. Scott let everyone know our meeting schedules. Freddie, I'll need you to brief me every morning. Since you want to limit paperwork, just brief me over breakfast in my office every morning at 7:00. If there is nothing else, we have a lot of work ahead of us, let's get to it."

As everyone was getting up to leave, the Director called after Christine. "Christine, can I see you, Scott, and Tom?"

Christine made eye contact with the director and indicated in the direction of ASAC Young.

Director Flynn, understanding her intent, called after Young.

"Kevin, why don't you hang around for a couple of minutes as well."

While the others were leaving the room, Christine was mentally preparing herself. She knew she had to give them something substantial and something that could be verified down the line.

"Ok Christine, you have our attention. What is it that's so sensitive?"

"I'm sorry to be so melodramatic, Mr. Director, but these rumors could be damaging if they got into the wrong hands."

"We understand—let's have it."

"The rumor is that there has been an entire power shift in the largest families in the country. If what we hear is correct, they're no longer individual or loosely knit units. In Wall Street terms, there has been a consolidation in the industry. As in many global industries, the consolidation left about six major players throughout the world. The new dispersion of power has left the majority of the Americas under the control of NASA-FEC. Which stands for North American & South American Free Enterprise Cooperative. They are run like a conglomerate with wholly owned subsidiaries throughout North and South America. They have government officials in high posts placed throughout the world, which includes federal judges and legislators here in the States. They even use lobbyists to get bills passed that make it more difficult for them to be tracked." Christine cleared her throat and took a long look at ASAC Young before continuing. "Sir, we're hearing rumors that these new syndicates have turned towards legitimate businesses and have worked out deals with some of the militias to be their strong men. In fact, it's our belief that the bombing of the Archer complex was not a terrorist act as such, but was instead motivated primarily by business reasons."

Young was furious. "Damn it Christine, if you know anything about that bombing you should be bringing it to us!"

"Relax, let's hear Christine out," the director said.

"Like I said, we don't have all of the answers nor do we have the verification we would like. I do believe that basically this information is reliable. We think that the white supremacist shot escaping from the bombing was actually hired to do it, and didn't do it for ideological reasons."

"How could you possibly know that? The security guard shot him before anybody had a chance to talk to him" Young asked.

"One of our men tailing a young lieutenant from what we believe to be the new West Coast syndicate, spotted the head of his militia, meeting with our lieutenant a week before the bombing."

"Why am I just now hearing about this?" ASAC Young demanded.

"Right now everything is still circumstantial. We don't have anything that we can go on yet. We think these new cooperatives are even stronger and more heavily entrenched than the Chicago mobs of the twenties and thirties and their ties to the militias make them even more dangerous."

"What do you mean more entrenched?" ASAC Young asked.

"It's our contention that members of the Cooperative can be found in some of the highest levels of state and Federal Government, and from there it wouldn't be a stretch to believe that they have people in influential positions in law enforcement including the FBI. We believe that HQ for this new cooperative is right here in the United States. I don't know exactly who or where yet. I also don't know if they had anything to do with the president's murder."

Young was shaking his head in disgust. "Why on earth didn't you guys come to us with your information. We have known for awhile that some of the latest actions of the militia have been influenced by outside sources. Some of their latest targets aren't traditional militia targets, and they've been getting an unusually large inflow of cash. We just couldn't tie anybody to them. If you guys had told us what you knew, between us we might have been able to prevent some of these bombings."

Flynn had no intention of allowing a split to occur this early in the project. "Kevin has a point, Christine, information like that should have been shared with the people monitoring the militia."

"With all due respect, Mr. Director, our people have been working on this angle for the past six weeks. We just didn't want to bring them to anyone's attention until we had something more solid to present?"

"Your point is well taken, Christine, neither Kevin nor I want to be bombarded with every rumor out there. I'm sure Kevin will check this out when he gets back to his unit. What do you need to follow this up."

"We have a lead that we're working on right now. We have a tip on a high- ranking government official supposedly owned by this new cooperative. If you were to authorize video and audio surveillance on this individual, he might tip his hand within the next two to three weeks."

"We don't have two to three weeks, Christine. How high is this suspect?"

"He is a U.S. congressman."

Both Flynn and Young sat up in their chairs as if they had just been pinched. "A U.S. congressman!" The director said. "You expect me to authorize surveillance on a U.S. congressman based on a rumor? He would have all of our hides hanging on his wall if we were discovered. I think you're going to have to bring me something more substantial if you expect me to stick out my neck that far."

"I understand the risk and implications, Mr. Director, but that's the quickest way I have of verifying or disproving these rumors we're hearing."

"You'll have to find another way; I can't authorize that."

"Excuse me, sir." Tom interjected. "I think there is a way this could be done and protect everyone at the same time."

"I'm all ears, Tom."

"Christine, does this congressman have any children?" Tom asked.

"Yes, he has a nineteen-year-old son and a fourteen-year-old daughter."

"Perfect—I'm not saying that this has ever been done before, but in a high profile case like this, you could use the children to camouflage your real objective."

Director Flynn's curiosity was aroused. "Go on, Tom."

"We use the DEA for the surveillance project, we create a dummy file on the nineteen-year-old boy and if we get caught we tell the congressman that we were actually following his boy. We tell him one of our undercover agents observed him buying a large quantity of cocaine and we were hoping that he would lead us to other dealers."

Scott couldn't believe what he was hearing. "You have got to be kidding—if his son were clean, his father would never believe us. Even if the congressman were to believe us, we can't do that to this kid."

"Trust me on this, the congressman would believe us. Parents today are so afraid that their children are doing drugs that if the DEA were to tell them that their kids were addicts the parents would always believe us over their own children. Besides it would only come into play if any of our surveillance efforts were detected. At that time we would agree to turn the son over to the congressman and to lose any reports that we had of his son. I can guarantee you that the congressman would not pursue the issue any further."

"Except that he would probably put that poor innocent kid through a drug rehab program or ship him off to Europe somewhere." Scott replied.

Christine could see that Scott wasn't taking to this idea very well. "I know what you're feeling, Scott, but I think sending one innocent boy to a drug rehab program is worth it, if it can help stop this cooperative from infiltrating the highest echelons of our government."

Director Flynn was getting just a little uncomfortable with this conversation. "I don't think that the director of the FBI should be hearing any of this. I don't even want to know the congressman's name. Kevin, I think you and I have another meeting to go to and these people have more work to do."

As they were walking out of the room, Director Flynn turned to Christine and said: "You have one week to prove or disprove this theory and I want you to use Francine on this."

Outside the conference room, Special Agent Quantara was waiting for his boss. ASAC Young motioned Quantara towards him and then told him that his services were probably required in the conference room.

With everyone else gone, they had just created their first sub-committee: Christine, Scott, Tom, Quantara, and Francine English, who would join them later. Their first task would be to figure out how to get a certain U.S. congressman to tip his hand in one week and then to implement that plan.

Chapter 6

Andy McCall got up at 4:30 and began his morning routine. Getting up early and running along the empty beaches was what he liked most about coming home to San Diego. It was the only time he truly had to himself. His morning runs gave him an opportunity for uninterrupted introspection. After his runs, he usually returned home for a quick shower and by 6:00 o'clock was placing the first call to his office in Washington D.C. After about an hour-and-a-half of addressing the day's most pressing issues, he usually joined his family for breakfast. Today after breakfast, he had planned on reviewing the speech he was to deliver at the opening of San Diego's newest Youth Center and Job Bureau. Like most congressmen, Andy McCall's holiday recess would be filled with speeches and ribbon cutting-ceremonies.

This morning, however, as he was running along the beach, the only thing going through his mind was his current predicament and that when he sat down for breakfast with his family, his daughter would not be there. He was obsessed with having let his daughter down. How could he be so blind to not notice his own daughter drifting away from the family? How could he miss his daughter's pain as she fell deeper and deeper into the world of drugs and violence? He had spent all of his time and effort in the family making sure that his son stayed out of trouble, but had failed his daughter so miserably. It was unbelievable to him that his daughter had turned into an addict and a murderer. He still would not believe it had he not seen the tracks on his daughter's arms and legs himself, or if those men had not shown him the photos of his daughter standing above that dead boy with a gun in her hand.

He had failed his daughter and ruined her life; he would not let her down again. He was ready to risk everything—his career, his reputation, even his own life to save what was left of his daughter. She was so young and he had failed to protect her; he was not about to let that happen again.

Like most of Andy McCall's runs lately, this one also ended in tears streaming down his face and a burden of guilt so heavy that he knew he wouldn't be able to face his wife and son at breakfast.

Chapter 7

None of the FBI teams could find anything in Congressman McCall's finances or personal background that indicated any vulnerability to the cooperative. It wasn't until three days after their original meeting that agent Quantara found a possible chink in the congressman's armor.

DEA agents had uncovered his daughter's secret. Several undercover agents identified her as a heavy drug user. She was recognized as a regular at certain known junkie hangouts until three months ago, when her boyfriend overdosed, and she hadn't been seen since. She wasn't identified as the daughter of a government official until Quantara floated the pictures of the congressman's son and daughter to agents in San Diego.

Quantara, with the help of the DEA, established surveillance on the congressman's home in San Diego and his office and apartment in D.C. To everyone on the task force it was evident that if this syndicate existed, they were either holding the congressman's daughter hostage or leveraging her in some other way to gain his cooperation. After two days of electronic surveillance and eavesdropping, they still hadn't discovered the whereabouts of the daughter nor were they any closer to connecting the congressman to the new cooperative.

It had been five days since the initial meeting with the director and there had been no significant progress on any front. The White House and the Senate were pressuring the director and he, in turn, was pushing Tom, Christine, and the rest of the task force for answers. Christine knew they needed to provide the director with something very quickly or there would be hell to pay. Their best option was still the congressman.

Christine called an emergency session of the task forces subcommittee (Christine, Scott, Tom, Quantara, and Francine) to discuss her proposal. "We all reviewed the information and the surveillance tapes on Congressman McCall." As she looked around the room everyone nodded. "The director has given us forty-eight-hours to come up with something or move on. He's getting pressure from the White House, and our butts as well as his are on the line here. Does anyone have any ideas on where to go from here if we can't use McCall?"

There was a brief discussion but it generated no new ideas. Their best hope of finding a lead on this new syndicate, or on Hoover, was still Congressman McCall. With no other input Christine was going to have to put her plan on the table, and knew that she was going to have to ease this committee into it.

"Francine, what would happen if we picked up the congressman and confronted him with the information we have?"

"I wouldn't recommend picking him up. If you're going to confront him, you should do it in a less formal and threatening situation, such as his home. This is a powerful legislator; he has many friends on both sides of the aisle, so it wouldn't do us any good to get him upset at the FBI."

"OK, let's assume we approach him at his home. I wouldn't think that he would ever, in the comfort of his own home, admit to anything as sinister as conspiring with a criminal syndicate."

Tom proposed that they bring their case to the majority leader and have him summon McCall.

Francine didn't think that was such a good idea. She was not quite ready to confront him or any other high-ranking government official with what they had.

It was time for Christine's proposal. "It's obvious that we don't have the luxury of time or procedure on this one. If we don't make our move on McCall in the next thirty-six hours, we're back at square one and I for one sure don't want to tell the director that."

A slight smile crossed Scott's lips. "What exactly did you have in mind, Christine?"

"We do have the resources of the CIA available to the task force. I propose we pick up the congressman during his run on the beach and provide him with an all-expense paid cruise up and down the California coast while one of those CIA specialists asks him a few questions."

Francine was shocked. "You are talking about kidnapping a congressman! You can't do that! Even if he was involved with the syndicate, you just can't treat a congressman like that! There are laws against it, and they carry severe penalties!"

Tom jumped in to calm Francine. "Relax, Francine—no one is going to kidnap anyone. Christine was just making a point, about how desperate our situation is. The CIA doesn't run these types of operations any more than we do."

Christine was watching everyone's reaction. Francine reacted pretty much as expected, Scott and Tom were a little surprised but not overwhelmed by the idea. It was Quantara, however, who surprised her the most. He appeared neither shocked nor surprised; in fact he seemed to already be planning the operation in his mind. Christine said, "Don't be upset, Francine—Scott's right, I was just letting off some steam. My plan does, however require a confrontation with the congressman. I plan on meeting him on the beach and laying out what we have on him so far. I'm going to exaggerate some of our evidence and gauge his reaction. If he bites I'll offer him a deal to help both him and his daughter out of this situation with their reputations intact. If he doesn't bite I'll let him know of a couple of places where his daughter can get discreet help and we'll look for other ways to get Hoover. I'll do this alone—that way I can be declared a rouge agent if he decides to cause trouble."

After some discussion and with Scott and Tom's help, they were able to convince Francine that this was the only chance they had of confirming the existence of this crime syndicate before the director would end this line of investigation. It was also decided that Quantara should accompany Christine to San Diego.

After the meeting broke up, Tom put his hand on Christine's shoulder and whispered in her ear, "You'd better be right! People will overlook a lot of things if you're right, but it's your career if you're wrong," then smiled at her and walked away.

On their way to the airfield, Christine told Agent Quantara that they would be following her initial plan after all. He showed no sign of surprise or hesitation at the change in plans. Christine did change a minor aspect of the plan. They would not be utilizing the CIA to conduct the kidnapping and interrogation. Christine would head up the operation and asked Quantara to help find three undercover agents of Latino descent who he trusted implicitly. Quantara smiled and assured Christine that he had just the men for the job. Christine's last task was to convince the head of the west coast DEA to let her borrow a confiscated yacht.

Chapter 8

As Andy McCall left his house and walked toward the beach, he zipped up his jogging suit against the unusually cool morning air. The fog along the coast made it seem more like San Francisco than San Diego. Andy began his stretching exercises, which kept him from noticing the two dark shapes emerging from the fog. By the time he looked up and saw the two figures clad in black diving suits with black boots and gloves and black hoods covered with dark goggles it was too late. One of the figures had fired a stun gun, which left McCall conscious but unable to move.

McCall was aware of his surroundings but unable to struggle or scream for help. When he tried to move, his muscles refused to respond. The two dark figures grabbed him under his arms and dragged him towards the sea. The waves were slapping against his legs and back as two more sets of hands grabbed him and lifted him into a rubber boat. In the bottom of the boat, he looked up and saw four people all dressed the same, wearing goggles. The next thing he heard was a small engine fight against the waves. After a few minutes, on the small boat, he felt a rope being wrapped under his arms and then he was hoisted onto a larger boat where he was pulled over the railing and quickly carried below deck and locked in a small room. During this entire ordeal, Congressman McCall was unable to scream or lift a hand in his own defense. He also didn't hear a single word being exchanged between his captors.

Christine was impressed with Quantara's crew and the yacht.

She estimated the yacht to be between 90 and 95 feet long and over 20 feet wide. It had four Deutz 1400 hp engines that could generate almost fifty knots, making this one of the faster yachts on the West Coast and ideal for their needs. The yacht's state-off-the-art electronics would allow them to stay out for days if necessary, while maintaining contact with their colleagues in Washington.

The congressman was locked in the head of one of the cabins. Christine took over the master suite, and Quantara and his three fellow agents took over the other two guestrooms. Pushing all four 1400 hp Deutz engines to the max, Congressman Andy McCall was carried far away from his San Diego home, long before he was expected to return from his run.

Once they were safely at sea and could no longer see the San Diego coast line, Christine met with Quantara and his three agents to ensure that everyone understood the next phase of the operation.

The three agents were to spend the next several hours playing cards in the crew quarters where the congressman was locked in the head. They were to speak only Spanish while they were in these quarters or anywhere near them.

As the effects of the stun gun began to wear off, McCall started to pound on the door demanding to be turned loose. He could hear the men laugh and then continue their conversation in Spanish. Andy McCall was scared—he wasn't sure what was happening. Surely these couldn't be the same people who had approached him about his daughter. He had already agreed to cooperate with them.

After several hours of letting Congressman McCall listen to nothing but Spanish, One of Agent Quantara's associates opened the door to the head and pulled the congressman out and threw him on the bed. Before the congressman had a chance to respond, the agent threw a picture of the congressman's daughter, clutching yesterday's paper, on the bed next to him.

"Congressman, our mutual friends have asked me to remind you that your daughter has not quite kicked her habit."

"Look, I don't know what else I can do for you. I already told the other men that came to visit me that I would cooperate. I have put my entire life and political career at risk. All I ask is that you don't hurt my daughter or my family."

"Our friends want to know what you know about President Canfield's assassination."

"I haven't heard anything else. I've already given you guys everything the FBI has. I haven't received another briefing memo—they just don't have anything new. Look, I just got the Western Oil deal pushed through Congress. I'm cooperating as much as I can."

Christine and Agent Quantara watched Congressman McCall from the closed- circuit TV monitor in Christine's cabin. They had seen enough, and it was a lot easier than they thought it would be. Quantara's friends had set the stage well. Their language mannerisms and appearances led Congressman McCall to believe that they were representatives of the underworld. Christine and Quantara both agreed that the congressman would be easy to turn around. It was time for phase three.

Christine and Quantara went to the main lounge and put on a tape of helicopter sounds and cranked up the volume on the yacht's sound system. The entire boat shook and it sounded like an entire fleet of helicopters was attacking. Then, as they faded the sounds of the helicopters, the crew of the boat fired a couple of rounds into the air and the agents holding McCall acted panicked as if they were under attack. They grabbed the congressman and stuffed him back in to the cabin's head.

Within moments, McCall heard several shots being fired in the cabin and then footsteps approaching his door. The door to the head flew open and in the doorway stood a figure dressed in black, wearing a black ski mask and a black hat and windbreaker with large red and white letters that read "FBI."

The FBI agent removed the hat and mask and let her hair fall to her shoulders as she smiled and stretched out her hand. "Congressman McCall, you're safe now. We have the boat under control. Please come with me."

The congressman was still somewhat in shock but extended his hand and let the agent help him up.

"My name is Christine Peal; we're with the FBI. As soon as I get the all clear, we'll be going up to the main deck to wait for our airlift off this boat."

As they walked through the cabin, the congressman saw the three men that had only moments earlier been interrogating him lying on the floor with blood covering their bodies. As they were walking out of the cabin with Christine still on full alert and her weapon at the ready, Special Agent Quantara came running up to them dressed just like Christine (without the ski mask).

"Agent Peal, the boat is secure, the dead and wounded are being administered to."

Without missing a beat Christine played her role. "Good job, Agent

Quantara; we'll go up to the main deck and wait for the airlift. Check the men in here and see if they have any ID or papers that might be useful and then join us on the main deck."

Christine escorted the congressman to the main lounge while Quantara went back into the cabin, retrieved the photo of the congressman's daughter and thanked the agents for their help. He ensured them that they could expense their cleaning bills for removing the fake blood and gave them a week's vacation and the use of the yacht.

In the main lounge, Christine was comforting the congressman and trying to get him to open up about why he thought he'd been kidnapped. The congressman was not very forthcoming until agent Quantara joined them and handed Christine the photograph and whispered something in her ear.

Christine looked at the photograph and then at the congressman and then, as if she had never seen any of this before, she began her questioning.

"Congressman McCall, is this your daughter?"

"Yes."

"Are the people that kidnapped you holding her?"

"Yes."

"What did they say they wanted?"

"I. . . I don't know."

"Don't worry, congressman; Agent Quantara found some video equipment in your cabin with a tape still running; maybe there'll be some clues on it."

The congressman's face turned white and before the video even started, he was coming clean and trying to make excuses for what they were about to see.

"You don't understand, they had my daughter, what was I supposed to do? They wanted information I was in a position to give them. I only did it to save my daughter."

Christine and Quantara sat and watched the video in silence; constantly keeping an eye on the congressman who spent most of the time with his head in his hands, sobbing. Christine stood and turned the tape off as it showed the congressman being put back into the head. She turned and took a long look at the congressman before she responded.

"Congressman McCall, I think we have a serious situation here. Based on what we just witnessed and heard on that tape, you have been and are now committing treason. I understand there are extenuating circumstances that may help explain your actions, but your actions are none the less treasonous."

The look on the congressman's face was one of total defeat. They had him exactly where they wanted him and now it was Agent Quantara's turn to play his role.

"Agent Peal, the congressman was under a lot of pressure. They had his daughter, for God's sake! There is nothing we can do about what he told them, but surely it's more important to find out what he did tell them and to recover his daughter than it is to prosecute him?"

"I don't know, Quantara, collusion with known mobsters, effecting legislation for personal gain, and conspiring against his own government. For a man in a position of trust such as his it's reprehensible."

"Maybe so, but if your daughter was just kidnapped I'm sure you would bend a little as well."

"Maybe—I can't guarantee anything, but if he cooperates completely, I'll get the director to speak to the U.S. Attorney on his behalf. Although I'm sure he would have to resign from politics when this is all over."

Quantara was now supposed to go after what they really wanted: the congressman's total cooperation.

"OK, Congressman McCall, it's up to you. We can help you get your daughter back and keep you out of jail. We need to know everything, though—how you got involved with these people, who they are, how they contact you, and what information you've given them. Are you prepared to help us, so that we can help you?"

The congressman nodded. Christine pulled a tape recorder from her pocket, turned it on and placed it on the table in front of the congressman.

"OK, Congressman McCall, we need to read you your rights first." Christine read the Congressman his rights and then started the interview. "OK let's start with how you were first contacted."

"A friend of mine, a judge on the California Supreme Court, called me and told me that he had seen some very incriminating photos of my daughter. He said that I would be contacted by some gentlemen that could make this go away and help dry out my daughter."

"That doesn't sound like much of a friend. Tell us about the pictures."

"They were pictures of my daughter standing above a dead body with a gun in her hand."

"Did you recognize the body?"

"I think it was one of my daughter's old boyfriends."

Quantara knew exactly who it was. He also knew that the boy died of an overdose and not a gunshot. At this point, however, he didn't want to tip his hand.

"Congressman McCall, I think you were probably set up. We will look into this, but I doubt that your daughter killed anyone."

"Oh God, how I hope you're right. I let her wander into that world. This is entirely my fault. You have to help me get her back."

Christine was beginning to understand the why, now she needed the who.

"We'll do all we can, but for now let's get back to your so called friend the judge. We'll need his name. We also need to know when the first contact happened and who it was that first contacted you."

"My friend was Judge Howard Feldman of Orange County, he's now a State Supreme Court Judge in San Francisco."

Christine had heard of him—he was a conservative with a reputation for being tough on crime, hardly someone that would be suspected of being in league with a crime syndicate.

"How long after you talked to Judge Feldman were you contacted?"

"The very next day two attorneys from one of the large Washington law firms came to my office on Capital Hill. They showed me the picture of my daughter with the gun, along with several others of her shooting up. They said they represented a group that could make all of this go away and keep it out of the Washington Post. I told them that I had to return to San Diego and talk to my daughter. They told me not to bother, that my daughter had entered rehab and would be unavailable for several days. When I asked them what they wanted from me, they gave me a list."

Christine couldn't believe her luck. First a State Supreme Court Justice, then a prominent D.C. law firm, and now a list. These people must feel very secure and very protected.

"Do you still have this list?"

"Yes, I do."

"Good, we'll need that list. What was on it?"

"They wanted me to help confirm two Federal judges. Then I was supposed to vote against a bill that would further open the borders between Mexico and the U.S., and for a bill that would legalize the sale of encryption technology to foreign powers. They also wanted me to push for approval of an oil company buyout, and ask the president to step in and resolve the airline strike. The only other thing was that since I'm on the Judiciary committee, I was asked to look into what the FBI had on the murder of a security expert named Canon, an FBI agent named Ballard, and on President Canfield's assassination."

"I can understand the federal judges and the votes on the various bills, but how were you supposed to get information on those murders and the assassination? Being on the Judiciary committee doesn't entitle you to that."

"They didn't really care how I got it, they just wanted it."

"Where you able to get anything?"

"Only that the guy who killed President Canfield also killed the other two and left J. Edgar Hoover's fingerprints at the scene."

Christine and Quantara were dumbfounded. "How did you get that information?" Christine asked.

"One of my secretaries in Washington was dating an FBI agent involved in the investigation. She would fill me in on the FBI's progress."

"You mean to tell me that your secretary was dating an FBI agent and he told her top-secret information and she told you?"

"Yes, something like that. My secretary didn't know she was passing me any kind of classified information. I got her into a casual conversation about the case and then she would tell me in confidence what the status of the case was."

Christine could hardly believe her ears and her luck.

"You then passed this information to the two attorneys?"

"Yes, but I only gave them the information after they let me talk to my daughter."

"Do you know the name of your secretary's boyfriend?"

"Yes, but I don't want to get him in trouble."

"It's too late for that. We can find out easily enough, but it would be better, if you told us."

"I only know his last name. She introduced him once as Special Agent Gibson."

Christine and Quantara just looked at each other and let it go for the moment.

Christine only had a couple of remaining questions for the congressman before she would turn him over to Washington.

"Are these attorneys your only contact with this group?"

"Yes; they gave me a card with a number to contact them with progress reports."

"Good, I'll need that card. Now we need to know everything you told them."

"I didn't really give them anything besides the FBI progress reports."

Christine turned off the tape recorder and put it in her pocket.

"OK, that's all I need for now. Agent Quantara has some questions about your daughter and how we might be able to find her."

Christine was making her way to the communications room and couldn't believe her luck. Not only had she just gotten enough information to confirm the existence of a new syndicate, but she had also been handed one sitting judge and at least two more in the confirmation process. In addition to the judges, she may have been handed the legitimate front for this organization in the form of one of D.C.'s most respected law firms.

The director would be more than pleased; the only question now was how much of this they could share with congress or the White House. Obviously, the reach of this new syndicate went beyond a couple of judges and a congressman.

More important to Christine was that someone had connected the three murders and the fingerprints. Someone out there knew that the three were connected, knowing that someone was after them was bound to make them nervous. Christine needed to get back to D.C. and find the rest of Hoover's files. She was still missing something.

She was fortunate and reached Tom in his office. She filled him in on the congressman's interrogation. They decided, it would be best to return the congressman to his home. They didn't want to alert the syndicate until the congressman's daughter was recovered. When he returned to Washington on his regular schedule, a more comprehensive debriefing would be conducted. Tom also scheduled a meeting with the full committee as soon as Christine and Quantara returned to Washington.

Christine returned to the main lounge and explained the plan to the congressman. "I talked to my associates. We've decided that you should return to your home and continue your relationship with these people until we have recovered your daughter. We'll be assigning one of our people as your assistant in San Diego as well as one in your office in

Washington. Every time they contact you, you are to contact us for instructions."

"What about my daughter? How am I going to get her back?"

"We will locate and retrieve her. We believe she's somewhere in San Diego. Every time you talk to her it is important to try and identify sounds that could help us pinpoint her location. We will also have your phones tapped. We don't think they'd allow her to stay on long enough for a trace, but you never know. They don't seem to concerned about being detected."

"What about the rest of my family when this is all over. These guys don't seem likely to forget."

"There is a possibility that when this is all over, we can relocate your family under the witness protection program. That is, provided you continue to cooperate and we're able to bring them down."

"I'll do anything, to keep my family together and safe."

"OK then, a helicopter should be arriving any minute to take us back to San Diego. Agent Quantara and I will go with you as far as the airport where you will be met by your new assistant. If anything happens or you are contacted again, call me at this number any time of day or night. I will be your primary contact with the FBI."

Christine handed him a card with just her name and a telephone number. Moments later they heard the helicopter approach and within minutes, they were on their way back to San Diego.

Chapter 9

The conference room was silent except for the tape playing in the middle of the table. Christine was not happy about the makeup of the group in the conference room. She had argued with the director against having Martinez and Gibson present, even arguing that Agent Gibson should be excluded for security concerns. The director would have none of it. He decided that this information was important enough for the entire committee. He felt that Agent Gibson lacked competence but was not a security risk. Reluctantly Christine began the meeting.

Everyone sitting around the table was concentrating on what they were hearing and taking notes. For the most part they found it inconceivable that this was McCall's voice. As they came to the part where the congressman was about to explain how he got the information from the FBI, Christine stopped the tape and addressed the director one more time.

"Sir, this next part is extremely sensitive and could be quite embarrassing for one of our agents; I once again recommend it not be played in open committee."

"As I told you before, this information is too vital to withhold from any member of the committee, and I want everyone to hear the full report."

Christine turned the tape recorder back on. As the congressman was laying it out on the tape, everyone's attention turned to Gibson, the director's face became red with anger, until he finally exploded.

"Shut that damned thing off. God damn it! Christine, you should have told me about this when you first called in!"

"This is not something I wanted to discuss over the telephone and we have not had an opportunity to meet since I returned. I tried to get you to review it separately, sir."

"Damn it, Gibson, you're an FBI agent—not some god-damned high school kid that has to impress the girls with how much you know. Tell me this jerk is making it up! Are you dating this congressman's secretary?"

"Yes, I guess I am."

"Jesus Christ! Gibson, did you give her classified information?"

"It may have slipped out while we were together."

"You mean while you were in bed together don't you?"

"I guess so."

"Thinking with that head in your pants just cost you your job and maybe even some jail time." The director turned to ASAC Martinez and with fire still burning in his eyes and his voice still raised told him what he wanted done with Agent Gibson.

"He belongs to you, so you get him the hell out of here, and keep him in your office until I can figure out what to do with him."

The room was eerily silent until ASAC Martinez and Special Agent Gibson had left. Then the director took a deep breath and addressed the remaining agents.

"What do we do with the secretary?"

Christine had already thought of that. "I recommend we do nothing. She is unaware of the syndicate as far as we know. It was the congressman that got information from her and we have him firmly under control."

Scott supported Christine's recommendation. "Christine's right. We should do very little to change the current structure of the congressman's office. In fact, I recommend that we encourage Gibson to continue his liaison with her, at least until this is over."

The director nodded his head in agreement. "OK, for now we'll leave things as they are. I'm going to remove that idiot Gibson from this case, revoke his security clearance, and put him on some inconsequential administrative duty until this is over. Then I'm going to drum his ass out of the FBI."

The director returned his attention to Christine. "Unless you have any more surprises, let's get on with the rest of this briefing." Christine turned the tape back on and everyone listened to the rest of it without further interruption.

"Jesus Christine, this thing is a bomb shell. This was great work." said ASAC Young.

It was Christine's turn to give credit to Quantara and his people. "I think it's important to note that without the help of Agent Quantara and his people and equipment in San Diego, we would never have been able to break the congressman."

"I appreciate that, Agent Peal, exactly how did you get the congressman to confess all of his sins?" ASAC Young asked.

" Are you sure you want to know? It might put you in a difficult position down the road." Christine asked Director Flynn.

Flynn glanced at Scott, who shook his head and slightly rolled his eyes. "Are we going to be able to use any of this when we get to court?" The director asked.

"Probably the confession, I'm not sure we want to play the entire tape." Christine admitted.

"Of course not, and I'm probably better off not knowing the details of how you got that confession."

"Yes, sir."

Their next step was to figure out how to proceed. Christine had worked on the shell of a plan on her flight back from San Diego.

"I think what we need to do is to have Agent Quantara and me return to California and work on the judge. He's our best link to the next level. He may also be able to provide us with a lead on the congressman's daughter."

The director nodded his head and looked to Scott for his thoughts. "Scott, this is your team, what do you think?"

"I'm impressed with how Christine has handled this whole thing. I think we ought to let her run with it."

"OK, Christine, but I have to inject a word of caution. You did a great job on breaking the congressman, but don't expect this judge to be easy. He's probably much more deeply entrenched than the congressman and probably has a lot more to lose by giving up his associates.

"While you and Quantara see about the judge, Scott and Francine will find a friendly face on the Senate and House oversight committees and bring them into the loop. I don't want these people to come after us later for investigating one of their own without letting them know."

Francine had another thought along those same lines. "Mr. Director, I think it is essential that we also bring in the House Judiciary committee. We should give them the name of the judges under investigation and why they are under investigation. After all, we don't want them approved."

Tom disagreed. "I don't know about bringing in all of these people on this investigation. If this syndicate expected to get those judges through the confirmation process, then chances are they had more than one congressman on the payroll. It might also be in our interest to let them get approved and then monitor their activities on the bench. We could watch and see who ends up fighting the hardest for their confirmation. That could possibly flush out additional members of this cooperative!"

The director agreed. "Actually, you're both right. This is a great opportunity to gather more intelligence, but we need to let Congress know what we're doing, and at the same time keep this close until we know who all the players are. Let's notify the chairman of the Judiciary Committee and stress the level of security involved in this investigation. Scott, I'll leave that up to you and Francine—if you think you'll need my presence when you talk to these legislators let me know."

Scott nodded and made some notes and issued additional assignments. "Tom, I thought you could take charge of identifying the lawyers and putting them under surveillance. I doubt they'll make personal contact with any senior members of the syndicate, but we may be able to intercept their E-mail or phone calls."

"Do we have the names and descriptions of these attorneys?"

"Yes, they actually left a business card with the congressman." Christine replied. "They were obviously not too concerned about him giving them up."

"I think as long as they have control of the daughter, they figure they control him." Tom said.

"You're probably right, Tom. I'll get you the descriptions after we're finished here."

Tom made some notes on his pad and nodded in agreement.

The director could sense that the meeting was about to come to a close. "OK, there is a lot to be done before Christine and Quantara can head back to California. We still have to decide how much of this Scott can put in his briefing tomorrow to all of the department heads and how much of this I can release to the White House. We also have to line up all those warrants that we're going to need. It's not going to be easy to get judges to issue warrants on other judges."

Aside from the director, Scott had more experience in the political arena than any of the others. "The problem is not the CIA or the NSA, the problem is the State Department and the White House. The CIA and the NSA understand top secret, the State Department, and especially the White House staff, don't really understand top secret. If they think the information could help them politically they'll put it on the five o'clock news."

Christine knew this wasn't what the director wanted to hear, but she had to agree with Scott. "Scott's right, anything we give to the White House, we should be prepared to hear on the five o'clock news. We don't know how many senators, congressman, judges, or even White House staff members are part of this. I propose that anything we give to anyone outside of this room, we need to give to Congressman McCall to pass on, if we expect them to continue to believe him."

"Okay then, as the director of the FBI, I'll decide who gets what. For now, in our official briefings, we'll tell everyone that we have made some progress on the killer, but haven't gotten any closer to the people behind him. We're going to have to take our chances with the judge who's issuing the warrants. I'm sure he won't issue them without all of the facts. I think, Scott, you and Jim Brodrick should get all of the warrants for us. Jim can help you find the right judge and cut through some of the red tape. We don't want a huge paper trail. We also should bring in Wesley at NSA. This may have national security implications if it's as wide spread as it appears."

Everyone nodded their agreement.

"Unless anybody has anything else, we'll get back together here in forty-eight hours—that should give us plenty of time to get all of the warrants and talk to the people we need to."

Christine wasn't quite ready to table everything just yet. "Mr. Director, I do have one more thing. What about Deputy Director Martinez and Agent Gibson, how will they fit into this operation?"

"That's a good question, Christine. I think this information is important enough to let Martinez know about. It could only help his task of finding the Hoover killer. It might even support his argument that the Hoover killer is getting information from the FBI—maybe not directly—but it sure looks like this new syndicate has some long tentacles. I'll bring him up to date on everything and then let him run with it in his investigation. Agent Gibson is another story; we won't tell him anything."

Christine wasn't too keen about giving Martinez access to the information that she worked so hard to gather, but she also knew better than to argue with the director.

"Mr. Director, I understand the need to provide this information to the ASAC, but due to its sensitivity, might I suggest that it not be released to anyone else without the knowledge of this committee?"

"Very well, Christine. I'll tell Martinez it's for his use only and not to be shared."

"Thank you. Also, has ASAC Martinez uncovered any information on the Hoover killer that might assist our investigation?"

"No, up to now he and Agent Gibson haven't identified a definite direction to follow. If there is nothing else, I'll see everyone back here in forty-eight hours."

Chapter 10

The next forty-eight hours were busy for everyone. Scott and Director Flynn spent most of that time briefing various groups and committees and dancing around the more serious questions.

Jim Brodrick was as good as his reputation. He was able to connect Scott with a federal judge who provided the various warrants requested. He was even able to provide the warrants on the other judges. Judge Franklin was highly regarded by his colleagues and the correctness of his warrants would never be challenged.

Francine was also beginning to show her value to the team. She set up a meeting for Scott with Senator Franklin De Marco and Congressman Dorin Connelly. These men headed the FBI oversight committees for their respective legislative bodies. Neither was too eager to attend a "clandestine" meeting with FBI agents without more information. Francine, by using her skills of persuasion and playing to their political egos, was able to convince both men to attend the meeting. She was also able to convince Congressman Oscar Myers and Senator Ashcroft Pickford III (both chairman of their respective judiciary committees), to attend.

Scott had sent a limousine to pick up members for the meeting and bring them to the Hyatt Regency near the Capitol Building. As the men began to gather in a conference room on the top floor of the hotel, they were extremely curious and somewhat edgy. Francine did the best she could to keep them calm until Scott arrived.

Senator De Marco was all over Scott as he walked through the door.

"OK, Peterson, what the hell is going on here? What's all of this clandestine crap? Why the hell has the head of the Washington office of the FBI shuttled two congressman and two senators to this hotel when we could have just as easily met in one of our offices?"

ADIC Scott Peterson calmly put his briefcase on the table, pulled out four sheets of paper and handed one to each of the legislators.

"Gentlemen, I assure you this meeting was necessary and the confidentiality of the subject matter required a meeting away from Capitol Hill. Before I can answer the rest of your questions and provide you with more details, I must ask you to read and sign the documents in front of you."

They each scanned the document and Senator Pickford reacted first.

"This is insulting! I've probably created more confidential documents than you've seen. I'm a United States senator, which means that I have already sworn to keep and uphold the laws of this country. That includes keeping those secrets that need to be kept. By the expressions on the face of my colleagues, I think they feel the same way."

"Senator Pickford, believe me when I tell you that Director Flynn understands that. This subject matter, however, is of such sensitivity that we cannot proceed until we have signed statements from everyone acknowledging that you understand that the leaking or otherwise unauthorized disclosure of this information will constitute treason."

"I don't know about the rest of them, but I'm not signing anything until I know what the hell is going on."

Congressman Myers (the house judiciary committee) agreed with Senator Pickford. Senator De Marco and Congressman Connelly, however, decided that since they were already here, signing this one more time was not going to make any difference. Besides, all of this secrecy had made them extremely curious.

Scott picked up the signed documents from Senator De Marco and Congressman Connelly. He then motioned towards Francine who was standing next to a door at the side of the conference room.

"Senator Pickford, Congressman Myers, if you would please follow Special Agent English to the adjoining room, she has established a direct line to Director Flynn. Hopefully he will be able to explain why you should stay and hear this briefing."

As the two men got up and left the room, they were still cursing Scott and the situation. Francine had already placed the call to the director and put him on the intercom once the men were seated.

"Mr. Director, this is Agent English: with me are Senator Pickford and Congressman Myers."

"Thank you, Francine. Hello Pick, Oscar. I knew that at least one of you would balk at signing this. I guess with the two of you being lawyers and former judges, I should have expected it to be you two." Ashcroft Pickford and Martin Flynn knew each other from Director Flynn's days in the Senate and had become reasonable friends although they often found each other on opposite sides of issues.

"OK Marty, what's going on here? You've got your people bringing us down here all clandestine-like and then they won't tell us what's going on until we sign another secrecy document. You know I don't work like that— I work for the people not the FBI. If this is truly a matter of national security, then our common sense and our oath of office will make sure that we do the right thing."

"This is definitely a matter of national security. Right now, we have enough proof to charge one congressman with treason, and that's all I can tell you until you sign this document. I will tell you that this briefing directly affects how you and Oscar do business. For Connelly and DeMarco it's more informational since they're heads of our oversight committees, but for the two of you it's essential that you be in this loop. I have never lied or misled either of you; I strongly recommend that both of you sign this document so that you can be fully briefed and kept in the loop."

Both men looked at each other and Congressman Myers nodded his head to Senator Pickford.

"OK Marty, Oscar and I will sign your secrecy reminder, but this had better be good because it goes against all of my instincts."

Both men returned to the conference room and signed the security agreements.

Scott began his briefing.

"Thank you for your cooperation, gentlemen. What you are about to hear you will find hard to believe at first, but after reviewing our evidence, you will undoubtedly believe, as does Director Flynn, that we have a major security crisis in the legislature and Judicial branches of our government. A crisis, which to date implicates federal judges and at least one congressman. We believe these acts include at least two more congressmen and perhaps even a senator or two. Currently we have no proof beyond one congressman, one sitting federal judge and two candidates for federal judgeships that are currently in front of the House Judiciary committee."

Pickford and Myers were stunned.

"What judges?" Meyers asked. "We have six in front of our committee for approval right now. What's the nature of their treason? We're voting on two of them tomorrow afternoon, so you'd better be ready to give some names."

"We are ready to give you the names of the congressman, the sitting judge, as well as those in front of your committee, but first please let me explain the nature of the treason and how we would like to deal with it."

Scott explained Representative McCall's roll and how he was to ensure passage of certain legislation that would be beneficial to this new syndicate.

The congressmen found it hard to believe that any criminal organization this vast could exist in today's environment.

Scott reminded them that with today's technology, and the Internet, running a worldwide criminal enterprise is no more difficult then running a global corporation.

Scott played the tapes for the congressmen.

Myers was not amused when he heard the tapes of Congressmen McCall (who was a member of his committee) admit to manipulating legislation and pushing through the confirmation of judges positively linked to organized crime.

"That son of a bitch! I trusted him! I asked him to be on the judiciary committee! I'll have him removed the minute I get back."

"Representative Myers, I can understand your outrage, but that's not how we would like to handle it."

"I can't let him stay on the committee, every vote he makes would come under question."

"Not necessarily; Congressman McCall is now under the FBI's control. Before we charge him, we would like to use him to smoke out any other high-ranking members of this new syndicate and to feed false information back to its leaders."

"I can't leave him on the committee—every decision we make would be tainted."

"Representative Myers, it's our belief that there is at least one other member of your committee working with this syndicate. We would like to use Congressman McCall to help flush him out."

"What about those two judges you were talking about, the ones in front of my committee? Surely we can do something with them?"

"It is essential that the syndicate not be made aware of our knowledge. We recommend that you approve one of the judges and find some political reason to disapprove the other. The FBI will track every case and every decision of the one that you approve. When we're ready to close down the syndicate, he'll be easy to pick up. Meanwhile we may get a glimpse of how they operate and who their fronts are. We will also keep an eye on the other judge and pick him up when the time is right. If we can find a weakness in either one of them as we did with Representative McCall, then we should be able to expedite this investigation."

"OK, this is obviously bigger than my committee; I'll do what I can. I assume I'll be able to select which one to reject?"

"Of course, Representative Myers. You may not, however, use anything that you have heard here in your rejection process."

"Fine, I'll expect immediate notification as soon as you have a lead on the other scumbag on my committee."

"Of course, that goes without saying."

Representative Myers grumbled something, pulled out a note pad, and began taking notes. Scott reminded him that this was a secret meeting and as such nothing in writing would be allowed to leave the conference room. Representative Myers put the note pad away and reclined in his chair as Scott continued his briefing.

"Gentlemen, we believe that the people we have uncovered so far are only minor players, and except for Judge Feldman, have not been brought into the core of the syndicate. Senator De Marco and Representative Connelly are here today in their roles as overseers and advisors to the FBI. We are about to launch an investigation to include wiretaps and surveillance of several senators, judges, and representatives. Director Flynn felt that we should keep the oversight and Judiciary committees involved every step of the way.

"We believe that the corruption is extensive. Therefore, it's essential that you not discuss this with your colleagues or your staff. At least not until we have a better understanding of the depth of this problem."

Senator De Marco had been involved with oversight of the FBI for many years and was not always an ally.

"OK, let's say we buy everything you've said—what about possible leaks from your agency? You guys haven't exactly been pristine in that area in the past."

"That's a good question and a valid concern, Senator De Marco. In the interest of cooperation and full disclosure, I am prepared to admit that we have already been compromised on this project."

Senator Pickford's face turned red as he slammed his fist down on the table.

"You've been compromised? How the hell did that happen? You put us through all of this clandestine crap and have us swear in blood, and your own agency can't keep a lid on this!"

"It's not quite like that. One of our agents, through some pillow talk with one of Representative McCall's aides, revealed some information regarding the progress of our investigation. This information then found its way to the syndicate by way of a law firm here in Washington. Fortunately the investigation had not progressed much at that time."

"What are you doing with the agent in question?"

"For now we are keeping him in place but away from any sensitive material. When this is all over, the director may press formal charges. His career at the FBI or any other law enforcement agency is over for sure."

Senator De Marco leaned forward, his forearms on the table, cleared his throat and began to speak in a calm and somewhat hushed tone, requiring everyone to listen more closely.

"Agent Peterson, you have one heck of a problem here. You have to conduct an investigation that involves some of the most powerful and visible people in the country. Any leaks of unconfirmed allegations could ruin the careers of many innocent and good men. If your investigation is not thorough enough, you could leave a cancer in our government that could make us a third-world government in a matter of a few years. I have a proposal that might make your job a little easier. I propose that we add the leaders of both parties from the House and the Senate to this group and call it a "Legislative Advisory Panel." You can brief us on a weekly basis or as needed. We'll act as advisors and assist you in getting access to various senators and congressmen. In turn, this committee will want assurance that once an individual has been cleared, all the files regarding the investigation of that individual be destroyed. You are not to keep any of the records showing that there ever was an investigation. I'm sure that none of us on the advisory panel want any of the information you end up gathering to become political fodder. Once this is over, we would also like to have access to any information you have that implicates any member of either house, so that we may appoint an independent counsel and institute our own expulsion procedures."

"I'll have to discuss this with the director. I don't believe he will have any problem with it."

"Good, now how many people know the whole story?"

"Including yourselves, fourteen."

"That means ten FBI agents know about this. How are you going to keep a lid on this?"

"All of the agents involved have worked on many classified projects for the FBI. If there is a leak it would be easily isolated."

"I'm sure that you're fully aware, Agent Peterson, that as the FBI Agent in Charge, your career is on the line."

"Senator, I'm fully aware that all of our careers are at stake on this one. I am however working with the best team the FBI has. Our top agents are assigned to this case. That includes of course, agents West, Broderick, and Peal."

De Marco was taken a little off guard.

"Agent Peal? Doesn't she work for Martinez?"

"Yes, she does."

"With the visibility and sensitivity of this case, don't you think you should have someone more senior on this case? Someone like Martinez?"

"Actually, Senator, Agent Martinez is also on the task force. Agent Peal, however is ideal for this case. The director selected her, and Tom West and I wholeheartedly support his decision. In fact, it was her own operation that exposed Congressman McCall, as well as our internal leak."

"What's Martinez think about all of this? He does after all head up Organized Crime."

Scott thought long and hard before answering, then he decided "what the heck," the director did tell him to tell them the truth. This might be his only opportunity to let someone outside the agency know that Martinez now had the responsibility of bringing in the Hoover killer.

"ASAC Martinez is on the task force in an advisory capacity. His primary focus will be the identification and capture of the Hoover killer."

"I thought we already had a task force for that?"

"We do sir. ASAC Martinez, however, believes he has a new approach that will be more effective. He will be running an independent task force reporting straight to the director."

Senator De Marco nodded.

"In other words, Martinez believes that there is a leak in your agency, so he's not sharing his strategy."

"That is his belief."

Senator Pickford and Congressman Myers looked confused.

"Excuse us, gentlemen," Congressman Myers interrupted, "What exactly is the Hoover killer case?"

"In our routine briefings to Senator De Marco and Congressman Connelly and their respective committees, we discuss our top five cases and this is one of those cases." Scott explained. "It is not relevant to this situation, except for the fact that ASAC Martinez is involved in both investigations."

Scott's explanation seemed to appease all those concerned. He assured them the director would contact the individuals Senator De Marco had requested be added to the committee and then closed the meeting.

The attendees left as they arrived, one at a time in unmarked black limousines. Scott and Francine let out a sigh of relief, comfortable in the fact that they would be able to report a successful meeting to the director.

Tom's check on the two attorneys began to pay off right away. His investigation led him to "Burns, Roberts, Weisman and Cole", a D.C. firm with over 100 attorneys in Washington and another 250 spread around the rest of the country. Unlike most firms, "Burns, Roberts, Weisman and Cole" didn't specialize, but instead was structured more like a corporation with separate divisions focusing on different areas of the law.

Their largest division, the Criminal Law Division, is made up of more than thirty five percent of the company's U.S. attorneys. Retired Superior Court Judge Franklin Cole currently heads this division. Judge Cole is no longer a practicing trial lawyer, but his reputation and the firm's success has been able to attract some of the top trial lawyers in the country to the "Burns, Roberts, Weisman and Cole" banner. Over the past five years, his team of criminal attorneys had amassed an impressive eighty-two percent acquittal rate, making them the most highly-sought after criminal law firm for high-profile cases in the country.

Their International Law department, with twenty attorneys in the U.S. and an additional 165 abroad, competes with the top three in the world despite its smaller size.

Intellectual Property Rights and International Trade is the department that has been growing the fastest in the firm. Their most recent victory over Vogel, the second largest software firm in the world (based in Germany), helped establish them as a player in the Intellectual Property Rights field.

Their most profitable division however, is not a law division at all, but rather one that works hand-in-hand with the other divisions in presenting the appropriate image of their clients to the public.

The Professional Management Division (PM) is affectionately known as the Political Misconduct division since many of their clients are politicians and high-profile individuals.

Paul Cedes, a former ambassador and past director of the CIA, heads PM. It's to this division that Tom traced the two attorneys that visited Congressman McCall. Tom's research uncovered things that both amazed and confused him.

He met Agent Quantara and reviewed the photos of the two out-of-place participants spotted at the militia meeting. He wasn't surprised to find that they matched the surveillance photos of the two attorneys.

His research also uncovered that Judge Feldman clerked for Judge Cole when Cole served on the California Appellate Court. The more Tom researched the law firm, the more certain he became that they were involved with this syndicate up to their necks. Among the many names that served as clerks during Judge Cole's extensive career, was Judge Phillip Walker.

Tom got a sick feeling in the pit of his stomach as the possible involvement of Judge Walker ran through his mind. Could it be pure coincidence that Judge Walker's office was used by Hoover to assassinate President Canfield or was Judge Walker part of this syndicate as well? Tom liked Judge Walker and didn't want to believe he was involved, but the evidence, though circumstantial, definitely linked him to Judge Cole. For Tom there were still too many questions and not nearly enough answers.

Chapter 11

Christine was back in her apartment, reviewing her notes and tapes. She thought that once Ballard was gone, his face would no longer haunt her. This just wasn't the case. Every night while she slept, she still saw Special Agent Ballard shooting her father in the back and Agent Canon's bullet blowing open her mother's head at pointblank range.

When she first joined the shooting team at Michigan State, she knew that one day she would use these skills to erase the faces of the two FBI agents that were imprinted on her seven-year-old mind so long ago. When the FBI recruited her after she won Olympic Silver, she became convinced that it was her destiny to avenge her family.

Christine first met Special Agent Ballard at the FBI Academy in Quantico, Virginia. She had never know the agent's name, but when she looked up to check out their next speaker and saw that face, her heart stopped. She glanced at his coat and saw the FBI badge draped over the breast pocket of his dark blue suit. To Christine it was as if time stood still. His face was the same and it looked like he hadn't changed clothes since that night twenty years ago when he killed her father.

Her body was screaming with terror but her mind refused to send the sounds to her mouth. She was stunned and unable to move. All she could do was watch in silence. She watched every movement he made, how he walked, how he talked, the way he took a sip of water before he was about to make an important point. She watched him eat with the rest of the students in the cafeteria. She watched as he got into his green FBI sedan and drove out the Academy gates. Christine had met the devil at the tender age of twenty-five. It would be another two years before she would be able to slay at least one of her demons.

Listening to Ballard's pleas on the tape gave her a small sense of satisfaction. But remembering the man who shot her father, and watching him as he crumbled before her eyes, was even more rewarding.

Christine listened to the tape again as she had daily for the past ten years. Listening to Ballard explain that he was only acting on Hoover's orders. Explaining that he had no personal animosity towards her or her family; that he and Gannon were only acting in the interest of national security. Christine listened over and over and every time the name sounded the same: Gannon. For over ten years she searched FBI personnel rosters and archives for an Agent Gannon, never finding any reference to him.

It wasn't until she was reviewing recently released and computerized files from J. Edgar Hoover's "private collection of cases" that she found her first lead. A name she had heard around the FBI appeared in several of the cases dated in the late sixties.

Agent Andy Greenfield was the supervisory senior resident agent in charge of the FBI Resident Agency in Lewiston, Idaho for more than fifteen years. Christine remembered his name because he was called out of retirement to help solve one of the agencies most puzzling murder cases on the Nez Perce Indian reservation.

After finding his name, Christine was like a child at Christmas. She could barely hide her excitement as she traveled to Idaho to ask retired Agent Greenfield questions that had haunted her for thirty years.

Questions like: Who were her parents? Why were they so dangerous to Director Hoover? Who and where was agent Gannon? Where are the rest of Hoover's "Special Projects" files?

As she got closer, however, she realized that those were answers that she would have to discover for herself.

She instantly liked Agent Greenfield. He was a big man, over six feet tall with broad shoulders and a face with lines that each had a story behind them. He didn't look like a typical FBI agent, he looked more like a man who had spent most of his life in the mountains. He walked with a cane, although it was obvious that he didn't need it; perhaps a habit left over from an old injury.

His house was a large A-frame built just above the banks of the Snake River where towns of Lewiston and Clarkston split the Idaho Washington border.

His friendly nature put Christine at ease. Andy, as he preferred to be called, enjoyed reminiscing about the FBI. He'd enjoyed his time there. He was more reluctant to talk about the early days of his service with the Bureau. Those, as he put it, "were days I would just as soon forget."

Christine pushed and told him that they were working on a case that may be related to one of Hoover's "Special Unit" cases from the late sixties.

As Christine listened to the tape, she could hear the anguish and pain in the old man's voice as he recalled a darker time in his life.

"The Special Projects Unit was no more than Hoover's personal dirty tricks squad. We were responsible to no one except Hoover himself. We had top priority on everything. I had been with the unit since sixty-one. In the early days, the jobs were primarily borderline legal. A bad guy would thumb his nose at the system or at Hoover; it was our job to break his thumb and get him back in line. Sometimes we got information from suspects when no one else could. It was that kind of job.

"The sixties just got crazier and crazier. Vietnam was in full swing, we had the hippies and the beatniks, and we also had the blacks pushing for more rights. In retrospect, I'm sure Hoover was in the early stages of Alzheimer's. All he wanted was those communist hippies locked up and to keep those niggers from starting another revolution."

There was a brief pause on the tape before Andy continued. "I'm sorry if this offends you, Christine, but for you to understand the Special Projects Unit, you have to understand the times.

"By the late sixties, the unit was totally corrupt. I finally asked Hoover to let me out in '68. The unit had become no more than a bunch of spies, thieves and murderers. We had photos of every enemy that Hoover or the FBI had ever made. If the people were straight, we would create compromising positions to photograph them in.

"As the whole world now knows, Hoover himself was no angel. As a result, there were people that had him over the barrel, which led me to believe that the Special Projects Unit, at Hoover's direction, did some work for the mob. That's when I got out. Hoover was very gracious about letting me out. He even gave me my own Resident Agency in Maine. I don't think he wanted me anywhere near where the Special Projects Unit might be operating."

Christine had listened to this tape many times, and each time she could feel the man's shame for being part of something he had despised. She listened to the rest of the tape as she heard herself questioning the retired agent.

"Andy, did you ever hear of an Agent Gannon in the Special Projects Unit?"

"No, when was he there?"

"Probably in sixty-nine."

"I was gone by then."

"How about an Agent Ballard?"

"Of course I knew Ballard. We worked some cases together; when I left, he teamed up with some real cocky young guy. You know... come to think of it, his name wasn't Gannon, it was Canon. I remember, because he spelled it funny. He only used one "n." He was a real jerk; he had a thing for African Americans, every other word out of his mouth was nigger this, nigger that. He just didn't seem like the right person to be handling all those civil rights cases."

"Do you know whatever happened to him?"

"Last I heard he left the Bureau after Hoover died."

"Did you ever hear about any African American families in D.C. being wiped out in '69?"

"I'm sorry, but that was happening all over the country back then. I can't remember a specific family. Maybe if you told me a little about them, I could help you."

"We don't really know that much about them ourselves. We just had someone come forward and claim that the FBI killed their family in 1969. I was hoping that you might be able to tell us a little about what was going on back then."

"I'm sorry, there was a lot going on, but I was already in Maine by that time. I heard the rumors of course, but I had to believe that they were exaggerated."

"Maybe you can help me with the case files from that period. We haven't been able to find any of the Special Projects files."

Agent Greenfield chuckled. "If you find those files, you'll have the motherlode. With those files, you'll be able to solve the Kennedy assassination. I'll tell you something that very few people know. I'm sure there are files somewhere, but more importantly, Hoover was so enthralled with technology and so insecure that he not only ran illegal wiretaps for his investigations, but he also taped most of his friends and all of his personal telephone conversations. None of his personal tapes and only a few of his illegal wiretaps have ever turned up. If you could find those, you would own every secret this country had in the sixties."

"I don't suppose you know where I could look for them?"

"Hoover was paranoid; he would never let them get too far away. I would look in his old offices or at his home."

"I appreciate your help. If you think of anything else, please give me a call on my cell phone; I have it with me twenty-four hours a day." Christine gave him her business card and circled her cell phone number.

"I'll do that. By the way, what was the name of the family allegedly wiped out by the FBI?"

"The Barbers."

"Hmm, that name does sound familiar, I'm not sure why. I'll keep thinking about it, though."

Christine turned off the tape and sat in the dark of her apartment. Agent Greenfield had provided her the help she needed to find the FBI agent that shot her mother. She in turn tracked him down and exorcised the second demon from her mind.

Christine debated playing the tape of Canon's pleas for mercy. However, every time she did, she wondered when and where this would end. Canon confirmed Hoover's involvement, and tried to buy his life by laying out a conspiracy which included a deputy director of the CIA, the head of the FBI, the vice-president of the United States and his boss, a businessman named Walter Brooks.

Christine had promised herself many nights since that she wouldn't rest until she understood why her family was murdered and all those involved were dead.

Uncovering the close relationship between Hoover and Vice-President Canfield wasn't difficult. It didn't take much of an imagination for Christine to believe Canon's last words, in which he implicated Vice-President Canfield as a major force behind the assassination of the Barbers. She desperately wanted to question him about his motives, but knew he was too well guarded and couldn't risk it. She would have to get her answers from one of the other two murderers. There was no way, however, knowing that he was responsible for her family's deaths, that she could let this man enjoy another moment with his family.

Christine smiled at the irony of Canfield dying on his way to witness one of the proudest moments of his family.

For now, she had to console herself with her thoughts and find out more about this CIA deputy director and Walter Brooks.

The ring of her telephone interrupted her thoughts.

"Christine, it's Quantara."

"Ah, Special Agent Quantara, have you kidnapped any congressmen lately?"

"No, I only do that under direct orders. I just wanted to remind you about the meeting tomorrow. Actually I was calling to see if you wanted to get together for dinner tonight to compare notes before the meeting."

"I would love to except tonight's not a good night. I'll take a rain check, though."

"OK, just thought I'd ask. I'll see you at the meeting."

"Thanks for calling; I'll see you there."

Chapter 12

The meeting started a few minutes late as everyone waited for Director Flynn to arrive. Noticeably absent from the meeting was Special Agent Gibson. ASAC Martinez, however, was sitting to the right of the director's chair frantically scribbling something in his notebook. When the director walked through the door, Martinez started to rise from his chair until he realized that no one else was standing, and feeling a bit foolish he quickly sat down. The director greeted the committee as he was settling in.

"I'm sorry I'm late, I got called to the White House. Brian Hunt, the president's chief of staff, seems to believe that we're holding back critical information from them.

"As you know, there's going to be a U.S.–African economic and technology summit in Washington next month. This will be the first time this many African leaders will be in the same place, at the same time. The president is headed to Africa in two weeks to convince some of the holdouts they should attend. He wants the Canfield assassination cleared up before he goes.

"The White House has already received calls from several of the African leaders concerned about their safety. They're afraid that if we can't protect our own former presidents, how are we going to protect so many of them.

"Hunt made it clear that the president wants to be able to assure everyone that they'll be safe on American soil."

Christine voiced what everyone was thinking. "That doesn't give us much time, boss. We still don't know what the meeting between Cedes and the militia was all about and we don't have a clue where to find Hoover. This could still get very complicated."

"That's a good point, Christine. Before we leave here, we'll have an aggressive plan of action, but we won't risk the entire operation for one political moment. This is an important summit for this administration, but we are not going to rush into any mistakes. This investigation will go wherever the facts and the evidence take us. We won't contaminate the investigation, not even for this summit.

"If at the end of the investigation we don't think we can guarantee the safety of the African delegations, then we'll let the White House know. It'll be up to the Secret Service to decide what to do with the information."

The director looked around the room and saw nods of agreement and understanding from everyone.

"Good, then let's get down to business. It's been a hectic forty-eight hours; Scott and I have spent most of our time in briefings and dodging the tough questions. Tom, where are we with Hoover? Any luck finding him?"

"I'm afraid we don't have much more than the last time we talked. We tracked the janitor to the train station. We've had men there every day since the assassination, circulating photos and computer-enhanced images in hopes that one of the regulars may have spotted him. We tracked him onto a train, which he took to the Rhode Island station several stops away. There we were able to track him in to the men's room. After that we can't find a single witness or surveillance camera that saw anyone that even resembled our janitor. We believe he changed his clothes in one of the stalls, removed his mustache, maybe even put on a wig and emerged as someone totally new and just disappeared into the crowd."

"What about fingerprints in the bathroom?" Martinez blurted it out before he thought the question through; it was a rookie mistake and he knew it.

Tom responded with some irritation in his voice. "That bathroom is used by thousands of people every day—even if there were prints, they were smudged and unusable long before we got to the scene. Besides, knowing our man, he wouldn't chance it; he would have worn gloves even into the bathroom."

Christine decided to play this game for a few minutes. "Have you found the weapon yet? From the surveillance photos we saw the janitor didn't take anything out of the building with him except the mop and the bucket."

"No we haven't; Christine, our experts tell us that for the accuracy he needed from that distance, the barrel of his weapon had to be at least thirty inches long and one continuous piece. A barrel that screws together could leave a seam, which could affect the trajectory of the round. Based on that analysis, we believe the janitor took the barrel with him inside the mop handle. The rest of the equipment he probably had hidden on his body somewhere. He never expected the guard to search him. He knew the guard would be focused on the mop bucket once it set off the alarm.

"The guard never once considered the fact that none of the other janitors took their mops and buckets home with them. There are several maintenance rooms throughout the building where their equipment is usually stored.

"In my opinion, Hoover brought everything he needed with him and then took it all out the same way. I don't believe we'll find his weapon until we find him."

Christine agreed. "You're probably right; did the tape of him entering the building give you anything new to go on?"

"Not really; it showed him entering with his mop and bucket through the same entrance that he left from. This just confirms our analysis that he brought everything with him and then took it back out with him. I still can't get over the fact that the guard didn't pick up on the fact that he was the only janitor to bring his own mop and bucket."

Director Flynn just smiled. "Hoover's no fool—I would guess that he has a psychology background. He was counting on the simple human association that a janitor with a mop and bucket is never out of place." The director then turned to Martinez. "How about you, Freddie, anything new on your hunt for Hoover?"

"No, not really. I still think he's getting his information from inside the FBI. I just haven't been able to make any headway in that direction. Since you pulled agent Gibson off of my detail, I'm a little short on manpower. I was hoping that Congressman McCall would be more help."

"What about Agent Gibson's relationship with Congressman McCall's secretary—have we been able to exploit that relationship anymore?"

"No, not yet, but Agent Gibson is being extremely cooperative,"

Martinez offered.

"Okay, anything else we need to know about Hoover?" The director waited a second before going on. "Good; Scott, how did you and Brian do with those warrants?"

"Judge Franklin signed off on all of the warrants. We don't have all of our teams in place yet, but we're working on it. Due to the resource restrictions, I have to make some priority decisions."

"How you doing with that?"

"We have audio and visual surveillance in place on Congressman McCall's phones, his home in San Diego, and his home and office in D.C. We're using three teams for around-the-clock surveillance in each location, so for the congressman alone, we have nine teams committed. We're also hoping the taps on his phones will give us a lead on his daughter's location. We have taps on the two judges before the Judiciary committee and have committed a total of four teams for-around-the clock surveillance on them. Those teams should be in place by tonight, tomorrow morning at the latest."

"Scott, should we put taps on the entire Judiciary committee?" Tom asked.

Scott got a slight smile on his face as he thought about Congressman Myers. "We had one hell of a time getting Myers to sign the confidentiality document. If he thought we were taping him, he'd have all of our hides. I think he's clean, but even if he isn't, we've already alerted him, so he's not about to say anything over an open line. Anything we could get from him won't be worth the hell we'd catch if he caught us spying on him."

The director agreed with Scott. "He's right, Tom, put a tap on the rest of the committee but leave Myers alone. I think we've got at least one more bad apple there."

Scott continued, "We've had some problems getting our resources in place in San Francisco. We should have Judge Feldman fully covered within twenty-four hours."

"Good; what about all the contacts that these people will be making?"

"I've given that some thought, considering all the people we're tracking, we'll have an extensive data base of people to check out. My recommendation, with the SACS approval of course, is to use the Organized Crime Division to run down the contacts that our subjects are in contact with. They would more than likely recognize those with organized crime ties and they also have extensive experience in uncovering questionable ties and backgrounds."

The director looked at Martinez for confirmation. "That sounds great; you don't have a problem with that do you, Freddie?"

Martinez was furious with Scott for committing his resources without discussing it with him first. He knew however that he had no choice but to go along. "Of course not, the Organized Crime Division is the logical choice to pursue that portion of this investigation."

The director smiled and went on to another topic. "Good—Tom, how about those attorneys the congressman put us on to?"

"I believe we identified a direct link to this new syndicate. It however, also provide us with a lot of new questions.

"To start with, Agent Quantara and I were able to identify the two attorneys as the same two who met with the militia. These guys work for a well respected mid-size D.C. law firm: Burns, Roberts, Weisman and Cole. They work in what's called their professional management division (PMD). We believe the PMD is their fix it division.

"They're billed out as image management and media relations. I have a strong belief that they go far beyond running a few PR spots for their clients. The head of this division is a Paul Cedes; we're working on getting his vitals right now."

Director Flynn looked at Scott and shook his head. "Tom, If this is the Paul Cedes that Scott and I know, then you may just have stumbled onto one of the key players in this syndicate."

The entire conference room fell silent as everyone was waiting for the explanation. "Paul Cedes was a deputy director over at the CIA. President Canfield later appointed him ambassador to one of those small African countries. That was a strange appointment; it came in the last two years of Canfield's second term and CIA deputies don't usually become ambassadors. It tends to make the host country nervous.

"In the late seventies and early eighties, we were having trouble stabilizing some of the governments in that part of the world. A good portion of the African continent was threatening to nationalize foreign-owned companies. It was Cedes who put together a plan that would help stabilize those governments and allow the U.S. to maintain control over their investments in these countries. Most of the European and Asian companies, of course, lost everything they had invested.

"It's widely believed but has never been proven, that Cedes, with the backing of the CIA, organized several military coups. Then with the help of the CIA propaganda machine helped get the people he wanted elected to influential governmental posts. In turn, once they were in power, this group stabilized their government's monetary and economic systems and upgraded their relationships with the United States.

"There are even rumors that as part of the deal, Paul and a handful of U.S. businesses got extremely lucrative life-time leases on some of the oil and mineral deposits in that part of the world."

All in the room except for Christine were stunned. Christine was simply amazed. After all this time, could it be this easy? This had to be the same Paul Cedes of the CIA that Canon told her about. It made sense; he was obviously a friend of Canfield's. The cheap leases on the oil fields made his friend Walter Brooks a billionaire. The thread connecting the conspirators to her family's murder became clear, even if the motive didn't.

"Has Cedes ever worked for any of these companies?" Christine asked.

"Not that I know of, but he may sit on the board of several of them. What are you looking for, Christine?"

Christine decided to take a chance. "Sir, I was just thinking that it's odd that we would have two staff members of Paul Cedes, who is a former ambassador to an African country, meet with the leader of known white supremacists just before the largest meeting in history of African leaders."

"What are you implying, Christine?"

"Sir, if we believe that Cedes is part of a sophisticated criminal network, which it sounds like he is, then we have to consider that he may be using the militia to somehow derail the meeting or maybe even assassinate one of the leaders at the summit."

"That's a pretty big leap, Christine. What if he's just meeting with the supremacists to make sure that there's no trouble at the meeting? So far all we know is that two attorneys who work for Paul Cedes were spotted with some militia people. Cedes no longer works for the government. We have to assume that his people were down there on his company's behalf."

"Sir, based on what you told us about his exploits in Africa, I believe that Paul Cedes and several of the businessmen for whom he struck those sweetheart deals—and in the process made exceedingly wealthy—have been in collusion to control the African economies ever since."

"Even if we bought your assumptions, there is nothing to indicate that Cedes and his pals have anything to worry about from any of these leaders."

"Sir, with all due respect, I think it's a theory worth investigating."

"Christine's right," Scott said. "It's certainly worth investigating. This is the best theory we have on any of this so far. I don't know how Hoover or the assassination of President Canfield fits into all of this, but Paul Cedes has definite links to Canfield, Congressman McCall, the militia, and Africa."

" Ok, I'll get the Secret Service to give us the background on each of these leaders. Then we'll pull the CIA reports on their political and economic positions. We should be able to determine whether any U.S. companies are in jeopardy of losing their standings in any of these countries.

"Tom, I'm going to put you in charge of analyzing all of this data and reporting back to the committee. For now I want complete around-the-clock surveillance on those two attorneys and on Paul Cedes."

Christine nodded: she had planted the seed and was sure that it would take root.

"OK, what's next?"

Tom addressed what he knew to be another sensitive topic. "Once we linked the two attorneys to the law firm, we went back and dug a little deeper. We found that both Judge Feldman and Judge Walker had clerked for Judge Cole in the past. Cole is the senior partner at the law firm."

Scott found this hard to believe; he liked Judge Walker, and in his mind there was no way that he could be dirty. "Tom, that's one hell of an implication. Just because Walker clerked for Cole doesn't make him part of his criminal enterprise, if there is one. I just don't see him dirty, let alone a murderer."

Director Flynn had had several dealings with Judge Walker and found him to be a bit headstrong at times but always a straight shooter. Like Scott he found this hard to believe. "OK, let's not jump to conclusions until we have the facts. Christine, what do you think?"

"I don't know the judge and have never had any dealings with him. It may all be just coincidental or he may actually be dirty. We really don't have much of a choice—we have to investigate."

"Tom, you take the lead on this," Scott said. "I'll back you up during the interview."

Everyone was in general agreement about the next stage of the investigation as it began to take shape. There were now enough players under surveillance that one of them was bound to provide a new set of leads.

Director Flynn was confident he would be able to provide the president some answers before the meeting with the African deligation. He just wasn't as confident that the president was going to like the answers.

The rest of the meeting covered details and assignments. Christine and Quantara would return to California, where Quantara would oversee the surveillance of Congressman McCall and the search for the congressman's daughter. Christine would head to San Francisco and try to find a way to get to Judge Feldman.

Scott and Tom would oversee all of the surveillance operations in the D.C. area. Francine was asked to dig more deeply into Judge Walker's background and case history.

ASAC Martinez was to continue to pursue the Hoover killer and any links to anyone on this investigation. It was also agreed that the group would reconvene in five days or, if the situation warranted it, earlier.

Chapter 13

Christine's flight west was uneventful. She flew through San Diego to get to know Agent Quantara better. She liked Quantara. He had a good mind, he believed in his work, and wasn't afraid to bend a few rules. She knew he could be counted on in tight situations, it would be good to have him as an ally down the road.

After she left Quantara in San Diego, she continued on to San Francisco. When she arrived at the Fairmont Hotel in San Francisco, the head of the FBI's San Francisco office, Bob Lambert, met her. This wasn't necessarily unusual in itself, but the look on his face was one of concern.

Without so much as a greeting, he walked up to Christine, grabbed her elbow, and led her away from the registration counter.

"I'm sorry to greet you like this, Special Agent Peal, but we have a situation that requires your immediate attention."

Christine forced a slight smile to cover her surprise. "It's good to see you too Bob—now what is so important that brings out the ASAC of the Bureau's San Francisco office to greet little old me at 12:30 in the morning?"

"As soon as you called, we put agents on the judge. We've been on him now for about twenty-four hours and I think we may have a bit of a problem developing."

Bob Lambert handed Christine an envelope as they sat down in a quiet corner of the hotel's lobby.

"These are a series of surveillance photos taken earlier today. Those two guys in the first photo, we believe are the Judge's bodyguards. We ran a check on them, and they appear to be relatively clean. They have a couple of assault charges that were dismissed and some misdemeanor permit violations, but that's about it."

"Okay Bob, so the Judge has bodyguards, that's nothing to get excited about."

"Believe me, if it stopped there, I wouldn't bother you with it. Take a look at the next two pictures. Those two were spotted down the block watching the judge's house. We don't think they're there to protect the judge. We have them on tape going in the house with those little doctors' bags, after the judge and his bodyguards left, and coming out about thirty minutes later. We think they were planting bugs and installing surveillance cameras."

"Could they have been planting explosives?"

"It's possible, but highly unlikely. The judge has been home for a number of hours now and nothing has happened yet."

"Good point. Have you been able to identify them?"

"We ran their photos and their tags, but we don't have any hits yet. Which in itself is unusual."

"First thing in the morning, get these back to the organized crime division and let them have a crack at them."

"I'll have them there by the time they get to work in Washington. There are a couple of other things. First of all, we lost these guys. We think they're holed up in a house somewhere in the neighborhood monitoring the judge, much as we are. Second, those last two pictures are of yet another surveillance team monitoring the judge's house."

"You have got to be kidding? What's going on here? This is like a convention! Do we know who these guys are?"

"That's the good news—we do know these guys. They're a couple of freelancers who do excellent surveillance work. We know that because we've used them ourselves when we've had manpower issues. That bad news is that we don't know who they're working for and they're not likely to tell us."

"We're not going to give them much of a choice—pull them in first thing in the morning for questioning. I want to know who they work for."

"We would love to do that, Agent Peal."

"Would you just call me Christine? You're making me nervous."

"OK Christine, I would love to bring them in, but that brings us to the real reason I'm here tonight. At about 10:30 this evening, my people found both men in their car with their throats slit ear to ear."

"Jesus Christ, Bob! What the hell's going on here? I want their office and their houses sealed. I want somebody to go through every bit of information they find. I want all garbage cans in this city turned upside down if need be, but I want to know who the hell these guys worked for."

"What about the locals? To them this is just a straight murder and it's in their jurisdiction. They're not going to be happy if we start steamrolling them. If we make a lot of waves about this, the judge's people will know that we're watching them."

"Of course you're right Bob, and maybe it's too early to tip our hand, but I want to know who these guys were working for, who killed them and why."

"That's fine, I want the same thing. Let my people handle it a little more discreetly and I'll get you the answers and I'll still be able to work with these people after you're gone."

"Okay Bob, it's your home court, handle it any way you see fit, just get me those answers. I haven't even been here two hours and this has already turned into a three-ring circus. I feel like somebody is constantly two steps ahead of us. Look, Bob, I need to get my beauty sleep, I need at least a couple hours or I won't be any good today at all. Is there anything else that I should know about before I head up to my room?"

"Just that I'm bringing in a triangulation unit tomorrow to try and find where that other surveillance unit is holing up."

"Good, this is quite a mess, Bob. Including us, there are at least three different groups desperately trying to keep an eye on this one judge. Makes you kind of wonder, doesn't it?"

"That it does, Christine. I'll go and let you get that beauty rest, not that you need it. I'll meet you here at 6:30 for breakfast."

Christine's night was anything but restful. Things were suddenly much more complicated than she had counted on. Somehow she knew that the people who killed her family were involved in something much bigger and much more sinister. She was certain her Hoover identity was safe. So she committed herself to uncover whatever was going on and follow it wherever it led. The only thing she was sure of was that Paul Cedes would not survive this investigation alive.

As she drifted off to sleep, her final thoughts were: besides the FBI who had an interest in watching the judge's movements and why?

At breakfast the next morning it was evident to Christine that Bob got less sleep than she did. His sleepless night, however, provided more results than hers did. His men had gone through the records of the two independents killed the night before. They found encrypted E-mail on their computers as well as a stamped and addressed envelope containing negatives of their stakeout. Bob was not amused by what his people had found and with a little more sleep he might have been a bit more tactful in the delivery of his findings, but for now he just needed to lash out and Christine was an easy target.

"What the hell were you doing last night? You really had me fooled, I hope you enjoyed making a fool out of my guys and me, because it won't happen again. Did you really think that we are so incompetent out here in the field that we weren't going to be able to figure out that those two stiffs from last night were working for you? Even with Washington stonewalling us on our information requests, we were still able to tie them to you. We're not complete idiots out here."

Christine was stunned at Bob's outburst but even more so at what he was saying. "Jesus, Bob take it easy. I'm not in charge of this investigation, but I can guarantee you that I don't know what the hell you're talking about! I would never withhold vital information from you or intentionally make your people look bad. We're all on the same team here. I can promise you that neither Scott nor I, nor the director has issued any outside contracts of any kind on this project."

"Somebody sure as hell has; we traced their reports back to the Hoover Building."

"That's impossible, Scott would have let me know if there was a surveillance team already on the scene."

"Unless he has a different agenda or somebody didn't tell him about it."

"I find both of those options highly unlikely. Were you able to trace the reports to a specific department or office?"

"Yes. That's why we thought you hired these people. We traced the reports to the Organized Crime Division."

"That's impossible, I would know about anything like this going on in my own division. Did your guys find any kind of office code? I'm sure something like this wouldn't just be left in the general mail."

"I don't know about any office code, but I brought a picture of the envelope. My guys are still working on deciphering the E-mails. They should have that complete in the next hour or so, then we should know the actual recipient of the E-mails."

Bob handed Christine the envelope and watched as her face turned bright red. Then she slammed her fist on the table and looked back up at Bob.

"You have my sincerest apologies, Bob, evidently someone at the FBI is running a separate and unauthorized surveillance of the judge."

"Are you able to tell who from the envelope?"

"Yes, the OCD181 code is that of ASAC Martinez. I'll try to get the details and I promise to bring you up to speed as soon as I can. Believe me, Bob, I was as blindsided by this as you were."

"Christine, I'm sorry I blew up at you. I didn't get much sleep, which is no excuse, but it really looked like you were playing us."

"Bob, there's no reason to apologize; I would feel the same way if I was in your situation. In fact, I'll probably go and blow up at the director myself now. Our immediate concern hasn't changed any, though. We still need to know who killed them and why. Now we also need to know whether or not the judge is aware that those two guys were working for the FBI."

"What you're really asking is, is our cover blown?"

"You've got it Bob—if our cover is blown, we're not going to get anything else from our taps or surveillance and we'll have to shift tactics."

Christine's first call, after leaving the meeting with Bob, was to the director. He assured her there was no other surveillance operation going on involving Judge Feldman. She then told him of the independent surveillance team, their deaths and how their trail led back to the FBI. The director became furious, but he damned near exploded when Christine told him about the routing code on the envelope. Without even saying goodbye, he slammed down the phone and Christine could imagine him storming down the hall to have it out with Martinez.

Christine knew she had to get in contact with the other surveillance teams around the country. It was obvious that whoever was protecting the judge was not above killing surveillance teams. If it was this new syndicate and they traced the team killed in San Francisco back to the

FBI, then they would certainly alert all of their members in the United States to be on the lookout. That, in turn, could cost the lives of many good agents.

Christine placed a conference call to Tom and Scott and brought them up to date on what looked to be Martinez' private operation. Both Tom and Scott were as furious as the director with Martinez' independent actions. Their primary focus now, was to develop a plan by which they could continue their surveillance while ensuring the safety of their agents.

While Christine was working on the revision of the surveillance plan with Tom and Scott, Bob was working on identifying the third party surveilling the judge. His triangulation vans were driving around the neighborhood and had isolated the equipment receiving the transmissions from the judge's house. It was a two-story house with an attic. It was situated on the corner of the block four houses from the judge's home on the opposite side of the street. The location was perfect for monitoring the neighborhood. Bob was a little embarrassed that his team hadn't selected that location first.

Once located, it was easy to piggyback on the frequency of the surveillance devices planted at the judge's house and to establish a separate listing post targeting the surveillance house. Now the watchers became the watched. It was just a matter of time before they would reveal who they were and who they worked for.

There was not much activity in the judge's house or in the house on the corner, until the evening shift change. Then, as the two men in charge began to discuss the day's activities, a few things became clearer.

"Anything happening?"

"No, not really, the judge just got home. He's in his office, one of the bodyguards is in the kitchen stuffing his face, the other one is out on the front porch having a cigarette."

"Good, anything new on this morning's activities?" The incoming watcher asked.

"No, the police came and questioned Norm and Sam and left when they told them they were asleep all night and didn't know anything about anyone being killed on their block until they saw it on the news."

"What about the surveillance equipment found in the car with the bodies? Has it been traced back to anyone?"

"Not yet; the only place it could be traced back to is the FBI. As instructed, we're using only FBI-issued equipment on this mission. We left several of the bugs exposed enough so that even those clowns the judge calls bodyguards could find them." The outgoing watcher said.

"Good, I still think it was a dumb idea to expose those two poor schmucks. By just finding the bugs, they knew they were being watched. Eventually they would have been able to trace the equipment to the FBI."

"I agree with you, but nobody expected the bodyguards to actually kill the surveillance team. I believe Washington was thinking that at most they would pull the bugs and trace them to the two guys parked in the car down the block and then find out who they were working for."

"Maybe so, but now thanks to two bodyguards that have more muscles than brains, we've got two dead PIs and a judge who still doesn't know the FBI is monitoring him. He probably thinks some mobster, whose case he is handling, was setting him up."

"What bothers me about this whole thing is undermining an FBI operation like this. If this judge is so important, why can't the boss just go to the FBI and tell them to back off? It's not like he doesn't have the power to do it." The incoming watcher said.

"I don't know, but there is something fishy about this whole thing—why would the FBI hire independents for a job like this? They have plenty of their own people in San Francisco a lot better than these guys." The outgoing watcher wondered.

"What ever is going on, it's obviously very political. I for one don't want to be caught in the middle of it."

"Look, all we did was place some bugs in the judge's house where those clowns could find them and then put the receivers in the PI's car. It's not our fault those goons overreacted. Besides we were acting on orders." The outgoing watcher said.

"Who do you think is going to back us when we get in front of a senate hearing?"

"All I know is that the judge is in there now and you have the reins until morning." The outgoing watcher said.

After hearing the tape, Bob decided that Christine needed to hear this right away. He contacted Christine and asked her to wait for him at her hotel. He then assigned one of his agents to visit the police station and look at the surveillance equipment recovered at the crime scene. The police assumed the equipment belonged to the PIs and had logged it into the evidence locker. The FBI agent copied down all of the serial numbers so he could later compare them against the FBI inventory.

When Bob replayed the tape for Christine, she was stunned. It was obvious to her and Bob that the other surveillance team was from some other government agency, such as the CIA or the NSA. It could even be some other governmental agency that worked far from the public eye, reporting directly to the White House. One thing was for sure, whoever these guys answered to was extremely high-placed in the government. There are just not that many people in the country that could tell the director of the FBI to back off on an investigation. It was also obvious that whoever they were, their main job seemed to be to expose the FBI surveillance regardless of the cost or consequences.

After carefully listening to the tape again, Christine concluded that this group wouldn't act without orders and anything out of the ordinary would probably be reported immediately to their superiors. This, she decided, was the edge she needed to get them to lead her to their boss. She also believed that the judge was sufficiently spooked now that any more irregularities would probably force him into some kind of action.

Christine decided that it was time to force the action and unless she totally misread Quantara, she knew she could count on him. She contacted Quantara in San Diego and asked him to be on the next flight to San Francisco. She also asked him to bring one of his DEA friends that helped out with the congressman and knew the value of discretion. She was determined to initiate her operation by 2:00 a.m.

Christine knew that whatever action she was about to take, it would have to be without FBI resources. ASAC Bob Lambert and his staff would never get involved in an operation like the one she was contemplating. If anyone at the FBI ever found out, She and anyone else involved would be fired immediately. To her the risk was worth it, after all the main reason she joined the FBI was to track down and kill those responsible for her families murders. Pushing Judge Feldman into action might get her a step closer to that goal. Quantara however was another matter. This was his career, his life, if he were fired, it would probably kill him. Yet she was sure that he wouldn't hesitate to help her. She would just have to develop a plan that was fool proof.

As the plan developed, Christine's version called for her and Quantara to conduct the actual mission themselves with Quantara's friend acting as driver. Her intent was to limit exposure to the three of them.

At exactly 2:00 AM, a sedan with Illinois license plates driven by

Michael Fox, Quantara's DEA friend pulled out of the Mark Hopinks parking lot on Golden Gate Avenue in downtown San Francisco. At exactly 2:15, the sedan slowed down next to a dark blue panel truck parked more than twenty blocks from the Mark Hopkins. Without stopping the sedan, Christine and Quantara jumped out. They were covered from head to toe in black, including black tennis shoes, black gloves, and black ski hats pulled down over their faces.

Christine quickly moved to the front of the van, removed the license plate, and then to the rear to removed the rear plate. Quantara picked the lock to the driver side door, got inside, and unlocked the other doors. He put the van in neutral and Christine pushed it down the hill. In less than a minute from exiting the sedan, the van was rolling downhill when Quantara popped the clutch and the van was off and running with them inside.

Quantara drove around the corner picked up his friend and then drove the van to within four blocks of Judge Feldman's home. At this point, Fox moved into the driver's seat, Christine removed the interior light bulbs, then slid open the side door through which she and Quantara disappeared into the night.

The plan was to approach under cover of darkness through the alley, which was the only blind spot from the surveillance house on the corner. They were halfway down the alley when Christine's jacket pocket started to vibrate.

She put her arm out to stop Quantara from moving forward. "Damn it, somebody is calling me."

"Well you can't answer it now." Quantara whispered.

"I have to if we want to maintain our alibi."

Christine punched the talk button and answered the phone in a whisper. "Who the hell is this, it's two in the morning."

"I'm sorry Christine, its Bob Lambert. The hotel said you had the do not disturb sign on your phone and wouldn't put me through so I had to call you on your cell."

"I didn't want to be disturbed because I haven't had any sleep in three days."

"I'm sorry Christine, but you're not going to get any now either. There's a problem at the judge's house. Someone is approaching from the alley. Our friends have a camera watching the alley!"

"Who has the camera, the judge or the guys on the corner?"

"The guys on the corner; our people monitoring them overheard all the commotion when they spotted two people in ninja outfits sneaking down the alley."

"What are they doing about it?"

There was a thirty-second pause before Bob returned. "They're actually calling for instructions."

"Great, I'll see you at headquarters as soon as I can get there."

Without waiting for a reply Christine hung up and she and Quantara were off. Christine climbed the trellises attached to the side of the house and waited for Quantara to signal her that the alarm had been disabled. As soon as she received the signal, she picked the lock and found herself standing in the upstairs hallway.

Quantara, meanwhile, entered through the rear door into the kitchen. As he entered the living room, he found the first guard right where he expected him, asleep on the couch. Before the guard knew what hit him, Quantara had him chloroformed and out for the night. The second guard was also where they expected him, sitting in a chair outside the judge's room.

Christine didn't want to use chloroform, she needed this guard awake and on the job. She made enough noise on her approach to startle the guard; before he could react, she had her Berretta pointed between his eyes. She kept him seated with his hands in the air until Quantara arrived from below. While Quantara held his gun on the guard, Christine kicked in the door to the bedroom and found a startled judge rolling off the bed. She quickly fired two shots with her un-silenced Berretta into the bed.

When Quantara heard the shots he stepped back and tumbled down the stairs. As he fell, he fired two rounds into the ceiling. Christine heard the shots and retreated to the hallway.

She found the guard in a prone position, taking cover from Quantara's shots. As the guard attempted to get to his knees, Christine gave him a quick kick to the face, which sent him reeling back to the floor. She stepped over him and ran down the stairs. Quantara, having recovered from his fall, was poised at the bottom of the stairs providing cover fire for Christine as she made her way out the door. Christine then assumed the cover position as Quantara made his exit.

As soon as both hit the front step, Fox pulled up in front of the house with the van's sliding door open. Christine stopped just short of the van, turned toward the house, kneeled and provided cover for Quantara until he was safely in the van. As she was about to move from her cover position, the bodyguard, with blood gushing from his face, emerged from the doorway with his pistol at the ready. Christine aimed and fired and watched the guard collapse. She got into the van and they were gone.

In the van, congratulations were flowing and the post-mission rush was evident. Christine expressed her congratulations to everyone, especially to Quantara, who had once again proven that he could be counted on when needed.

Quantara smiled and stretched his back. "I have to tell you, Christine, I didn't think I could pull off a convincing fall when I saw how steep those stairs were as I was going up."

"I never had a doubt; we needed that fall so that the guard could chase me out of the bedroom. It worked perfectly."

Agent Fox lost the smile on his face as he remembered their getaway. "It was almost perfect. No one was supposed to get killed. You killed that guard in the judge's doorway."

Christine put her hand on Fox's shoulder. "Relax, I didn't kill anybody. I shot that guard in the right shoulder. It should be a pretty clean wound. My kick to his face did him more damage than that bullet did. He'll be out of the hospital by tomorrow afternoon. Besides, we had to provide a touch of realism and sincerity."

By 2:45 the van with its license plates intact had been replaced exactly where it had been taken only forty-five minutes earlier. By 3:00 a.m. the sedan driven by DEA Agent Michael Fox was pulling up in front of the Mark Hopkins Hotel. Christine emerged less than ten minutes later minus her "ninja attire" wearing a white blouse with a light blue jacket and matching pants. When she entered the FBI building on Golden Gate Avenue downtown San Francisco at three twenty in the morning, gone also were the black tennis shoes and in their place white open toed high heels.

Bob just shook his head as Christine walked into his office. "I'm sorry for bringing you out here in the middle of the night, but this is your case."

Christine smiled; "That's no problem Bob, I was just sleeping."

Just then Bob's private line rang. There were very few people who knew he would be there; one of those was the man in charge of watching the judge and the house on the corner. Bob pushed the speaker button on his phone. "Ed, I've got you on the speaker, what's going on over there?"

"All hell is breaking loose. I think you ought to get over here right away."

"Ed, this is Christine Peal, I don't think that would be wise right now. If we come over now, we may blow the stakeout. You'll just have to continue to be our eyes and ears and stay on top of it for us. What kind of messages have our friends at the corner been sending?"

"When they spotted someone in the alley, they called a Virginia number; we should be able to put a name to it in the morning. He told them to hold their positions and just observe for now, that someone would call them right back with instructions. Nobody actually called them back until the van was pulling away from the judge's house. At that time the caller instructed them to intercept the prowlers; under no circumstances were the prowlers to be allowed to enter the judge's house. When he was told that it was too late and that shots were fired, he was furious. He told them to find out if the judge was dead and gave them a phone number to call for further instructions."

"Great, did we get that number?"

"Yes, we did. I recognized the country code as England, but that's as far as we've gotten with it so far. This number must be in some kind of code; it appears to have four extra digits."

"That's great work, Ed. Don't worry about the number, we'll run the trace from here."

Ed gave them the number and Bob started working on his computer while listening to Christine talk to Ed.

" What about the judge—have you heard anything about him?"

"He's alive, in fact he came out of this unharmed. Evidently the body-guard overpowered one of the assailants and threw him down the stairs and then chased the other one out of the judge's bedroom into the street."

Christine fought of the urge to smile as she was listening to the description of the guard's "heroic" actions. "How about calls—has the judge made any?"

"He made two calls, one to 911 and one to 202-536-4741. The 911 call was actually pretty calm for someone who had just been shot at. He told the dispatcher that he had intruders in his house, and that shots were fired and then gave him his address.

We have both of the calls on tape, I think it would be best if I just played the second call for you."

"Walter, this is Feldman."

"It's five-thirty in the morning."

"Get your ass out of bed, Walter, this is Feldman."

"What the hell are you doing calling me at home, get off of this god damned line."

"Listen, you son of a bitch, somebody just tried to kill me. I want to know what the hell is going on?"

"Get off of this God damned line, you fool. . ."

"That was it—he hung up and then the police and ambulance arrived and he's been with them ever since."

"That's great work Ed, keep your ears up, someone is going to have to give our friends on the corner more instructions. That should give us a great opportunity to find out who they're working for. Also the judge sounds spooked, so he's going to reach out to someone for help again and we want to know who that is."

"We'll stay on it. How about the video that our guys got of the failed assassins getting away?"

"What did we get?"

"All we really have is a shot of the van and two people coming out of the house. I don't think we're going to be able to identify anyone from what we have. We probably won't even be able to trace the van. There were no plates on it and the best we could tell was that it was a dark-colored Ford panel wagon somewhere from the mid sixties. Washington can probably get more from the tapes."

"There's no rush on them, just send them over with the regular courier at the end of your shift."

Christine knew that the director needed to be brought up to date on the night's activities, but he wouldn't be in his office for another two to three hours. This gave her an opportunity to run down the numbers that they got from Ed.

Bob was having some problems tracing the overseas number, as Ed mentioned, there were too many digits in the number. Christine was about to dial one of the other numbers when the proverbial light came on.

"Bob, what numbers do you have to call when you try to reach me at the Mark Hopkins?"

"The hotel's telephone number."

"Yes, but that only gets you to the hotel."

Bob got a big smile across his face as the light came on for him as well. "Of course, the last four digits are an office or hotel room extension."

Bob pushed the speaker button on the phone and dialed the number (minus the last four digits). The phone rang and everyone in the room held their breath until the phone was picked up on the third ring.

The accent was undeniably British; Christine could just imagine a tall Brit with dark hair, a dark suit, white shirt, and dark tie standing stiff as a board as he spoke into the telephone. "Hotel Europa, may we be of service?"

Bob was about to ask for the room number when Christine reached across the desk and hung up the phone. "Let's not expose ourselves just yet. We now know whoever stayed at the Hotel Europa in London in room 1634 last night is pulling the strings of our friends on the corner. It should be very easy to find out who that was without letting them know we're onto them. In a couple of hours we should also be able to put a name to that number in Virginia. When we have the name, then we'll be able to tie it all together and present it to the director."

Bob found himself caught up in Christine's energy and wasn't tired even though he hadn't slept in over thirty-six hours. He could see now why Christine had moved through the agency so quickly. She was the youngest agent in her position and he speculated that she would become the youngest deputy director ever. She was the type of agent who forced the action; nothing stood still around her for very long. This kind of agent also constantly lived on the edge of the law themselves and often risked entrapment charges when making their cases.

Bob couldn't believe their luck. If someone hadn't tried to assassinate the judge, it would have taken months to get the information that they just gathered in a couple of hours.

Christine saw an opening and knew this would be her best chance to act on it. "We still need to find out who the judge was calling. I'd like that name, before we call the director. I think the judge will be very nervous now, which will make those controlling him very nervous. We should have a team ready to go in and extract him should the need arise."

Bob suddenly was part of the meeting again, as he was stunned by Christine's comment.

"Just a minute, you're talking about kidnapping a State Supreme Court Judge!"

"No, I'm not, I'm talking about saving a judge's life. If the judge makes his handlers too nervous, they'll just eliminate him. We're in a unique position to prevent that. When the order comes we can save his life or we can sit by and watch him get killed. My guess is that none of us want to sit by and watch a judge get killed. Especially, if by saving his life and protecting him, he may become the most important witness the FBI has ever had."

Bob found it hard to argue against Christine's logic. He knew they didn't really have a choice but to protect him if it looked like he was about to be taken out.

Christine's plan was working to perfection, by faking the assassination attempt on the judge, she not only created the phone activity, but also put the judge's life in danger from his own people, forcing the FBI to rescue him.

Chapter 14

By the time the first morning sunbeam found its way through the maze of highrises and into the office of Bob Lambert, Bob and Christine had already put in a very long day.

Bob Lambert, had been working on the computer for hours attempting to run down the Virginia and 202 telephone numbers. Christine had spent her early morning hours recruiting help from Quantara and his friend Michael Fox of the DEA as well as Tom and Scott in Washington. She called Fox and Quantara who had temporarily moved into her hotel room and asked them to clean up and join her in Bob Lambert's office.

Christine got Scott and Tom on a conference call and was bringing them up to speed on what they had learned so far. She told them about an unknown party that attacked the judge and the subsequent flurry of telephone calls from both the people watching the judge and the judge himself. She also told them that their attempts to trace the calls so far have been unsuccessful.

When she mentioned London, it struck a chord with Tom; something reminded him of a news broadcast from the previous evening, but he just couldn't pin it down.

"Scott, did you watch the news last night?"

"Yes."

"There was something going on in London—do you remember what that was?"

"Yes, the president landed in London. He and Prime Minister Blair are going to meet and they're going to do a first ever joint address to the House of Commons."

"Of course! Now I remember, and the first lady had a photo op with the Queen. They were having tea."

Christine's mind was already connecting the dots. "Do you know where the president's party is staying?"

Neither Tom nor Scott was aware of the president's itinerary, but they knew they didn't like the direction this conversation was taking.

There was only one way to see if Christine was on the right track. Tom had a friend working the political desk at the Washington Post—if he wasn't with the president in London, he would be at home or at his desk at the Post.

"Christine, what's the name of that hotel that your people tracked the number to?"

"The Hotel Europa, suite 1634."

"Ok, you guys, hold on a minute, I'm going to call an old friend and collect on a favor. He should know where the president's party is staying; let's hope it's at the Windsor."

Tom called his friend and as expected, he was in Europe covering the president's trip. It took some persuasion but he finally got the number from his friend's secretary. Two minutes later, he was on the phone with his friend.

"Mac, how are you doing? I see you're hobnobbing around Europe again."

"Somebody has to let the folks back home know what our president is promising this time. Can I assume that's why you're calling me; to find out what the Europeans want?"

"Well, not exactly. I just have a question and it's too early over here to call anybody, but I knew you would be up."

"Alright Tom, what's going on? What do you want?"

"Is that anyway to talk to an old friend?"

"Okay, now you've got me curious. What's up?"

"I was just trying to find someone with the presidential detail and didn't want to go through all that crap at the White House. For security reasons, they won't give us any room numbers at the front desk."

"So how is it that I or maybe my paper can help the bureau?"

"This has nothing to do with the bureau, Mac, I just need to know what floor the president and his senior staff are on so that I can get a message to one of them."

"I'll tell you what, Tom, if you give me the message, I'll make sure they get it."

"I appreciate that, Mac, but you know me—I like the personal touch."

"Is there a story, here Tom? My reporter's nose tells me there is."

"No story here, Mac; I just need to reschedule a tee time."

"Hell Tom, who do you expect to buy that?"

"Are you going to help me here or not?"

"Okay don't get huffy. It's no big secret, the president and a couple of his senior staff are on 16 and the rest are spread between floors 12 and 14. Are you sure one of them didn't stay out too late or something?"

"I'm sure, thanks for your help Mac. I owe you one."

"Let's just say that, when you're ready, you call me for that exclusive. I'll see you when I get back to D.C."

Tom hung up from his call and returned to his conversation with Scott and Christine.

"Well, it's confirmed, the president and his party are staying at the Hotel Europa. It gets even worse—only the president and his very senior staff are housed on the sixteenth floor."

There was a deafening silence on the phone as all of the possibilities and scenarios were playing out in everyone's minds. Scott was the first to say what everyone was thinking.

"Okay, I'll say it. The president, a senior member of his staff, or both are hip deep in this thing."

Tom was trying to keep an open mind; after all it was the president of the United States that they were talking about.

"Maybe there's something here, maybe not. All we know for sure, is that a room on the sixteenth floor of the hotel the president is staying in was left as a contact point for a surveillance team observing the activities of the same judge we're keeping an eye on."

Christine felt they now had enough information to present to the director. "The way I see it, someone knowingly impeded an FBI investigation, and that's a crime. If its linked directly to the president, it's an impeachable offense. We need to take this to the director now."

Tom could feel his blood pressure starting to rise again.

"Everybody just relax; nobody is going to impeach the president simply because someone on his staff exposed an illegal and unauthorized investigation. Remember, what they actually did was expose an unauthorized, renegade investigation launched by our buddy Martinez. Let's keep this 'need to know' for now. Scott and I will get to the director and brief him on what we have, and then we'll call you from his office in about an hour. Where should we reach you?"

"I'll be right here in Bob Lambert's office trying to run down those other numbers."

"Do you want our people here to work on those?" Tom asked.

"Thanks Tom, we'll stay after it here, at least until our next call. I'm afraid of who we'll find on the other end of those numbers and I want to keep that knowledge down to as small a group as possible."

"Okay Christine, we'll check back with you in about an hour." Tom signed off.

Christine joined Bob at the computer and told him the bad news. He wasn't too surprised; he believed all along that the other surveillance team was from another government agency like the NSA, CIA, or even some heretofore-unknown group working out of the executive office. There had been rumors for a long time about the White House having its own investigative unit.

What did surprise him, but also totally shocked and dismayed him, was Ed's call from the surveillance house moments later. Bob, Christine, Quantara, and Fox were gathered around Bob's speakerphone listening to Ed, who could barely contain himself.

"Jesus Christ boss! You've got to hear this tape! They're going to do it, they're actually going to kill a federal judge!"

Without waiting for comments, Ed switched on the tape.

"9613"

"I have new instructions for you."

"Go ahead, I'm ready to copy."

"Negative. You are not to write down or tape these instructions under any circumstances. Is that clear?"

"Yes sir! The line is scrambled and the recorders are off."

"Good. First, you are to forget the contact number given to you this morning. Is that clear?"

"Yes Sir!"

"Next, you are to prepare a plan to terminate the subject."

"Are you saying that you want us to terminate the surveillance or that you want us to terminate the subject?"

"You are to prepare a plan to terminate the subject. Is that clear enough?"

"Yes, sir."

"You are to complete your plan immediately and be prepared to carry it out within the next six hours. If and when the word is given, you will complete your assignment and return to Washington. This will be our last contact until you return to Washington. Use the emergency numbers if contact is absolutely necessary. Any questions?"

"Yes sir; how will we be notified of the go code?"

"Tune your TV to CNN and watch the news at the top of the hour for the next six hours. You'll be listening for the phrase "jurisprudence." If the go code is not given within the next six hours, then you'll continue surveillance for the next twenty-four hours and then pack your gear and come home. Any other questions?"

"No, sir."

"Good luck then, and I'll see you back in Washington."

"I think somebody in Washington has flipped!" Ed yelled over the phone. "This call came in less than two minutes ago. That idiot on the corner is on the phone right now recalling his people. It sounds like he has his TV tuned to CNN. In case you guys haven't checked your watches lately, it's about fifteen minutes before the hour. Boss, I've got a feeling these guys are really going to do it."

"Ed, I think you're probably right—give us a couple of minutes to figure out our next move and we'll get right back to you."

"Don't spent too much time figuring things out, because I don't think that judge is going to be around much longer."

Bob got up from his desk and walked to his bookshelf to turn on a small TV. He tuned it to CNN and turned down the volume and looked at the others.

"It looks like that attempt on the judge this morning has really stirred up a hornets' nest. Christine, I guess you've got your wish; we have no choice but to go in and get the judge out."

"Martinez's operation being exposed, is what probably touched all of this off." Christine said.

"Whatever the reason, we need to put a plan together to get him out, before they kill him," Bob grumbled.

Even though she hadn't had any real sleep in days, Christine felt alive and alert.

"We know about the camera in the alley, so we should take advantage of that. We also know the judge hasn't had time to replace the bodyguard that went to the hospital and that the police increased the frequency of their patrols.

"We need to plug all that in to our plan and get a schedule of the patrols. We're also going to need some of your city contacts, Bob. If you can get us a garbage truck with its crew, I think we can pull this off."

"I don't know what you have in mind, but it'll take me about half an hour to arrange for the garbage truck."

"That's good; I don't think we're going to have much more time than that. If they get the go-ahead at the top of the hour, then they'll need at least another hour to get everyone in and briefed and they'll probably go at the top of the second hour." Christine was now in her element as she continued to direct the operation. "That gives us a little over two hours to get the judge out. I think we need to be ready to go within thirty minutes of them receiving the go code."

Bob still wasn't one hundred percent behind this plan. "I'm not sure that's going to be possible, Christine. We have to pull a team in, brief them, and then run our plan by the director."

Christine challenged Bob. "We don't have time for all that, Bob. We know the layout of the house and we have a way around the alley camera. We can't afford to bring another team in at this stage. Special Agent Quantara and Agent Fox will make up the rest of our team, and I'll handle the director afterwards."

"Agent Fox isn't even with the FBI, we need approval from the DEA to use him on this mission."

"We don't have time for a lot of paperwork. If Agent Fox is willing to volunteer for this mission then we'll work out the paper trail with the DEA later. Are you volunteering for this mission Agent Fox?"

Michael Fox got a big grin across his face as he answered. "I am volunteering my services to the San Francisco branch of the FBI to use me as the ASAC and Special Agent Peal see fit."

Bob didn't have an alternative plan and knew it was too late to get one of his regular units in, so he reluctantly went along. "Okay Christine, it's your hide. You guys had better get busy and tighten up the plan then, while I see about your garbage truck."

For the second time in a matter of hours Christine was getting the adrenaline rush she always got before a major operation.

Quantara and Christine polished the plan while Bob lined up the garbage truck, and Fox worked out the transportation details and the police patrol schedule.

They all stopped what they were doing at exactly 7:00 a.m. to listen to Hanna Barberra give CNN's top-of-the-hour news report.

"In London today the president began his European tour with a historic address at The House of Commons. We now go live to Marta Hingle, our London correspondent. Marta...."

"Thank you Hanna, I'm standing here in historic Parliament Square with Brian Hunt, the president's Chief of Staff."

"Mr. Hunt, the president has had many triumphs during his term; how would you rate his performance in front of the House of Commons?"

"Thanks for having me here, Marta. As you know, our president is a history buff and though our government was founded by a group of very courageous and far sighted individuals, we are still young in terms of our own history. So for the president, watching the British system of governance and jurisprudence still going strong is like stepping back in time to before our own independence. His performance in the House of Commons is one of the major triumphs of this term. You would have thought they were all democrats."

There was a stunned silence throughout Bob's office. The air suddenly seemed colder and a chill ran up everyone's back. They couldn't believe what they had just heard.

They had just watched the second most powerful man in the country, the one man who can sway the president's policies, give the order to kill a federal judge.

Chapter 15

Tom and Scott were with the director in his office when they placed a call to Bob Lambert's office. The director was already agitated by what he heard from Scott and the fact that neither Christine nor anyone else was available to take his call didn't help matters much. When the phone rang back at the switchboard, they were informed that Christine had left a number where she could be reached. Tom dialed the number and immediately realized that he had gotten through to Bob Lambert on his mobile phone.

"Hello Bob, its Tom, I've got Scott and the director here with me; we're trying to track down Christine. She was supposed to be expecting our call—is she there with you?"

"Well, kind of. She is with me but not available right now."

"Bob, this is Director Flynn, what do you mean she's not available? What the hell is she doing?"

"Mr. Director, this is a car phone and it's not secure. If you'll give us thirty minutes we'll be able to explain everything over a secure line."

The director looked at Tom and Scott in frustration but he really didn't have much choice. "This had better be good. Call me here in thirty minutes. We won't be going anywhere until we hear from you or Christine, so don't leave us hanging."

The San Francisco Sanitation District truck number 173 was making its way down the alley of the 4200 block of Rivera, street in the Sunset District. To the casual observer, it looked like any other garbage truck going about its appointed rounds. However, if you were to look closely, you would notice that this truck was carrying two extra collectors. At every stop two collectors would retrieve the cans on the left and two would retrieve the cans on the right.

Christine was counting on anyone monitoring the alley seeing only a garbage truck and garbage men. Much like not being alerted by a janitor with a mop, she was betting on the natural association of the garbage men and the truck. Once they were at the judge's house and she and Quantara didn't return to the truck, she knew the race would be on.

As the truck pulled up behind the judge's house, Christine and Quantara jumped off the running boards and headed in the direction of the trashcans. This time, however, they passed up the trashcans and headed for the rear of the house. The other two garbage men emptied the cans on their side and returned to the truck. The garbage truck then continued its rounds with the usual two men working the back of the truck.

Before entering the judge's house, Christine checked with Bob (who was in constant contact with Ed) for any unusual movements from the house on the corner. Although there was none, everyone was certain they had completed their plans to assassinate the judge and were all set to go in less than twenty minutes.

Christine knew those observing the alley would notice the missing garbage men any moment now. When they did they would be on top of them in a matter of seconds. There would be no time for explanations; the judge would have to be taken by force.

Christine kicked in the back door to the kitchen and Quantara burst through, surprising the bodyguard, caught with his head literally in the refrigerator. Christine rushed past the bodyguard and up the stairs, while Quantara subdued and tied the guard.

Christine broke through the judge's bedroom door, and found herself staring down the barrel of a .45 held firmly in the hands of a very large security guard who looked much more professional than the judge's other security people. Somehow Bob's surveillance team had missed a vital piece of intelligence.

Behind and just to the right of the security guard, standing next to his bed dressed in pajamas and a robe, stood Judge Feldman.

The judge moved beside the security guard before he spoke.

"Who the hell are you? Who sent you?"

Christine knew that there wasn't much time, but she saw an opportunity to gather some vital information and she decided to take it.

"It doesn't really matter who I am; what matters is that my orders come from the same place as yours."

"Cedes sent you to kill me? That son of a bitch. You tell him that I want a meeting. I want to know why all of a sudden I'm a marked man. Does Walter know about this?"

Just then Christine heard Bob in her headset. "You guys have been made. They've realized two of the garbage men disappeared; they're on their way to the judge's house—get out, now!"

Before Christine could react, she heard the sound of a shotgun explode behind her and watched as a bean bag slammed into the chest of the guard with enough force to lift him off of his feet and throw him five feet back onto the bed. Quantara rushed through the door and secured the .45 from the guard. He bound the guard's hands and feet with plastic ties and spoke into his open microphone. "We have the judge and we're headed out now."

Christine grabbed the judge, moved down the stairs and to the front door. By the time they reached the front door, Quantara was by their side to lead them into the street.

The hesitation in the judge's bedroom had thrown off their timing, and agent Fox was forced to go around the block. When they stepped onto the front porch, they saw several men running down the street towards them with small arms in their hands, dodging early morning commuters.

Agent Fox had seen the assault on the judge's house and switched to the alternate extraction plan. By the time Bob was relaying this information to Christine, she and Quantara with the judge in tow were already back in the house and on their way out the back door. The van pulled up just as they were entering the alley. Christine shoved the judge in the van while Quantara covered them. Quantara had barely entered the van before Agent Fox began accelerating down the alley. Fox had almost cleared the alley when another van appeared blocking their exit. A quick peek into the rearview mirror told Agent Fox that he was being squeezed by a second van coming from behind.

Christine grabbed Quantara's .45, loaded a fresh clip into her Berretta instructed Quantara and Fox to get the judge to safety and then rolled out the side door of the van into the alley.

She surprised the occupants of both attacking vans. She came to her knees and with Quantara's .45 in her left hand and her Berretta in her right, she fired into the driver's compartment of the van in front of them. The driver's dead body fell forward, landing on the horn. With the horn blaring and Christine firing into the van, the assailant on the passenger side of the van made the fatal mistake of attempting to flee the van while returning fire.

Christine would have let him escape had he not fired at her or the van containing the judge. As it was however, she had no choice but to kill the assailant before he reached cover. She quickly turned on her heels and fired at the second van, shooting out its tires and disabling it.

Agent Fox, seeing that there was no one at the controls of the van in front of him, put his van in gear and began pushing the other van out of the way.

Christine was now exchanging fire with the second van and was able to keep them from pursuing Agent Fox. She was drawing heavy fire herself and was pinned down, only able to watch as her means of escape disappeared down the alley and into one of the main streets.

Christine heard Quantara in her headset talking to Bob Lambert, but was too busy herself to respond.

"Bob, all hell is breaking loose out here. We had to leave Christine in the alley; she's under heavy fire and needs help right now! The opposition has two dead but there are at least six more shooters headed her way."

"What the hell happened?"

"Later! Christine needs help in the alley behind the judge's house. Get a team there right now!"

"I'm on my way—we went without a backup, remember? You guys stay with the plan; I'll get her out."

When Christine heard that there were six more on the way, she knew she didn't have time to wait for support. "You guys can't help me, there's no time. Just call the cops and get some sirens blaring around here that may get these guys to back off enough to give me room to get out. I'll check back with you as soon as I get a chance."

Christine made her decision to move; she rolled onto her stomach and began firing down the alley toward the second van. She continued to fire as she got to her feet and started making her way backwards to the other van. She reached the driver side door just as she ran out of ammunition, pulled out the dead driver, and took his place.

The windshield began to shatter from the bullets being fired at her. She crouched below the dashboard and covered with shattered glass form the windshield, began blindly backing out of the alley. She could feel the tires being shot out from under her as the van ran over a curb, but fewer bullets connecting with the front of the van.

She took a quick look and realized that she was in the street. With all of the tires shot out, the van was too difficult to turn and Christine had no choice but to get out before the chase caught up to her. She kicked open the rear door and ran down the street, around the first corner and disappeared into the suburb as morning traffic was beginning to get heavier.

Christine jumped a fence and found herself in the backyard of an upscale neighborhood. She hid in the garage and stripped off her garbage collector's coveralls. Her first job now was to call off any armed support that may be on the way. She hadn't heard any communications over her headset in a while and was wondering if it was still operational.

"Bob, it's Christine—can you hear me?"

"Thank God! We can hear you, Christine—are you alright?"

"I'm Okay and for now I'm out of immediate danger. Call off any backup, we don't need this thing any bloodier than it already is."

"Consider it done. Where are you? I'll come and pick you up."

"I'm not exactly sure. I'm hiding out in a garage and can hear the sirens coming from my left and going to the right. This neighborhood is starting to come alive. I'm going to see if I can get a ride out of here in one of these cars, somebody here is bound to be going to work soon. I assume Quantara and Fox are out of range?"

"Yes, they continued with the mission and should have the judge on the way to headquarters by now. I'm only a few blocks from you, if you can tell me exactly where you are I can pick you up."

"That's no good, Bob, you can't afford to be seen anywhere near here. Head back to your office and I'll see you back there as soon as I can."

"I could hang around just inside of the five-mile range of our headsets just to keep the lines of communications open."

"That's not necessary, Bob; besides somebody has to call the director."

"If you think I'm calling the director, you're crazy. I'm staying away from the phones until you get back."

"I thought you guys were old friends?"

"We are, but that won't keep him from shooting the messenger; besides this is your operation. I don't think he's going to want to hear from me that we just killed two federal agents."

"I doubt that these deaths will ever be acknowledged by anyone."

"You may be right, just the same I think I'll wait for you before calling him."

After disconnecting with Bob, Christine evaluated her situation. She found herself in a garage with a typical Yuppie setup: one minivan and one BMW. Somehow she figured that the minivan would not be headed to the office. So she climbed into the back seat of the BMW and waited. She only had to wait about fifteen minutes until she heard the garage door open. She curled herself up on the floor behind the passenger's seat to avoid being detected when the driver entered the car.

The driver had barely backed out of the driveway before he was on his cell phone. The first call was to his office; evidently he was running late and needed his secretary to cover for him. The second call was to his mistress to cancel a date for that evening. It appeared that his wife insisted on going to dinner at the home of friends. He assured his mistress that he would make it up to her.

The commute to his office lasted about thirty minutes, all of which he spent on the phone. It took Christine only about one minute to figure out that this guy was a real jerk. She spent the rest of the trip figuring out a way to make sure that he got what he deserved.

When he finally parked his car in the garage at work and went inside, Christine got revenge for the wife. She slipped off her dark pants and then her panties. She reached around the seat, got a pen and paper out of the glove box, and wrote a note.

Danny,

I wore these the last time we made love in your car. Bring them with you the next time you come to see me and I'll let you rip them off me on the kitchen table.

Love and Kisses
Pammi

Christine put the note inside the panties and put the panties above the passenger seat visor. Christine was sure they would take this car and not the van to dinner that evening. She also knew that the last thing the wife would do before getting out of the car would be to pull down the visor to check her makeup in the mirror.

Christine could barely keep from laughing as she was putting her pants back on and imagining this jerk's surprise when his wife found the panties.

After exiting the parking structure, Christine found herself downtown in the heart of San Francisco's financial district. Still dressed in her black pants, shirt, and tennis shoes, she was sure to draw attention, even in San Francisco. She attempted to reach Bob on her headset, but the system was either shut down or no one was monitoring it. Although she carried no identification on her missions, she did carry a $100 bill, a $20 bill, and two $1 bills tucked in to her socks. She got change for one of the $1 bills and called Bob's office to have someone come and pick her up.

Both Fox and Quantara came to pick her up. They were glad to see her unharmed and in good spirits. She was pleased to hear that the rest of the operation had gone well and that the judge was safely tucked away in a high-security conference room in the basement of the FBI building.

Christine wanted to stop by her hotel for a change of clothes and to clean up, but Quantara told her about the director's impatient calls. He also told her that Lambert was avoiding the calls until she returned.

As Christine entered Bob Lambert's office, Bob got up from behind his desk walked around to the front and gave her a hug.

"Man, am I glad to see you in one piece."

"I know why you're glad to see me—you just don't want to have to explain any of this to the director!"

As they broke the embrace, Bob smiled and returned to the chair behind his desk.

"That sure as hell is part of it. Now that you're here, should we give him a call?"

"Jesus Bob, give a girl time to catch her breath! What happened at the surveillance house after they lost the judge?"

"All hell broke loose. Ed has the tapes. He's bringing them over now. It got bloodier after you got out of there. An SFPD patrol car responded to a 911 call and when they got to the scene, they saw three guys dressed in dark clothes loading two dead bodies into the side of a van. When they ordered them to stop, two more guys appeared from the other side of the

Van and shot the officers."

"Oh my God! Are they dead?"

"We overheard the government people at the surveillance house say that they thought they killed them. The local media has been broadcasting special reports on the shooting. They're saying two SFPD officers have been killed. The video camera inside the police car caught the whole thing on tape and somehow its already found its way to the media. There's been no mention of the judge and speculation is that the officers ran across a drug deal gone bad."

"What about the guys at the corner—what are they doing?"

"They packed up and split. Ed says he got some good pictures of several of them as they were coming back from the alley and he thinks he got a clean shot of the guy in charge."

"Okay, as soon as Ed gets here with the tapes and pictures, let's review them and get copies to Washington. What about the judge, how's he holding up?"

Bob got up from his desk, walked over to the TV, turned it on and pushed a button on the VCR. A few seconds later a picture of the judge sitting at a conference room table appeared.

"See for yourself. That conference room doubles as an interrogation room. We can see anything he does and the microphones are so sensitive that we can almost hear what he's thinking. We had him brought in blindfolded, so he doesn't know who we are or where he is."

"Good, has he said anything that could help us?"

"Not yet, he just keeps asking to see somebody in charge."

"When his bodyguard had the drop on me in his house, he mentioned Cedes and a Walter. Cedes we have a handle on but let's see what we can find out about this Walter. Anything else I should know before we call the director?"

"Just that he's called a couple of times and my secretary says he sounds very agitated."

Christine placed the call and as promised, the director, Tom, and Scott had all been waiting. Thirty minutes had stretched to two hours and the impatience could be heard in the director's voice.

"You know Christine, when I was in the field and I told the director of the FBI that I would call him in thirty minutes, I always called him in thirty minutes. Even if I was out having breakfast with Bob Lambert, I always took time to call. I digress, however—I'm sure you were doing more important things than having breakfast with Bob."

"Mr. Director, please believe me when I tell you that this delay could not be avoided."

"I was just explaining to Tom and Scott that you would have an excellent reason for not calling me back."

"I do sir, but before I go on, I'd like to let you know that in addition to ASAC Lambert, Agents Fox and Quantara are also in the room."

"Quantara—what's he doing there? I thought you sent him to San Diego?"

"I did, sir, but I had to recall him to San Francisco for a special assignment."

"I'm sorry Agent Fox but I don't believe we've met."

"No sir we haven't, I'm on loan from DEA."

"Okay Christine, maybe you just better get on with it and tell me what the hell is going on."

"Of course, sir. Things have changed considerably since our last conversation. I'll assume that Tom and Scott have briefed you on our friends at the corner and who we think may be pulling their strings."

"They did, but I don't want anybody jumping to any conclusions."

"I understand that sir. As you know, we've been monitoring the surveillance house on the corner. Early this morning they received a call telling them to forget the contact number they were given and to prepare a plan to terminate the judge."

"Terminate the judge? Are you sure you got that right?"

"Yes sir, the order was repeated and a go code was planted on CNN. We immediately put a plan of our own together to pull the judge out before the other side could kill him. When we recognized their "go code" on CNN, we jumped into action and rescued the judge."

"You didn't think that was important enough to call me?"

"Sir, we really didn't have a lot of time. We had to organize the rescue, line up the personnel and equipment and execute all in a matter of minutes."

"You can't tell me there wasn't time for a one minute phone call. Bob where the hell were you when this was going on? Don't tell me you lost my number too."

"No I didn't, but we really did have our hands full."

"We'll talk about this later, somebody better tell me what the hell happened out there."

Christine picked up where she left off before the director interrupted her. "Unfortunately, things didn't go as smoothly as planned. Either the assassination team was already on the way or their reaction time was quicker than we expected. Either way, they were on top of us during our extraction and a firefight ensued leaving two dead."

"Christ, Christine, please tell me you guys didn't have anything to do with those two SFPD officers that were killed this morning."

"No sir we didn't, at least not directly. We were being squeezed between two of the attack vans, when I jumped out of our van and shot the driver and passenger of the van ahead of us. Agent Fox then pushed their van out of the way with his, but by that time I was out of position and pinned down and wasn't able to get back to the van. I instructed agents Quantara and Fox to get the judge to safety. I exchanged gunfire with the assassins until I was able to get away myself. When I did get away, the police hadn't arrived at the scene and I was able to confirm that the driver and passenger I shot were both dead.

"From what we heard, the squad car arrived while the team of assassins was trying to clean up the mess and got killed when they challenged the assassins."

There was a momentary silence on the phone before the director came back on.

Then a calmer director came back. "Are you OK, Christine?"

"Yes sir, I'm fine."

"Thank God for that. How about Quantara and Fox, are you guys alright?"

"Yes sir."

"Yes sir."

"Good. I guess you guys know this is one hell of a mess. Bob, do you have anybody from your office working on this thing with the locals?"

"Yes sir I do, I have our local liaison on this per SOP. We have a solid firewall up on this thing. Only the people in this room and now those with you know that we had any involvement at all."

"Good, what about the judge? What's his reaction to all of this?"

"We have him locked in the basement; he doesn't know where he is or who has him." Bob Lambert told the director.

"You mean to tell me that you guys took him by force?"

Christine knew that Bob was about to catch hell if she didn't jump in and help him. She was probably going to need his help down the road and wasn't ready to burn that bridge.

"Actually sir, that was my idea. This judge is very dirty and very deeply entrenched in this organization. As long as he thinks we're bad guys, we have leverage. The minute he finds out that we're the FBI, he'll lose any fear of us and clam up. He knows that the FBI can't really do anything to him. Besides that sir, it was either grab him or let him be killed. We really didn't have much of a choice."

"Did anybody try to explain his predicament to him and get him to come with you on his own?"

"Sir, there really wasn't any time for a lot of discussion. By the time we got to his house, the bad guys were already on their way."

"Okay, but remember this is a judge and not some homeless junkie."

"Of course, sir."

Tom had been listening carefully, but was hung up on the 'go code'.

"Christine, how was the 'go code' delivered?"

"Via CNN in a speech given at Parliament Square in London."

"Who gave the speech?"

"You guys aren't going to like this, but the speech was given by Brian Hunt, the president's Chief of Staff."

The phone went silent for what seemed like an eternity before the director finally broke the silence.

"Can I assume that there is no way that this can be a mistake or a coincidence?"

Bob used his friendship to emphasize his point. "Marty, I don't think we can avoid it any longer—we have something very wrong in the White House. The code they used was 'Jurisprudence'. That's not exactly a phrase that works its way into a conversation very easily. I analyzed the tape of the speech very thoroughly and Hunt really had to stretch to make the phrase fit. The way I see it, the only way Hunt didn't know what he was saying is, if he has a speech writer who enjoys trying to trip him up."

"Okay Bob, we'll run the tape through the stress analyzer and take a closer look at Brian Hunt."

Christine didn't want to leave it there. "Mr. Director, I know no one wants to think or talk about this, but what about the president?"

"It's a large leap from Brian Hunt to the president of the United States. Let's investigate the leads we have. If they take us to the president, then we'll be entering a whole new arena."

"That's good enough for me sir—how about the judge, how should we proceed with him?" Christine had made her point.

"Follow your instincts, Christine, they've been pretty good so far. Tape the session in case we need it later. What about that group of government people you were monitoring, the ones who tried to kill the judge?"

Bob had been following their activities. "They packed up and left. Their last instructions were to return to D.C. I have a man on his way over here with their photos and he should be here any minute. As soon as they get here I'll E-mail them to you."

Director Flynn didn't like how fast everything was moving. "Okay, send the photos directly to Scott. He'll start identifying them as soon as he gets them. For now, we'll just keep them under surveillance. It would be counterproductive to pick them up at this point. Bob, make sure you stay on top of your local situation and let me know if there's anything we can do from here."

"Of course. What do you want us to do with the judge once Christine is done with him?"

"That's a good question, Bob. Since Martinez's rouge operation probably set all of this in motion, I'll put him in charge of babysitting the judge and anybody else needing it as this investigation unfolds.

"I still don't understand why discovering the FBI had the judge under surveillance was enough to spook this syndicate into having him killed. If they're that sensitive, we'd better make sure that none of our other surveillance operations are discovered."

Christine and Quantara looked at each other, knowing full well that the director didn't have all of the information.

"I'll provide you with a full written report when I return to D.C. and perhaps that will clear things up for you, sir." Christine assured the director.

After a few more moments of light banter everyone signed off and Christine headed to the basement to interrogate the judge.

Chapter 16

Christine wasn't particularly interested in preserving the judge's rights for a clean prosecution: She was more interested in extracting information and as such behaved accordingly. The fist thing she did when she entered the conference room was to shut off the video camera. She then took out a tape recorder and put it on the conference room table.

The judge watched her curiously and then marched toward her and demanded in his most judicial voice to see the man in charge. Without missing a stride, Christine thrust the heel of her right palm into the judge's chest, sending him flying backward to land squarely on his back. The judge was stunned. He was still gasping for air when Christine jerked him off of the floor and threw him into a chair. As he was beginning to gather himself and breathe more deeply, Christine leaned within an inch of his face and reinforced her authority. "You wanted to see someone in charge, Feldman; now you have. I'm going to have to strap you into a stress analyzer, it's kind of a sophisticated lie detector. Then I'm going to ask you some questions and I'm only going to ask them once. If you don't answer or if the machine tells me that you're lying, I'll put a bullet in your foot. The next time you lie I'll put a bullet in your other foot, and then in your hands. If I don't think that you're going to cooperate at all, I'll put a bullet in your brain. I hope we understand each other."

The judge was almost back to normal and was about to challenge Christine but got only got as far as "Who are…" before Christine slapped him across the face hard enough to knock over both him and the chair he was sitting in.

"Feldman, I told you that I would be the one asking the questions. I'm not going to tell you again. You will speak only to answer my questions. Now, I'm going to put you into one of those nice comfortable high-back chairs and get you ready to answer some questions. I don't want any trouble. Just nod your head if you understand."

The judge dazed and frightened wiped blood from the corner of his mouth and nodded his head. Christine walked to the door opened it and brought a roll of clear plastic into the conference room and spread it out on the floor. Then she walked over, grabbed the judge, tore off his robe, and put him into one of the executive-type, high-back chairs, which she then rolled on top of the plastic cover. She tied his feet to the chair legs and his hands palm down to the armrests. His head was put into a neck brace and taped against the chair by running several strands of electrical tape around the chair and across the judge's forehead, pinning his head firmly against the back of the chair.

Bob Lambert was in his office furious. "Why the hell did she shut off the surveillance cameras? What's she going to do that she doesn't want us to see? Quantara get down there and turn that camera back on."

Quantara could imagine what she was doing. "Sir, she is doing what she has to, to get information from the judge. The judge thinks like you do sir, that you just can't mistreat a judge. There's no way we'll get this judge to talk as long as he thinks he's above the law. So the first thing she has to do is get rid of his arrogance and make him believe that she'll do anything she wants, to him."

"Okay, I can buy all of that, but she'd better remember that she's an FBI agent and he's a suspect? If she touches a hair on his head, he's going to sue the FBI for millions and he'll win. I better go down there and remind her of that."

Bob Lambert stormed out of his office headed to the basement with Agents Quantara and Fox close behind him.

After Christine had the judge all tied up, she went back into the hall and retrieved a machine that looked like an EKG printer. She set it up on the conference room table, attached two electrodes to the judge's chest, and plugged them into the machine. Then Christine, holding a glass of water, walked in front of the judge positioning herself so that all he could see was her face.

"Okay Feldman, I think we're ready. Let's start with something simple. What's your name?"

Without hesitation and only a hint of defiance in his voice the judge answered. "Judge Rupert Feldman."

Christine tossed the glass of water in his face and got within an inch of the judge's face. "Did your mother name you Judge Rupert Feldman?'"

This time the judge answered with a barely audible and intimidated "No."

"Then why are you already lying to me? Do you remember what I said I would do if you lied or didn't answer?"

Christine backed away from the judge, walked over to the conference table and picked up a mouthpiece. She walked back to the judge, held up the mouthpiece in front of his eyes so that he could see it and then continued.

"I told you that I would shoot you in the foot for your first lie. The machine said you lied, so now I have to keep my word. I'm going to put this mouthpiece in your mouth so you don't bite your tongue off from the pain when I shoot you. We have a lot of questions after this one. Consider telling the truth from now on and maybe you'll be able to walk out of here under your own power."

The judge started to protest but Christine shoved the mouthpiece in his mouth and secured it with a piece of tape. She then went to the table, picked up a pistol, lifted it up so that Judge Feldman could see it, then lowered it and fired a bullet into the left foot of the judge. The last thing the Judge remembered before passing out was the penetrating pain of his left foot.

Bob Lambert was about fifteen feet from the basement conference room when he heard the shot. He was momentarily stunned and then bolted toward the interrogation room with Quantara and Fox right behind him. "Jesus Christ, she's out of control. My God! You can't shoot a judge—I don't care what you think he did. We're the FBI—not the CIA."

Quantara was somewhat surprised himself but wanted to give her the benefit of the doubt, at least until they had a chance to see what actually happened. "Sir, sir, let's not go charging in there, let's bring her out. Let me go in and get Christine to come out and talk to us."

"There can be no excuse for shooting a judge. She crossed the line.

Get her the hell out of there."

Before Quantara had a chance to enter the conference room, Christine came out, holding a blood-soaked towel over a wash basin with about a half an inch of blood in it. Bob Lambert ASAC of the San Francisco office of the FBI was unable to control himself when he saw Christine. "What the hell do you think you're doing? You're out of control—you can't shoot people as part of an interrogation! I'm relieving you of your duties."

Christine smiled a disarming smile; "Relax, Bob, nobody got shot."

"We heard the shot and what about all this blood?"

"What you heard was a starters pistol. As I shot the starter pistol I dropped a large piece of ice on the judges bare foot. His imagination did the rest. He won't even have a bruise when he wakes up."

"What do you mean when he wakes up?"

"He passed out when the ice hit his foot."

"What about this blood?"

"I got it from the cafeteria, I think they're having lamb today."

Bob relaxed a little but was still furious. "You can't just go around making up your own interrogation rules. My God, you could have killed that man, you could have given him a heart attack. You damn near gave me one. He'll probably still sue us."

Quantara actually started laughing. "For what, dropping ice on his foot, or for firing a starters pistol in his presence? This has to be one of the best illusions yet. This lamb's blood makes it complete."

"That's right, and if I want to pull this off, I need to get back in there before he comes to. Bob, we can have this out later, right now I have an advantage that we have to pursue. If I'm going to get fired at least let me make it worthwhile."

"Okay, but I want that camera back on and I want someone in there with you."

"I'll go with her." Quantara volunteered.

Without waiting for Bob's approval, Christine and Quantara went back in to complete the illusion. When Quantara saw the judge tied up the way he was, he wondered of Bob Lambert was right and Christine had gone over the edge. Christine put the basin down next to the judge's foot and wrapped the blood soaked towel around it. She then stood up and threw a glass of water in the judge's face to bring him around. The judge was still hazy and that's just how Christine wanted it. She removed his mouthpiece and motioned for Quantara to unwrap the towel and hand it to her. She lifted it to the judge's face.

"I didn't know a foot could bleed this much. I guess it was a good thing that we put that plastic down. We'll also have to have more bandages ready next time. Now that you know I mean what I say, we can start again. I'm going to ask you some questions and you're going to give me some answers. If you're not telling the truth you know what will happen.

"Let's try that first question again, what's your name? Before you answer, think about your answer—remember I want the truth and only the truth." Christine picked up the tape recorder and turned it on. She then put it back on the conference room table.

This time the judge stopped to think before he answered. "My name is Francis Rupert Feldman."

"Very good. Now to show you that I can be understanding when you cooperate, would you like a shot to help numb the pain in your foot?"

The judge without hesitation responded in the affirmative. Christine took a syringe from the table and injected it into the judge's arm. She smiled at the judge and continued in a softer tone. "OK now, back to business. How long have you been working for Cedes?

"Five years."

"Who recruited you?"

"Paul Cedes."

"What do you do for him?"

"I recruit other judges and pick and chose which cases we should fix and which cases we let go through a regular trial."

"Where does Paul Cedes fit into the organization?"

"He's the chief advisor to the council."

"What about Walter, what are his responsibilities?"

"He's a member of the council."

"How many members are there on the council?"

"I'm not sure; Walter is the only one I know."

Christine leaned back as if to look at the monitor to verify the accuracy of his answer.

The judge reiterated his answers to assure her that he was telling the truth.

"I'm telling you the truth—Walter Brooks is the only council member I know."

Christine was temporary knocked of balance. The billionaire oilman—here he was again. If Christine believed in destiny, she was beginning to believe her destiny was not only to avenge her family or rid the world of Walter Brooks and Paul Cedes, but also perhaps to save the country. She had to gather her thoughts. She couldn't let up on this judge. He may be the link to finding out about her parents.

"How do you know Brooks is on the council?"

"Paul Cedes, Walter Brooks, and I often meet to discuss strategy and future recruits."

"So Walter Brooks is one of the key members of the council?"

"I'm not sure; he may be representing someone else."

"Who?"

"I don't know, honestly I don't know."

"If you had to guess, who would it be?"

"I've always thought that it was someone high up in the White House."

"Brian Hunt?"

"Maybe, I don't know."

As Christine was working the judge over, a thought flashed through her mind. She may never have this opportunity again.

"Who ordered the hit on Michael Peron?"

The judge hesitated but only long enough for Christine to remind him that she still had a bullet left for his other foot.

"I met with Paul and Walter and we discussed the ramifications of Peron's testimony."

"Are you talking about Paul Cedes and Walter Brooks?"

"Yes, we decided that Peron was going to strike some kind of deal with the Attorney General. Laura Kinsman told Paul that she had no choice but to deal, there were just too many people watching the case. If she didn't deal up the ladder, she probably would've been exposed."

"Are you telling me that Laura Kinsman is part the organization?"

"Yes, they needed someone high up in the Attorney General's office. They just recently asked her to become an advisor to the council. So I'm sure they didn't want to expose her. When Peron attempted to make a deal with Laura, he ordered his own hit."

"So, you, Paul, and Walter actually ordered the hit?"

"No, we made a recommendation that Walter took to the council. That was my last involvement."

"Why was it so important to get to Peron? If I remember right, Peron was only looking at price-fixing charges?"

"That's true, but he could've exposed the entire operation. He was the key man in Mexico."

"So who was responsible for calling the assassin and giving him his instructions?"

The judge hesitated and Christine could see in his eyes that he was about to lie.

"I don't know."

Christine took a step back pretending to look at the monitor.

"Rupert, Rupert, Rupert, you were doing so well; I thought we were getting to understand each other and now you go and lie to me." She cocked her pistol in front of Rupert's face so that he could clearly see it and then hesitated just long enough to give him a chance to beg her not to shoot him.

"Please, please don't shoot me, they'll kill me if I tell you."

"I guess you have a choice to make. I'll kill you right here, right now, or you can tell me and live awhile longer hoping they don't find out you told me. The choice is entirely yours."

"I honestly don't know for sure, but Paul Cedes implements all of the council's directives. He would be the logical choice for making such a call."

"Did he ever say where he might find such a person?"

"No, but he used to be with the CIA, so I'm sure he has many of those kinds of contacts. He could also have done it himself, he can be pretty ruthless."

Christine looked at the monitor and then lowered her pistol.

"Did you ever hear the name of Hoover while you were with Paul Cedes?"

"No, I swear, I never heard anything about anyone named Hoover."

"Okay, now tell me about Judge Walker; what is his involvement in this thing?"

"As far as I know, nothing. We recruited his clerk years ago, but he assured us that Walker would never join us, so we never approached him."

Just as Christine was thinking how well this was going, Quantara cleared his throat to get her attention.

"Christine, see if he knows where Congressmen McCall's daughter is."

"OK." Christine walked back to the judge.

"Just a couple more questions, Rupert, and you'll be able to get cleaned up and we'll get a doctor to look at your foot. You've probably figured out by now that we're not in the same organization that you are. I do however represent some very angry people and if you ask me who and I tell you, then they'll have to kill you. This way you'll be able to walk away when we're all done here. These people owe a certain congressman a favor, and they want to know where his daughter is. For your own sake, I hope you know where she is and that she's still alive."

"She's still alive. She's being held in a house on Coronado Island. She's being treated very well and undergoing a detox program. We had no intention of harming her; she was just a tool to recruit Andy."

"OK Rupert, one more question and then you're going to give this man the names of everyone you know in your little family. After that you'll get to clean up and see a doctor."

Christine knew that she was about to take a big chance, but she may never have this opportunity again. "What do you know about a man named Barber?"

"Nothing; I've never heard of him."

Christine paused for a moment and then decided not to pursue it.

She got Quantara started and then headed back up to Bob Lambert's office. When she entered Bob's office, Bob was still upset.

"I told you guys to turn the camera back on when you went back in there. Damn it, what are we going to tell Flynn? He wanted this interrogation on tape."

"Don't worry Bob, it's all on tape. I had an audio tape recorder running the whole time."

"I don't know what to say, Christine, your technique is unusual to say the least and for all I know, everything you did in there was as illegal as all hell. We'll probably never be able to use any thing you got in court. Please tell me you got something."

"Yes Bob, we got quite a bit. He'll go away for the rest of his life as will several other prominent officials. Quantara is still down there getting more names."

"Will we be able to use any of this in court?"

"Come on, Bob, this has never been about getting anybody to court. This is about uncovering treason at the highest level of government. I doubt that any of these people will ever go to trial. But to answer your question, yes we'll be able to use his entire confession in court. Aside from a few mind games, nothing illegal happened in that interrogation."

"My report is still going to have to have the part about the shot and the lambs blood in it."

"So will mine Bob. They put me in charge because they know I'll get the job done. They also know that I work within limits. My boundaries may be a little broader than most, but my conviction rate is the highest in the organized crime division."

After another few minutes of banter, the screen displaying the conference room came back on. There was Judge Feldman sitting in his robe in a highback chair rubbing his left foot. Just minutes later Quantara joined them in Bob's office. "I have to hand it to you, you definitely get results. That poor bastard doesn't know if he's coming or going. He just handed us a gold mine."

"He's giving us everything we need except who's running this thing," Christine said while staring into the monitor.

"He did give us Paul Cedes, Walter Brooks, which I still can't believe, and an assistant attorney general," Quantara said.

Christine turned from the monitor. "That's true, he did confirm Paul Cedes and gave us our next rung on the ladder and we now know that they have a council and we know the name of one of the council members. What we don't have are the other council members and the head of the organization."

"I want to hear this tape. Less than forty-eight hours ago you came to me with a simple surveillance job and now I've got dead people all over town and find myself in the middle of a treason case that reaches into the White House. Remind me to be busy the next time you call for help," Bob said with a smile.

"If it will make you feel any better, we're almost done in California. A quick stop in San Diego and we'll be out of your hair, at least for a while."

"What was that stuff about Michael Peron? Wasn't he the guy from Mexicana Oil assassinated about six months ago?" Quantara asked.

"That's the guy."

"What on earth made you ask about him?" Bob wondered.

"Think about it. You've got this syndicate and one of its chief players is one of the richest men in the world, who just happens to have made most of his money from oil. Then the head of the second largest oil company in Mexico is assassinated, just as he's about to testify on corruption in the oil industry. It just seemed like a logical question."

"Judging by the response, it was the perfect question. What about Barber, how does he fit into this?" Quantara asked.

"He doesn't, that's an unresolved homicide that I thought I would throw into the mix."

"What about the judge, what's going to happen to him?" Fox asked.

Christine thought a moment before replying. "The director wants him tucked away until this is over, so I guess we'll do as he said and turn him over to Martinez when we're done."

"This judge is going to have a fit when he finds out you're an FBI agent." Bob told her.

"Don't let him get too high and mighty—after all, he just admitted to multiple counts of treason and kidnapping. Let's call the director and brief him on the results of the interrogation."

The director was pleased with Christine's complete and relatively quick success. He did get a nasty feeling that their investigation was just getting started. It had already led them into the legislative and judicial branches, and now it looked as if they were about to uncover corruption in the upper echelons of the attorney general's office. That would be more than enough for any investigation, but now Christine's warnings about the White House had to be taken seriously. The mounting evidence was pointing to a trail of corruption could lead through the corridors of the White House—maybe even right into the oval office. The more they found the less he wanted to hear.

The director was not surprised at Paul Cedes' involvement. He was, however, taken by total surprise when he heard of Laura Kinsman's involvement. She was highly regarded and well respected as one of the top prosecutors in the attorney generals office; in addition he also considered her a friend and often a confidant on difficult cases. The one piece of good news was that Judge Walker didn't seem to be involved.

Things were beginning to move very quickly. Decisions needed to be made within the next few days, some of which included who to pull into the loop and who to leave out in the cold? How much could they tell the White House? Was it time to bring in the attorney general or Congress?

There was much to do and it was time to reevaluate their position and next steps. He needed to get all of his key people back to Washington for thorough analysis and recommendations.

The director's big concern right now was Christine. She was a key investigator on the case and yet had acted like a field agent, exposing

herself to more physical danger than she should. If anything should happen to her, there was a good chance the case would be seriously delayed
or maybe even totally derailed. She kept the case moving forward. He
knew that she pushed the procedural envelope from time to time, but it
was difficult to argue with her success. Despite his concerns, he approved
Christine and Agent Quantara's plan to rescue the congressman's daughter. He was also eager to hear the interview with the judge. He was disappointed that video wouldn't be available but was assured there was plenty
on the audiotape for everyone. He was rather curious to see how Christine got the judge to open up the way he did so quickly as he did.

Chapter 17

After the judge had given the FBI agents all the information he could, Bob Lambert, accompanied by two additional agents, came to take official control of him and place him under arrest. Bob did the honors.

"Francis Rupert Feldman, I am Special Agent in Charge Bob Lambert. I'm with the FBI and you, sir, are under arrest for the crimes of treason, kidnapping, murder, conspiracy to commit murder, receiving bribes, and offering bribes. Once we get back to D.C., I'm sure we'll be able to add several charges stemming from your work on the bench."

As soon as he realized that he was in the custody of the FBI, Judge Feldman exploded.

"You son of a bitch! You guys are with the FBI? You can't treat people like this! I'm going to have all of your badges; every one of you is going to end up in jail! Anything I said here is inadmissible—you can't prove a thing. That crazy bitch shot me in the foot, I would have confessed to anything."

Bob ignored the outburst and looked at the judge's foot. He could barely make out a red mark where the ice had hit it.

"Well, Rupert, it looks like you're going to have a tough time convincing anybody that you were shot."

"Where is that crazy bitch? I'm going to have her hide! I'm a god damned Judge—you can't do that to a judge."

To his own surprise and the others in the room, Bob forcefully slammed his index finger into the judge's chest.

"Listen here, you sanctimonious SOB, that "crazy bitch," as you put it, saved your life. The rest of us wanted to finish you off and dump you in an alley somewhere, for what you and your friends did to the congress-man and his family. She's the one who talked us out of it. Thanks to her, you'll probably get to start your live over in the witness protection pro-gram somewhere instead of ending it in the electric chair with your friends. So from now on, you keep your mouth shut and speak only when your spoken too, is that clear, Rupert?"

This time, with somewhat less conviction, he tried to rise out of the chair in one last act of defiance.

"I'm a federal judge, you can't talk to me like that."

Bob shoved the judge back into the chair, then leaned over and put his finger in the judges face and let him know where he stood.

"If I ever hear you refer to yourself as a judge again, I'll finish the job Agent Peal started and I won't be using blanks. You don't deserve the honor of being called a judge." Bob turned his back on Rupert Feldman and addressed himself to one of the Agents as he walked out of the room. "Get this jerk cleaned up, get him some clothes and food and then put some guards on this room until we're ready to move him. Get rid of that phone on the wall and if he gives you any trouble, bind and gag him."

Chapter 18

Christine wasn't wasting any time—she knew Bob Lambert would be able to handle Feldman's transfer and that Quantara wouldn't be able to rest until they at least tried to rescue the congressman's daughter. Quantara and Michael Fox made arrangements with the DEA for their support from their San Diego office to scout out the area on Coronado Island where the congressman's daughter was being held.

Coronado Island had two things going for it: Hotel Del Coronado and the U.S. Naval station. Posing, as busboys from the hotel seemed silly, so Christine, Quantara, and the DEA agents dressed in navy uniforms and requisitioned one of the navy's official vans from their motor pool.

Based on the DEA's observations, security in and around the house was fairly loose. There were never more than three guards at the house and they didn't appear to be expecting any trouble. The plan, therefore, was simple. They would launch simultaneously stun grenades into the kitchen, living room, and the bedroom where the congressman's daughter was being held. Quantara would burst through the front door and Christine through the rear door. They would make their way to the bedroom, retrieve the girl and exit the house through the front door while being covered by the DEA agents. At least that was the plan.

The first thing they noticed when they were close enough to see the target house, was all the unusual activity on the front steps of the house. There were three men and a woman standing on the steps and two more men just getting out of a dark sedan appeared to be joining them. One of the men was on a cellular phone while another was handing out night-vision goggles. The one on the phone finished his call and started giving instructions to the others, using his hands to make gestures and point in different directions. They seemed to come to an agreement as they split up and went off into different directions in the neighborhood.

Christine wasn't sure whether to laugh or cry. It was obvious that the girl had escaped. This would make their job much more difficult. They had two choices—they could join the search and hope they found the girl before the bad guys, or they could wait for the girl to be recaptured and proceed with their initial plan, making a few adjustments for what was certain to be tighter security. Christine decided they should do a passive search of the neighborhood by just driving through the streets and acting only if someone actually spotted the girl.

Christine was riding shotgun, watching the bushes and alleys as they slowly approached the target house, when all at once a skinny young girl darted from the bushes in front of the house and ran straight for the van yelling at the top of her lungs.

"Help me, please help me! I've been kidnapped—please help me!" The van came to a sudden stop, Quantara jumped out of the back door, pulled the girl inside and closed the door behind them just in time to hear a bullet ricochet off it.

"Nobody shoots back." Christine yelled at her crew. "Michael, you'd better drive like hell and get us out of here."

"We've got a dark sedan on our tail." Quantara yelled from the back of the van.

"Is this Dejavu or what." Michael Fox yelled over the noise of the shattering windshield.

"Except this time I don't want anybody killed. Shake that sedan." Christine told Michael as she brushed the glass out of her lap.

Michael turned down an alley and yelled for everyone to hold on. As soon as the sedan turned into the alley behind him, Michael slammed on the brakes, threw the van in reverse, and began backing up as fast as he could, still keeping the van on the road. The sedan kept coming until the final seconds when the driver decided that this girl just wasn't worth it.

He cranked the wheel to the left, but was too late. The back of the Navy van broadsided the sedan on the passenger side and spun it into the ditch. Michael and Christine were held in place by their seat belts but Quantara and the girl were thrown against that back door. Fortunately neither was seriously injured.

Michael quickly recovered and drove the van out of the alley and back to the naval station. The navy was put out by the damage to their van, but Christine assured them they could bill the FBI.

Michael Fox took Christine, Quantara and the girl to Christine's car. The congressman's daughter was frightened and wasn't sure if she had improved her situation or made it worse.

"Who are you guys? Where are you taking me?"

Christine showed the girl her FBI badge. "We are with the FBI and we're working for your father. He is very worried and has had us looking for you for quite some time."

"Oh, thank God! Where is he? When can I see him?"

"We're going to the airport right now. We'll get you cleaned up and put you on an airplane to D.C. to see your father."

"Why do we have to go to Washington? Why can't you just take me to my house in San Diego?"

Quantara felt sorry for this girl. The last few weeks had to have been a nightmare for her. Her drug use kept her down, and then to be yanked off the street without knowing why had to have been extremely frightening. Being put through a cold-turkey detox program under the best of conditions is difficult, but to do it without a support group and while a prisoner is enough to make most drug users suicidal. This young girl, however, was a fighter. She had come through all of that and more; she'd escaped from her captors, and now found herself among more strangers who from her point of view, may or may not have her best interests at heart.

Quantara hated drugs and what they did to people; he especially hated what they did to children like this one; but most of all he hated those who sold the drugs or otherwise took advantage of innocent children. As far as Quantara was concerned, Feldman was the worst—he was in a position to help these kids but instead used his power to hurt them.

The congressman was not without fault, first as a father and then as a legislator—Quantara believed the congressman had failed on both counts. His primary concern now, however, was to make sure this girl got the chance she deserved. He let her know that her entire family was in Washington and that for now she would be safer there with them than in San Diego by herself. He spent the entire trip to the airport talking to her as an equal: gaining her trust and helping her regain her confidence.

He was surprised to find that her captors had run a pretty effective detox program on her. She appeared to be over the hump and with a proper supervision and maintenance program, she could be one of those rare success stories. He found it ironic that had they not run such an effective program on her, she probably would never have escaped.

While Quantara was spending time with the congressman's daughter, Christine was arranging an FBI charter to meet them at John Wayne Airport in Orange County and fly them to D.C. The only thing the FBI had available was a flight which was already headed to D.C. from San Francisco.

When the plane arrived, Christine and Quantara walked to the plane with the congressman's daughter between them. The copilot met them at the bottom of the steps.

"One of you Agent Peal?"

"Yes, I am," Christine replied.

"Ma'am, you have a message from the director. He would like for you to call as soon as we're airborne, regardless of the time."

"Very well, thank you."

"There's one other thing ma'am," the copilot said. "We have two people in custody on board, so I'm required by regulation to take your weapons for safekeeping."

He held out a canvas bag and Agents Quantara and Peal placed their service revolvers in the bag. Neither made any move to give up their backup weapons. The copilot thought about challenging them for a moment, but let it pass.

As they stepped inside the converted 737, they were greeted by a friendly faces grinning from ear to ear. Bob Lambert and two other agents were on the flight escorting Francis Rupert Feldman and one other prisoner to Washington.

The four refused to let their reunion be affected by Feldman's curses and protests when he saw Christine enter the plane. That was until Christine heard him try to talk to the girl.

"Julie! What are you doing here?"

The girl was surprised to see Feldman and then she saw his hands and feet were chained.

"Judge Feldman, what's going on here?"

Before Feldman could respond, Christine answered her.

"Julie, this is the man who had you kidnapped. This man was using your life to blackmail your father. These men are taking him to Washington to be charged."

"I don't believe it—he's one of my dad's friends."

"No Julie, he's not one of your dad's friends," Christine insisted. "He's one of his most dangerous enemies. This man is a criminal, a kidnapper, and a murderer. When you get to Washington, I'm sure your dad will tell you all about it." Feldman tried to protest, but Christine quickly shut him up and threatened to have him gagged if he said another word without being asked first.

Bob Lambert told Christine and Quantara about the other prisoner. He was one of the team assigned to assassinate Feldman and in the same group that fired at Christine and killed the two SFPD officers. Ed caught him on film as he was returning to their surveillance house. He was later spotted and arrested at the airport, attempting to board a plane for Washington. Christine was curious if he had given them any information.

"No, he hasn't given us anything except his name, Terry Burns'". Bob told her. "He claims to be working for the government and to have immunity. He gave us a number to call to verify his immunity, but as yet no one has answered the number. We plan on tracing it as soon as we get to D.C."

"Your people did great work, Bob, this may be the break we're looking for," Christine told him.

"It could be, but I don't think we're going to get much out of him. By the way, you had better call the boss. While you're at it, find out why he insisted that I come to Washington. I had plenty to clean up back in San Francisco."

"I'll check with him. As far as this guy is concerned, if we've got the number that's probably all we need. I hope we don't plan on offering him any kind of deal," Christine added. "He killed two cops—we'll get our information some other way."

Her call to the director was short. He wanted to make sure that everyone was on board safely and to let her know that Tom would be at the airport to take custody of the prisoners.

The prisoners would be interrogated, and after everyone got some rest, there would be a meeting of the full committee. The congressman's daughter would be reunited with her family at FBI headquarters just prior to the meeting. It was eight in the morning by the time Tom took charge of the prisoners and Christine was headed home with Julie, the congressman's daughter, in tow.

Christine showed Julie to the spare bedroom, then set the alarm for the doors and windows and turned on her tone-activated recorder attached to the phone. If Julie attempted to escape or use the phone, Christine would know.

Christine didn't get much sleep; there was too much going on. The murder of her family had turned into some kind of massive crime conspiracy lasting over three decades. She had to follow it to its conclusion: she knew now, that Paul Cedes and Walter Brooks were involved in her family's death—but would this investigation lead her to others?

From here on, it was essential that she be able to closely monitor all the developments in this case and be able to act quickly if she needed to. Her mind was filled with possibilities. Perhaps her father was an oil baron and was killed by Brooks to take over his fields. Or perhaps he was a land baron killed so that the oil companies could take his oil-rich land. Whatever her father was, she knew he had been rich—how else could he leave her so much money with only a note saying, "You will know what to do with all of this money when the time is right."

Christine finally did drift off to sleep. When she woke up, she found Julie at the kitchen table eating half a dozen scrambled eggs and several English muffins. Christine listened to the tape on her phone and found that Julie had indeed placed two calls. The first was to her home in San Diego where a machine answered, and the second to her father's office where she was told he hadn't yet arrived. Christine didn't have any problems with Julie making these calls and joined her for breakfast even though it was already past noon.

She spent her time with the Julie trying to get whatever information she could about the kidnappers. She urged Julie to recall anything she may have overheard or seen, specifically any names she may have heard. Except for a couple of first names (which were pretty much useless) the only name possibly useful was a Mr. Kessler. Julie had heard his name mentioned several times and her captors seemed very respectful to him on the phone whenever he called.

Julie was stronger and surer of herself. She wanted to be reunited with her family and was eager to get going. Christine assured her that she would see her father soon.

After a few phone calls and a couple of hours later, Christine and Julie walked into Christine's secretary's office where they found Congressman McCall and Special Agent Scott Peterson waiting. Julie for the moment forgot what drove her from home and to drugs and ran into her father's open arms.

Christine moved them to her office, giving them some privacy, and returned to her secretary's office to share a smile with Scott. "It's good to see you, Scott."

"It's good to see you too. It sounds like you just finished a couple of rather intense days."

"To say the least. Has the congressman been very helpful?" Christine asked.

"Since he heard that we retrieved his daughter, he's been extremely helpful. He's even come up with a plan to cover our involvement and get his family out of harm's way, while he continues to work with us."

"Do you trust him?"

"I guess I do; I think he's basically honest and just got caught up in a terrible predicament," Scott said.

"OK, if you think he can help let's give him a chance," Christine said. "Maybe the boss will let him serve out his term if he gives us enough help in this investigation."

"Speaking of the boss, we have a briefing in about an hour. Be prepared—I think he wants to know everything that happened while you were out West. I think he's blocked off a full hour for you and Bob."

"I guess I should put it in some kind of sequence then. I'd better get busy. Can you find a place for the congressman and his daughter until then?"

"Sure, I'll take them with me."

So much had happened in the last couple of days, it seemed like months since the task force's last meeting. The director decided on a full meeting, which included Martinez, Bob Lambert, and Francine.

"I'm glad everyone could make it. We've come a long way from our last meeting just a few days ago. Bob, it's good to see you here. I don't know how much you know, but in the next couple of hours, you'll probably hear things that you wished you hadn't. I'm glad you're here, because from what I hear, we owe your group a round of gratitude for their work in San Francisco. Christine, I think your last couple of days have been the most active, so why don't you lead us off?"

"Thank you, Mr. Director. With the help of Special Agent Lambert and Agent Quantara, I would like to lay out what we discovered over the last couple of days. I think it's also important to note that to gather the information we did, in such a short amount of time, we had to stretch procedure a little bit. ASAC Lambert and Special Agent Quantara did not indorse, approve of, or in any way participate in any of these procedures."

"OK Christine, you got your disclaimer in, how bad is it? You didn't kill anybody to get this information, did you?" The director joked.

"No sir, but I'm sure you'll get some complaints from one of our suspects."

"I understand Christine, did you break any laws."

"I don't believe so sir."

"Did you violate his civil rights?"

"Except for the fact that I didn't identify myself as an FBI agent until after the interview, I don't believe that I did anything illegal."

"How do you expect to prosecute him if he didn't know you were FBI when he confessed everything? Nothing he told you will hold up in court if you didn't merandize him."

"I know that sir. To be honest, I didn't think that he'd give us anything if he knew we were FBI. I felt getting a complete layout of this syndicate was more important than prosecuting one crooked judge. Besides, we can come back at him now that he's been officially arrested and from information we gather after arresting other members of this syndicate."

"You're probably right. It doesn't sound like you did to much damage, I still want you to meet with our legal people to see what we can salvage from this interview. I don't like leaving crooked judges running around free."

Christine was relieved at the director's attitude and laid out the last couple of days in complete detail. She included the deaths of the PIs and pointed out that it was probably their deaths that somehow set in motion the first attempt on the judge's life. She conveniently forgot to mention that it was her and Quantara that made that attempt. She told the group about all of the radio and telephone traffic they monitored shortly after that attempt.

She explained how the president's chief of staff sent the coded message to kill the judge and how with the help of the San Francisco Bureau they went in and rescued him.

The more she said the more unbelievable it all became to everyone in the room. When it became time to play the tape she glanced at Bob Lambert to make sure that he wasn't about to make a last minute protest.

"Sir, as you know, the interview with the judge was extremely successful. I have a transcript of the interview if you prefer not to sit through the tape."

"Is there something on this tape that you don't think I should hear?"

"No sir, its just a lengthy interview."

"This is the top priority on my schedule, so let's get on with it."

Christine turned on the tape recorder and watched everybody's reaction. Bob Lambert gave Christine a disapproving look when he realized that the tape didn't begin until after the gunshot. Most everyone else showed their surprise and became extremely uncomfortable as they listened to Judge Feldman explain how deep in to the various branches of government the reach of this syndicate had become.

They listened to the tape in silence with Francine frantically taking notes. At the end of the recording, Christine turned off the recorder and waited for comments.

"I wish we had gotten all of this after we read him his rights." Director Flynn said. "I hate the idea off letting this jerk off."

"Tom, you've been with him this morning, how's he behaving today?" Scott asked.

"Actually I think he likes me; but he doesn't like Christine much. We have the perfect opportunity to play good cop/bad cop. I have a feeling that he'll cooperate with us across the board as long as he doesn't have to talk to Christine anymore."

"Good, then you run with it." The director told him. "Get him to tell you everything he told Christine and make sure you read him his rights first. I want to be able to use this confession. You can use the tape to refresh his memory, but make sure he reiterates everything on there. Also make sure you have a stenographer in the room and video the whole thing. I don't want any way for him to wiggle out of this later."

Tom agreed, while smiling mischievously at Christine. "Christine may have to stop by and say 'Hi' if he doesn't feel like cooperating."

"Christine, I tried to write down all of the names that the judge was giving up, but I'm afraid that I may have missed some—could I review that part of the tape later?" Francine asked.

"That won't be necessary, Francine—in your briefing packet, there's a complete transcript of the tape and a list of everyone he mentioned including as much background information we could gather in so short a time. That brings up another problem though, what do we do with all these names? We can't afford to put them all under surveillance nor can we pick them up yet." Christine told her.

"I think we do what we talked about in San Diego," Bob said. "We identify the high-profile ones and those most likely to have major influence in the syndicate and work them, letting the others go for now. We can always pick them up when we're ready."

The merits of Bob's proposal were discussed and then it was decided to identify the top five and add them to their active list and add the rest to their monitor list. There were just two other major issues to take care of from the West Coast trip. First, how to cover the judge's disappearance, and second, how to cover the congressman's daughter's rescue.

The congressman took care of the latter concern himself. He would call the number on the card the attorneys had given him and give them his cover story.

His daughter ran away and made her way to some friends of theirs in San Diego. They contacted him, he in turn had two of his old Marine Corps buddies that still lived in San Diego bring her to him. He would go further and let them know that, he had hidden his daughter and the rest of his family. He would serve out his time and then retire from politics and would no longer be of service to them.

The judge's disappearance would be more difficult to explain, especially to those watching him. It would have to look like a competitor and not an FBI operation. To that end, Christine had been working on an idea.

"What I'm about to say sounds far-fetched and maybe even a little crazy. Our biggest problem is in not letting Brooks and his friends know that we're onto them. That becomes increasingly more difficult as we begin to monitor more and more of their people. So we need good covers for each person that we monitor or bring in. Instead of developing multiple cover stories, why not just create a single cover story for the whole operation."

The director looked doubtful. "Just how do you expect to do that?"

"Let's create our own syndicate. Let's make them think they have competition. We can run a sting that could provide cover for all our activities. We might even be able to infiltrate our people into their hierarchy to discuss a merger, cooperation, or territory."

The room fell silent as they tossed the idea around in their own minds. Christine didn't hear any objections so she pushed on.

"Think about how much easier it would be to pull people off the streets without tipping anyone to the fact that the FBI was onto them. We could even make the judge the first victim. We put pressure on some of the minor players the judge gave us and force them to switch their allegiance to the new syndicate. If enough of these people start defecting, their committee is going to have to get together and figure out what to do about the new player in the game. When they do, we'll be tailing Paul Cedes and Walter Brooks, who'll lead us to the rest of the council. If somehow we can get audio or video of that meeting, we'd have all the proof we need to shut down this operation.

"As a by-product we might even uncover the Hoover killer—somebody in that group has to have hired him."

The director's mind was working double time as Christine was talking. "I think you have something here. I can see only one major flaw. This isn't your typical crime syndicate. This group operates in the white-collar world. They probably run a few drugs, and have some high priced prostitutes working for them, but their primary focus is in the legitimate business world. There's just no way that we could put together a corporate front that would be a convincing challenge to whatever resources Brooks could throw at it. A project of this nature would take quite some time to develop and evolve to the point where we could get a glimpse of their board. I don't think we have that kind of time."

"Don't shelve it yet, sir; let's give it some serious consideration over the next twenty-four hours." Christine pleaded.

"Alright, Christine, we'll think about it. In the meantime, is there anything else?"

"Not from the West Coast, but we still have several other issues that need to be resolved. What's going to happen to the congressman? What about Judge Walker, and how long can we hang onto the assassin?" Christine asked.

"We're allowing the congressman to stay in office until his term expires, then he'll drop out of politics and public life for personal reasons.

In the next forty-eight hours, his family will be relocated to a safe house outside the country. They'll remain there until it's safe to return or until the congressman joins them."

Everyone agreed this was reasonable since the congressman agreed to help as much as possible.

Scott brought them up to speed on Judge Walker. "According to Feldman, Judge Walker is as clean as they come. There's, however, a bad apple in his court. His clerk's name is on the list of names Feldman gave us. We already talked with Judge Walker; he's prepared to run any kind of sting or misinformation campaign that we would like. He's also volunteered to kick the shit out of him for us whenever we're ready."

Martinez addressed the question of the assassin. "Legally we can only hold this assassin for forty-eight hours before booking him. We're going to hold him as a material witness, which gives us more time. His bosses, however, are going to be looking for him long before that."

Christine saw an opening for her idea. "This is exactly the type of thing our sting could be used for. We could send Cedes some clothing from this guy and maybe a picture that looked like we really worked him over. We could tell him that if he doesn't get his people out of our business, they'll all end up looking like this. Cedes' people would stop looking for him, thinking that the competition had killed him. Meanwhile we can hold him and extract everything he knows."

The director nodded his agreement. "It's a good idea, Christine, let me sleep on it. I'm still not comfortable with us trying to set up that kind of undercover operation. The cost alone would wipe out our entire budget."

"Sir, maybe we don't have to create a new corporation," Quantara interjected. "What if we found one of the companies that Brooks and these people were trying to squeeze out? We could put a couple of people inside and basically reverse the process on them."

"That's a good idea, Quantara, let me think on it." The director's tone of finality closed that topic. Martinez continued his briefing.

"Tom's turning the judge over to me after this meeting, and I'll keep him in a safe house outside town until we determine his final disposition. I think both he and the hit man have more to tell us so I'll keep after them. I'm hoping that they can help me track down a lead on 'Hoover'."

Christine couldn't resist. "How is that investigation going?"

"I haven't made much progress so far, but I still think that we're dealing with someone with access to FBI computers who knows our internal procedures. I should know more after interviewing our two guests."

Scott had been interviewing the assassin most of the morning and wasn't quite as confident. "I'm not so sure you're going to get much out of their guys. We identified him: his real name is Andrew Mitchell. He's a decorated war hero; he served with both the Rangers and the Green Berets. He let himself be captured in Vietnam just so he could infiltrate a prison camp and bring out one of our intelligence officers. Most of his work was behind the lines. He joined the CIA in '84 and disappeared during an operation in Iran in 1996. He was presumed dead and that's where his records end, until this morning of course. I just don't see us breaking this guy down."

Director Flynn had another idea. "I see a guy like this as a patriot, and can't believe that after serving his country the way he has, that he would knowingly destroy it. I think he believes that he's still working for our government and that he's doing the right thing."

"So what are you suggesting?" Martinez asked.

"I think instead of breaking him, we try to turn him. Show him the truth; show him he is actually working for and protecting a group of people that are destroying the country. Next time you interview him, Scott, bring in one of our shrinks and let's get a profile on him."

"Okay, that makes sense. If you're right and he's still working for the government, there's a good chance he's a member of that rumored special White House security force. His disappearance coincides with the assumption of power by this administration."

Christine agreed. "If all of this is true, then there'll be several other disappearances of soldiers or CIA personnel with his kind of background around the same time. I recommend that we run a profile through the computer and see what we come up with. We may be able to identify more members of this security force. If we can find out who Mitchell reports to, we'll have another route to finding out or confirming who's running the show and whether or not it's being run from the White House."

The director agreed and tasked Scott to head up the research and report back to the committee with his findings.

"Have we been able to get a confirmation on that hotel room in London?" The director asked.

"No sir," Tom said. "The best we can do is narrow it down to the president's senior staff. We're pretty sure though that the president himself wasn't in that room on that night."

The meeting went on for another hour before most of the issues were resolved or tabled until later.

Against the committee's advice, the director decided to bring certain trusted members of Congress into the loop. This was strictly a self-defense measure—in case the White House and the presidency were found to be involved, the FBI would need the help of Congress and the Justice Department to sort it all out.

They also decided that Paul Cedes would be a major focus of the investigation. He enjoyed protection from many different sources on Capitol Hill so he would have to be handled with kid gloves.

The next couple of days would be killed with tedious legwork. Each name on the list would have to be researched and examined in more detail. Then a decision would have to be made as to what level of surveillance to assign to each name.

Christine's main concern was to get everyone focused on uncovering the cancer in the White House. She was convinced this conspiracy led all the way back to her family's death. The only problem was, the further back they traced this conspiracy, the closer they would get to her.

Chapter 19

Following the meeting, Christine called it a day and to take a well-deserved rest. Since she first assumed the role of Hoover, she'd been reading various mercenary magazines, always enthralled with the idea of assassins for hire. She knew, of course, that she would never be able to do this, but it nonetheless excited her to go through the magazines and imagine what these people would be like. She no longer read the magazines, but she did find all kinds of Internet sites looking for mercenaries or wanting to hire someone for a job. The FBI constantly reviewed these sites and in recent months had even closed down some of the more dangerous ones. This time when she arrived home, she logged on to her computer and started scanning several bulletin boards.

Her attention was drawn to the screen when she found a site that specifically sought out the help of "Hoover." There was even an E-mail address to reply to. Christine marked the bulletin board and continued scanning. She found several other bulletin boards with requests for Hoover's services, all with the same E-mail address.

Christine was confused and curious, but cautious. There were not many people that knew of Hoover's existence. Those who did wouldn't attempt to hire him.

Christine decided she had to chance it. She had to find a way to send these E-mails without being traced. She kept asking herself, "How would those mercenaries do it?" Then it came to her. She went to the public library in the Congressional Building where thousands of people passed through daily. She walked up and down the rows of computer tables until she spotted a man logging into AOL. She watched as he typed in his screen name and then watched his fingers move over the keyboard as he entered his password. She then went to a nearby stack of books and waited.

After about an hour, the man passed by her, heading toward the library exit. Christine found the computer he was working on, logged on to America on Line, entered the screen name of "Maniac," and typed "winner" into the password field. Seconds later she was in AOL. Christine had prepared her message ahead of time and now typed it in.

"To: Looking for help
From: Hoover

Got your message. Am interested.
Reply with Target and Fee!
Reply within thirty minutes or I'm history."

Christine sent the message, closed down the computer, and walked out of the library.

Her next stop was the Charles Schwab brokerage house on 34th street. Christine was aware that the computers set up in their lobby were intended for their customers to check their portfolios but she also knew that a simple click of the mouse would get her to an AOL screen.

It had taken her forty minutes to get to the Charles Schwab building, which was just in time to retrieve her message. Her only concern was that "Maniac" didn't come back to retrieve his messages.

She logged on and found her reply.

Christine was shocked at the request and the dollar value of the job. This was the most expensive contract that she had ever heard of. It seemed extremely rich. Someone wanted to make sure that "Hoover" took this job.

The message read: "Congratulations on your last job. We have multiple problems, which we would like you to handle. We are prepared to pay $5,000,000 per problem.

"Exactly two hours after this message is accessed or downloaded, another message itemizing the problems will be sent to this address. Each message will remain for exactly thirty minutes or until it is downloaded, whichever comes first. A virus placed in the messages will delete them ten minutes after they're accessed.

"Should you decide to handle any or all of these problems for us, place an ad in the 'On-line Penny Shopper.' The ad should state, your problems can be handled for ($5) for each assignment you elect to accept. Include your account number in reverse order and in the next ad put the country and bank into which the initial deposit can be made. We will then deposit $2,500,000 for each assignment into your account within two hours of your post unless we are instructed otherwise."

Christine couldn't believe what she had read. She tried to print out the message but the computers at the brokerage firm were not connected to printers. She attempted to save it, but before she had a chance the message dissolved.

She had to believe the authenticity of the message and that someone in the syndicate wanted somebody else removed.

Something about the message told her to proceed with caution. The technology behind the message was sufficiently sophisticated to require a programmer to build. That meant someone other than the sender knows about these assassination requests and who was behind them. Of course that person, if he were still alive, would be as hard to find as the sender himself. For now she would just wait for the next message and see who the targets might be. Instead of heading home, she waited out the two hours at a local park.

She found a cyber café, sat down at one of the computers, logged on, and waited for the message. The second message was right on time. It contained no introductions or small talk, it just listed four names, their home addresses, their place of employment and their private telephone numbers: Paul Cedes, Laura Kinsman, Judge Francis Feldman, and Walter Brooks.

Christine was stunned, the FBI had only had those names for less than forty-eight hours and somehow this syndicate was already aware that its people were exposed and, as such, potential loose ends. Someone on their task force was communicating with them either knowingly or unknowingly—either way, the entire operation was now in danger.

As Christine was contemplating this new twist, she realized that her belief that Cedes and Brooks were two key players in this syndicate was now in doubt. She was brought out of her thoughts as she watched the message on her screen explode into a rainbow of colors and then form into a crescent moon before it disappeared.

Her first thought was what a beautiful way to trash a message, her next thought was that this could be a recognizable signature of the programmer. Christine was now faced with two other problems; what to do about these contracts and what to do about the leak on the task force?

The leak had to be plugged; the director had to be made aware of it. The question was, how best to do that without exposing herself. Several options presented themselves, but the one she liked most was planting a rumor of the contracts with a couple of known FBI snitches and let it work its way through the system. That would allow someone else to break the news of the contracts without them being able to track it back to Christine. She accomplished her objective with two phone calls.

The question of the assassination contracts was another matter. Her plans were to eliminate Cedes and Brooks anyway, so why not get paid for them? One contract like this requires a tremendous amount of monitoring, patience, planning, and resources. Two would be next to impossible, especially now while she's so highly visible within the FBI. The upside was that by using the data gathered by the FBI, she would know exactly when and where her targets would be most vulnerable.

Though all her instincts warned against doing this, she decided that this is would be her best chance of getting revenge for her family. This would also be the biggest challenge her Hoover persona ever faced. Her mind was made up; she'd accept the contracts.

Leaking the story of the hits was not a problem for Christine. Establishing procedures for moving funds without leaving a trace was somewhat more complicated.

Her experience in tracking organized crime money movements told her that there was no way to avoid a trail if she used wires to move the money. She had no choice but to do it the old-fashioned way.

She placed several calls to Switzerland setting up a series of accounts. Then she called several other countries and set up additional accounts. She placed a final call to a courier service, which had the reputation of discretion and, for the right commission, would perform highly confidential services. This service was often used by organized crime to move sensitive information. She gave the service their instructions and three hours later had her procedures in place.

The courier would pick up the funds from the bank (using the proper codes) and redistribute it to four other Swiss banks (which Christine just set up). For this service, the courier would be paid a commission of $500,000. Christine would then wire the funds from those banks in smaller amounts to financial institutions in the Bahamas. Then it would be further transferred to financial institutions in Costa Rica under the protection of three different law firms: the first being the client of the second, and the second being the client of the third. Costa Rica provides stronger client protection and account secrecy for their banking relationships than even the Swiss. They also have an additional impenetrable layer of protection for attorney-client privilege. So if funds are deposited through an attorney on behalf of his client, it provides two very strong veils behind which to hide funds. Christine further protected herself by placing two additional layers of attorneys between her accounts. Even the primary attorneys knew Christine only by an account number never having met her.

Once everything was in place, Christine placed the appropriate ad in the "Penny Shopper." She would give it two hours and then check her account in Costa Rica to ensure that the deposit was made. Since all along the way, everyone would be taking a small commission for their discretion, the final deposit in Christine's account should be for $8,500,000.

Christine finally got home and took the long shower she had promised herself. She didn't feel like going out, so she prepared some soup and heated up leftover spaghetti. She finished her soup and spaghetti and went straight to bed. She was planning on her first complete night's sleep since this case started. Her wish was coming true until the ringing of the telephone on her nightstand rousted her from a deep sleep. She pulled a pillow over her ears in hopes of drowning out the ringing. She was mostly successful until she heard Scott Peterson's panicked voice on her answering machine. "Christine, it's Scott—if you're there you better pick up. I think we have a problem."

Christine threw the pillow against the wall, checked the clock on her nightstand and against her better judgment she picked up the phone. "This had better be an emergency, Scott. It's three in the morning, I need some rest."

"I'm sorry Christine, but you're not going to get any rest tonight. Something's got the boss really peeved. He's called an emergency meeting for this morning; it's mandatory, and he's not accepting any excuses. It sounds like one or all of us are on his shit list."

"When and where?"

"The conference room; he wants everybody there by five."

"Five! Jesus Scott, what could be so important that couldn't wait until business hours?"

"I have no idea, but he sounded pretty pissed. I wouldn't be late."

Christine hung up the phone and set her clock's alarm to three forty-five. She would try to get another forty-five minutes of sleep before heading in. While tossing in bed trying to go back to sleep, she kept trying to figure out what could have set the director off. Surely the assassination rumor hasn't found its way to his desk already.

On her way to the meeting, Christine accessed her Costa Rican account and found that $8.5 million had been deposited. She knew she shouldn't have been surprised but at a certain level she was. Whoever sent those funds had a tremendous amount of confidence that Hoover wouldn't just skip out on the contracts. Christine was still trying to figure out who could put up that much money for these contracts as she pulled into the near empty parking lot of the FBI building. She noticed only a few cars including the director's and ASAC Martinez's. It was still several hours before the thousands of FBI employees that worked in the Hoover building would be arriving.

She entered the conference room, and found the mood somber. It was obvious that no one wanted to be there. The director's attitude didn't help the mood any. He appeared disgusted and angry.

"I apologize for bringing all of you in this early, but I was woken out of a deep sleep myself this morning at about one o'clock. What I heard bothered me enough to get all of you here as soon as possible. While I was still in my pajamas, I was briefed by the DEA on some intelligence they acquired from one of their deep-cover field agents.

"It would appear that this syndicate or international gangsters or businessmen or whatever the hell we want to call them, the ones that I didn't even know existed a few days ago, have a source inside this very room. As you might guess, that's not something I wanted to hear at one in the morning from the head of the DEA."

The room fell silent as everyone was checking out each other through the corners of their eyes. After pausing a moment for effect, the director continued. "These businessmen, and I use that term very loosely, to ensure their continued secrecy, have put out a contract on the lives of Paul Cedes, Judge Francis Feldman, Assistant Attorney General Laura Kinsman, and our own prime suspect, Walter Brooks." The director paused again as he searched the room with his eyes. "For those of you not with me yet, let me tell you my problems. First of all, we've been aware of these names for less than forty-eight hours. So how in the hell could anybody out there already know that these people have been compromised?

"Second, only the people in this room and Feldman know that we have these names. Feldman hasn't even gone to the bathroom without one of our people since he gave us the names—so that leaves the people in this room.

"My third problem is that now, I have to figure out a way to protect these people. That's not going to be easy to do if we have a leak on this task force.

"So guess what people, we're going to find and plug this leak, before anyone goes home. We may all be living in this building for the next few days, but nobody is leaving here until I'm convinced that this leak is plugged!"

Not a soul stirred as the director made his point. He softened his tone a little as he continued. "Okay, I find it hard to believe that we have any traitors or intentional criminal misconduct going on in this group. So for now let's assume that this was an unintentional leak. If that doesn't work, then we'll go to more drastic measures, including polygraphs. We're going to start by pairing off and having you review your last forty-eight hours with your partner down to the last detail."

ASAC Martinez's face turned bright red as he attempted to get the director's attention. "Excuse me chief, can I get a couple of private minutes with you?"

"Not now, I want to get to the bottom of this."

"I think I can help get to the bottom of this."

"If you know anything about this Freddie, for God's sake let's hear it."

"I don't think we have a leak here sir; if I could just ask where we got the information regarding the contracts."

All eyes, though confused, quickly focused on Martinez.

"All I can tell you is that the DEA's man got the information from a highly placed member of one of the largest drug organizations in the U.S.," Director Flynn replied. "Their man has been in place for over two years and has been a key player in one of the most successful drug enforcement operations in DEA history. His information has always been extremely reliable."

"I don't doubt his information sir, in fact I can confirm his information. What I need to know is where he got it." Martinez insisted.

"I don't understand—if you can confirm his information, why does it matter where it came from?"

"It's vital that we know where he got the information; it could provide a prime lead to Hoover."

"My understanding is that he only makes contact every seventy-two hours unless there is an emergency like last night. We can have them check his sources when he calls them back. I'm pretty sure it'll be someone high up in the U.S. drug scene, but I'm not going to push him to dig any deeper and jeopardize his cover," Director Flynn said.

"I understand sir, but it's vital that I find out who told him about the contracts."

Director Flynn was getting irritated. "Freddie, what do you know about this? How can you confirm the information? What do you know about these contracts?"

"The syndicate didn't exactly sanction or contract for these hits. The fact is, they probably don't even know about them."

"What the hell are you trying to tell us, Freddie?" The director insisted.

"Sir, there really is no contract on these people. I was able to track down a way to leave a message for Hoover. I needed to get his attention and get him to reply so that we could trace him. In order to do that, I placed ads for him in places where someone like him might be looking for his next job. The jobs had to be enticing enough and financially rewarding enough that his ego and greed couldn't refuse."

The director and the rest of the room were stunned and in a state of utter disbelief. Christine was most stunned of all; this was a development she hadn't anticipated. Martinez' ploy had worked; he had lured her into contacting him, which put him closer to discovering Hoover than anyone had ever gotten before. As she was contemplating her next move, she could hear the director lashing out at Martinez.

"What in the hell did you think you were doing? Have you totally lost your mind? You're an FBI agent for God's sake—you can't go out and pull a stunt like this, especially not without running it by me first.

"I can't believe you put a price on four people's heads to catch a single killer. It just doesn't make any sense. Besides that, you don't have that right—hell, I don't have that right, in our system nobody has that right. Please just tell me that Hoover didn't accept the contract, because if he did, you know those people are as good as dead."

"No sir, Hoover will never come close to these people. If I'm not able to track Hoover in the next forty-eight hours, then I'll call off the hit."

"This is the dumbest thing I've ever heard an FBI agent do. Where have you been while this agency's been tracking Hoover? From past experience, we know that he can get to anyone and has the best information network of anyone we've ever been up against. How could you possibly think that once you hired him you would be able to control him?"

"Sir, this is the only way that we're going to get him to come out in the open. As you well know sir, sometimes we have to go outside of the FBI's regular procedures."

"Are you insane, Freddie? There is a hell of a lot of difference between pushing the procedural envelope and hiring the top assassin in the country to kill four people. We are not the CIA; we don't run covert operations. If anything happens to any one of those people, I'll personally file charges against you. I'm totally speechless; I don't even know how to handle this or where to take it from here. The one thing I do know is that you're not waiting forty-eight hours to call this thing off. As soon as we get out of here, you're going to do whatever you have to, to get hold of Hoover and tell him the contracts are void and you're going to put all four of those people under protective custody. What the hell ever came over you to make you do such a dumb thing?"

"Sir, Hoover is the single most dangerous man the FBI has ever hunted. He just killed a former president, and we need to do whatever we can to put him away. The book doesn't always work with people like that."

Director Flynn suddenly looked very tired. "Martinez, how did you get so far off track? Hoover is only a weapon, the people hiring him are the dangerous ones."

"I understand that, sir, but I'm so close to catching him. We're tracing the advance I wired him and tracking the bulletin boards and any E-mails that come and go from the bulletin boards. We're also tracking his postings to the 'Penny Shopper.' Sir, I know we'll have him in the next twenty-four to forty-eight hours."

"What makes you sure you're going to have him in forty-eight hours? Have you been able to track his location?"

"No sir, not exactly, but the bulletin boards are so basic that we should be able to trace anyone that posted to them within a matter of days. Plus we have E-mail messages that we'll be able to trace."

"You're talking about several days—by that time Hoover may have fulfilled the contract you issued. You better have more than this! If you don't, we'll have four dead people on our hands. What about this advance? How much was that for?"

"I wired $10,000,000 to a numbered account in Switzerland."

"Ten million dollars? Jesus, Freddie you're not authorized to make that kind of disbursement! Who signed off on that and how the hell did you get that much money without my countersignature?"

"Sir we have those seized organized crime assets; we have close to forty million in that fund. I believe that was exactly how Congress intended those assets to be used."

"I kind of doubt that Congress expected those funds to be used to put contracts on our own citizens," the Director snapped.

"No sir, but I'm sure they intended them to be used to track down criminals of Hoover's stature," Martinez retorted.

"Freddie what's going on inside your head? Hoover is just another case. You jeopardized your entire career and four lives just to get at this guy. You better get this guy and you had better get these hits called off and me my $10 million back."

"We traced the money to a numbered account in Switzerland which was opened only hours earlier."

"Good, than we can get our money back!"

"I don't know. After we traced the money to the bank, we began monitoring the bank for large wire transfers. We were expecting the money to be wired through a series of different banks until it got to its final destination," Martinez said.

"So the money is still there?" The Director asked.

"Yes sir, or at least we think so. Like I said, we were expecting the money to be wired through a series of banks but so far it hasn't moved. We intercepted several wires that were approximately the same size as our deposit but they were all legitimate. So we believe the money is still there. We're trying to gain access to the account now."

"Okay, what about other leads—you mentioned a penny shopper, what's that about?"

"We asked Hoover to place a reply in the 'Penny Shopper' so that we would have an additional avenue to track him down."

"Did he reply?"

"Yes, he accepted all four contracts through the 'Penny Shopper'."

"Just tell me that you got some leads from it."

"Not yet sir, it looks like the ad was placed by a large black kid in baggy clothes and it was paid for in cash. It's highly unlikely that we'll ever find this kid. We were expecting the ad to be placed by phone and credit card. Those we could have traced."

"I guess you forgot to tell Hoover that" the director snapped sarcastically.

"Sir, I'm still confident that we'll be able to bring Hoover in, in the next couple of days. Especially if we can talk to the undercover agent and find out where he got his information. Whoever told him about the contracts is in direct contact with Hoover. If I can get to that person, I can get to Hoover."

"I doubt that the DEA is going to give you access to their man. They have a lot of time, money, and not to mention a man's life invested. If they can get you more details without raising suspicions that's fine, but I'm not going to push them."

"Sir, if they're concerned about protecting his identity, we can protect him."

"I doubt they'll be concerned about his identity, because they're not going to let anyone get near him."

Martinez wanted to talk to the undercover agent himself, but it wasn't the time to push his already quite upset director. He knew he was going to have enough trouble just keeping his job. The director seemed pretty upset over the $10 million. He was about to acknowledge the director's last comment when a phone on the conference room wall rang.

Francine answered the phone and then turned to the director. "Sir, it's Special Agent Gibson, he's calling for ASAC Martinez."

Director Flynn could feel his face get red. "Gibson! Tell him we're in a meeting, and Martinez will call him back as soon as we're finished."

Francine passed the message on to Gibson and then turned back to Director Flynn. "Sir, he said it's urgent, he said that ASAC Martinez asked him to interrupt the meeting if he had any new information on the money."

"Is he talking about my ten million?" The director asked Martinez.

"Yes sir."

"If he has an update on the money tell him to get over here and share it with the rest of us."

Francine did as the director asked and Gibson was on his way before she even got back to her chair. The director returned his attention to Martinez.

"Freddie, I'm really worried about your judgment lately. What on earth made you trust Gibson with any part of this investigation, especially after I dismissed him for security reasons?"

"I needed help tracking Hoover and he was available. He also has extensive experience in banking and was quite helpful in setting up the technology that will allow us to track the money. I don't believe we'll have a repeat of his previous incident. I'm also not allowing him access to any classified information."

"What do you mean he doesn't have access to classified information? The fact that you contracted for a hit on four US citizens and used $10 million of the governments money to pay for it had better be classified."

"Yes sir, it is, what I meant was that it's the only thing he's working on."

There was a knock at the door and Francine got up and let Agent Gibson in. He looked intimidated and didn't look anyone directly in the eye. He was walking towards Martinez when the director stopped him. "Gibson, if you have information regarding my $10 million, I want you to share it with all of us."

Gibson suddenly felt uncomfortable, he owed it to Martinez to brief him first, but there was no way he could ignore the director's instructions. He gave Martinez a look that said, "I'm sorry for what I'm about to do," and then addressed himself to Director Flynn.

"Sir we just received an update on the account number into which we made the deposit. We didn't get access to the account, but one of the vice presidents of the bank checked the account and told us that there was no money in it."

"What the hell do you mean there's no money in it?" Director Flynn retorted.

"Apparently the money was withdrawn fifteen minutes after it was deposited."

"Freddie, you told me they couldn't get the money out without us knowing about it!"

Martinez was stunned and at a loss for words as Gibson continued. "Sir, we had the most sophisticated electronic tracking equipment standing by. We have the ability to trace any wire transfer to the furthest corners of the earth."

"OK, so you're telling me you know where it is?"

"Not exactly sir. We were expecting the money to be moved by wire through a number of different locations until it ended up in its final destination. Unfortunately the money wasn't moved by wire."

"Exactly how was the money moved?"

"Somebody came in and withdrew it."

"You mean somebody just walked into the bank and withdrew 10 million dollars?"

"Yes sir."

"Freddie, please tell me you had a man in the bank."

Martinez shook his head no and Gibson continued. "We do have a pretty good description of the man that withdrew the money."

"At last we finally get a break. Did you get his description out to the local police and ask them to pick him up for questioning?"

"Not yet sir, I wanted to check with ASAC Martinez first."

"Could this have been Hoover?"

"No sir, from the description we got, this man didn't look anything like the man that shot the president. This was an older white man about seventy with long white hair, a longish white goatee, glasses, wearing a white suit with a red bow tie, and carrying a pearl-handled cane."

There was a slight snicker throughout the room, which the director quickly cut off. "I don't find this amusing, people. Gibson, do you know why they're snickering? They're snickering because you just described Colonel Sanders from Kentucky Fried Chicken. I think we can pass on having the locals pick him up. It's my guess that underneath Colonel Sanders we would probably find Hoover. Is there any way of tracking the money now?"

Martinez shook his head, "No sir, Hoover is very intelligent; we were expecting a sophisticated transfer procedure, weren't prepared for a live in-person withdrawal. I never expected Hoover himself to show up and make the withdrawal. I'm afraid, sir, that we won't find him through the money now."

"Jesus Christ, Freddie—you set in motion this elaborate and highly illegal operation just to flush out Hoover. Then when you have him flushed you don't even have a man in the same place where you set the bait? We should be focusing on finding whoever is behind this syndicate and un-covering just how high this goes in our government, but thanks to you we're going to be using all of our resources for the next couple of days keeping four people alive. Can you call Hoover off?"

"I don't know sir, we still have several avenues to get at Hoover."

"Please enlighten me, because from where I sit, I see it like this: You hired the deadliest man in the country, perhaps the world, to kill four U.S. citizens, then you paid him 10 million of the governments dollars for the hit, which you illegally took from the FBI. You then lost track of the money, you can't track him through the ad or the Internet, so unless Hoover sends you an E-mail with his return address underlined, you're no closer to finding him then you were before you started all of this. Does that about sum it up?"

Martinez tried to salvage what he could. "We do know that since Hoover probably picked up the money himself, he's still in Europe. So we have a chance to catch him as he tries to reenter the States. Even if he gets through Customs, we still have a couple of days to prepare for him here."

"Freddie, have you heard anything I've been saying? You don't have any more time. You better find Hoover, cancel this contract, and get that ten million back or I'm personally going to lock you up. Do I make myself clear?"

"Yes sir."

"Tom, you and your people are back in charge of Hoover. Freddie, you'll give everything you've got to Tom and I mean everything. After you've handed over all of your research and notes, then I want you to see to the safety of the people you targeted.

"Scott, I want you to oversee and approve all of his plans. Understand this Freddie—your career is over! The only question now is whether or not you're going to jail. If anything happens to any of those people that's exactly where you'll be headed."

Christine was still reviewing everything she just heard. Despite what the director thought of Martinez's actions, he had gotten closer to discovering Hoover and his true identity than anyone ever had before.

Martinez had outwitted her. She had fallen for all of his traps. Fortunately she also listened to her instincts and created very cautious procedures by using a courier service in Switzerland and a double blind for the ad.

Her only loose end was the drug dealer she leaked the contract information to. He had been a good resource in the past, but was very susceptible to being squeezed. If the information was traced from the undercover agent all the way to Christine's contact, it would be a stretch, but it could eventually establish a link to her. Her contact was listed in the informant's master log as being one of her paid snitches.

Sitting at the conference room table listening to the wrap-up discussions of the meeting, Christine wasn't sure how she would handle this loose end. She would wait to see how things developed before she acted.

Christine's only other fear was that Martinez would end up interviewing Paul Cedes and Walter Brooks. She was having second thoughts about Martinez; maybe he wasn't that slow after all. If he ever compared notes with Brooks and Cedes, chances were that one of them would be able to put it all together and remember that little black girl who got away thirty years ago.

They would still be a long way from putting her and Hoover together, but they could probably narrow it down to a government employee with access to classified materials. From there it would just be a matter of grunt work, pulling calendars, schedules, and vacations and comparing them to the timing of Hoover's various jobs to determine opportunity. To protect herself, Christine had to complete at least one of Martinez' contracts sooner than she wanted to. It would be her most dangerous job yet; Martinez and half of the FBI would be waiting for her.

Her big advantage was that the director was extremely upset with Martinez and probably wouldn't allow him the opportunity to interview Cedes. As long as the director kept Martinez on a short leash, Christine still had a pretty good shot of covering her loose ends.

The director didn't know it, but Martinez had done a pretty good job of flushing Hoover out. Christine was glad that he was so poorly staffed or she may have been locked in a room with Judge Feldman right now.

She smiled to herself as she sat there, realizing that she was the only one that would ever truly appreciate the outstanding job Martinez had done. Martinez could have gotten them close, but it was highly unlikely they would have traced Hoover to her. The FBI, for all of its civil rights and equal opportunity talk, was still a male, macho-driven organization. The thought that someone as effective, efficient, and illusive as Hoover could be a woman, let alone an African American woman, was as foreign to the FBI as the thought of walking on land was to a fish.

Christine could hear the director reminding everyone that although they would be focused on getting Hoover and protecting the four targets, the real mission was still to break this unholy conspiracy. Before the meeting broke up, he tasked Tom to heighten security at all custom and passport checkpoints and make sure that the only way Hoover sets foot on American soil was in handcuffs. Realistically however, the director knew that with no more than the video from the Canfield assassination, catching Hoover at the airport was unrealistic.

He asked Christine to stay after the others had gone. "Christine, we're about to make history. I'm going to appoint you as Acting Assistant Special Agent in Charge of the Organized Crime unit replacing Martinez. I'll make my permanent decision after this case is closed. You may end up being the youngest ASAC in the Bureau."

This was what Christine had wanted since she joined the Organized Crime unit— now all she could do was stand there and manage a "Thank you, sir."

Chapter 20

Fourteen hours after the meeting, Director Flynn still had trouble believing everything he'd heard. He was about to sit down for lunch with someone who, in just a couple of days, had gone from being considered a good friend to being a traitor to her country and the target of an assassination contract. He decided to try the soft touch first and try to turn her instead of having her handcuffed and hauled to FBI headquarters,. Deep down he was hoping to get her to help him bring down this syndicate. That was the only way he could see keeping her out of jail for the rest of her life.

Assistant Attorney General Laura Kinsman was not only bright and well respected for her abilities as a litigator, but she was also very attractive and turned every head whenever she entered a room. Director Flynn was well aware of that which was why he had reservations at "MonCheri," where the booths were almost soundproof and the atmosphere was dark, and it had no bar. As she walked towards him, her body was silhouetted against the light behind her, and for a moment he forgot why they were there.

On several occasions Director Flynn felt there was some kind of spark between them. He almost asked her out once, but decided that would make him look as foolish as some of his colleagues on the hill. He always snickered to himself whenever he saw those old geezers running around with women less than half their age. He just wasn't ready to be laughed at behind his back, at least not for that reason.

Maybe it was the setting—a romantic restaurant, the dimmed lights, or the whispers and gentle laughter, but to Director Flynn, Laura somehow seemed friendlier than usual. For the first time, she kissed him on the cheek when they met and seemed to hold his hand longer than usual before they sat down.

He was reluctant to intrude on the mood, so he allowed the small talk to continue through lunch and until after the waiter had served their coffee. He then reached across the table gently grasping Laura's hands and pulling them to the middle of the table. He looked her in her eyes and let out a deep breath before starting. "Laura, I have something very serious that we need to discuss."

Laura nodded her head to encourage him to go on and didn't make any attempt to withdraw her hands. "Laura, I'm sure you're aware that I'm very fond of you. That's what makes this even harder."

It was obvious that Laura had no idea what he was talking about. "Martin, I thought you asked me here to finally ask me out, but now you're beginning to frighten me. What is it?"

Martin Flynn locked on Laura's eyes and took a firmer grip on her hands. "Laura, what I'm about to tell you I find very hard to believe, but my office has uncovered conclusive proof that you're involved in some really bad stuff that includes conspiracy to commit murder, kidnapping, and bribery. We know that you're part of a very powerful crime syndicate."

Director Flynn expected Laura to register shock, avert her eyes and attempt to pull her hands free. To his surprise, she did none of those. There was a pause that seemed to last for minutes before Laura lowered her eyes to the table. "How did you find out?"

Director Flynn was taken aback by the question. "That doesn't really matter now, does it? The important thing is that you're not even attempting to deny it."

"You said you had proof and I believe you. We wouldn't be here now if you couldn't prove it, would we? The real question is what are you going to do about it? You do have some options?"

"I'm sorry Laura, but if you're thinking about me looking the other way or even joining you and your murderous band, you can forget it.

"I have no choice; I have to take you in. You'll be facing charges of murder, conspiracy to commit murder, and racketeering, but if you help us collapse this syndicate, I would recommend leniency and maybe even the witness protection program. But only if your testimony helps us put some of the big players away. Otherwise, you'll be the most beautiful women behind bars for a very long time and we would never be able to have our first real date."

Laura withdrew her hands from Director Flynn's and when she raised her head, the soft light of the room reflected a slight smile bringing her face and eyes to life. Director Flynn sat intoxicated by the lights reflection on her face and almost missed what she was saying.

"Martin, would you mind if I made a call before you take me in?"

"This is an unusual situation, Laura. If you get your attorney involved, I'm not going to be able to help you as much. If you cooperate, I'll probably be able to get you into the witness protection program, in which case we don't want anyone to know about this, not even your family or your attorney."

"I understand that, Martin. Believe me the call I want to make is not going to compromise any of your efforts. There's someone I want you to talk to before you take me in."

Director Flynn nodded his agreement and Laura took her portable phone out, got up from the table and moved just out of hearing distance from Director Flynn before placing the call. She returned to the table, put the phone back in her purse, and this time looked Martin Flynn in the eyes. "Believe it or not, I'm glad that it was you who found me out and even more relieved that you're going to take me in. I only have one request, don't take me in until you've had a chance to talk to a couple of friends of mine. They're on their way over here now."

"Laura, I don't know what you've got in mind, but if these guys are going to try and recruit me, I'm going to take all of you in. If they're coming to convince me to let you go by force, that won't be that easy. I have two agents waiting in cars outside."

Director Flynn pulled a small walkie-talkie out of his pocket and instructed the agents to move inside the restaurant and keep an eye on his table. Laura smiled and patted his hand. "Relax, Martin, it's nothing like that. They're just going to share some information with you that I'm not authorized to discuss. It might be best though if you ask your people to leave. I don't think it would be good for all of us to be seen together. I'll personally guarantee your safety."

"No offense, Laura, but we both know your friends have no qualms about killing. They've proven that on too many occasions."

"All I can tell you is that once you meet my friends, everything will become clear. You really don't need your men."

Director Flynn thought about it for a moment and then walked to the front of the restaurant talked to his agents and took one of their guns. The agents turned and left the restaurant, and the director returned to his table. Not knowing what to make of Laura, he just sat there and wondered what she was up to. She was about to go away for the rest of her life yet she seemed totally in control of the situation. Director Flynn had consumed two cups of coffee and was just starting on his third when he noticed two figures coming towards him in the dimmed lights of the restaurant. Laura saw him withdraw his weapon and place it on the bench next to him. "Relax, Martin, you won't be needing that."

As the figures got closer, the director thought he recognized one of them. By the time they were standing next to the table, Director Flynn did recognize one of the men as Peter Eagelton, the United States attorney general. The other man also looked familiar although he couldn't place him.

Peter Eagelton stopped at the edge of the table and extended his hand. "Martin, it's good to see you; Laura it's nice to see you getting out of the office some."

Though still a little confused, Director Flynn rose and shook his hand. "Peter, it's always good to see you, although I must admit I'm a bit surprised to see you here."

"This wouldn't have been my first choice to meet, but sometimes circumstances dictate these things. Oh, where are my manners, this is Federal Judge Clayton Powell. Judge Powell tells me that the two of you have worked together before."

"Of course, Judge Powell, it's a pleasure to see you again. Won't you gentlemen join us."

As Peter sat down, he caught a glance of Director Flynn's pistol sitting on the bench. He smiled at the director and nodded down towards the pistol. "You won't be needing that. We come in peace. In fact we're all on the same side. I brought Judge Powell because I wanted someone to confirm what I'm about to tell you.

"Laura tells me that you're about to arrest her for several charges including murder."

The director looked around the table and nodded his head. "That's right; my people uncovered enough proof for us to guarantee an indictment as well as a conviction."

"Might I ask where you got this proof?"

"You know better than that Peter. I'm not prepared to release any of that information until you tell me what the hell's going on!"

"It's not what you think Marty. Six months ago, a colleague at the Attorney General's office approached Laura with a very financially rewarding proposal. She did what we would expect any loyal assistant attorney general to do. She brought the proposal to my attention. I wanted to see how deep this corruption ran, so I asked Laura to pretend to go along. Laura, being the wise and cautious attorney that she is, insisted that I put these instructions in writing. At the time I thought she'd watched too many spy movies, but now I'm not so sure. I not only put my request in writing, but I also brought Judge Powell in on it.

"Judge Powell, as you know, is the judiciary advisor for the justice department and came aboard our little sting to make sure we obeyed all the rules so that we could prosecute the little shit that's polluting my office." Peter Eagelton smiled at Laura as he continued. "Laura, as you know, handles primarily white-collar crime. We deduced that's what they wanted her for, so I assigned her more of the high-profile cases just to see where that took us.

"We quickly found that this was no small operation. Laura outgrew her contact and quickly moved up the ladder. After two months and throwing two cases she was invited to a lunch in New York City. There she met an inner circle of judges, attorneys, and a couple of congressmen. We knew we'd stumbled across something major, but we also knew that Laura still hadn't met the people who ran this organization so we couldn't pull her out just yet.

"Judge Powell wanted to bring in the judiciary committee since there were so many judges and lawyers involved, but I argued against it. I needed to know how widespread this was before we brought somebody else in on the investigation." Peter Eagelton paused to gauge Director Flynn's reaction.

The director was getting hot under the collar. "Let me get this straight, Peter; you're running an investigation in my backyard without bringing the FBI in on it?"

"I didn't have much choice, Martin, we didn't know who was part of this conspiracy. There weren't too many people we could trust."

"Even if I buy that, I have proof that Assistant Attorney General Kinsman recommended the assassination of that oil man Peron."

Laura quickly jumped on the defensive. "Look! I did no such thing! All I did was tell them something they already knew. I told them I had to make a deal with Peron or I would be uncovered. I'm sure the hit was in place long before I passed on that information. Besides, I warned your people that something was going to happen and that they should double their security. I expected you guys to be able to protect him. Letting them know that Peron was going to name names bought me a invitation to their council meeting. I'm scheduled to be an adviser at their meeting next week."

"No one is blaming you Laura; I'm blaming Peter." Director Flynn turned to Peter not making any attempt to hide his anger. "You should have brought me in on this a long time ago. Instead I'm wasting my resources keeping an eye on people that you're telling me are part of the investigation. How many people have you got on this job and how much money am I wasting chasing after your staff? For God's sake please tell me you didn't have anything to do with that mess out in California!"

"I don't know what you're talking about. We don't have anything going on in California. As far as how many people I have on this? You're looking at the entire team except for my confidential secretary. Before you shoot me, I think we should compare notes. I'm especially curious as to how you got to Laura."

"You may have forgotten this, but it is my job to find out who killed Peron and President Canfield. Laura and her pals made it to the top of the list."

"Look Martin, I screwed up by not bringing you in on this from the beginning, but I think we should join forces now. I'm sure we have information you could use and I am very curious to find out how you uncovered Laura's involvement."

"I have a task force working on this, and they're not going to be to happy to find out about your operation. Especially since Laura could have provided us with information that cost the lives of two San Francisco police officers, two private detectives, and damn near one of my top directors."

"Jesus, I'm sorry Martin, I really didn't know. We would've given you anything you needed." Peter Eagelton said.

"Let me run it by my committee, they're not going too be happy."

"Let Laura and me come by and brief your committee. We can give them everything we have."

"I'll let you know where and when. There's one other thing we ran across that you guys may not be aware of yet." All eyes turned to Director Flynn as he looked at Laura. "There is a contract out on Laura's head." The table was silent for a full minute before Director Flynn continued. "The shooter goes by the code name of 'Hoover' and to the best of our knowledge he's never missed and we've never been close to catching him. He's already been paid $10 million, in advance, for four hits and expects to be paid another $10 million after the job is done."

Laura slumped back in the booth totally taken by surprise. Peter reached over to comfort her and Judge Powers leaned forward on his elbows to challenge Director Flynn. "How could you possibly know all of that?"

"That's what we get paid for, Judge. This information is extremely reliable. On that same hit list, are three more of Laura's friends. You'll probably recognize these names: Paul Cedes, advisor to Presidents, Judge Feldman from the California State Supreme Court, and Walter Brooks, industrialist and one of America's ten richest men, according to 'Forbes.' Hoover has been promised $20 million to kill the four of you, $10 million up front and another $10 million when the job's done."

Laura was recovering her senses. "How is this possible? Paul Cedes is the concigliary to their committee. He's their link to the legitimate world. There's no way they would have him assassinated. I met Judge Feldman a couple of times; he seemed full of himself but he was one of their big recruiters, at least that's what he told me. Walter Brooks I've never met, and only know what I've read about him. This makes no sense, Martin— are you sure of your information?"

"I'm positive. Laura, we're prepared to put you under protective custody right now, if you'll agree to it."

Laura looked at Peter, who nodded his head in agreement. "I think Martin and I have a lot talk about, but I agree with him about this. You need to be placed in protective custody right away. I got you into this; I'll find away to get you out of it." Peter turned his attention to Director Flynn. "Have you got a place you can stash her until this thing is over?"

"I did when I thought she was part of the cartel," Director Flynn said. "I was going to put them all in one safe house together. It would make protecting them a lot easier. Plus, it would make interviewing them easier as well. Now that I know she's not part of them, I obviously don't want to put her up with them. We have other safe houses, but this guy is real good; I wouldn't be surprised if he has all of their addresses."

Laura had heard enough. "Why are you guys talking like I'm not here? I still have cases that are not going to just disappear. I also have a cover to maintain and I want to find out why there is a contract out on me. I can't do any of that sitting in some safe house. Give me a bodyguard and let me do my job. I'll start calling my contacts and find out what's going on. Something major has to be going on to justify contracts like these."

Director Flynn didn't like that idea much, especially since he knew who sanctioned the hit. The task force also had to debrief her; she was sure to have information they needed. "Laura, here is what I recommend; I don't think you should be continuing with your cases. Peter is going to have to reassign them or get continuances for you. You should come with me to FBI Headquarters; I'll bring the key task force members in to debrief you. At that same time, we need to figure out how we're going to protect you. I also don't think you should meet with anyone in the syndicate until this thing is over. The one thing you can't do is underestimate Hoover. If he gets the slightest opening, you're dead."

Peter nodded his agreement. "Martin's right, if this guy is that good, you can't be running around the courthouse or the streets for that matter. You would be too exposed plus you could put a lot of innocent people in jeopardy."

"Okay, you guys have sufficiently scared me. I'll go with Martin to his office and let his people grill me. In turn I want to know what the FBI has and I want to be part of the investigation and the decision-making process about my protection."

Director Flynn looked at Peter who just shrugged his shoulders. "You've got a deal" Director Flynn offered. "As long as you both understand that from here on, the FBI is in charge of the show and Laura takes her orders from me and my taskforce leader until this thing is over."

Peter spoke for Laura. "We agree as long as the judge and I can be at the meetings."

"Peter, you can be there, but Your Honor, please don't take this the wrong way, I'm already working with an oversight committee and really don't want to expose this crucial information to any more people than I have to. Plus it would provide Hoover one more way to locate Laura."

"Martin, you have an excellent reputation in Washington, if you tell me that you're working with an oversight committee, I'll take your word for it and not insist on being at the briefings. Besides I wouldn't want to put Laura in any more danger than she already is," Judge Powell offered.

"Thank you, Your Honor, be assured that we'll bring you into the loop at the appropriate time." Director Flynn told Judge Powell.

Everyone seemed appeased for now, although Director Flynn was still furious with Peter for launching an investigation without at least alerting him.

Chapter 21

While Director Flynn was talking to Laura, Scott and Tom were to retrieve Paul Cedes and take him into protective custody. Christine's task was to drive to Maryland where Quantara would meet her and help her bring Walter Brooks to FBI Headquarters. Before Christine could head to Maryland however, she had to attend to another matter.

Scott and Tom knew that picking up Paul Cedes was not going to be easy. Cedes was an advisor to presidents and a former CIA field operative. As former ambassador he wouldn't be going easily. If not handled properly, there might even be the possibility of a physical encounter. They were prepared to take him by force if they had to, but it had been a long time since either one had been involved in any kind of serious physical altercation. That's why they decided to bring two field operatives to Paul Cedes' office with them.

Paul Cedes office was on the 34th floor of the Emerson Building on the southeast corner of 3rd street and Constitution Avenue and it fit his stature. He occupied a corner office with floor-to-ceiling windows on two sides, giving him an unobstructed view of the U.S. Capital and the Supreme Court on one side and Union Station on the other.

Dressed as a UPS deliveryman with a dark wig, a heavy dark mustache, a brown shirt with padded shoulders, long brown pants, heavy boots (with lifts), and carrying several packages, Christine entered the Wakefield Building on the northeast corner of 3rd street and Constitution Avenue.

Christine took the elevator to the 34th floor. Once there she found the office she was looking for. There was one receptionist on duty at the front desk; Christine quickly neutralized her with a tranquilizer dart.

The private secretary outside the office she needed to access, was about to challenge Christine when she shot her with her second tranquilizer dart. She burst through the door of the office, shot the executive with her third tranquilizer dart, and quickly scanned the room. She inspected the floor-to-ceiling windows and found the view she was looking for.

From her pocket she produced a glasscutter and cut a hole three inches in diameter into the window. With a small suction cup, she made sure that the cutout piece didn't fall into the street below. She placed the piece next to the window, putting the Hoover print in its center.

Christine opened one of the boxes she brought with her and unpacked her M40A1 sniper rifle and scope.

From another pocket she pulled the five round magazine loaded two rounds and inserted it into the rifle. She chambered the first round and waited. Christine was 34 floors up, dealing with an unpredictable wind whipping around the buildings and had no idea what type of security was built into the windows of the target office. She debated on preparing additional rounds, but decided instead to rely on her backup plan.

Paul Cedes' office, along with his extra large executive desk, also had a small conference room desk at which he and three of his colleagues were having lunch when Scott and Tom arrived. When his secretary announced them, Paul Cedes turned around in his chair and greeted them.

"Gentlemen, come and join us. How is good old Martin these days?"

Scott, ever the politician, replied in kind. "The director sends his best wishes. Unfortunately, however, he will not be able to join us"

"That's too bad, what can I do for you then?" Cedes asked.

"Mr. Cedes, I think it might be best if we talked in private."

Paul Cedes nodded to his associates who got up and left the room. As the others left, Paul Cedes rose from his chair and walked toward Scott and Tom. "OK gentlemen, we're alone, so what's this all about?"

"Sir, the director was hoping you would join him at FBI headquarters to discuss an urgent matter."

"Why did he send you guys? Martin's got my number."

"He just wanted to make sure you arrived safely."

"What the hell are you talking about, arrive safely?" As he was talking, Paul Cedes bent over his desk to open his cigar box when his window facing Constitution Avenue shattered and the picture of him and J Edgar Hoover on the opposite wall fell to the floor. The suddenness of the moment and the confusion caused by the noise and the wind thirty-four floors above the street momentarily froze all three men.

Scott was the first to recover and threw himself on top of Paul Cedes. His action was instinctive but a fraction of a second too late as he heard the thud of the bullet as it entered Paul Cedes' chest.

As the door to Cedes office burst open, Tom yelled to the agents accompanying them to get an ambulance, while Scott worked on stopping the bleeding.

Across the street, Christine watched through her scope and realized that Paul Cedes was still alive. She wasn't sure what went wrong with her first shot—even accounting for the wind, she shouldn't have been that far off target. Her second shot hit Paul Cedes but didn't appear to have killed him. She knew that something like this was possible; that's why she always had a backup plan.

She left the rifle on the floor, picked up all of the unopened packages and made her way out the office and down the delivery elevator. She reached the street, got into the UPS van, changed her clothes, and emerged as a businessman with medium length black hair, a neatly cropped black mustache, and a slight bulge around his midsection. Christine was now wearing a dark suit, white shirt, burgundy tie, black shoes, wire-rimmed glasses, and carrying an overstuffed legal briefcase. She easily blended into the crowd now beginning to grow around the ambulance parked in front of the Emerson Building, with its siren blaring.

Christine watched the crowd and the building until two FBI agents stepped out the front door with two EMS technicians escorting a stretcher behind them.

Scott and Tom were only a step behind the stretcher, with Tom on one side and Scott on the other. As they were about to lift the stretcher into the van, Christine pressed a remote control button in her pocket, which was followed by a loud explosion and a cloud of smoke a block away.

While everyone's attention, including that of those attending the stretcher, was diverted to the explosion, Christine removed her silenced Berretta and shot Paul Cedes in his right temple. She turned and walked quickly with the rest of the crowd in the direction of the explosion. Once she was around the corner, Hoover was gone.

Scott and Tom helped put Paul Cedes into the ambulance and as soon as the door was closed, one of the technicians saw the new bullet wound.

"Oh shit, this wasn't here before. This guy has a bullet in his head. I think he's dead."

Scott checked his pulse and the new wound. "God damn it Tom, that son of a bitch Hoover just shot Cedes in the head with us standing right there."

Tom yelled at the driver to stop the ambulance. "Scott, get on the phone, we've got to seal off this entire area."

They both stepped out of the ambulance and looked around before Scott stated the obvious. "He's long gone. He was right there in the crowd. Damn it, I can't believe we let this happen."

Tom kicked the ground in disgust. "I can't believe we fell for that, it's the oldest diversion in the book. Just think how close he had to be to get that shot off without us seeing or hearing it. Let's get hold of all the cameras that were in the crowd."

"We need to get some teams out here and see what we can find. We have to lock down this whole area. He had to fire those first two shots from one of those buildings across the street."

"Okay, I'm on it; meanwhile Scott, you get the privilege of telling the boss that we just lost Cedes."

"He's going to kill us. Cedes was probably the most important of the four people on that list."

"Not only us, Scott—Hoover just fulfilled the first part of Martinez's contract. I think Martinez just served his last day in the FBI."

"Damn Tom, we better contact the director and Christine so that they don't walk into a mess like this. They're going to have to put on extra security to get Brooks and that assistant attorney general to the shop."

"I doubt Christine has even made it to Braddock yet," Scott replied. "We should have the locals provide additional security until she can get there."

"OK Scott, but even Hoover couldn't get to Braddock, Maryland in time to hit Brooks at his own place before Christine can secure him. We definitely need to alert her, but our focus needs to be on the assistant attorney general. The boss is picking her up at a restaurant on First Street. and New York Avenue. It would be stretching it, but Hoover could have time to get to her."

"OK Tom, you call Christine and I'll call the boss. I guess I better call the local homicide unit as well."

Chapter 22

Director Flynn was still with Laura Kinsman, Attorney General Eagelton and Judge Powell when Scott called.

"Chief, I got some bad news."

"I can't take anymore bad news today Scott, do I have to hear this?"

"I'm afraid so chief. Paul Cedes was just shot."

"Shit, please tell me he's not dead."

"I'm afraid he is."

"What the hell happened? Where were you and Tom?"

"I'd like to get into that at the debriefing, chief. It does have Hoover written all over it."

"You guys saw him?"

"No, I just know it was him. Sir, we really need to focus on getting you out of there safely. If Hoover has a secondary target for today, we think it's got to be Assistant Attorney General Kinsman. You guys are only about twenty minutes from here. It would be a pretty ballsy move but Hoover is the one person that could pull it off."

"OK Scott, what did you have in mind?" The director asked.

"We secure the perimeter, bring in a UAV (Urban Assault Vehicle), some body armor complete with helmets and face shields and then drive the van up on the sidewalk, right to the front door. We then get you into the van, exposing you for no more than two seconds. It would take Hoover more than two seconds to figure out who was who under those suits." Scott told the director.

"What about the attorney general or the judge?"

While Director Flynn was talking to Scott on the phone, the rest of the party at his table was hanging on his every word sensing that something was wrong.

Scott explained to the director that "Hoover" had never even wounded anyone that was not his specific target. He was certain that once Laura Kinsman was out of the restaurant, everyone else would be safe.

The director bought off on the plan and explained the latest developments to the others while Scott made the arrangements.

"As you may have guessed by my conversation, Hoover started to fulfill his contract. A few minutes ago Hoover shot and killed Paul Cedes." Director Flynn paused for effect and watched as Laura's face turned white as a sheet. "I don't know all of the details yet, but Paul Cedes is definitely dead and my people are certain it was Hoover. They'll have confirmation by the end of the day."

Laura lost all of her strength and resolve. "Oh my God, he's coming after me next, isn't he?"

"It's highly unlikely that he would attempt two high-profile assassinations in one day, but we should be ready just in case. My people have a plan to get us out of here." Director Flynn told them about the assault van and the protective clothing. He assured them that the UAV would be pulling up to the front door and all he and Laura had to do was step in it.

Laura was concerned about the rest of the people in the restaurant, but Director Flynn assured her that it would be safe for them to leave. "Hoover is very dangerous, but he's also very professional, he's never caused any collateral damage, and he'd never injured a bystander." The director told them.

Laura was still visibly shaken. "If he can get to Paul Cedes, then he sure as heck can get to the rest of us."

Peter Eagelton held Laura's hand for support. "That's not necessarily true. Paul Cedes wasn't expecting him but we are, isn't that right, Martin?"

"He's right, Laura, once we get you out of here and to the compound, you'll be safe. Even Hoover can't get to you there." The director turned to Peter Eagelton. "I think this would be a good time for you and Judge Powell to leave."

"I don't know about Peter, but I'm not leaving until I know Laura is safe," the judge shot back.

"Look Judge, we can protect Laura better if we don't have to worry about protecting the two of you as well."

Peter Eagelton nodded his agreement. "He's right, Judge, there's no use for you to be here. I think you should go and make Martin's job easier."

"Okay, but I want to know Laura's safe as soon as you get her to safety."

"You have my word sir." The director replied.

The judge got up to walk out but Peter Eagelton didn't follow him.

"Peter, aren't you coming?"

"No, Judge; I got Laura into this, I'm going to make sure that she's safe."

As the judge walked out the front door, the others sat and watched.

Director Flynn didn't expect any problems, but he was still relieved when the street remained calm.

"How long will I have to stay there? I need to be able to continue my life," Laura asked.

Director Flynn lowered his eyes. "Laura, I'm not going to kid you. If we don't bring down this crime syndicate or whatever you want to call it, you may never be able to resume your normal life."

"Millenium," Laura said softly. "They call themselves the Millenium. It has something to do with wanting to be the major economic force in the world by the end of the millenium."

"Those are the kinds of things that don't sound like much, but with that information, my task force will have a better idea of how to focus their investigation," Director Flynn chided. "Look Laura, even if we bring this "Millenium" to its knees, you're still not safe unless we capture Hoover. Hoover has already been paid $10 million. He'll complete the job just to protect his reputation."

"I'm not spending the rest of my life in hiding," Laura insisted. "Let me talk to my contact and see what's going on. It doesn't make any sense that the Millenium would want these people dead. I'm sure Walter Brooks provides most of the funding and many of the legitimate fronts. Paul Cedes provides contact with the Washington crowd as well as running their security. This just doesn't make any sense."

"Since your name is on the list, you have a right to know what I'm about to tell you," Director Flynn said. Then he addressed Peter. "Part of this is your fault so I expect you to stand back and let me handle this my way. Unless I have your word on that, I'm not going to continue."

"That's probably the least I owe you after keeping my investigation from you all this time. You have my word that no matter what, I'll leave it in your hands." Peter Eagelton promised.

"Laura doesn't need to go back undercover to find out why the

Millenium wants to do away with this particular group of people. We know who issued the contracts and why." Director Flynn paused just long enough to check Peter's reaction.

"My people have been under tremendous strain ever since President Canfield was assassinated. We know Hoover did it, we just can't find him. Hell we don't even know who he is. We also know that Hoover was behind two other assassinations. We know it was him, because he always leaves a fingerprint behind. The reason we call him Hoover is because it's J. Edgar Hoover's right thumbprint that he leaves behind."

Peter and Laura looked at each other with amazement. "Hoover's thumbprint? How the hell did he get that?" Peter asked.

"That's one of the problems, we're not sure how he got it. He may have an accomplice in the FBI."

"So what does all of this have to do with the contract on me?" Laura asked.

"As you might guess, our people have been under tremendous pressure to bring in Hoover and whoever hired him. I put Special Agent Martinez in charge of hunting down Hoover. I guess the pressure just got to him so he set a trap for Hoover. The bait in his trap was you, Cedes, Brooks, and Feldman."

"Christ Martin! Please tell me that this hit wasn't put on by the FBI!"

"I wish I could Peter, but the fact is that ASAC Martinez contracted with Hoover for these assassinations in hopes of getting him into the open so we could pick him up."

Laura was still in shock. When she did speak it was with a hint of hope in her voice. "This is good, isn't it? This means that your guy can call it off."

"It's not that easy, Laura. Martinez is trying to cancel the contracts but as you can see with what happened to Cedes, Hoover has already started working on them."

Peter still couldn't believe what he heard. "Why on earth would a senior FBI agent do something that stupid?"

"Peter, it won't do us any good to try to figure it out now. Believe me, I've been trying to figure this out ever since he told us about it. What we have to focus on is getting Laura to safety until we're sure that Hoover's no longer a threat."

"My God Martin, I can't even imagine anything that stupid. I hope you've got him locked up."

Just then the director's phone rang. "Yes."

"Sir, it's Scott, we're outside. If you're ready, we'll pull up to the front door in exactly two minutes!"

"OK, we're on our way!"

Director Flynn motioned for Peter and Laura to slide out of the booth. He led them to the front door, keeping close to the wall and away from the windows.

Their wait wasn't long. Exactly two minutes after the phone call, the restaurant windows began to rattle. The tables began to shake and move across the floor, glasses began to shatter as they fell off the tables, and then the UAV appeared, no more than four feet from the front door. It looked like a tank without the gun turret, only completely square. It was solid black and made of three-inch steel. Its doors opened not like a regular car but rather more like a steel wing rising to protect anyone that walked underneath it.

From underneath this wing four agents in full body armor emerged and entered the restaurant. Once inside, they raised their helmet shields and director Flynn recognized Scott and Tom. "That's one hell of an entrance guys. I don't suppose we could have done this a little more discreetly?"

"To tell you the truth sir, we were more concerned about safety than discretion." Scott told the director.

"What are you guys doing here anyway? We have special units for this kind of stuff. You guys aren't field agents anymore."

"You didn't think that we were going to miss a chance to pull our boss's chestnuts out of the fire, did you?"

"I think you guys have been hanging around Christine too much. Let me introduce you to everybody."

After brief introductions, the rest of the men handed out the additional suits and helped the others into them. Laura had to bunch her skirt around her waist to fit in to the bulletproof coverall. Once everyone was secure in their suits, the agents formed a circle around Laura, Director Flynn, and Peter Eagelton. Scott then pulled them out of the middle of the circle and put two of the agents in the center and everyone else around the edge.

Laura Kinsman was on one side of the circle, Attorney General Eagelton on the other side. Director Flynn was to the rear, Scott Peterson was leading the way, and Tom West was between Scott and Laura. With the two agents in the middle of the circle, Scott opened the restaurant door and in less than five seconds seven heavily bundled and protected figures made their way into the vehicle. Once inside, everyone removed their helmets and breathed a sigh of relief as the UAV made its way down the street.

Laura attempted to act calm but was curious about what just happened. "I thought you guys came to protect me. Why was I on the outside of the circle?"

Tom smiled. "First of all, behind these suits and face shields, it's impossible for anyone to distinguish us from each other. The killer would assume that we put you and the director into the middle of the formation so that our bodies could protect you. Any shots fired therefore would be directed at the center of the formation. By putting you and Mr. Eagelton at the side of the formation, that put you out of the direct line of fire. We also had another agent in front of you for additional safety."

"Quite ingenious, Agent West."

Scott Peterson, not being fully aware of what transpired at the restaurant, wasn't ready to exchange compliments with Laura. "We try not to lose anyone in our custody."

Director Flynn backed him off. "Relax Scott, it's not what we thought. I'll get into it when we get back. We'll need to call a meeting of the task force. What's happening with Brooks and Christine?"

"Last time I talked to Christine, she was still on her way to Braddock. I'm sure she'll call as soon as she can." Tom said. "I also have the State Troopers parked outside of the Brooks estate until she gets there."

Chapter 23

Christine walked for two blocks before she slipped down into the metro. There she entered the men's room and transformed Hoover from a clean-cut businessman into a young black rapper with baggie pants worn low on her hips, a large loose baggy shirt, and untied tennis shoes. She also wore a Chicago Bulls' baseball cap pulled down over her face. On her back, she had a knapsack that contained the clothes she'd been wearing and the briefcase. Christine got on the Blue Line at Federal Triangle and switched to the Red Line at Metro Central.

She got off the Red Line at the Woodley Park Zoo. Christine walked to the side of the Zoo ticket booth and emptied her backpack into the large Dumpster. Without looking up, she handed three dollars to the booth attendant, got her ticket, and entered the Zoo. Once out of view of all cameras and making sure no one was around, she entered a lady's room. She stripped off her baggy clothes, under which she was wearing a dark slim-fitting lady's pantsuit. She removed her hat, fluffed out her hair, and emerged as Christine Peal. She exited the Zoo through a different path, walked to the bus stop and took the bus to the Bethesda stop. There she picked up her Volvo and entered the Beltway heading toward 270 and Braddock Heights.

While Christine was still on the bus, Tom had called and alerted her to Cedes' assassination and cautioned her to take extra security measures. Christine told Tom that she was having car problems and would be slightly delayed. They agreed to have the Maryland State Highway Patrol watch the house until she arrived.

At a rest stop near Germantown, she stopped and dropped the knapsack into a trash bin and then continued on. Christine covered the usually difficult forty miles in record time. She was still more than twenty minutes late meeting Quantara.

As expected Quantara was waiting at the Roy Rogers Restaurant on Highway 40 just four miles from Braddock Heights.

"Did you run into some traffic on the way up here?"

"Not really, I just had a flat tire."

As they walked to Quantara's Chevy Blazer, he noticed that all four tires on Christine's car were the same size. "Great! You've got one of those cars where they still give you a full-size spare."

Christine was mentally kicking herself. She had thought of everything except to put one of those little spares on her car. She hated the slightest things going wrong with her plans. "Actually, I had to make that a special request when I bought the car."

Before Christine could stop him, Quantara opened her trunk to retrieve the flat tire.

"Let's grab your flat and have it fixed while we're at Brooks.'"

When Quantara looked in the trunk all he could see was one small spare, still strapped in.

"Where's your flat tire?" Quantara asked.

"I already dropped it off," Christine replied. "I'll pick it up on the way back."

"Good," was all Quantara said as they got into his Blazer and drove to the Brooks estate. They pulled up behind the State Trooper and Christine got out to talk to him. She showed him her badge; the trooper didn't seem too impressed with either Christine or Walter Brooks. "So what are you guys doing for Brooks this time?"

"I don't know what you mean? We're just here to check out Mr. Brooks' security."

"You mean all those goons he's got up there aren't enough? Now he's got the FBI protecting him as well?"

"You don't sound like you like him much, officer."

"Let's just say that he's not a favorite of the people that live out here. Somehow he got the state to agree to privatize Highway 17 all the way from Highway 40 to Interstate 70 and the Old Hagerstown Road from 17 to 70. That forces anybody that wants to go north to go at least twenty miles out of the way. He also doesn't spend any money in either Braddock or Fredrick. He doesn't even bother to drive to Fredrick to use their airport. So his neighbors have to put up with those helicopters that he's got coming and going all day long."

"Sounds like he's just a rich guy flexing some muscle."

"Well ma'am, I guess that's why you're here; he just flexed some more muscle."

"We're just here to check his security. I guess his neighbors make him nervous."

"Ok ma'am, I guess you don't need me anymore then. The gate to the estate is about a mile down Old Hagerstown Road."

Christine got back in the Blazer and Quantara drove to the gate of the estate. She could see that there were two cameras covering the gate and the fence had a sign with a lightning bolt on it, indicating that it was electrified. Before they could even call the house from the speaker outside the gate, they saw two Jeeps coming down the dirt road with what looked like two armed guards in each.

"Well Christine, it looks like we have a welcoming committee," Quantara said.

"I wonder how big this place is to have two Jeeps patrolling it?" Christine thought out loud.

"That's one of the things we can ask Brooks when we bring him in."

"I hope we don't have to take him by force. We could have trouble getting out of here," Christine said.

"Hopefully, Francine did her job and he's ready for us," Quantara offered.

The guards escorted the Blazer to the main house, where Christine and Quantara were escorted to an office, which to Christine looked to be a replica of the Oval Office of the president of the United States.

Behind the desk in the center of the office, sat a man Christine knew had to be between sixty-five and seventy. His hair was almost white, his face lacked the wrinkles and lines that you would expect in someone of his age, and his smile showed a gleaming crop of white teeth. As he stood to greet them, Christine saw a man who took care of himself. His shoulders were still broad and looked strong and he lacked that midsection expansion that most men his age so proudly displayed. His grip was firm as he introduced himself.

"Good afternoon, I am Walter Brooks. You must be Agent Peal and Agent Quantara. Welcome." Walter Brooks smiled at Christine as he returned to his desk and took his seat.

"Francine called earlier to let me know that you would be out. She said something about a threat to my life."

Brooks didn't offer the agents a seat, so Christine stepped to the front of his desk and towered over him. "Yes sir, we have information that there has been a contract placed on your life."

Brooks was feeling a little uncomfortable with Christine towering over him. "Please, both of you have a seat. Certainly you noticed as you were driving in that I have my own security force. They're quite effective. I also have a security system that even your best people would not be able to crack. This house is three miles from the nearest public road. I have five two-man security teams in Jeeps, constantly patrolling the estate. At night I have a dozen highly trained guard dogs running the grounds. Inside, I have motion sensors, lasers, and three guards. I'm safer than the president of the United States."

"That's quite impressive Mr. Brooks, but I think until we get a handle on this contract you would be safer at the FBI compound. At least until we can run security checks on your staff."

"I appreciate that Miss., however I prefer my own home to some room at the FBI. I will be happy to provide you with the names of my entire staff and you may run your security checks, but you will have to do it while I remain here."

Christine had to find away to get Brooks out of his fortress. Force was not an option. They needed to get him back to FBI HQ if they ever expected to get anything out of him. "Mr. Brooks, the director instructed me to make sure that you return to the FBI complex with me. The man after you is a most accomplished assassin. The president himself has warned the director about letting anything happen to you."

"Then let me call Norman and take your director off of the proverbial hook."

"Sir, before you call the President, perhaps I should call the agency and have you talk directly to the director?"

Before Brooks had a chance to reply, Christine was already dialing the number. The director wasn't in, so Christine dialed Francine and was immediately connected to her office. "Francine, I'm here with Mr. Brooks and he seems to be somewhat reluctant to return to the Hoover Building. with us. Would you explain the urgency of the matter to him?"

Christine handed the phone to Brooks. "Sir, it's Agent English."

Brooks took the phone and a big smile crossed his face. "Francine, how is it that I am lucky enough to talk to you twice in one day?"

"Mr. Brooks, you really should listen to Agent Peal."

"Francine, how many times do I have to tell you to call me Walter?"

"OK Walter, you really need to go with Agent Peal; the director is very concerned about your safety."

"You and I both know that my compound is safer than any place in the country."

"But not as safe as the Hoover Building."

"Francine, you know I would do almost anything for you, but I have too much to do to leave now."

"Walter, I don't want to pull out any old IOUs, but you do owe me."

Walter Brooks momentarily lost his pretentious tone. "You wouldn't!"

"I would. This is your life we're talking about."

"OK, I'll come in, but only long enough to meet with Martin, and only if you promise to meet me."

"OK Walter, I'll see you when you get here. Would you let me talk to Agent Peal please."

Walter Brooks handed the phone back to Christine. "Thank you, Francine."

"I just used a chip that I've held for ten years. This had better be worth it."

"It is Francine, I'll see you when we get back."

Christine hung up the phone and she and Quantara rose. "Sir, we have Agent Quantara's car outside and we're ready to leave as soon as you are."

Walter Brooks leaned back in his chair making no move to come with them. "Here is how we are going to do it. I promised Francine that I would come to the Hoover Building. I did not promise her that I would be getting there in your car. I am going to freshen up, then I will have my pilot pick me up out back and fly me to the Hoover Building."

"Sir, there is only one problem with that; the Hoover Building, is in the Federal Triangle and I doubt you'll be able to get clearance to land there."

"You let me worry about that, Agent Peal. If one or both of you would like to come along in the helicopter, that would be acceptable to me. We will be ready to go in about thirty minutes."

Christine wasn't about to argue with him, she was just glad that he was going. She decided to ride in the helicopter and return for her car later.

Quantara headed back to D.C. in his Blazer. Christine gave him her keys so that he could make sure her car was secure.

Christine was surprised when she got into the helicopter and found Walter Brooks at the controls and the pilot in the copilot's seat. Walter

Brooks turned his head and smiled at Christine as she strapped herself in. "Just hold on, young lady. This is only going to take a couple of minutes."

Christine sat back and put on the headphones. She could hear the pilot getting all of the clearances and trying to slow Brooks down as he was lifting off. "Sir, remember that we're in Washington airspace here; we really should wait for all of the clearances before we lift off. Remember, sir, there are hundreds of planes in this area."

"You worry too much Joe; we're only going high enough to land on the Hoover Building."

Christine was beginning to wish that she had gone with Quantara. She wasn't a stranger to helicopters; in fact she even had unofficial flying lessons from one of her friends. She was however getting nervous with Walter Brooks a weekend pilot and a man probably in his late sixtys flying into one of the country's most restricted airspaces without waiting for proper clearances.

As they climbed to two thousand feet, Christine could hear the pilot tell Brooks that they had been cleared through 2500 feet and gave him a heading to follow. Brooks wasn't impressed.

"Can you believe this Agent Peal? I can see the Hoover Building right in front of me and they want me to fly all over the place to get there. This should be like driving on the street—if the road is clear go for it."

With that Walter Brooks banked the helicopter and headed straight for the Hoover Building. As they were dropping altitude, Christine could see the top of the Hoover building, and men scurrying around one of the helicopters. Then she heard the pilot in her ear.

"Mr. Brooks, they're not ready for us. We're not cleared to land. The helipad is occupied, sir."

Walter Brooks laughed into his headset. "Look Joe, that helicopter will be off of the pad before we get down there."

Christine could only sit and watch as this crazy old man was about to land on top of the FBI building, blocks from the White House, without clearance. It was as if he was playing chicken with the helicopter still on the pad. Then all at once, the helicopter on the pad lifted off and Brooks slid into the empty spot.

Christine could see Scott running out of the glass door onto the roof flanked by two mechanics. The mechanics helped Christine and Walter Brooks out of the helicopter and signaled the pilot to take off.

Walter Brooks made a gesture across his throat signaling to the pilot to shut down the helicopter. Scott then walked up to the front of the helicopter put his FBI shield against the window and signaled the pilot to lift off. Without further discussion, the helicopter lifted off and Scott grabbed Walter Brooks under the arm and escorted him into the building.

"What the hell do you think you're doing? I want my helicopter and pilot back here," Brooks snapped.

Scott took it in stride. "I'm sorry Mr. Brooks, but we don't have room for the helicopter. We'll call it back when you're ready to go."

"Then you better call it back now. After I say hello to Francine and Martin, I'm getting back in the helicopter and heading home."

Christine had been watching and listening to Walter Brooks closely. This was a man who had it his way his entire life. He obviously wasn't used to anyone's rules but his own. He would be tough to break. She did noticed that every time he got upset or overly excited, his speech would slip and lose that superior edge.

Tom led them to Director Flynn's office where the director and Francine English were waiting. Walter Brook's mood changed considerably when he saw Francine. He walked over to her and gave her a hug. "Francine, my favorite FBI agent, how are you? Are you ready to quit this thing and join me?"

"I'm fine Walter and I love my job."

Walter Brooks released Francine, turned to Director Flynn and lost the smile from his face. "Martin, what is going on? Why did you send my helicopter away?"

"Walter, we just don't have room for it up there. We have a lot to go over and we have to figure out how we can best protect you."

"You can best protect me by leaving me alone at my estate."

"That may be what we decide in the end," the director said. "For now though, let's try to figure this thing out. I have a meeting with my security team and Attorney General Eagelton starting in about two minutes. We'll get this sorted out. Before I go into that meeting, is there any reason you can think of why anybody would want to put a contract out on your life?"

"I run businesses all over the world. There are probably several dozen people that would like to see me dead."

"But no one specific?"

"No one I can think of."

"Okay Walter, we're going to meet with Eagelton and we'll be back in about twenty minutes or so. Francine is going to take you to my conference room and make sure you're comfortable until we get back."

"I flew out here specifically to talk to you. How dare you go off and leave me?"

"Walter, before you and I can discuss this thing logically, I need to know what the attorney general and the rest of my staff have."

"Then I should come with you."

"That's not possible Walter. Wait in my conference room and I'll be back as soon as I can."

Francine took Walter Brooks by the arm and led him into the next room as the director, accompanied by Scott and Christine, headed to the task force meeting. Along the way they stopped at Scott's office and collected Attorney General Peter Eagelton and Assistant Attorney General Laura Kinsman.

When they entered the conference room everyone except Agent Quantara, who was still on the way from Walter Brooks' estate, was already there. This included a very sheepish Freddie Martinez.

Attorney General Eagelton, having worked with Martinez on other cases, spotted him before he even had a chance to find his seat and immediately unloaded. "What the hell is he doing here? He should be locked up somewhere."

"Maybe so, but you agreed to let me handle it," the director shot back. "He's been relieved of his duties and he is technically under house arrest. He can't leave the compound and that guard outside goes wherever Freddie goes."

That didn't seem to appease AG Eagelton. "Well, that's just great—meanwhile my top prosecutor has a price on her head, put there by this idiot."

Director Flynn wasn't about to leave it at that. "I'm not going to make any excuses for Martnez, what he did was stupid and criminal. But, if you and your people had followed procedures and notified us of your investigation and undercover operation, Laura's name would never have been on that list. As far as any of my people knew, Laura was part of one of the largest and most dangerous criminal organizations this country has ever seen. Our information has her as part of the team that decides who lives and who dies. So don't put it all off on Freddie." Director Flynn paused just long enough to let his words sink in, before pushed on.

"That leads us to why we called this meeting. For those of you who don't know, this is Attorney General Eagelton and Assistant Attorney General Laura Kinsman. They're going to tell you a little story that I think you'll be interested in." Director Flynn didn't bother to hide the edge in his voice.

Peter Eagelton explained how Laura found herself undercover and her subsequent rise in the syndicate's hierarchy. He explained her role in the assassination of the oilman Peron and being appointed to the inner sanctum.

Most of the agents present showed their displeasure with how the attorney general handled his information. It was Bob Lambert who was perhaps most upset of all. "Director Flynn is right, you guys are as criminally liable as Freddie. If we had this information even forty-eight hours ago, four more people would be alive today, including two San Francisco police officers.

"You have no right to point a finger at anybody. You have at least four lives on your hands already. Hell, I wouldn't be surprised if the two of you knew about President Canfield's assassination ahead of time and just didn't bother to warn anyone." Bob Lambert's face was still red with fury when Director Flynn cut him off.

"Okay, that's enough. There's plenty of blame to go around on this one. Both agencies have made some costly mistakes. What we have to do now is get our heads together and see exactly who and what we're dealing with."

The door opened behind the director and Francine English joined the meeting. The director asked her about Walter Brooks. Francine assured him that although he was still irritated, he would be fine. Director Flynn continued with the meeting as Francine found her seat.

"I suggest that Laura brief us on everything she knows about this syndicate and who some of the major players are. Then Scott can recap our operation thus far and exactly where we are and how we got Laura's name. Once all of that is out of the way, I'll want to hear from all of you about the status of your investigations and how the hell we let Hoover get to Cedes this morning."

The director started to rise and told everyone that he was going to check on Walter Brooks and for them to continue.

It took Laura almost forty-five minutes to cover what she knew about the organization including a listing of the names of the people that she had been exposed to and their relative place in the organization. Director Flynn returned to the meeting with Agent Quantara at his side, just as Laura was wrapping up.

The director walked in with his hand on Quantara's shoulder. "Look who I found coming up the steps. Christine, I bet now you're glad you took that helicopter." Then he turned his attention back to Laura. "Did you tell them about the name of this syndicate and what's behind it?"

Laura nodded indicating that she had. Director Flynn then continued. "Good, so now we have something to go on. Millenium is obviously not our typical organized crime family. While I was talking to Walter just now, it occurred to me that if he is one of the key people in Millenium, he's just cocky enough to set up an actual corporation to run it. Peter, I think this is something best investigated by your staff."

AG Peter Eagelton nodded in agreement as he took down a note.

Director Flynn had another piece of bad news to share before the meeting continued. "Freddie, I don't know how to tell you this, but I just found out the drug dealer that the DEA agent was undercover with was killed when a rival dealer attempted to rip him off. The agent was only slightly injured and will be fine. This all unfortunately happened before the agent had a chance to find out where the dealer got his information about the hits. I'm afraid that lead to Hoover is shut down. It doesn't look like Hoover had anything to do with the dealer's death."

Freddie's face turned white and his shoulders sagged even more. His last hopes were being shattered one at a time. First with the loss of Paul Cedes and now with the death of the drug dealer that could have led him to Hoover.

To Freddie it was as if someone knew he was getting close and was shadowing his every move and then cutting him off whenever he got close. Now more than ever Freddie thought that Hoover had some kind of tie to the FBI, maybe even someone in this room. He also knew that Hoover had won and it would be useless to voice his theory of a Hoover collaborator sitting at this very table. After today he would get very little if any support for any of his ideas or opinions. There was, in fact, a good chance that he would be the one locked up and Hoover would still be free.

Against his better judgement, Freddie Martinez decided to put his opinion on the table, especially since this might well be his last opportunity.

"Sir, before I'm silenced forever on this matter, I would like to tell this committee my opinion of the Hoover matter."

"Like I told Peter, I still believe that you have valuable input for this task force. So let's hear it," Director Flynn instructed.

"As you know sir, it has always been my contention that Hoover has a partner in the FBI. For Hoover to have been able to avoid detection during a massive worldwide search like the one we conducted ten years ago after the assassination of ADIC Ballard, his partner must be a senior agent. That, plus the fact that every investigation that either Tom or myself have undertaken, has been cut short before they've even had a chance to get going, leads me to believe that Hoover's partner is on this task force."

The conference room erupted. Director Flynn had to shout to get control back. "Damn it people, everyone just quiet down. This is a task force. We don't have all of the answers; the whole idea is to throw out your thoughts and opinions and then for everyone to discuss them logically. Freddie has done just that, now it's up to the rest of us to discuss them."

Director Flynn waited for everyone to settle down before he continued. "Now does anyone have anything reasonable to add to this?"

Tom West took this opportunity to present his own theory on Hoover. "Sir, as you know, I've been with this Hoover case as long as anyone. I haven't said this before, but I believe, that Hoover does have someone on the inside, maybe Hoover is a FBI employee himself. I don't believe, however, that Hoover's contact is on this task force."

Tom continued. "We have proof that Hoover was involved in four assassinations. If he had been involved in more, I think we would have known about it. He does make it a point to leave his calling card. With the help of Jim Brodrick and his people at the National Center for the Analysis of Violent Crime and some recently released Hoover files, we found one common connection to all of the victims." Tom made sure he had everyone's attention.

"In 1969 an FBI Agent Mark Ballard and an FBI Agent William Canon both worked on a special projects task force answering only to FBI Director J. Edgar Hoover. They worked together for about nine months.

"In the investigation of President Canfield's assassination, we found records of his vice presidency showing that he and Hoover and another individual had several lunches at the vice president's home during the fall of 1969. On two separate occasions, there are records of incoming calls from Africa during these lunches, and on one occasion both Ballard and Canon accompanied Hoover to the lunch."

Director Flynn's curiosity was aroused. "This is great work Tom, but it doesn't really link Paul Cedes to the others unless he was the other man at the lunches."

"No sir, the other man was not Paul Cedes; we believe that Paul Cedes was the man calling from Africa."

You could hear a pin drop in the conference room as Tom had captured everyone's attention and imagination. "Paul Cedes at the time was the CIA's man in Africa," Tom continued. "This is particularly interesting since the other man at the vice president's lunches, is the same man in your office, Walter Brooks.

"At that time, he was a minor oilman with a minor stake in a minor country. That country was Cameroon.

"In September of 1969, the Cameroon government was overthrown and its current government began to form. By the spring of 1970 Walter Brooks had exclusive drilling rights and lifetime leases on most of the Cameroon oil fields. He also received mining rights to two major diamond mines.

"Why Canfield, Hoover, and his men are associated with Cedes and Walter Brooks we're not sure. We do know that Canon went to work for Brooks as his head of security after Hoover died in seventy-two, and Walter Brooks started getting filthy rich after he started meeting with Canfield, Hoover, and Cedes. I believe the reason behind the assassination of Canfield, Cedes, Canon, and Ballard has something to do with the lunches at the vice president's place in the fall of sixty-nine and the oil field leases that Brooks got that following year."

The director pushed himself away from the table and leaned back in his chair. "Jesus, Tom that's one hell of a story. Why haven't I heard it before?"

"Agent Brodrick and I have just been kicking it around. This is actually the first time I've put it together this succinctly. I guess I just needed to dispel agent Martinez' contention that Hoover's contact is on this committee."

"How does what you just told us dispel that?" The director asked.

"Sir, these are obviously not contracted assassinations. Hoover wants us to tie all of them together. That's why he's using J. Edgar Hoover's prints. J. Edgar Hoover was the only one dead out of this group. So in order for the assassin to feel like he's getting even with everybody, he's in affect blaming everything on Hoover. The fact that there was ten years between the first assassination and the second demonstrates that our "Assassin" was not hired to do these hits.

"I believe Hoover is doing this on his own, for revenge. Whatever happened at those lunches in sixty-nine made Hoover very unhappy."

"How does the assassination of Michael Peron fit in to your theory?" Christine asked.

"I don't think Hoover had anything to do with it. He didn't leave his calling card. We already know that Paul Cedes had his hands in that one. I can't see our assassin working for that bunch." Tom replied.

The director turned to Jim Brodrick. "Jim, do you buy off on Tom's assessment?"

"Yes sir, I do. I would even go a step further and say that Hoover's actions are totally independent of this Millenium bunch. He probably isn't even aware of its existence."

"OK, so now we have a definite theory about Hoover, one that in its own weird way even makes sense. You still haven't answered why it couldn't be anybody at this table," Scott Peterson asked.

"Take a look around the room—most of the people here were still in high school in sixty-nine," Tom answered.

"Not all of us," the director said.

Tom smiled as he replied. "No sir, in nineteen sixty-nine you were serving on a battle ship in the south China sea in the middle of the Vietnam conflict. Agent Martinez spent all of sixty-nine and part of nineteen seventy monitoring Castro and the Cubans in Florida. Scott spent sixty-nine and seventy at the language school in Monterey, California, learning how to speak Mandarin Chinese. Even back then he was thinking way ahead of everybody else. The rest of us were either in high school, college, or, some like Christine, were just barely starting grammar school."

"I'm not sure whether to be insulted or impressed that you checked us all out." The director said.

"Sir, like Agent Martinez, I had my concerns. I'm glad to report however that this committee is clean."

"Even if we believe everything you just said, that only means that Hoover himself isn't at this table. He could still have a contact here,"

Martinez insisted.

"Maybe so, but I believe its highly unlikely." Tom replied.

"Okay." The director interjected. "Where do we go from here?"

"If Tom is right, we have two separate investigations here," Scott offered. "First we have Hoover, who is going around killing people for some reason that we may never understand. Then we have the Millenium that wants to take over the world. I think we should let Tom continue the Hoover investigation. The rest of us need to focus on the Millenium; they could do irreparable harm to our country. From what Tom told us, I would bet anything that they were founded back in '69, and its founding members were Paul Cedes, Walter Brooks, then Vice President Canfield, and maybe even J. Edgar Hoover."

"I would hate to think that Hoover had anything to do with this," the director said. "He's been maligned enough since his death, something like this would destroy what's left of his reputation."

"At this point it really doesn't matter who started this organization," Christine said. "This thing has grown to the point where it's seeped into places it has no business being. We're talking about judges, senators, and congressmen, all part of this Millenium. All corrupt and all in a position to guide or even overthrow the government. Maybe our assassin was around in '69 to see what happened in that African country and just didn't want it to happen here." Christine looked around the room for reactions before she continued.

"Sir, I think we have to find a way to break Walter Brooks. He's the only person still alive who knows the whole story and he's certainly the money behind this Millenium."

"He does seem to be the key," Director Flynn said. "Francine, you know him best, do you have any ideas?"

"No sir, this is a man that makes and breaks presidents. He's a widower with no children, a self-made billionaire, and a man that owns not only companies but many say even countries; it won't be easy. But I'll give it serious thought, sir."

"OK Francine, get us something. I'm sure we have other things to cover. I want to hear what went on at Paul Cedes' office," the director said.

Scott told everyone about the first attempt at Cedes while they were in his office. He explained that Hoover failed on that attempt because of the sniper-proof windows. These windows were constructed not only with bulletproof glass, which Hoover was able to penetrate without problem, but they also had a prism built between the panels of the glass that actually made everything appear three inches further to the right than it actually was. That's what made Hoover miss his first shot.

Christine sat amazed as she listened to Scott. She had counted on the bulletproof glass, but she had never heard of this offset glass.

Scott speculated about what he and Tom thought happened outside of the building. "We think that Hoover was disguised as a businessman and walked right up to Paul Cedes' gurney and shot him in the head while we were distracted by an explosion a block away.

"We confiscated all the video and film in the area. We have lots of pictures of the smoke from the explosion and a couple of shots of a black man in business attire walking away from the scene. We're pretty sure it was Hoover because he was immune to the explosion and smoke. Human nature would be to at least look."

"I assume that Hoover was responsible for the distraction," the director asked.

"We think so." Tom said. "He set off a smoke bomb in a UPS van. We think he stole that van and got into the building dressed as a UPS courier. The security cameras spotted a UPS man entering the building with several packages and they showed the same guy leaving with packages."

"Do you really think that he had time to change from his UPS outfit into a business suit and come out of the building and position himself to shoot Cedes?" Director Flynn asked.

"Yes, we do." Scott answered. "We think that he exploded the van by remote control as he was standing next to Paul Cedes, walked to the nearest Metro station, and disappeared into the crowd."

"That's how he got away last time," Martinez added.

"Okay Tom, it looks like you have your work cut out for you. I guess this means he wasn't the man that withdrew my money from that bank in Switzerland. Get this guy; I want him stopped and I want the money back and I don't want any more headlines." Director Flynn emphasized his words by tossing the evening addition of the Washington Post into the center of the conference room table. The headline read; "Ambassador Shot Dead in DC Streets."

As the task force moved on to other topics, the phone rang. Francine answered it and handed it to the director. "Sir, it's the White House. It's

Chief of Staff Hunt."

The director took the phone from Francine and answered with a hint of annoyance in his voice. "What can I do for you, Hunt? I'm in the middle of a meeting, we'll have to make this quick."

"I'll get right to the point then." An obviously upset Brian Hunt continued. "I understand that you have Walter Brooks over there."

Director Flynn was surprised that the White House already had that information, but he refused to let it show. "Yes Brian, Walter's over here visiting."

"Well he doesn't want to be there so turn him loose." Brian Hunt insisted.

"I don't think that would be a good idea. He has a contract on his head and if he leaves here, he'll be dead within a day."

"People like him get death threats all the time. He can take care of himself." Brian Hunt was emphatic.

"Look, Brian," the director said. "Get your hand out of his wallet and think with your brain for a minute. The same man that's after your money machine killed Paul Cedes earlier today. If this guy can get to Paul Cedes, he sure as hell can get to Walter Brooks and then where're you going to get your campaign money?"

The line went dead for a minute before Brian Hunt returned. "I'll have to call you back in a couple of minutes."

Director Flynn handed the phone back to Francine and looked down the conference room table. "The cat's out of the bag. The White House knows about both Cedes and Brooks. That and the activity in California should spook them if Christine's theory of White House involvement holds up."

AG Peter Eagelton was taken off guard. "You mean to tell me that you guys expected this conspiracy to reach into the White House?"

"Yes," Christine said. "If there's no conspiracy in the White House, then they'll leave Walter Brooks with us for his own protection. If someone over there is in this thing with him, they'll want him out of here before we can break him or hear something that we're not supposed to. They're not dummies, they have to know that the judge is gone and now with Cedes dead and Brooks in our hands, they're going to start to panic."

"I still don't buy it. I think you guys are way off on this," Eagelton said.

As if on cue, the phone rang, and Francine handed it to the director.

"Sir, it's the president."

Director Flynn took the phone as the entire conference room fell silent. "Mr. President, how can I help you today?"

"Hello Martin, I actually just have two things that we need to discuss today. The first one is the Canfield assassination, are you making any headway on it?"

"Yes sir, we have some very strong leads."

"Will I have anything to take to my meeting with me?" The President asked.

"It may not be what you want to hear sir, but we should be able to provide you with a good deal of information by then."

"Damn Martin I was hoping you'd be able to give me some assurances. Oh well just give me what you have. Don't wait until the last minute, we may have to spin whatever you come up with."

"Of course not sir, I'll try to have it to you at least four days before your meeting."

"That'll be just fine Martin. Now about this other thing, Brian tells me you're holding Walter Brooks."

"Holding is a bit strong, sir. We had Walter Brooks come in so that we could protect him better, Mr. President."

"Exactly what are you protecting him from, Martin?"

"Mr. President, I'm sure Brian Hunt told you that there is a contract on Walter Brooks' head. It looks like Hoover is the assassin that holds the contract."

"Hoover? Isn't that the same guy you think shot Canfield?" The president asked.

"Yes sir."

"Why would someone want to kill Walter?"

"That's what we're trying to find out, Mr. President," Director Flynn replied.

"I haven't had a chance to talk to Walter yet, but Brian tells me that Walter doesn't want to stay with you guys. Can't you protect him just as well out at his place?"

"We don't believe so, Mr. President. If Hoover can get to Paul Cedes in his office, he can get to Walter Brooks in his home."

"Paul Cedes? What the hell has he got to do with this?"

"I phoned your office about his assassination earlier today."

"Damn it Martin, I know he was killed, but nobody told me anything about this Hoover being involved in it again."

"Sir, Paul Cedes and Walter Brooks were on the same contract accepted by Hoover. Hoover has already made good on the Paul Cedes portion. We don't think we can stop him from killing Walter Brooks if he leaves the Hoover Building."

"Jesus, Martin! Are you telling me that the Cedes and Brooks assassinations are somehow connected?"

"Yes sir."

"God damn it Martin, why haven't I been kept abreast of all of this?"

"Sir, I believe Brian Hunt has been briefed on most of this information."

"Who do you have running this investigation?"

"Scott Peterson, Tom West, and Christine Peal, and I'm personally supervising it."

"Isn't this the same group that's also in charge of the Canfield assassination?"

"Yes sir it is," Director Flynn replied.

"Martin, I would never tell you how to do your job, but don't you think having the same team running two such high-profile cases at the same time is asking a bit much?"

"Believe me, Mr. President, I would never assign two such high-profile cases to the same team at the same time unless they were related."

"But you just told me that . . . " The president interrupted himself in mid-sentence before he continued. "Martin, can you come over here this evening?"

"Yes sir, should I call Brian Hunt to set up a time?"

"No," the president replied abruptly. There was a slight pause before the president came back. "I have an opening at 7:15. Bring the three agents you have running this case with you. I want to hear what they have to say about this as well."

"We'll be there at 7:15. Sir, what about Walter Brooks?"

"Do you really think he's in that much danger, Martin?"

"Yes sir, I believe if he returns home, he'll be dead in a matter of days."

"OK, then have him cool his heels there for now. If he gives you any trouble, I'll talk to him."

The president hung up and Director Flynn handed the phone back to Francine and let out a deep sigh of relief. "Thank God, from that conversation I would say the president has no clue about what's going on here."

Director Flynn relayed the president's side of the conversation to everyone in the room. They all agreed with the director about the president's apparent lack of involvement.

They did pick up on Hunt's selectivity on what he passed on to the president.

There were several concerns about how they would approach the meeting with the president. "Exactly how much are we going to tell the president tonight?" Christine asked.

Peter Eagelton and Laura Kinsman felt that it was time to tell the president everything, including their suspicions about the White House. Some of the others were not sure the president was ready to hear that his Chief of Staff and his biggest political contributor, and friend, are suspected of being part of a worldwide-conspiracy of racketeering and murder.

The task force decided they should play it by ear and tell the president whatever felt appropriate at the time.

Before the meeting broke, Francine had a report on the purchase of Western Oil. "As you requested sir, I tracked down the sale of Western Oil. Midland Enterprises was the buyer. Midland is a subsidiary of Underground Technologies, which is owned by Venture Drilling, which of course is owned by Venture Global."

"It looks like Walter Brooks' stake in the world-wide oil reserves just increased." Christine observed.

"It increased by about three percent," Francine said. "That's why he needed help in Congress and the justice department to get it through. Walter Brooks now owns about forty percent of the oil reserves outside of the Middle East and Russia. Although we think he just recently took a position in the Russian fields."

Scott smacked himself in the forehead in a sign of recognition. "Damn, that's why they wanted Congressman McCall's help to push the Encryption Technology bill through. They're going to trade Encryption technology for a stake in the Russian oil fields. Holy cow, they're trying to corner the oil market."

"If that happens, they'll be able to put a stranglehold on most governments around the world, including the United States," the director said.

"At least we have the mastermind next door. If we cut off the head, we may be able to stop this juggernaut," Tom said.

Christine was still uneasy with Hunt's role in all of this. "We really can't do too much until we figure out how the White House fits into this. We also still have that white supremacist group out there. I'm certain that they're planning something with Brooks and his people."

"Christine's right. There's still a lot we don't know," the director said. "Tom, have you had a chance to track down anything else on that African connection?"

"No sir, not yet," replied Tom.

"Okay then, I think it's time to talk to Walter Brooks," the director said. "Christine, you and Francine join me. Scott, I want you and Tom behind the mirror observing. Everybody else, I'll see you tomorrow at the briefing. Peter, if you and Laura want to wait in my office, we'll get her to safety as soon as we finish with Walter."

Prior to going to meet with Walter Brooks, they stopped by the director's office to discuss strategy. Christine wasn't too excited about Francine sitting in on the questioning, she knew that would make it less intense. On the other hand, Francine's presence for some reason did seem to make Walter Brooks more cooperative.

As they entered the room, Walter Brooks hung up his cellular phone and launched into a tirade directed at Director Flynn. "Martin, who the hell do you think you are? I've been here for over four hours without so much as a peep from you. I talked to Brian Hunt a couple of hours ago and he said the president was going to order you to let me go."

Director Flynn tried to calm Walter Brooks. "Listen Walter, I'm sorry I haven't had a chance to catch up with you. We've been trying to figure out what's going on here, and if you'll be patient for just a few more minutes, I'll lay it all out for you."

"All you have is a few more minutes," Walter Brooks huffed. "I just ordered my pilot to get his butt back here to pick me up."

"I wish you hadn't done that, Walter, at least not until we've had a chance to talk."

"Martin, you have thirty minutes to make your case. If I don't leave on my helicopter when it gets here, there will be hell to pay."

"Nobody wants to cause you any trouble or inconvenience, Walter, but your life is in real danger."

"So you say. You seem to forget, I have over twenty security people at my estate."

"That's not going to protect you from this assassin," Christine said.

"Then what makes you think I would be safe here?" Brooks snapped back.

"Even Hoover wouldn't risk an assassination attempt inside an FBI compound," assured the Director.

"OK, if everything you say is true, what are you going to do about it? I'm obviously not staying here forever. I have companies to run."

This was the perfect opening for Christine to start working him. "To start with sir, we are going to have to find the connection between you, Paul Cedes, Judge Feldman, Laura Kinsman, President Canfield, and an oilman named Michael Peron."

As Christine, Director Flynn, and Francine stood back and watched, they got the reaction that they were expecting: first shock and then anger. "What the hell do you mean connection, I don't even know these people. What do they have to do with an assassination attempt on my life?"

Christine could tell that she was getting to him. Walter Brooks' practiced speech pattern was starting to break down. She continued to press. "President Canfield was assassinated by the assassin we've dubbed 'Hoover.' Your name and those others were all found on the same contract that 'Hoover' is currently working on. Also, we believe Hoover killed Michael Peron."

Christine paused for effect but not long enough for Walter Brooks to respond. "We already connected Laura Kinsman and Michael Peron. Ms. Kinsman was working with Mr. Peron on allegations of corruption in the oil industry. We know that Mr. Cedes and Judge Feldman had several dealings with each other, and of course we know that you and President Canfield had been good friends over the years. What we need to know is what your relationship is with all of these other people. How you are all connected?"

"What the hell is she talking about, Martin?" Brooks demanded. "I don't know any of those people, especially if they have anything to do with anything illegal. Have you brought in this Laura Kinsman or this Judge Feldman to talk to them?"

"Yes we have, Walter, they're both in the building right now," the director told him.

"Well what do they have to say about all of this?" Brooks asked.

"That's kind of interesting," Christine said. "Laura Kinsman still maintains her only association with Peron or Paul Cedes is through her job as assistant attorney general. We have, however, tied Judge Feldman much closer to Paul Cedes, and even Peron." Christine paused long enough to let her comments sink in with Brooks before she continued. She was about to corner her prey. "When Judge Feldman found out he was on a hit list, he told us a story about worldwide corruption and an attempt through a criminal conspiracy to take over the world's energy markets. He's talking to one of our interrogation teams right now.

"The judge is looking for immunity and a guaranteed place in the witness protection program. He should be able to give us most of the names involved in this conspiracy and hopefully why this particular group of names should end up on the same hit list." Christine had put Walter Brooks on notice.

They watched as Brooks began to unravel. They knew his survival instinct would be to get out of there. He didn't disappoint them.

"That explains how Feldman may be involved but it doesn't explain why my name is on that list with them, unless somebody is out there trying to take over my oil companies. If what Feldman said about some-one trying to corner the energy market is true, then my companies are in serious danger. That's probably why my name is on that list. That's an-other reason why I can't stay here.

"You guys haven't convinced me that you can protect me any better than my own people. So unless you're going to hold me at gunpoint, I'm leaving when my helicopter gets here."

Director Flynn kept the pressure on. "We still don't think that's a good idea, Walter. Let Christine and her people spend some time with the judge; maybe he can tell us how you fit into this."

"I don't need anybody to tell me how I fit into anything. I just need to get back to my place and right now. Did you talk to the president?" Brooks asked.

"Yes Frank, I did."

"Then just follow your orders and let me the hell out of here."

Christine was watching for Walter Brooks' reaction waiting for the director to tell him that the president told him to keep him there. What she got instead was her own mouth dropping to the floor when she heard the director's response.

"All right Walter, it's against my better judgment but somebody will be here in about fifteen minutes to take you to your helicopter."

"Good, don't worry Martin, I'll make sure you're relieved of any responsibility if anything happens to me."

Director Flynn wasn't quite finished. "Walter, I'm only agreeing to this if you accept two of my agents to go with you to review your security."

After a brief pause while he thought it over, Walter Brooks agreed to director Flynn's conditions.

"Okay Martin, you've got a deal, but only if Francine is one of those agents."

Director Flynn thought about it for a moment and though Francine wasn't a security specialist, he knew she could handle Walter Brooks better than anyone, so he agreed.

Once back in his office, the director cut off the questions he knew were coming.

"I made a tactical decision in there. Walter has too many friends to try to hold him on what we have. I also don't think we're going to break him the conventional way. Christine did a good job of pushing him to the edge, and the best way to take advantage of that is to send him home where he's comfortable and have our people there see what he's up to." When the director didn't hear any dissension he continued. "Christine, you're going to coordinate his security, and Francine, I'll be getting wiretaps in the next fifteen minutes; it'll be your job to bug his cell phone and the main junction to the house.

"Christine, you tap the PCs and whatever other communications equipment he has at the estate. If we play our cards right, we could wrap up this whole organization through him.

"Christine, remember that your primary job is still to keep him alive. If anything happens to him, you may have the shortest career as a ASAC in FBI history."

"What about the tails when he's off his estate? He uses that helicopter of his quite a bit," asked Christine.

The director turned to Scott. "You take charge of that. The three of you coordinate before you head out. Francine, you should go out with Brooks in the helicopter and Christine will join you after our meeting with the president."

As they were about to leave, the director called after Christine. "Christine, that was good work in there. I think you set him up nicely. He should be panicked enough to make a move soon."

Chapters 24

Christine needed time to think. She did that best in her car. Tom West and Jim Brodrick had given her a lot to think about. They had solidified the connection between Hoover, Canfield, Cedes, Brooks, Ballard, and Canon. Even though Ballard and Canon committed the actual murders of her parents, she was now certain that the rest of these people were in on the planning of it. She was also convinced that the murder of her parents had something to do with the African country of Cameroon.

Questions about her father and mother were still running through her mind as she was driving through the streets of Washington. Did one or both of her parents witness something that got them killed? How did they get all of the money? Did they own the oil fields in Cameroon? What was she supposed to do with that money?

After trying to unravel the mysteries for about an hour, Christine found herself in the community of Kettering, Maryland—a small bedroom community outside D.C. This was a place she hadn't been to in several years. As she drove the streets in her Viper, she felt strangely out of place in this conservative middle class community. She turned off Central Avenue onto Lake Arbor Way, and wished her Volvo wasn't stranded in Braddock.

Christine pulled up in front of a well-manicured yard with a half-moon driveway leading to the front entrance of a large brick home and back out onto Lake Arbor Way. She paused for a moment, then committed herself and drove down the driveway to the front entrance. Christine took a deep breath, stepped out of the car, walked up and knocked on the door.

When the door opened, she was face-to-face with a slightly stooped small black woman in her late sixties, drying her hands on her apron. The woman paused for a moment as she looked at Christine and then a let out a scream of recognition.

"Oh my goodness—Chrissy it's you!" The old lady grabbed Christine by the hand and pulled her into the house. She turned and yelled to her husband. "Honey, Honey, you'll never guess who's here. Come here, hurry." The woman turned back to Christine and gave her a big hug. "Oh Chrsisy, where've you been? Let's look at you." The woman stood back as she checked out Christine. "You look so good. We haven't heard from you in so long. We didn't know what happened to you."

Christine just smiled as she followed the old lady into the living room. She could hear the heavy feet of a large man coming up the stairs. Turning toward the stairs, she saw a large black man in his late sixties wearing an FBI hat, overalls, and work boots.

When he spotted Christine he slowed down and the smile on his face disappeared. "Hello Christine, I see you found our address."

Christine let go of the woman's hand and walked toward the man in the FBI hat. "I never lost the address, Virgil. I'm sorry I haven't been by. I just haven't been real proud of myself lately and couldn't bring myself to look you guys in the eye."

"Christine, it's been over ten years; nothing could be that bad."

"I did try; I even pulled up in front of the house, I just couldn't bring myself to come in."

"Your mother has been very worried about you."

The woman walked between the two and grabbed each of them under the arm and led them back into the living room. "The two of you sit down, let me get some coffee. Oh Chrissy, it's so good to see you."

"Your mother's right, it is good to see you," Virgil said.

Christine sat on the couch as Virgil planted himself in his favorite recliner. "Virgil, believe me, I'm glad I finally had the courage to come in," Christine said.

"Christine, this is and always will be your home. When we took you in, we didn't do it just for the good days. We want to be there for you on your not-so-good days as well. We love you as our very own, you should know that by now. Can't you tell how much Eleanor missed you?"

Just then Eleanor walked back in the room and sat next to Christine on the couch. "Don't let him fool you, honey. He's missed you as much as I did. He wears that hat you gave him when you graduated from the FBI academy every day."

Christine was fighting back tears. "I've missed both of you. After my parents got killed, you were the only people I felt safe with. You brought me up and shared everything you had with me, even your values. That's why I couldn't come to see you earlier. I've done things that I'm not proud of and I would do them again if I had to."

"Christine, we're your family now, you can come to us with any-thing," Virgil assured her.

"Honey, we love you no matter what." Eleanor said as she took Christine's hands in hers. "We pray for you every night. No matter what you do, we're gonna be proud of you."

Christine was losing her battle against the tears as they began to seep out of the corners of her eyes one at a time. "We've never really talked about my real parents. Can you tell me a little about them?"

Christine could tell that Virgil got a little uncomfortable, but Eleanor wasn't derailed by her question. "Honey, you were seven years old when your parents died. You have to remember what good people they were. Always helping everybody. They were the most generous people in Virgil's congregation, both with their time and their money. If they hadn't been dead when Virgil retired, I'd have sworn that they'd been the ones that donated the money to the church to buy this place for Virgil and me. You know Virgil tried to turn down this house, but the church elders said that if he didn't take it, the church wouldn't get an additional $250,000 that this anonymous donor promised."

"That's right, and as soon as we moved into this house, the church got the $250,000," Virgil added.

"I know my parents were good people, and I'm sure in a way they had something to do with you getting this house." Christine got up and looked out the large picture window facing Lake Arbor as she talked. "What I've been wanting to know for a long time, is what did my father do for work, how did he make his living? I want to know why he died?"

Virgil was about to light a cigarette when Eleanor gave him a dirty look. He put the pack of cigarettes back in his pocket and stood up.

"Why don't you and I go for a walk down to the dock," Virgil said to Christine. He then turned to his wife. "Mother, while we're out why don't you go and get that suitcase that Winston asked us to hang on to."

Christine was suddenly alert. "Are you talking about Winston, my father?"

"Yes, I am, Christine. Your dad gave me a suitcase to hold a long time ago."

"What's in it? Let me see it."

"I don't know what's in it. I've never opened it. Let's go for a walk and then you can take it with you or open it here or whatever you want to do."

They went down the steps and out the back door into the yard. As they were walking through the yard, Christine could tell that the plants and flowers were meticulously cared for. A stone step led to the dock, where a small fishing boat was moored. Christine could read the name on the back of the boat: "Christine." She realized how much a part of their life she was and began to feel bad about the way she had cut them out of hers. Without thinking she wrapped her arm around Virgil's as they stood watching the ripples of the lake.

"So tell me why we had to come out here for you to tell me about my parents?" Christine asked Virgil.

Virgil lit a cigarette before he began talking. "I didn't want your mother to get upset. The sixties were difficult times to be black in America. Your father was a very proud man. He ran his own business, a small investment firm in downtown Washington. In those times, that was probably not a good thing for a black man to be doing. His business was ransacked several times, but he just kept rebuilding it. He always said that he ran an investment company because money knows no color. I'm afraid in the end money did have a color. He was making good money for several black families. Most of us at that time didn't have any money for him to invest, but those who did, gave it to him gladly and he made more for them." Virgil took a long drag on his cigarette before continuing.

"I don't know much about your family before you arrived in our community, but I do know that if there was a family in need, black or white, your mom and dad were there to help. They also worked with the civil rights movements. The night your parents were killed, they had just been to a rally. The FBI concluded that some Klansmen broke into your house and shot your mom and dad and probably dumped you in the woods somewhere."

Virgil exhaled a series of smoke rings into the air and continued. "Friends of your family found you hiding in their garage the next day and brought you to the church.

"Eleanor and I decided not to turn you over to the police and waited instead for relatives to show up to claim you. When none did, we decided to officially adopt you about a year later.

"Back then, there wasn't a lot of paperwork if a black family wanted to adopt a black child. The officials really didn't care, they figured it was just one more black kid off the streets. To us, you became the daughter that we could never have. We gave you our last name, but we never wanted you to forget your natural family. That's why when we adopted you we just added Peal after Barber."

"I know, Virgil, but Christine Barber Peal just never felt right. I've been going only by Christine Peal for a long time now." Christine wanted to change the subject. "What about the suitcase?" Christine asked.

"Your father came to the house one night after he'd received another death threat. He said that he wanted to leave this suitcase with us along with a letter for you. He said it was a precaution in case anything ever happened to him and your mother. I was to give the letter and the suitcase to your guardian to hold until your thirtieth birthday."

"That was seven years ago, Virgil! Why haven't you given me the suitcase and the letter?" Christine demanded.

Virgil took another deep drag on his cigarette before answering. "Stop and think about that for a minute Christine. When was the last time you came to see us?"

Christine was embarrassed and answered sheepishly. "I'm sorry, Virgil, I should have called to let you both know I was OK. Ten years is a long time."

Virgil flipped his cigarette butt into the lake and stepped onto his boat. "Now tell me what you've done that you haven't come to see us for so long. Remember, I'm still a member of the cloth, and confession is good for the soul."

"I wish I could, Virgil, I really do—maybe someday. What I can tell you though, is that I know the Klan didn't shoot my parents. I was there; I saw who did it."

Virgil kept fiddling around on the boat and without looking up said, "I know you did Chrissy, I know you did. We just never wanted to push you about it. We figured that when you got ready you'd tell us about it. Do you want to talk about it now?"

Christine thought a moment and then decided against it. "Not yet, Virgil, maybe later."

Christine extended her hand to help Virgil out of the boat. "Let's go up and see what's in the suitcase."

Christine's heart was racing. Would she find the key to her past or just an old pair of socks and pajamas? She felt like a kid at Christmas, wanting to run ahead and open her presents.

When they got back to the house, Eleanor was waiting for them in the living room with what was more like a footlocker than a suitcase in front of her. Her face lit up when she saw Christine and Virgil. "I forgot how heavy this was. I almost didn't get it up here by myself."

Virgil leaned down and kissed his wife on the forehead. "I'm sorry honey. It's been a while since I've moved it. I should have been here to help you."

Eleanor waved her husband off and encouraged Christine to open the suitcase. "Come on, honey, I've been dying to see what's in there for over thirty years."

"I told her that she could take it with her and open it in private," Virgil told his wife.

Christine dropped to her knees and ran her hands over the top of the case. "No, I want to open it here with my family."

Virgil pulled his wallet out of his back pocket and withdrew a key. "Then you'll need this, it's been in my wallet since the night your dad gave it to me."

Christine took the key and unlocked the case. All three held their breath as Christine lifted the top of the case. She wasn't sure what to expect, but she knew it wasn't what she found.

As they looked into the box, they saw African masks, statues and drawings. Christine was confused as she picked up the artifacts and carefully inspected them. "What's all this, Virgil?"

"Do you think these are worth a lot of money and that's why your family left them for you?" Eleanor asked.

"I don't think so. They left me a lot of cash," Christine said without thinking.

Virgil picked up on the off-handed remark. "What do you mean they left you a lot of cash? This and the letter are the only things that your parents left for you."

"I'm sorry Virgil, but they did leave me a lot of money. I was tracked down by an attorney just after my thirtieth birthday and he gave me access to a fund that they had set up for me when I was still a baby."

"So it was you that bought us this house?" Virgil asked.

"Yes, I wanted to give something back to you, since you guys gave me so much."

Eleanor came off the couch, kneeled beside Christine and gave her a big hug. "We love you honey, you didn't need to do this for us." Eleanor looked at the contents of the box and then at Virgil. "Virgil, honey, why don't you give her the letter; maybe it explains what some of these things are."

Virgil Peal walked to the fireplace and took a framed picture of the three of them at Christine's high school graduation from the mantel. He flipped it over, took the back off and removed a sealed envelope. As he handed the envelope to Christine he gave her one final word of caution. "Christine, whatever's in that envelope, I want you to remember that you have family right here. We'll be here no matter what. Also remember that the times were very different when your father wrote that letter."

Christine took the letter and began to open it trying not to tear the envelope. She could tell by its feel that this letter was several pages long.

She unfolded the letter, took a deep breath and began to read.

Dearest Christine,

If you are reading this, two things have happened. First, your mother and I are no longer with you, second it is your thirtieth birthday.

Your mother and I have written this letter to you every year on your birthday since you were born.

Today is your seventh birthday; we hope to be able to continue to write this letter every year until your thirtieth birthday. At which time we will sit down with you and explain all of this in person.

Due to the volatility in our own country, and the hostility here in America, your mother and I wanted to write you these letters in case anything were ever to happen to us.

I hope that you're seated.

Your name is not Christine Barber. Barber is the name we took when we came the United States. Your real name is Etina Boinya, you are the daughter of Winston and Marita Boinya and the only niece (so far— your mother and I are working on getting you a brother) of Mafani Boinya, president of Cameroon.

You and your cousins are the future of our country.

Christine had to read that last paragraph several times before it sank in. Her family came from Cameroon, the same country that Tom talked about in the briefing. She just found the link between the conspiracy and her family. It was Cameroon. Christine wiped a tear from the edge of her eye as she continued to read the letter.

Mafani, my older brother, and I were born to Shamba Boinya, the son of King Amuela Boinya, the last of the great African kings. He was the leader that united the tribes under a centralized system of government.

We are members of the Fang tribe from southern Cameroon. You are a descendent from a long line of leaders, chiefs, and kings of the Fang people.

Your grandfather Shamba Boinya who succeeded Amuela saw that Cameroon's political structure had to change if Cameroon was to be part of the twentieth century. In order to meet that change, he sent my brother and me to be educated in England.

It was soon discovered that Cameroon was rich in natural resources, especially oil. Your grandfather fought against western interests taking over the country's natural resources. He believed that the resources were the property of the Cameroonian people and that they should reap their rewards.

Due to his strong beliefs, your grandfather was assassinated in 1956 and Ahmadou Lido of the Bamoun tribe assumed the throne. Your uncle and I were exiled.

In nineteen-sixty Cameroon was once again to have a democratic election after the French and British government granted us our sovereignty. During this election, although we were no longer in Cameroon, our family name had such strong standing that your uncle Mafani was elected president.

Things changed for the better in Cameroon after he became president. I decided I could help my country more by better understanding those wanting to own its resources, than I could from within. With that in mind we moved to America.

Christine's hands were shaking as she was holding the letter. She stopped to gather herself and handed the pages she had already read to Virgil, who with Eleanor looking over his shoulder began to read them in silence. Christine continued reading.

America is a tough country to live in if you are not white. Many here have heard of Africa, but few know of its many independent nations.

Being the son of an African king is not something you want to let people in this country know about.

The assumption in America is that we are all still banging on our drums in loincloths. There is a core hatred and evil toward all those with black or dark skin. The special hatred for anyone of royal African lineage forces us to continue to use the name of Barber.

Most American corporations are aware of the vast resources that exist on the African continent. Their goal appears to be to steal as many of these resources as possible, before our people learn what we have.

Within the past year, Mafani has come under extreme pressure to turn several of our prized offshore oil fields over to American and British oil companies. Mafani has refused unless they guarantee the use of only Cameroonian labor and return fifty percent of the profits to the Cameroonian economy. Opposition to his policies has been so strong that he fears for his family's life, but he dare not send his family away during this crisis. This would be a sign of weakness and show fear to his countrymen.

To protect the family name and the right to lead Cameroon should anything happen to him, Mafani sent several of the family's most prized possessions to me for safekeeping.

Over the last few months he also moved over twenty million dollars out of Cameroon to be used to set up a government in exile until we are able to return to Cameroon, if it should come to that.

Since you are now reading this letter, we have to assume that something happened to us before your eighth birthday. If my brother has not contacted you in the past twenty-two years, then you are bound to be very confused.

Christine had to stop reading her mind was racing. She wasn't as confused as her father thought she might be—in fact things were becoming clearer. She now knew why her parents died. It was all for oil. Her parents died so that Walter Brooks could get to Cameroon's oil. All she could think of was to get to Walter Brooks and cut him to pieces, but not until he knew who she was. Christine's thoughts were broken as she heard Eleanor shriek.

"You're a princess, you're a real live princess!"

Christine just sat there for a moment and then continued reading as her tears fell on the page, smudging the words.

Should anything happen to us, I have left instructions with friends telling them what to do and how to help you. Please don't be angry with them; I left strict instructions that you were not to be given access to this letter, the arti-

facts, or the money until you were thirty. Your mother and I believed that you should not be burdened with your heritage until you have had a chance to enjoy your own life first.

In a few days you will be contacted by someone and given access to some money. Our hope is that you will have to share this with your cousins. If you receive the full amount, then your cousins are no longer alive.

There should also be a large block of money. This money is to be used to fight for Cameroon's independence if it is controlled by outside forces.

If Cameroon is a democratic society, then you may use these funds to establish charities that benefit the people of Cameroon. If you believe Cameroon has drifted from the ideals of your uncle and grandfather, then you may use these funds to start a political party or run for office yourself.

Attached to the end of this letter you will find a list of names and cities: these are all Cameroonian refugees who have come to America in the last six months. Those still alive when you read this letter will help you better understand your homeland and then you'll know the right thing to do.

If you are reading this letter, then you are probably also looking into a box of statues, masks, tapestries, and photographs.

These will prove to the world and to your countrymen that you are truly the descendent of King Amuela Boinya.

The statue of the king sitting on a low throne wearing the projected visor as his crown and holding the sword of state in his left hand is King Amuela. The terracotta tobacco pipe was a gift from the Bamoun tribe to your grandfather, King Shamba. The Royal Elephant Mask was a gift to King Amuela from the Tikaar the grasslanders. The bronze mask is the Batcham mask from the Batcham tribe. The Batcham chair, of which there is a photo in the box, along with all of the other large items in the photos, is in storage in England. If you find Cameroon to be a safe and developed country please place these items into a museum for the people of Cameroon.

There is so much more that your mother and I wish to say to you. Perhaps on your next birthday we'll be writing to you and your brother.

Always know that we love you and always remember that you are a Boinya, direct descendant of the great kings of Africa. The right to lead Cameroon is in your blood.

Love Always: Prince Winston Boinya
Princess Marita Boinya

Mom & Dad

Christine put the letter down and without thinking picked up the statue of King Boinya—this was her great grandfather, ruler of a proud people. She just stared at the statue until she heard Virgil's voice.

"Christine, are you OK?"

"I'm better than I've been in a long time. I finally know who I am, and why my family was murdered."

Virgil didn't know what to think, all he could do was ask. "Why?"

Christine put down the statue of King Boinya and picked up the terracotta pipe as she talked.

"I found out today that in 1969 the president of Cameroon was assassinated and the current regime was put into power. I didn't understand it then, but I do now.

"According to this letter, my father's last name of Boinya would have been enough to get him elected to replace his brother after his assassination. So the people that assassinated the president of Cameroon also killed my father in 1969 to keep him from returning to Cameroon."

"Christine, with what you know now, and this letter, you have enough to go to the authorities." Virgil said.

"It's not that easy, Virgil. I saw who shot my father in the back and who put a bullet into my mother's head; believe me, going to the authorities wouldn't help."

"Christine, the times are different. You more than anyone should know that. Look at you, you're an FBI agent. In 1969 it would have been unheard for a black woman to be FBI agent."

"I know times have changed, but in some ways they really haven't. That reminds me, I'm meeting with the president tonight, I should get going."

"The president? My baby is a princess and she's meeting with the president. Oh, I'm so proud of you!" Eleanor exclaimed.

"What are you going to do with all of this?" Virgil asked, pointing to the artifacts.

"I was hoping to leave them here for now."

"Oh, we wouldn't know how to take care of this kind of stuff. This has to be worth millions of dollars, what if we break it?" Eleanor insisted.

"It's no different than it has been for the past thirty years. It's important though that no one finds out about any of this until I'm ready."

Virgil and Eleanor agreed; Christine packed everything away and helped Virgil move the box of artifacts back into the basement closet. She put the letter and list of names in her pocket and said her good-byes.

Christine felt like a new woman, she really was of royal lineage. She also, for the first time in over thirty years, felt that she had an understanding of who she was.

Christine had a lot to think about. Right now though, she had a meeting with the president to get ready for.

Chapter 25

The drive back to the Hoover Building went too quickly for Christine. Her mind was trying to absorb and connect everything she just learned. Her original plan had been to follow Greenfield's advice, go to Hoover's home or office, and find his secret files. Greenfield was right—a man like Hoover would never be too far from those files.

Driving by the Department of Justice, the FBI's headquarters in Hoover's day, Christine decided the risk was too great. Especially since she already knew most of the things that would be in those files.

It was more likely that Hoover would have secret storage places in his home anyway. If the opportunity presented itself she would still attempt that search.

Christine pulled into the FBI building and went straight to her office, where she found her secretary, Doris, waiting for her.

"Everyone is waiting for you; the director is having a fit."

"What's the problem, Doris?"

"You have a meeting with the president tonight and the director wants to review it first."

"Oh, is that all? Where're they meeting?"

"In the director's office. Ms. Peal, you should also know that the official notice naming you ASAC of OCD came through today. Congratulations!"

"Thank you, Doris, but it's just Acting ASAC."

"No ma'am, I think you should look at the memo. It definitely says 'appointed to the position of Assistant Special Agent in Charge of the Organized Crime Division. Should I have facilities come by and move your stuff to the ASAC's office?" Doris asked with an ear-to-ear grin on her face.

"No, I'm sure it's an error. The director told me himself that he wasn't making the final call until after this case is wrapped up. Besides, I want to stay down here."

Doris acted disappointed as she handed Christine a folder. "ASAC Peal," Doris teased, "you will need these files for your meeting. This is the latest on Hoover, Judge Feldman, and the number the assassin from California had with him."

"Thank you Doris, and don't forget to start interviewing new assistants for me. As an ASAC you surely don't expect me to make do with the same assistant I had as a mere special agent," Christine teased Doris.

When Christine entered the director's office, Scott and Tom were already sitting at a small conference room table reviewing documents. The director from behind his desk acknowledged Christine's entrance.

"Well look at this, your first official function as ASAC of OCD and you're late. Tom promised me that if I made him ASAC, he'd be on time to my meetings."

Christine looked around the room, saw the smiles on everyone's face, and relaxed. "I'm sorry sir, I wasn't aware that we had a meeting scheduled, and had some personal business to take care of."

The director stepped out from behind his desk and shook her hand. "Congratulations, it's now official; you are the FBI's youngest assistant special agent in charge heading a major division."

"You mean acting ASAC sir?" Christine asked.

"No, Christine, I talked it over with some of my key advisors including these two right here, and they all thought I should make it permanent."

Christine was shocked—she hadn't expected this. Too many good things have happened to her today. She was waiting for someone to pinch her and wake her up. "Thank you for your confidence, sir," Christine said. "I assure you, I will make the best of this opportunity."

Tom and Scott congratulated Christine and after all the backslapping and handshaking was completed, they got down to business.

"Do we have anything more than we did this afternoon?" the director asked.

"Not really, AG Eagelton traced most of Walter Brooks' companies, and he thinks that the entire criminal enterprise is being run out of a holding company called 'Global Ventures'." Tom said.

"Has he got any proof?" Scott asked.

"No, but Cedes and Canfield were on its board, as well as some of the major bankers and oil men in the world."

"That doesn't mean much, Tom," Christine said. "In a company that size we would expect that quality of board members. Cedes was an ambassador and Canfield a president—what company wouldn't want them on their board?"

"You have a point," Director Flynn said. "But, it does give you and Francine something to look for while you're at Brooks' house. I bet if you find a Global Ventures file, you'll have taken your first step to replacing Scott or myself."

Christine smiled as she volleyed back. "I wouldn't want to force either of you into retirement before you're ready."

Tom had also tracked down the number the assassin gave them to call for his immunity. "We traced the number to a switching unit in an empty office in Boston. From there we tracked it to a warehouse on Telegraph Road outside the Beltway. The switching machine was off but the warehouse phone is still turned on. We're sitting on the warehouse; if we don't get anything by morning we'll go in and dust the place."

"Good, pass all of this on to the guy we got it from and let's show him that he's on the wrong side." The director said.

There were no additional developments and the director told them he would take the lead with the president and they should talk only if the president addressed them directly.

Their strategy hadn't changed much from the afternoon meeting. They were still going to determine how much to tell the president based on his reactions.

Tom, Scott, Christine, and Director Flynn arrived at the White House together in the director's car. Director Flynn's driver dropped them off at the Northeast Gate where they entered the White House from the rear. They were escorted down a hall and into the library on the first floor.

This was Christine's first visit to the White House, and like most Americans she was impressed just to be there. In the library the others treated it like any other library and sat to wait for the president. Christine walked around the room and couldn't help but be in awe of everything around her. With her back to the entrance she stopped at the fireplace and closely examined a lamp on the mantle. Without turning around she commented on how pink this room was. Not at all what she expected for a library in the White House. A strange voice answered.

"That's not really pink; my wife tells me that this library is 'highlighted with Rose Tones.' That lamp you're looking at is an 'Argand'—it was a gift from the Marquis de Lafayette to General Knox, the secretary of war under Washington."

Christine turned around and found herself staring at the president of the United States. The president turned and greeted Director Flynn who along with the others had stood when the president entered.

"Martin, I'm glad you could make it."

"Thank you, Mr. President. I believe you know Scott Peterson and Tom West."

The president shook both men's hands and then walked over to Christine.

Director Flynn introduced her. "Sir, this is Assistant Special Agent in Charge of the Organized Crime Division Christine Peal."

The president looked confused as he greeted her. "Welcome to the White House, Ms. Peal, but excuse me if I'm not up on the latest personnel changes at the bureau, did ASAC Martinez leave us?"

"No sir, we just made some personnel adjustments," Director Flynn said.

"In that case, congratulations ASAC Peal. Why don't we all sit down and you can start with your briefing," the president said

As Director Flynn was about to start, a valet entered with coffee. The president thanked him and said that he didn't want to be disturbed.

Director Flynn knew that at a meeting like this, there was usually at least one advisor with the president.

"Sir, will Brian Hunt be joining us?" The director asked

"No, not this time Martin. I thought it would be best that I hear what you have to say myself, before we involve the rest of the staff.

"We're meeting here instead of the Oval Office, because I want to hear the truth. I don't want anybody to be concerned about tapes or history or anything like that. I want to know what the hell is going on. You can start with what you alluded to on the phone. Exactly how are Canfield's and Cedes' assassinations related to the contract on Walter? "

"Sir, we believe President Canfield, Ambassador Cedes, and two FBI agents were all assassinated by the same person," Director Flynn started.

"What FBI agents? I haven't heard about them," the president demanded.

"One was actually a former agent who, at the time of his murder, was serving as Walter Brooks' head of security; the other one was ADIC Ballard about ten years ago."

"Are you trying to tell me these murders go back ten years?"

"Actually sir, it's our belief that these murders are related to a series of meetings in the fall of 1969 between then Vice President Canfield, Director Hoover, head of African operations for the CIA Paul Cedes, and a young maverick businessman named Walter Brooks."

"That's one heck of a group; what exactly happened at that meeting?" The president asked.

"We're not sure sir. Those meetings are the only things we know of that tie all of those people together. The only time the two FBI agents worked together was during the time period when they worked on Hoover's special cases. Canfield's vice presidential papers showed that the same two agents attended one of the meetings with Hoover."

"So you think that what ever happened at those meetings is behind these murders thirty years later?" the president asked with a hint of doubt in his voice.

"Sir, Tom and Jim Brodrick over at NCAVC have taken a long look at this and these meetings are the only common denominator they've found. The same person is definitely responsible for all of these assassinations. Why there was a ten-year gap we don't know.

"We do know that during the fall of '69, there was a coup in Cameroon and then shortly thereafter Walter Brooks received exclusive rights to the bulk of the Cameroon oil deposits. We also know that in the last few years of Canfield's administration, he appointed Paul Cedes as ambassador to Cameroon. Which, as you know, sir, is highly unusual."

"Are you trying to tell me that President Ackerman's administration conspired with the CIA and an American businessman to overthrow Cameroon for its oil?"

"No sir, we don't believe it was officially sanctioned. We don't believe President Ackerman or the CIA were even aware of it," the director said.

"You think Canfield ran this by himself?"

"Yes sir, we do. With Cedes controlling the U.S. resources in Africa,

Canfield as Vice President had certain resources available to him, and with Walter Brooks providing the funding it would have been easy for them. ”

"OK Martin, what about Hoover and the FBI? At that time their responsibility didn't reach that far. How could Hoover possibly fit into this?”

"I don't know sir. Our best guess is that it was Hoover's job to keep whatever Cameroonians were in the United States from causing any trouble," the director said

"This is incredible. Why is all of this surfacing now, and why does this assassin, the one you dubbed Hoover, want to kill all of these people?” the president asked.

"We don't know, sir. Perhaps it has something to do with the gathering of the African states.”

"I think I need to get my African analysts in here," the president said.

"Before you do that sir, there are a few other things you should know.”

"You mean it gets better than this?”

"I'm afraid so sir," the director said. "We believe the same people who plotted the overthrow of Cameroon, forged a white collar crime syndicate with the express purpose of taking over the economies of the world.”

"Christ, Martin, are you listening to yourself? Now you've got one of my biggest contributors taking over the world.”

"I know it sounds far-fetched sir, but the pieces are all there. We are on the trail of a criminal conspiracy that leads to the halls of Congress and courthouses throughout the country. I believe what we have here is larger and more pervasive than ABSCAM, GREYLORD, and ILLWIND combined.”

As the director was talking, Christine remembered ABSCAM as being the investigation that led to a large number of convictions of U.S. Congressmen and GREYLORD being the undercover operation that brought down corruption in the judiciary, but she couldn't remember ILLWIND.

"Do you have any proof that any of this is actually happening?” The president asked.

"Yes sir, we have a judge at the Hoover Building that confessed to a good portion of it. He implicated Walter Brooks and Paul Cedes as being part of this syndicate." The director waited for the president's reaction.

The president sat in silence for a minute as he thought about what he had just heard. "OK give me the bad news—you can't run an operation like this without somebody in the administration. Don't tell me that my vice president is running me like Ackerman's did him."

"No sir," Director Flynn said. "It's not your vice president, we believe it's your chief of staff."

"Hunt!" the president, exclaimed. "You think it's Brian Hunt?"

"Yes sir, we have evidence that proves Brian Hunt ordered an assassination while he was in London with you."

"What do you mean you have evidence? If you have evidence why isn't he in jail?"

"Sir, we have Brian Hunt on tape giving a prearranged signal to a hit team in San Francisco to kill a judge."

"I can't believe this; if you know all that, why haven't you come to me before this?"

Director Flynn looked at the floor as he answered. "Sir, to tell you the truth, until this afternoon we were not sure if you were involved or not."

The president got out of his chair, paced up and down the room for several moments before turning around and pointing his index finger at the director.

"God Damn it Martin, you know me better than that!"

"Yes sir," was all the director could say.

The president was about to make another point when there was a knock at the door.

"I told you I didn't want to be disturbed," the president yelled at the door.

Without opening it the aide informed the president that Admiral Karcher was here for his eight-thirty meeting. The president opened the door and asked his aide to reschedule the meeting with the admiral for six in the morning. The president then returned his attention to Director Flynn and the others.

"I find all of this hard to believe, but for now I'll take your word for it. The first thing I have to do is fire that weasel Hunt and we better get justice and the attorney general in here."

Director Flynn interrupted the president. "Mr. President, I think we need to proceed with caution. There is still a lot we don't know. We know they call themselves the Millenium but we don't know everyone on the council."

"I can't pretend I don't know about this," the president said.

"Sir, it's imperative that you give us a couple of more days to work out the rest of this case. We believe your meeting with the African states is in danger."

"Not this Hoover again?" the president asked.

"No sir, it's not Hoover. Sir, would you mind if I asked you how this meeting came about?"

"My staff's been working on it for over a year."

"Would you remember whose idea it was, sir?"

"Come to think of it, it came out of a meeting with Brian Hunt, our ambassador to Chad Ambassador Carmichael, our ambassador to Nigeria Ambassador Fellows, and myself." All of a sudden the president didn't feel quite right about this meeting.

"Would you mind telling me why you think this meeting is in danger?" The president asked.

"Sir, we have surveillance on many of the militia groups in the country; one of our teams caught two of Paul Cedes' people in discussions with a white supremacist group. It's our belief that they intend to assassinate one or several of the African leaders."

"Then just pick them up for God's sake," The President snapped.

"Sir, after Ruby Ridge and Waco, we can't just go in and start arresting people. Neither one of us would want to be responsible for the ensuing riots."

"Okay, so which leader are they after?"

"We don't know, sir," Director Flynn admitted.

"Okay, unless you guys have something else I think it's time to get my African analysts down here. They might be able to give us a better idea on the African angle. I also want to get Eagelton and Sidney March in on this."

"Sir, Peter Eagelton is already aware of all of this and had in fact launched a separate and independent investigation into these matters before he was briefed on our efforts."

"Jesus Christ! Am I the only person that doesn't know what's going on?"

"No sir, but we are working with the oversight committees from both the house and the senate."

"Jesus, Martin, you got congress involved and you didn't bother to see me?"

"Sir, we were investigating several judges and congressmen; we were required by law to inform the oversight committee."

"Does Sidney March at justice know?"

"No sir."

"I recommend you brief him first thing in the morning. For now I want everybody to wait here while I get our analysts. I want to put this African question to rest."

When the president didn't hear any objections he walked to the door gave his aide some instructions and returned to the others.

"Okay, while we're waiting, why don't you tell me how you want to proceed from here," the president said.

"I would like forty-eight hours sir. During that time I'll have two agents in Walter Brooks' home looking for any information, especially electronic, that could tie all of this together. He has to be maintaining records somewhere."

"How are you going to get your agents into his house?" the president asked.

"That has already been arranged. One of my agents is on the way out there with Walter right now and ASAC Peal will join them in the morning."

"Agent Peal, what do you think about all of this? Do you think this all goes back to 1969?" The president asked.

"Yes sir I do. I think everything happened the way Director Flynn outlined it."

"What about this assassin, this Hoover? Surely he hasn't been holding a grudge since then?"

Christine had thought about what she would do if this moment came. Would she send everyone down this path or would she obey her director and not tread on new ground before testing it out with him first. She decided to go for it. "Sir, this last twenty-four hours has been extremely informative; I've formulated a theory about Hoover that I've not even shared with the director yet."

The president looked at Director Flynn and smiled, then looked back at Christine. "I'm sure Martin won't mind if you share your theory with all of us."

"My theory requires the assumption that these men were involved in the overthrow of the government of Cameroon in 1969. It's my belief that Hoover is not one person. I think Hoover is the nucleus of a guerilla force in Cameroon that's seeking revenge on those who illegally took over their homeland." Christine heard no one telling her to be quiet so she continued. "That's why Hoover could be in Switzerland and Washington, D.C. at the same time."

Tom looked at director Flynn and nodded his head. "It does make sense sir. It would also explain how Hoover was able to shoot at Paul Cedes from the 34th floor of a building and then set himself up to shoot him on the street. It's humanly possible for one person to do it, but much more practical for a two or even a three-man team."

"That's why she's the youngest ASAC in the bureau," the director said.

"But why would they wait thirty years for their vengeance?" The president asked.

"That sir, I don't have the answer to yet. Perhaps your analysts can help us there," Christine countered.

"Mr. President, while attempting to save this judge in San Francisco from Brian Hunt's assassin, ASAC Peal and her team encountered a well-trained and very professional assault force." Scott knew he was on treacherous ground but decided to continue. "After we captured one of them, he claimed immunity. Unfortunately we have been unable to trace the number he gave us to verify his immunity."

"You're wondering if they're part of that secret White House police force that is rumored to exist." The president said.

"Yes sir, I guess I am." Scott said.

"Until we sat down in this library this evening, I would have told you in no uncertain terms that such a force doesn't exist. After what you've told me however, I wouldn't rule anything out." The president sat in silence for a moment then got up and stood next to the fireplace.

"Martin, as you were telling me about this conspiracy and how it may go back thirty years, I got to thinking about Brian and how he got on my staff.

"I was introduced to him about fifteen years ago while running for my second term as governor of New York. Walter Brooks introduced us. He told me he knew this high energy, brilliant young lawyer, just graduated from Harvard Law and could do wonders for my campaign. Walter was right, I've won every campaign I've been in since then."

"Mr. President, I think that Brian is being developed to take over this organization after Walter," the director said.

"Not if I can help it. I personally am going to cut his balls off," the president said through clenched teeth. Then glanced at Christine and smiled.

"Sir, if Hoover gets to Walter Brooks, we may need to make a deal with Brian Hunt in order to get his cooperation," the director said.

"Then you had better make sure that Walter doesn't get killed, because I'm not making any deals with Hunt."

There was a knock at the door and the President let in his aide and two other men. One was a tall skinny black man wearing a suit that looked too baggy for him and the other was a shorter white man with long blond hair held back in a ponytail.

"Good evening, gentlemen," the president greeted the men. He dismissed his aide and invited the men to join them in the library. The president made the introductions and then addressed the tall black man. "Jon, my friends and I have been discussing the upcoming economic summit. They're concerned for the safety of some of our guests. They're going to ask you some questions and I would appreciate it if you helped them out." The president turned the meeting over to Director Flynn.

"What we need to know Jon, is what countries are the least likely to want to do business with the west or are even thinking about displacing western companies."

"Ean and I split Africa into two parts," Jon said. "I handle primarily the Sub-Saharan Continent and Ean handles the rest. In the Sub Sahara, the Congo is probably the most anti-western. They've recently gone through significant political change and are trying to nationalize many of their resources. In the mid-nineteen seventies, the Congo government gave away exclusive rights to many of their natural resources to foreign companies. Their new government realizes this was a mistake and is trying to get them back. Namibia and Angola are undergoing similar transformations." Jon stopped and looked at Ean.

"In Northern Africa, you are looking at Ghana, Senegal, and Togo. They're the most active in trying to regain their economic independence." Christine thought she could detect a slight British attitude in Ean's tone. Christine was surprised to hear Tom cut in before the director was finished with his questions.

"Where would you put Cameroon, in the north or the south?"

"Technically in the south, but it's kind of on the dividing line," Jon replied.

"Great," Tom continued. "Where would you say Cameroon stands today?"

"Very solidly pro-American and western business. They're probably one of our strongest allies in that part of the world," Jon said.

"Who is their current leader?" Tom asked.

Jon thought for a moment and then answered, "Bellos."

Ean corrected him. "Actually his name is Bello, Furandi Bello."

Tom kept on his line of questioning. "How long has he been in power?"

"About twenty years." Jon said but this time he looked to Ean for confirmation, who gave it to him through a nod of his head.

"Well that blows that theory." Tom said to no one in particular.

"What theory is that?" the director asked.

"The theory that whoever had overthrown the government in sixty-nine is still in power and working with Brooks," Tom replied.

The two African analysts looked at each other and then Jon said what they were both thinking. "We're not quite sure what you guys are looking for, but Furandi Bello is the son of Biya Bello who took power after the coup in 1969. In fact it was Furandi that led the raid on the palace and put his father in office. Many in Cameroon believe that it was Furandi who slaughtered the entire Boinya family. Furandi took over after his father's death in 1987. He's not a very popular leader, in fact it's widely believed that he killed his father because he didn't want to wait for him to die to take over. Nobody ever claims to have voted for him, yet somehow he manages to continue to win the elections."

"You're forgetting a big part of the legend," Ean said.

"There's a legend?" Scott blurted out.

"In Africa there's always a legend," Ean said.

"I'm not sure that this would qualify as a legend, but the leader that they assassinated in sixty-nine was a Mafani Boinya. The Boinyas have been rulers in Cameroon, Gabon, and the Congo for centuries. There are historical statues of the Boinyas throughout that part of Africa. They depict them as chieftains, elders and kings. Mafani Boinya was the eldest son of Shambia Boinya, the last king and first president of Cameroon. He transformed his people."

Tom interrupted Jon. "You said the eldest son of this Mafina. Does that mean there is another one?"

"The name is Mafani," Jon corrected, "and, yes there was another son. At the time of the coup he was living abroad. The last records of him placed him in England, but many believe that he came to America when things started to turn bad in Cameroon and got killed here. Others say he was killed in England on the same night his brother was killed in Cameroon. Either way, he's never been heard from since."

"I think we just heard from him," Tom said, "You were talking about a legend."

Jon was excited about what he was hearing. A Boinya alive, it didn't sound possible. "Yes, the legends say that a Boinya will rise to avenge the blood of the family and sit on the throne again. Many of the older people of Cameroon still believe that Winston Boinya, that's Mafani's brother, or one of his offspring will return to lead Cameroon out from under the tyrannical grip of the Bellos."

The African analysts weren't sure what they had done, but they could tell it had a tremendous impact on everyone in the room, especially the female agent.

"Did Winston Boinya have any children?" the director asked.

Jon and Ean looked at each other deep in thought before Ean answered. "I would have to do more research, but I believe they had a little girl. She would have been five or six at the time of the assassinations."

"That would make her about thirty-five or thirty-six now." The director said.

"My God we just found Hoover!" Tom exclaimed.

"Do you really think so?" Scott asked. "Why would she surface now and why would she kill an FBI agent ten years ago and then not kill another one until now?"

Jon and Ean felt like they just walked in on the middle of a movie, but neither dared interrupt.

"Think about it Scott, it makes sense. We were wondering why Hoover and the FBI was involved; they had to track down this other Boinya and his family. My God, this means that Hoover probably had Canon and Ballard kill the Boinyas!" Tom was putting it all together out loud. "If the girl was five or six, she probably saw who killed her parents and then one day ten years ago she saw one of the murderers in the street and recognized him. She followed him, stalked him or whatever, and then killed him. She may have even known that he was FBI and have been looking for him. Then she just didn't find the other one for ten years. Maybe she sweated him and got the rest of the names, or maybe she's just a better researcher than we are, but somehow she figured this whole thing out and is now taking her revenge."

"What about your theory that Hoover is actually several people?" Scott asked.

"I still believe that. I think she put together some kind of Cameroon freedom force and they plan to kill President Bello when he arrives for the summit," Tom said.

"What about the supremacist that Cedes' people were talking with?" the president asked.

"Mr. President, I think they are two totally separate issues. I'm convinced that the Millenium is going to take out one if not more of the leaders that Jon and Ean told us about.

"If we researched Walter Brook's oil leases, I'm convinced we would find many of them came after some kind of violent coup. We know he's trying to corner the world oil reserves; he can't afford to let any African countries break away from his grip.

"I think this summit was set up for the specific purpose of bringing some of these countries back in line." Tom sat back and watched the president for a reaction.

The president turned to director Flynn. "Martin, you've been awfully quiet, what do you make of your man's analysis?"

"Mr. President, he's here because he's the best. My mind doesn't work as fast as his; I'm going to have to go back to my office and work through all of this, but off hand, I'd have to agree with everything he's said.

"There are two threats to the summit out there. I definitely agree that one or all of the leaders of the countries that Ean and Jon were telling us about are in serious danger.

"Walter has a long reach. We know he reached all the way into congress to get the encryption legislation passed just so he could trade that technology for rights to the Russian oil fields, so I'm sure he'll try to protect his interests in Africa any way he can.

"I also know that Hoover, whoever or whatever he or she is, is very dangerous. If Hoover is after Bello, then we have a problem, because so far Hoover hasn't missed.

"That's what I think, Mr. President; I'll give you a more definite opinion after I've slept on it and heard from my agent with Brooks."

"Okay Martin—ASAC Peal, we haven't heard your opinion."

Christine was fighting for control, her entire life had just been pulled together in a single day. That same day, though, could be her undoing. Tom really was the best investigator the FBI had, he would put the rest of the puzzle together in a matter of days. He'd already concluded that Hoover might be a woman and that she was in her mid-thirties and of African descent. Her only hope was that he wouldn't be able to trace her family to the United States.

She heard the president's question but her mind was still trying to figure out her next step.

"Sir, much like Director Flynn, I feel like I'm two steps behind Agent West. This is a lot to think about, but on the surface, I can find very little to argue with in Agent West's analysis. I still believe, though, that our emphasis must be on Walter Brooks and the Millenium. They are the larger threat to our country right now."

"You're right of course, but I don't want anything to happen to President Bello, especially not on American soil. I also don't want to have to make a deal with Hunt, so you had better bring Brooks in alive." As soon as the president finished speaking, he realized that the analysts were still in the room.

"Jon, Ean, what you guys heard in this room this evening is top secret. You are not to discuss it with anyone, not even each other. That is a direct order from the president of the United States. This is a matter of national security.

"I'm going to loan you to Director Flynn until the economic summit is over. Give him and his people whatever they ask for." The president then turned to Director Flynn. "Martin, I want an update by noon tomorrow. I'll tell Cindy to put you straight through. Don't forget to call March over at justice." The president got up and everyone understood that the meeting was over.

Chapter 26

It was after eleven before Christine got home. She was emotionally and physically exhausted. Her meeting with her adopted parents after more than ten years, finding the artifacts, the letter, and listening to the president's analysts had all taken their toll.

Christine was reluctant to make decisions whenever she was in such a state, but she had to make some decisions before morning that could effect the rest of her life and perhaps even the future of two nations. Once Tom tracked down the migration of her parents from England to America, it would only be a matter of days before he identified Christine Barber Peal as Etina Boinya.

Christine pulled out the letter Virgil had given her and read it again. She reviewed the list of names and understood that these people had been in America for over thirty years and may no longer have strong ties to Cameroon.

The list had both the individual's Cameroonian name as well as the name they were going under in the United States. She scanned it for names she might recognize. Of the entire list, she recognized two names: Malcolm Singer, a congressman from Chicago, and William Cook, head of the NAACP. Christine made a note of their names and decided to track them down in the morning.

She was still faced with the question of what to do about Walter Brooks. By tomorrow morning, his security would be even tighter than ever. If she was going to kill him without getting caught, she would have to act soon.

Christine's priorities had changed over the last twenty-four hours; she could no longer take unnecessary risks. She needed to concern herself with Furandi Bello, who was responsible for the death of all Boinyas in Cameroon. She also needed to focus on finding a way to carry out her family's wishes and return Cameroon to the people and to free and democratic elections.

The next several days would be extremely busy for Christine. Tom would come by to pick her up at seven in the morning and take her to her car in Braddock. Then they would verify the security at Walter Brooks' estate.

Christine could only see one window of opportunity to take out Brooks. After tonight the security would make the risk too high. She had no choice, she had to make her move tonight and get back before Tom came by to pick her up in the morning.

Christine had never attempted anything of this magnitude without a properly worked-out plan and backup plan. She could hardly believe that she was about to drive to the heavily guarded compound of Walter Brooks and attempt to kill him, without any idea of what weapon she would use or how she would even get in to the compound.

There was no time to waste; Christine always destroyed her clothing and equipment after each assassination, not wanting any evidence lying around for someone to stumble across, so she had to make do with whatever she could find. She managed to find a pair of black tennis shoes, a black spandex running suit, and a black ski mask. She added some long black dress gloves and looked at herself in the mirror. This time there was definitely no doubt that Hoover was a woman.

Christine slipped purple NIKE sweats over the spandex running suit, forwarded her home phone to her cellular phone, picked up her service revolver, her special forces knife, and as an afterthought, she grabbed her competition dart set and a roll of duct tape. Before she left her condo, Christine went back into her bedroom and got a small jewelry box and a black fanny pack.

By the time Christine had her Viper headed down 395 toward Braddock, a plan was beginning to take shape. As she got further away from the city lights, Christine realized that she was getting her first real break. There wasn't much of a moon and what moon there was, was hidden behind heavy storm clouds. The night was dark, which Christine knew gave her a better chance of approaching undetected.

She pulled off the freeway and onto the main road that led to the private drive of Walter Brooks. She came within a half mile of the private drive and stopped.

She removed the fuse for the interior lights of the car, took off her sweats and slid out of the car. Christine put the box of darts, the tape, and the jewelry box into her fanny pack. She strapped the shoulder holster with her service revolver over her running suit and her knife to her leg. She jogged the half-mile to the private road and made her way down the road until she was within a hundred feet of the main gate. When she was within a hundred feet of the gate, she dropped down into the ditch alongside the road and crawled to the gate. Once she was at the gate, she could see the security cameras covering the estate entrance. The cameras were set on a pole twenty feet off the ground facing each other on opposite sides of the road, providing full 360-degree coverage of the gate area.

Christine was lying in the shadows of the ditch trying to figure out how she was going to neutralize the cameras when a dead bird lying at the bottom of the ditch gave her a way in.

She gathered several rocks from around her and tossed a couple at the cameras to gauge her range. She had to throw a rock approximately thirty feet across the road, twenty feet up in the air and hit a video lens about one inch in diameter with enough force to break it. She had to do all of this while staying low and in the shadows.

It took her fifteen attempts before one of her rocks finally found its target. The lens of the camera shattered and the rock along with the broken pieces of glass fell to the ground.

Christine moved from her position in the ditch to the side of the road directly underneath the still functioning camera. She took the dead bird and tossed it into the middle of the broken lens pieces scattered underneath the camera. Christine made her way along the road to the gate staying out of view of the remaining camera. She lay down in the shadows next to the gate and waited.

With heightened security, she knew that it would only be a matter of minutes before one of the roving patrols would be sent to check out the malfunctioning camera. Lying in the shadows next to the gate she waited—it was a full fifteen minutes before a patrol arrived. "Security isn't as tight as it should be," Christine thought as she saw a two-man team pulling up to the gate.

The headlights of the Jeep were set on bright and pointed down the road. The Jeep came to a stop on the other side of the gate and the passenger stood up and pointed his flashlight at the camera.

"The camera is busted," he said into a walkie-talkie.

"Find out how it got busted," an irritated voice came back over the walkie-talkie.

The passenger pushed the remote control and the gate rolled back. From Christine's position, she could see the passenger jump out of the

Jeep and, with the beam of his flashlight running along the barrel of his pistol and out in front of him, he walked toward the camera. When he reached the camera he relaxed his gun hand and directed the flashlight beam around the area until he spotted the dead bird in the middle of the pieces of the broken lens.

"I found the problem," the guard yelled back to the driver. "One of those stupid black birds ran into the camera and broke its frickin' neck."

"Can you fix the camera?" the driver yelled back.

"No, the lens is broken, its going to have to be replaced."

"Okay, wait there. I'll call for some instructions," the driver told his partner.

While the driver was getting directions and the other guard was still preoccupied with the camera, Christine, staying in the shadows and on her stomach, crawled around the edge of the electric fence and inside the compound.

As far as Christine was concerned this security team already had two strikes against them. They were too slow to respond to a broken camera at a sensitive infiltration point, and they had allowed the grass around the entrance and the fence to grow too tall. It was obvious that the loss of Michael Ballard was already beginning to show.

Christine settled into the tall grass off the side of the driveway no more than ten feet from the Jeep, waiting for her next opportunity.

"They're going to send a replacement camera. We're supposed to wait here," The driver yelled to the guard.

"Tell them to bring a ladder." the other guard yelled back.

The driver pulled the Jeep forward, blocking the entrance to the estate. He shut off the engine and had his headlights pointed down the road.

Christine's plan was simple—once inside the gate, she would make her way to the house. That was when she thought the guards would see the broken camera and leave. She hadn't planned on a new camera being installed that very night. She considered that a plus for the security team. Not only did this change mean that she would have to wait in the tall grass longer for everyone to leave before she could make her way to the house, but she would also have to find another way out. It was crucial to her plan (such as it was) that Walter Brooks not be found dead until she was back in her apartment. If she got caught going in, she could always claim she was testing their security, but on her way out she would have no such excuses.

This time the security team's response was actually quicker. It was no more than six or seven minutes before Christine heard the panel truck roll past her.

The Jeep was blocking the entrance, so the van had to park behind it. Two men got out of the van, one grabbed the ladder attached to its side and the other went around the back and retrieved the camera. They left the rear door to the van open and joined the other guards.

Christine saw an opportunity and a way she could save herself a three-mile walk. She slipped into the van while they were in front of the Jeep changing out cameras. She then slid behind the passenger seat and pulled a drop cloth over herself. It was only a matter of minutes before the technicians returned. They loaded up their equipment and headed back up the road to the house.

Christine had accomplished the first part of her plan; she had gotten onto the compound. While she was crouched in the back of the van trying to figure out how she was going to get into the house, the answer was provided for her.

"I'll go to the control room and test the camera; you put the equipment away," she heard the driver tell the other technician in the van.

"Okay, but if anything's wrong, you'll have to go back down and fix it yourself. I'm going back to bed."

The van pulled up to a building about fifty feet from the house. The driver got out and walked to the main house while the other tech went to open a large rolling shop door. Christine took this opportunity to sneak out of the van and follow the tech to the house. She watched as he entered a code and then place his thumb on a screen. She heard a heavy bolt retract and as the tech opened the door, Christine came up behind him and hit him in the back of his head with the butt of her pistol. The technician collapsed in her arms and she pulled him into the house. She taped his feet, mouth, and hands with duct tape and then made her way to the control room.

Fortunately from her earlier visit she had seen the layout of the house and had no problem finding the control room. There was another code box at the entrance to the control room, but Christine didn't bother to try and break it. Instead, she simply knocked on the door. She heard someone coming toward the door, the door unlock and then the man on the other side. "Did you forget the combination again, Fred?"

As the man opened the door, Christine burst through and took him by surprise. Before he knew what hit him, his mouth was taped and he was wrapped in his chair by several strands of duct tape. Christine pulled the other tech into the control room and tied both to a large pillar so they couldn't move once she was gone. She scanned the monitors.

She found the room she was looking for: the only room with a guard posted outside the door. It was on the second floor and the guard appeared to be asleep with his chair tipped on its rear two legs against the wall. She also spotted the second guard. He looked asleep in the kitchen. Checking the rest of the monitors, Christine found a blue screen with about a dozen red dots moving around it. When she looked at its label, it said "dogs." She had forgotten all about the dogs. It was a good thing she hadn't tried to run or crawl to the house. They would surely have found her. She also found a switch on the control board labeled "fence." She knew this had to be the on/off switch for the electric fence.

Christine could avoid the roving patrols as she tried to make her escape, but the dogs would be another thing. There had to be a way to collect all of the dogs quickly on a property this size. She scanned the monitor again and found a button that said "recall" next to the blue screen that showed the dogs running around the property. This had to be the button to push to collect the dogs. Christine's question now was, is this one of those high-frequency recall signals that only the dogs will hear or is it a siren that will wake up the entire neighborhood. She decided that if this were her security system, it would be a silent recall.

Christine flipped the fence switch to the "off" position closed her eyes, put one hand over her right ear, held her breath and pushed the recall button. When she didn't hear a wailing siren, she sighed in relief and checked the screen. She saw all of the red dots moving in the same direction, to what she had to guess was their kennel. Christine let go of the button and the dots stopped moving in the same direction and started dispersing around the property again. This could be a problem; Christine obviously couldn't be holding down the button for the recall while she was making her escape.

Christine decided to take care of that on her way out. She had to neutralize the two guards before she could enter Walter Brooks' room. She went to the kitchen and found the first guard face down on the kitchen table sound asleep. Without attempting to be quiet or careful, Christine walked up to the guard. As he was beginning to wake up she hit him over the head with her pistol and he was out again. She found some rope and tied him spread-eagled on the kitchen table. She wrapped his mouth with duct tape and set out to take care of the other guard.

This time, making every attempt to move quietly and cautiously, Christine made her way up the stairs until she was standing in front of the guard. He was sound asleep with his mouth open, leaning back in his chair in front of his boss's room. Christine stuck the barrel of her gun in his mouth and he woke immediately, almost falling out of the chair. She motioned for him to lean forward in his chair and to drop to his knees. When he did, Christine pulled the gun out of his mouth and before he could move, hit him on the side of his head with the butt of the gun, knocking him out cold. She tied him to the railing and taped his mouth closed with the duct tape.

She was almost there; now nothing stood between her and Walter Brooks. She opened the door and found herself in the sitting room of a large bedroom suite. She could see a trail of both men and women's clothes on the floor leading to the next room which Christine figured to be the "bedroom." This was a complication she had not counted on. Walter Brooks was very attractive to women and obviously very rich, but she had failed to count on him having female companionship tonight.

She walked around the corner and found Walter Brooks lying on his back under a single sheet with a woman lying face down next to him with one arm draped across his chest and one leg sticking out from under the sheet.

Christine acted on instinct. She came up behind the woman, put her knee in her back, and stretched her neck back. She slapped a piece of duct tape on the woman's mouth and across her eyes. She leveled her gun on Walter Brooks, who was dazed but waking very quickly.

"What the hell is going on here? Who are you?"

Christine pushed her gun further into Walter Brooks face and told him to "shut up." She bound the woman's feet and hands and rolled her off the bed. When Christine rolled the naked women over she was momentarily stunned. What she saw wasn't just the face of a frightened woman, but the face of Special Agent Francine English.

Christine recovered and taped Walter Brooks' mouth shut and made him drag Francine into the other room. She had him string her up in the closet, taping her hands to the closet rod and her feet to the bottom of the shoe rack. There they left a naked Special Agent Francine English hanging like a side of beef in a slaughterhouse while Christine forced Brooks back into the bedroom.

She wrapped his hands and feet with tape and sat him in a chair near the bed. She removed her ski mask, made sure he saw her face, and ripped off the strip of tape covering his mouth.

"You? You bitch—what the hell do you want? This isn't funny." Brooks yelled at her.

"Listen, you sniveling little prick, I'm going to tell you a story and then you're going to fill in any blanks, understood?"

"You're not going to get away with this. My people won't let you out of here."

"Maybe not, but I want to tell you a little story. In 1969 you and some friends of yours got together and decided that you wanted to control the world oil supply. To do that, you had to get your hands on some oil. You and your friends decided that there was oil to be had in a little African country named Cameroon. All you had to do was overthrow the government and put your own in place. So you got together with the CIA and killed the president of Cameroon and his entire family. But, there was a brother in the United States, so you had Hoover's people kill the brother and his family. Then you just put your puppet in place and life has been great for you ever since.

"There is only one thing keeping this story from having a happy ending for you. You forgot to make sure that Hoover's people got everybody. You see, the brother had a daughter that got away."

Walter Brooks face went white. "Oh my God, you're the little girl."

"That's right, I'm Etina Boinya!"

"Look, this is bigger than you know, we can make it up to you."

"How are you going to make up taking my parents from me?"

"I can give you anything you want; I can make you rich. I can make you FBI director, I can even make you president of Cameroon. Just tell me what it is you want."

Christine stepped up to Walter Brooks, put her hand over his mouth and said, "This is all I want!" As she cut his throat from one ear to the other.

Blood was shooting from his throat onto Christine's spandex running suit. She could feel the blood seep through her suit even as she heard the gurgling sounds of a dying Walter Brooks.

Christine pulled the jewelry box from her fanny pack, withdrew the thimble, placed it over her right thumb and pressed it into the blood gushing down Walter Brooks' chest. She then pressed the blood-soaked thimble onto the forehead of Walter Brooks, leaving a bloody outlined thumbprint of J. Edgar Hoover's right thumb. She put her ski hat back on, pulled it down over her face, and returned to the control room.

Christine took three of her darts, pushed the recall button for the dogs and wedged the darts into the side of the button housing using them as nails to hold the button down. She saw the red dots all move in the same direction and when she removed her finger the darts held and the dogs continued to return to their kennels.

Christine was out the front door and about a mile down the driveway before she spotted the first patrol. She fell to her stomach and stayed there until the Jeep passed. It took her another twenty-five minutes and two more stops to avoid patrols on the way to the fence. She was sure the body hadn't been found yet, but decided to test the fence just in case. Christine threw the knife at the fence and when it didn't spark, she climbed it. The inside of her thigh got caught on the top strand of barbwire. She reached back, wiped off the blood left on the fence, and jumped to the other side. She made her way to her car, took off her hat, and headed back toward the highway.

As Christine drove, she reviewed everything that had just happened, looking for anything she might have done to give herself away. Her only concern was Francine English. Christine only said two words in front of her, but it might be enough for Francine to recognize her voice.

Christine had a whole new set of questions. "What was Francine doing in this man's bed? For how long had they been sharing a bed? Was Francine part of the Millenium?"

On her way back to D.C. Christine pulled into the rest area near Germantown. She changed out of her blood-soaked spandex running suit and into the NIKE warm up. She cleaned off her knife and tossed the running suit into the trash. As she entered the city, she stopped at the first Dumpster she saw and threw her remaining custom darts and duct tape away.

By the time Christine got back to her condo and cleaned up, it was 5:00. Expecting Tom at seven, she decided not to try and sleep.

The last five hours had been some of the most intense of her life. Her only regret about killing Walter Brooks, was that she wasn't able to savor the moment longer and that she didn't have a chance to find out who the other members of the Millenium were.

Christine's adrenaline wouldn't allow her to think about sleep. Instead she spent the next couple of hours putting together a plan to kill the last remaining member of the conspiracy that wiped out her family.

She was certain that once Furandi Bello was executed, Cameroon, with the help of expatriates still living in the United States, could be returned to the people of Cameroon.

Chapter 27

Tom West spent most of the night tossing and turning; when the phone rang at six, he was already showered and trying to figure out what tie to wear for the day. He got the phone on its second ring and immediately felt his energy being drained when he heard Scott on the other end of the receiver.

"Tom, it's Scott."

"Scott, please don't call me in the morning. Every time you call me this early it's bad news."

"In that case, this won't hurt my average any. We just got a call from the Brooks estate."

"Oh God no, don't tell me Hoover got to Brooks!"

"I'm afraid he did Tom. They found him this morning with his throat cut from ear to ear."

"Damn it Scott! I thought that place was locked down tighter than a drum. How the hell did Hoover get in?"

"We don't know yet. I need you to get up there as soon as you can."

"I was on my way to pick up Christine—we were headed there to check out the security."

"You can forget about the security, but you might as well take Christine with you. Make sure you guys secure the computers and all of Brooks' files."

"How's Francine? Has she got the place secured for us?"

"That's part of the problem. We can't find her. There's an ex-agent running security for the Brooks estate now. His name is Brian Defore; as soon as he found Brooks, he backed out of the room and locked the door. He's keeping the scene sterile until you get there. I'll send a crime lab and forensic team to the scene, but I want you there before anything is touched."

"I'm on my way; I'll swing by to pick up Christine and we'll be there within the hour."

"My next call is going to be to the Director. I don't have to tell you how unhappy he's going to be about this. He's going to want to know what the hell happened, so give me a call as soon as you've looked at the crime scene."

Tom was in his car on the way to Christine's when he called her.

"I'm on my way over there now, can you be ready and out front in ten minutes?"

"Good morning, Tom, You're half an hour early and you don't say good morning— that's pretty rude."

"I'm sorry Christine, my mind was on other things. Walter Brooks just got killed."

Christine used the best-surprised voice she had. "What? How? When? Damn it Tom, what happened to all that security?"

"Those are all questions we'll find out when we get there. I'll be in front of your building in about seven minutes."

Christine looked at her watch; it was six-thirty that's about the time she thought that they would find the security breach. There had to have been a shift change at the estate some time between six and seven-thirty. She was a bit surprised that the missing dogs hadn't alerted someone earlier.

Christine, wanting to be as far removed as possible from her outfit the night before, was standing in front of the building in a white tailored pantsuit, a pink silk blouse, and a single gold chain necklace when Tom arrived with the flashing siren on the dashboard of his car.

"How can you possibly look like you just stepped out of a 'Vogue' fashion shoot this time of morning? You do know we're going to a crime scene?" Tom said with a smile as he checked out Christine.

"A newly appointed Acting ASAC has to look the part," Christine said, returning Tom's smile. "Besides we know it was Hoover, so it was probably a long distance shot with a sniper rifle with very little mess. I probably won't even get my hands dirty."

"Not this time." Tom told her. "This time Hoover did it up close and personal. Scott said that Brooks' throat was cut from ear to ear. I think Hoover took some personal pleasure in this one."

Christine's cell phone rang as they were getting on the Interstate. She answered it only to hear Doris tell her that she was moving their office up stairs into ASAC Martinez's old office, and that she should check her messages at her new number. Christine knew that she would never remember the number.

"Okay, Doris, I'll try, but it'll take awhile to remember the new number."

"You don't have to remember it, you could write it down, people used to do things like that." Doris said a bit sarcastically. "Or you could check your phone. It captures the last ten calls received as well as the last ten calls missed. So unless you get nine more calls before you call me back, this number will still be there."

Christine hung up the phone and looked to Tom. "Does your assistant give you this much hell?"

Tom laughed, "Claire thinks she's my mother. I wouldn't survive this jungle without her, though."

The drive to Walter Brooks' estate went quickly. Tom's siren allowed them to get through the morning traffic and to the estate in less than an hour. At the gate to Brooks' private drive, they found two security guards with automatic weapons.

One of the guards approached and waved them through when he saw Christine's FBI badge. "A little late for that." Tom commented as he drove past the armed guards.

"I wonder who'll be coming to oversee the place. Brooks didn't have any relatives." Christine said.

"Oh crap, Christine, that's a good point. We need to call Scott and tell him not to let that weasel Brian Hunt know about this yet. He'll have some lawyer up here locking all of this stuff up so we can't access it."

Christine had Scott on the line as they were pulling up to the house. She relayed Tom's concerns and promised to call him back as soon as they had anything. A short stocky man greeted Tom and Christine in his late fifties or early sixties wearing wire rim glasses halfway down his nose.

"One of you Agent West?"

"I am." Tom answered.

"Good, I'm Brian Defore. Peterson said you were gonna take over."

"Do you know Scott?" Tom asked.

"I was with the agency for a number of years; Scott and I worked a couple of minor cases together."

"Good, then you should be able to help us quite a bit." Tom introduced Christine and they went into the house.

Brian Defore took them up stairs to Walter Brooks' bedroom suite. "Everything is exactly the way I found it. Except of course, I untied the guards. But I made outlines of where they were and they're waiting for you to talk to them."

"That's great work, Brian, this will help us a lot. What about Agent English? She was supposed to be staying out here evaluating the security," Tom asked.

"She was assigned a room a couple of doors down from Mr. Brooks. We found her stuff there, but we haven't found hide nor hair of her anywhere on the compound. My men have been looking since I called."

"Could she have left last night?" Christine asked.

"No ma'am," Brian Defore replied. "She wasn't signed out on the log and all the cars are still here and I would've heard if the helicopter had left."

Brian Defore unlocked the door to the crime scene. "He's in here."

Tom and Christine walked through the sitting room and what they saw even shocked Christine.

Taped to a chair was the naked shell of a man, with his eyes wide open, a wide gash running the width of his neck, dried blood clotted in his chest hair, sitting in a small pool of blood that hadn't yet completely dried. The carpet around the chair was red with blood.

"Damn, I'd say Hoover got his pay back on this one," Tom said as he carefully walked around the body.

"Who's Hoover?" Brian Defore asked.

"That's who you were supposed to be protecting him from." Tom replied.

Christine pointed to the thumbprint on Brook's forehead. "That's Hoover," she said.

Tom walked around the room several times. He looked under the bed, between the sheets and inspected as much of Brooks' body that he could without touching it.

"How many women are there on the compound?" He asked Brian Defore.

"Three: his private secretary, who is downstairs in the kitchen waiting for you, and two guards. They both came on duty this morning."

"How long has his secretary been with him?" Tom asked.

"I'm not sure, but it's been more than twenty years."

"Are they having an affair or a relationship?"

Brian Defore smiled at the thought "No, maybe a long time ago, but not anymore. Mr. Brooks likes his women a lot younger."

"How about the guards, could one of them be having an affair with Brooks?"

"Possible but highly unlikely," Brian Defore said.

"Call them in anyway, I'll want to talk to them." Tom said.

"What are you thinking?" Christine asked Tom.

"Well, those aren't all men's clothes lying on the floor, and from the looks of the sheets, Brooks didn't spent the night alone in this bed."

"You don't think that whoever did this slept with him first?" Brian Defore asked.

"No, she wouldn't have left all of these clothes lying around," Tom said.

"Damn, then we have another body somewhere." Brian Defore said as he kneeled down next to the blouse.

"That's not Hoover's style," Christine said, "Hoover wouldn't kill an innocent bystander."

"Christine's right, you'll probably find her tied up along the road somewhere," Tom agreed.

"Look, we may have blown it in here, but I don't think anybody got off this compound carrying a body for three miles." Brian Defore protested.

"You're right Brian, this woman is still on the premises. You said all of the women that were here are accounted for?" Tom asked.

Brian Defore thought for a moment before answering. "All but that agent of yours."

Tom looked at Christine, "What do you think?" He asked her.

"It's possible; there did seem to be something between them." Christine said.

Tom turned back to Brian Defore, "Brian, do you have any tracker dogs out here?"

"Sure, we have some of the best."

"Good, go get one, let him smell the clothes on the floor and then turn him loose. I bet that she's still in the house somewhere and alive."

Brian sent one of his guards to get the dogs while he took Christine and Tom to the control room. He had the technician and the guard that was on duty in the control room join them.

They explained the various functions of the control board and the layout of the monitors. The darts had been removed from the "recall" button on the dog's monitor, but the guard explained how the intruder had rigged it.

The crime lab people and the forensic team arrived while Tom and Christine were getting the tour of the control room.

Tom instructed them to start in the bedroom with Walter Brooks and to keep their eyes out for anything that might tell them where a missing woman might be stashed.

Tom turned his attention back to the monitors and then to Brian Defore. "Are all of these monitors hooked to video equipment?"

"Yes, and we have all of the tapes from last night's shift. This shift came on at eight and was scheduled to get off at eight this morning. I took a look at a couple of the videos while we were waiting. All of this seemed to have occurred around two o'clock this morning. I'm sorry to say that my guys look pretty silly on there," Brian Defore admitted.

"Am I correct in assuming that a black man about 5'11" is responsible for all of this?" Tom asked.

"I don't know about black or white, but this sure as hell wasn't any man. It looked to be a woman about five foot six, or five foot seven and she was in damned good shape."

"A woman? Damn it, why would Hoover reveal herself now?" Tom asked no one in particular.

"Maybe this was her last target and she no longer needed the disguise." Christine said.

Tom didn't think that was the case. "If my theory is right, she's not finished. She still has to get to Bello. There's no reason why she wouldn't continue to try and misdirect us, unless she knows we're onto her."

"But that's not possible, we only found out about her last night ourselves. Maybe she doesn't know about Bello," Christine insisted.

"There has to be a reason why she would shed her cover as a male Hoover. She's not dumb, she knows there were cameras watching her last night. She wants us to know she's a woman; why?"

The question lingered in the air, when one of the crime lab team burst into the control room. "You guys gotta see this, we found your missing woman."

Tom and Christine walked into the sitting room of the bedroom suite and found Francine bound and gagged, stark naked, with her hands taped over the cloth rod and her feet tied to the shoe rack. Tom lost his cool. "God damn it, get her down from there and get her a blanket. That's an FBI agent for God's sake."

Francine collapsed as soon as she was cut free. Christine grabbed a blanket from the couch in the sitting room and wrapped her in it. Scott called for an ambulance against Francine's wishes and decided to give her a chance to recover from her embarrassment without him present.

"Christine, I'm going to check the grounds, maybe we can figure out how Hoover got onto the estate."

"Okay, don't forget to call Scott and let him know what's going on. I promised him a call."

"I'll do it while I'm walking the grounds. Can I borrow your phone? My battery just died." Tom asked Christine.

"Sure." Christine said and handed her phone to Tom.

Christine helped Francine to her bedroom and got her cleaned up and dressed. Francine's feet and hands were red and bruised from being tied all night and she was embarrassed and exhausted. Aside from that, she was fine and would be as good as new in a couple of days. At least physically; emotionally could take a little longer.

"He's dead, isn't he?" Francine asked half sobbing.

"Yes, they found him this morning. It looks like Hoover cut his throat." Christine told her.

"It wasn't Hoover, it was a woman."

"We know it was a woman. We found out last night that Hoover is a woman, plus we found the Hoover print in the middle of his forehead."

"Oh God, Christine, what was I thinking. My career is over. My life is over." Francine broke down crying.

Tom was driving around the property with one of the security patrols filling him in on what they found at the scene.

Scott was with Director Flynn and they were furious when they heard about Francine. The director wanted her brought straight to the Hoover building for questioning, but Tom convinced him to let the doctors check her out first. No sooner had Tom hung up with Scott and Director Flynn, than Christine's phone rang. Scott thought about it for a second then decided to answer it.

"Hello, this is Agent West."

"I'm sorry, I must have a wrong number. I thought I was calling Agent Peal."

"This is Agent Peal's phone, can I take a message for her?"

"Yes, I suppose you can. Please let her know that Agent Greenfield called, and I have some information about that family she was asking about."

"Andy, is that you?" Tom asked, somewhat surprised.

"Yeah, it is, who is this?"

"It's Tom West."

"Tom, what the hell are you up to? What are you doing on Peal's phone?"

"We're working a case together, I had to borrow her phone. What are you doing? The last I heard, you retired to the great northwest somewhere."

"I did; I'm hiding out up here in Northern Idaho and Washington State. Or at least I was hiding, until that gorgeous young agent came and snooped me out."

"You mean Christine called you about a case?"

"No, she came up here to see me."

"Which case?"

"She said she was looking into one of Hoover's 'special unit' cases from the late sixties."

"When was this?"

"I guess it's been four or five months. Are you guys still working on that case?"

"Yes we are, in fact I'm at a murder scene directly related to that case."

"Well, tell her I don't have any more on those files, but I did find out that in late sixty-nine, there was a black family in D.C. that was supposed to have been killed by the Klan, with the same name as the one she was looking for."

"What was the name?"

"The Barbers. Tell her that people who were around in those days think that 'the Special Projects Unit' had its hand in that one. It seems that there was an extensive FBI search for a surviving child who was never found."

"I'll pass the message on to her. Do you have a number where she can call you back if she has any more questions?"

Andy Greenfield gave Tom the number and they said their good-byes. Tom had gotten off of the Jeep during the conversation and was just standing at the main gate trying to make sense out of what he had just heard.

Why was Christine asking about one of the old Hoover files from late sixty-nine five months ago? That's been a line of investigation for less than forty-eight hours. Was this black family the Boinyas? How would Christine know about them? Why hasn't she shared this information with the task force? What else did she know?

Tom decided that there was too much at stake. He had to dig into this further before confronting her or talking to Scott and the director.

Tom was still thinking about the call he just received, and almost missed the guard explaining how a bird ran into the camera during the night and that they had to change the camera out.

Tom stooped down to looked at the bird and shook his head. "Did your guys even bother to look at this bird? This thing's been dead for days. That camera was probably knocked out by one of these rocks lying around here."

"No offense sir, but it was about one in the morning when the camera went out. Not exactly the time of night anybody wants to pick up a bird and see how long he's been dead," the guard said with a hint of sarcasm in his voice.

"You're right of course, and that's exactly what Hoover was counting on," Tom told the guard.

By the time Tom got back to the main house, he had a pretty good idea of what had happened. He entered the control room in time to watch the rest of the security videos with Christine and Brian Defore. He was impressed with what he saw of Hoover. She had no problems neutralizing the guards. He was only sorry that there were no cameras in the master bedroom, because Tom was sure that Hoover had revealed herself to Walter Brooks before killing him.

Tom had done and seen all he could at the estate and was eager to move the investigation back to the Hoover Building to follow up on his hunches. He gathered all the tapes and made arrangements for Special Agent Quantara to meet Francine English at the hospital and bring her to the Hoover building as soon as the doctors cleared her.

He instructed the guards to load all of the computer equipment and all the files into his car. Without anyone there to tell them any different, the guards complied.

"Christine, I think I'm done here. You want me to give you a lift to your car?" Tom asked.

"Sure, there's nothing I can add here."

On the way to Christine's car, Tom explained to her how he thought Hoover got on to the estate and made his way to the house. In Christine's mind this just reinforced how dangerous Tom could be. He had already tracked almost her exact movements. She would have to keep a close eye on his progress.

Tom dropped her off at her car and started to pull away when he suddenly stopped and rolled down his window. "Christine, wait a minute, I forgot to give you your phone back." He handed her the phone but decided against giving her the message.

Christine watched Tom pull away and started her car. She was about to drive away herself when she stopped to call Doris to check her messages. As predicted, she couldn't remember the new number. She did remember Doris's instructions. She pushed the recall button and was given three choices, missed calls, received calls, and address book. Christine pushed the received call button and as the numbers began to scroll by,

the first number caught her eye. Her phone received a call from a 208 number after Doris had called her; Christine knew she didn't get any such a call. The call must have come in while Tom was using her phone. He obviously just forgot to give her the message.

Christine was about to call the number back, but something inside her told her to hold off. Instead, she dialed the operator and asked where the 208 area code was located. As soon as she heard the operator tell her Idaho, Christine knew her life as Christine Peal the FBI Agent was over.

She dialed the number and heard a man answer on the other end, "Yeah."

"Andy, this is Christine Peal."

"I guess you got my message."

"Yes, Tom told me you called. He just couldn't remember what you said. He was somewhat distracted at the time."

"Yeah, he said you guys were out at a murder scene."

"I'm actually getting ready to leave now. Did you have some information for me?" Christine asked.

"Like I told Tom, I don't have anything new on those files, but I did get some of my old friends to call me back on that name you were asking me about. It looks like there was a black family named Barber that was killed under suspicious conditions in late sixty-nine.

"The official record says the Klan did it, but my friends seem to remember rumors of Hoover's enforcers being involved."

"By enforcers do you mean the 'Special Projects Unit?'"

"Yes, and there was a hell of a fuss about a little kid that got away."

"Thanks Andy, did you tell all this to Tom?"

"Yea, that was OK, wasn't it?" Andy Greenfield asked.

"Yes that's fine; I was just wondering if I should call him and fill him in."

"Listen, if there's anything else I can do to help just let me know. You're always welcome to come up here and go fly fishing with me."

"Thanks, I'll keep that in mind." Christine hung up the phone and didn't move for about five minutes. She always knew this day might come, but she wasn't ready for it just yet. There was still so much to do. She had her plans in place for just this situation, but now that it was actually happening she didn't know what to do next.

At the most Christine felt she had four or five hours before Tom put it all together. She drove to her apartment as fast as she could. It was time for her to go underground and disappear.

Christine grabbed a few clothes, a large envelope, her computer, and her emergency cash. She always kept one hundred thousand dollars in hundreds, fifties, and twenties in her condo for this specific emergency. She changed into dark slacks and a dark loose-fitting shirt, put on the money belt, grabbed the packed gym bag and took one last look at her condo and her life as Christine Peal.

Chapter 28

Christine was in her less conspicuous Volvo, but she knew she would have to dump it soon. She placed two calls, the first to her father in Kettering, to let him know she would be by to pick up the artifacts and the second to Special Agent Quantara to see if he had heard anything from Tom.

The first call went smoothly enough. Virgil would have the box ready when she got there. The call to Quantara however, sent her back out to the Brooks' estate.

While at the hospital, Francine told Quantara that she saw Walter Brooks put two CD ROMs and a couple of files in a floor safe next to the bed. Those had to be what the FBI needed to tie up the rest of the Millenium.

Christine had to get her hands on those files. They could be the bargaining chips that could get her out of this alive.

Her time was limited, and she could feel Tom breathing down her neck, but she had to take the chance.

She drove back to the estate and the guards recognized her from her earlier visit. She had no problem gaining access to the crime scene or finding the safe. Once she knew what and where to look, it was easy for her to spot the safe, even under the heavy shag carpet. There were no keys to the safe, no one knew the combination, and safe cracking was not one of Christine's specialties.

In an act of desperation, Christine had the guards cut the two-by-two-by-three safe out of the floor and put it in the back of her car.

This entire event had taken over two-and-a-half hours before she was back in the city. She had no idea what Tom was doing but had to take a chance on retrieving the artifacts.

Christine drove to Kettering and called Virgil when she was less than three minutes away. Christine could detect no unusual stress or strain in his voice. She asked if anyone had called him looking for her, when he assured her no one had, she pulled up to the front door.

"Christine, what's going on—what's this all about? You sound so mysterious." Virgil asked when he greeted her.

"It's nothing serious. I've got to go away for a while. The FBI may come to see you. Tell them whatever they want to know. You have done nothing wrong. Just answer their questions to the best of your ability and I'm sure they'll leave you alone. I'm just sorry that I got the two of you involved in all of this."

"What are you talking about? What could be this bad? Does this have anything to do with you father's letter?" Virgil asked.

"Yes, I guess it does. I love both you and Eleanor very much. I don't have much time left, I really need to leave."

"What about your mother, she's at the store, I know she'd want to see you."

"I can't wait, Virgil. If I don't go now I might never be able to go anywhere ever again."

Christine and Virgil carried the artifacts to Christine's car and then Christine gave Virgil one final hug and with tears rolling down her face she left behind the only family she'd had for thirty years.

It was now two in the afternoon and Christine knew that Tom had to be right behind her. She found an old CONOCO service station with gas pumps that had long been abandoned. There were two men working on cars in the service bay. Christine pulled as close as possible to the bay. When she got out of her car, two black men covered in grease came out from under the hood of a car. One looked to be in his eighties, the other in his sixties.

Christine approached the men, making sure not to get any grease on herself.

"Would you gentleman be interested in making $500 for five minutes of work?"

The old man whistled. "Child the last time anybody offered me that kind of money, they wanted me to run moonshine for old Lester Williams. I'll tell you the same thing I told him. I ain't gonna do anything against the law. The same goes for my boy. Ain't that right Wilber?"

"That's right, Pa."

"This isn't illegal. In fact I'm an FBI agent." Christine showed them her badge. "I just need to open this safe and get one of those computer disks out or the whole city may be in danger."

"Why can't you just take it to your office?" The old man asked.

"There's just no time." Without waiting for a reply she opened the back door of her car and motioned for the men to come and take a look.

The men looked at the safe and at Christine's FBI identification again.

"Will we have to pay taxes on the money?" The younger man asked.

"I'm afraid so. Even the FBI can't get around the IRS." Christine replied.

"I guess if we have to pay taxes on it, then it's gotta be Okay." The younger one decided.

It took the men less than five minutes to open the safe with their welding equipment. Christine made the men give her a receipt for the five hundred dollars and left.

She bought an old beat-up and rusted-out 1968 Chevy Impala, transferred her artifacts; and gym bag to it and parked her Volvo in the parking lot of Bethesda naval hospital. She then drove to Alexandria where she did a little shopping and rented a $50 per night motel room, paying for a week in advance.

Christine pulled up the floorboards of the motel room and stored the artifacts under the floor. She opened the folders from Brooks' safe and began reviewing them. The first folder had photos of two white supremacists and one African leader. On the back of the photos were the names of the supremacists and what group they belonged to. On the back of the African's photo was the name Joachim Sassou, president of Congo. It also had a date, a time, and a place on it. Christine interpreted that to be the time and place that President Sassou was to be assassinated.

When Christine opened the second folder, she found the same photos of the supremacists but this time their photos had a date, time, and place on the back. In large red letters there was also a note that said, "Only after their mission is complete." Christine knew that meant that these guys would never live to brag about their exploits. The third photograph in the envelope is what shocked and scared Christine the most.

It was a photograph of the president. When she flipped it over, it had the same date, time, and place written on it as the others. Christine suddenly realized that the African leader was only a decoy and the real target along has been the president.

The white supremacists would be shot, leaving everyone to think that they killed the president by accident while they were trying to kill a black leader.

Christine had no choice, she had to get this information back to Tom and Scott— they had to warn the president.

The date on the back of the picture gave her two days to head off the assassination of the president and to secure her own freedom.

Chapter 29

After Tom dropped Christine off, he reviewed the last couple of days. He replayed every meeting and every conversation he'd had with Christine. He needed to make some calls and was cursing his phone for not working, until he realized that if his phone was working, he would never have taken the call from Andy Greenfield.

Tom got back to FBI Headquarters and went straight to his office. He had several messages waiting for him from Scott and Director Flynn. Before returning the calls, he sent the technicians from the computer lab to retrieve Brooks' computer from his car. He also had them bring all of the paper files to his office.

His first call was to Scott. They agreed to meet in the director's office. When he arrived, he was surprised to find Peter Eagelton and a fourth man waiting for him.

The director made the introductions. "Tom, this is Mr. Reynolds, the attorney for the estate of Walter Brooks, and you of course know our AG Peter Eagelton."

"That's pretty quick counselor, I just barely got back from the estate. I didn't realize anybody else had been called," Tom said.

"I'm sure you're aware that Mr. Brooks has interests throughout the world that must be protected. My job is simply to protect those interests." The attorney answered.

"Who notified you about Mr. Brooks death?" Tom asked the attorney.

"That's immaterial. What is material, is that you took some things from the estate this morning that you had no right to take. The estate would like them back."

"Those things are part of a homicide investigation, Mr. Reynolds. They may be evidence of the crime. We had every right to take them with us," Tom insisted.

"Unless the computer was used to hit Mr. Brooks over the head, you had no business taking it. From what I understand, Mr. Brooks didn't die of paper cuts, so the files must be returned as well," the attorney countered.

"We'll have to wait for a judge's decision on that," Attorney General Eagelton added.

Reynolds pulled out a folder and handed it to AG Eagelton. "We filed these papers with Judge Metzger forty minutes ago. My assistant should be in your waiting room by now with the papers requiring you to release these things to me."

Scott walked to the door, opened it, and a young man who looked no older than eighteen stood up. The attorney walked out took the papers from him and handed them to the attorney general. Peter Eagelton reviewed the documents and shook his head. "They're real, guys, give him back his things."

Tom was about to protest but Director Flynn raised his hand cutting him off.

Tom offered to have everything shipped to the attorney's office, but Reynolds insisted on taking it with him. Tom escorted Reynolds to his office where Reynolds's assistant and some FBI staff members moved the files to the assistant's car. Two computer lab technicians helped Reynolds move the computer equipment into his car.

By the time Tom returned to the director's office, he was furious. "Damn it, there went our best bet of figuring out this Millenium and who's behind it. I'd like to know who the hell called him?"

"It could have been anybody at that house, or maybe even somebody who just called in to talk to Walter." Peter Eagelton said.

"Just tell me what the hell happened out there and how Francine fits into this whole mess," the director said.

Tom told them what he had found, how he thought Hoover got into the estate and that he thought she got out over the fence, since she wasn't spotted leaving by the gate cameras.

The fact that Hoover was a woman was news to Peter Eagelton. The director explained about their meeting at the White House and Tom's deductions. They tried without success to figure out why Hoover decided to reveal that she was a woman. The director was especially upset about Francine's involvement with Walter Brooks. Tom assured her that Quantara would be bringing her in for questioning as soon as the doctors released her.

"What's our next move?" The director asked.

"I think we have to pull in Brian Hunt," Scott said.

"I would like to hold off on that for now. We know nothing else will happen until the summit. That's two days away. Let's put a tail on Hunt and see where he leads us. With Brooks dead, Hunt has to be beside himself; I'm kind of interested in seeing who he turns to," Tom said.

"What about taking another run at the judge and that shooter you have locked up?" Peter Eagelton asked.

"The judge is pretty much wrung dry, but we might be able to get a little more from the shooter," Scott offered.

"We've got less than forty-eight hours to break this Millenium and to find Hoover. Any ideas?" The director asked.

"Actually, I think I have some leads on Hoover, or at least who his inside person might be at the FBI," Tom said.

"Let's hear it," the director said.

"Sir, if you don't mind, I would like to check out a few more things before I put anything on the table that I won't be able to retract later."

The director nodded. "Fair enough, Tom. Scott, get us something from that shooter. We need it. Peter you ready to go talk to the president?"

With that, the meeting was over and Tom headed back to his office, eager to check out his hunches. He pulled all of the reports generated by the task force, especially those prepared by Christine or those in which Christine played any kind of role at all and went through them again. After reviewing the files for more than an hour, he replayed the tape of Christine's interrogation of Judge Feldman.

He replayed the tape several times where Christine was asking Feldman about Hoover. Tom couldn't detect any change in her tone. He did notice a slight change in her tone and the way she asked about someone named

Barber. The same name that she asked Agent Greenfield about.

Tom needed to talk to Greenfield again. He pulled out the number that Agent Greenfield had given him earlier and called it. Tom was actually a little surprised when the phone was answered on the first ring.

"This is Andy, speak," the voice on the other end said.

"Andy, it's Tom West. How are you?"

"Tom, I'm the same I was when we talked this morning. What's going on; I don't talk to anybody at the agency for months and then three times in one day?"

"What do you mean three times in one day? Did Christine call you?"

"Yea she did, right after I talked to you. What's going on?"

"This is going to sound strange and please don't ask me any questions, but I need to know everything she said and everything you talked about when she came up to see you."

"Look Tom, last I heard, you were both on the same team. I don't remember you being this competitive about a case."

"It's nothing like that Andy. Right now I'm investigating five homicides; they span a ten-year period and are all linked. I'm sure whatever you and Christine talked about when she was up there has something to do with all of them."

"Why can't you just ask her what we talked about?" Greenfield asked.

"Andy, you'll just have to trust me for now. I need to know exactly what you talked about."

"Okay Tom, but I hope she's not in any trouble, because I like her."

"I like her too Andy, but she may be into something pretty heavy," Tom said.

"She wanted to know about Hoover's 'Special Projects Unit.' She was particularly interested in the late sixties. I tried to explain to her that those were different times and unless you lived them, you really couldn't understand or judge them.

"She asked about cases that an Agent Ballard and an Agent Canon might have worked on together. Although I remember, she didn't have Canon's name right. She called him Gannon."

"You corrected her and told her that it wasn't Gannon but Canon that worked with Ballard in sixty-nine?" Tom asked.

"Sure, but like I told her Canon was a real jerk. I was gone by late sixty-nine so I couldn't help her much with those cases."

"This morning you mentioned something about a black family that was supposed to have been killed by the Klan, but it looked like maybe it wasn't so. What was all that about?"

"She said that someone had come forward and claimed that the FBI had wiped out their family in 1969. When I asked her what the name was of the family, she told me Barber. At the time I didn't have much for her, but I told her that I would make some calls."

"Did she say anything else about the Barbers?"

"No, but she was real interested in getting hold of Hoover's private files."

"What did you tell her about them?" Tom asked.

Agent Greenfield chuckled. "The same thing I tell everybody; whoever finds them will be able to solve most of our political mysteries including the Kennedy assassination."

"I appreciate all your help, Andy. If there's anything else you remember please let me know."

"I don't know if this will help you any, but I did tell her that she had a better chance of finding Hoover's tapes than she did of finding his files. Hoover taped everything back then."

"I don't suppose you told her where to look?" Tom asked.

"I told her he'd probably hide them at his office or his home; he would never have been too far from those tapes."

"Thanks again, Andy; I do appreciate this."

"What do you want me to tell Peal if she calls back?" Greenfield asked.

"I don't think she'll be calling you back."

"Are you ever going to tell me what this is all about?"

"Maybe someday when we're out on your lake fly fishing."

The puzzle was beginning to come together. Tom could see the picture forming; he just needed a couple more pieces.

He pulled up the Barbers' file on the computer but found it extremely sparse for a family that was wiped out by the Klan. There didn't appear to have been much of an investigation and it was closed a week after it was opened. Tom printed out what there was and was about to pick up the telephone when his assistant came in and told him that Agent Quantara was here with Agent English.

Tom asked his assistant to take Agent English to ASAC Peterson. His assistant thought that a strange request since Agent English was perfectly capable of finding ASAC Peterson's office on her own. Nonetheless, she did so.

Tom called Scott and let him know that Francine was on her way down. Scott wanted Tom and Christine there when he talked to Francine, but Tom convinced him that they had other priorities at the moment. Although Scott was curious, he didn't push it.

Tom knew what he was thinking was ridiculous. It just wasn't possible for Christine to be this missing Barber girl, because that would mean that she is actually Etina Boinya, niece of the assassinated president of Cameroon. More importantly, it would also mean that she's "Hoover." Tom just couldn't believe that Christine could be capable of murdering or plotting to murder five people, including a former president of the United States.

As Tom thought about the assassination of Walter Brooks, he realized that Christine was with them when they realized that Hoover was probably a woman. Hoover no longer disguised himself for the Brooks murder—why?

Because Hoover knew that the FBI knew Hoover was a woman. Besides Scott, the director, the president, and himself, Christine was the only other person that had that information. From the description the guard that saw her gave and from what came across on the video, it could be hundreds of women, but it could also be Christine.

He dropped her off before midnight and picked her up after seven. That would have given her more than enough time to do what she had to do and get back. She also had access to the security layout.

As much as Tom didn't want to believe it, he knew it was more than a possibility that Assistant Special Agent in Charge of the Organized Crime Division Christine Peal was Hoover.

He had Special Agent Quantara join him in his office and asked him several questions about his and Christine's work over the last couple of weeks. When he asked Quantara exactly where they were when he called them about Paul Cedes' death, Quantara told him that he was in Braddock waiting for Christine and Christine was still on the road. She had run into some car trouble and ended up being a few minutes late.

Tom's questions were making Quantara a little uneasy. "What's this all about? Why all these questions about our activities over the last couple of weeks?"

"I'm just trying to review some critical time sequences and where everybody was. Did Christine say what kind of car problem she had on her way to Brooks' place?"

"Yea, she had a flat tire. I remember because I noticed her car had all full size tires on it. She said she had to special order her spare to be full size instead of one of those little ones. It was odd though because she also had a little spare in the trunk. I guess with Volvo it really is safety first."

"Was the flat tire in the trunk?" Tom asked.

"No, she had stopped on the way out and dropped it off somewhere. She was going to pick it up on her way back to town."

Tom made a note and then got up and walked Quantara to the door. "Thanks," Tom said as he opened the door.

"Is there something going on I should know about? Brooks being hit wasn't Christine's fault. We didn't even have time to make any security changes out there," Quantara insisted.

"Nobody is looking for a scapegoat." Tom assured him.

Tom was now convinced that Christine had the opportunity to assassinate both Cedes and Brooks. It was a long shot and required meticulous planning, but it was possible.

In reviewing President Canfield's assassination, Tom remembered that Christine had to be called back from her day off. This, in Tom's mind, gave her an opportunity in Canfield's assassination as well and added one more piece in the puzzle. The puzzle was almost complete, and Tom didn't like the picture that was forming.

Finding out Christine's whereabouts during the Canon and Ballard assassinations would be more difficult and would involve other people. Tom decided that it was time to talk to Scott and the director.

Chapter 30

Christine pulled out the list of expatriates, found the names she was looking for, and called information. She got the number for the NAACP and placed her call. She wasn't sure exactly what she was going to say, so when the secretary answered, she almost asked for the NAACP executive director by his Cameroonian name. Catching herself at the last minute, she asked for Peter Brown.

There was a slight pause before Peter Brown came on the line.

"This is Peter—may I help you?"

"Mr. Brown, you don't know me, but I was told I could find Tande Makuna at this number." Christine said, using Peter Brown's Cameroonian name.

There was a long pause before Peter responded. "I'm sorry, you have the wrong number."

"My mistake, Mr. Brown; Mr. Boinya must have been in error." Christine hoped the Boinya name would have enough effect on Peter Brown to make him open up.

Peter had been caught off guard. That was a name he had not heard in decades. "Hold on just a minute, ma'am. What did you say your name was?"

"I didn't, but my father used to call me Etina." Christine waited for a reaction.

"My God, Are you saying that you're Etina Boinya?"

"Yes, Mr. Makuna, that's who I am."

"How do you know about Tande Makuna?" Peter asked.

"From my father; he has told me many things." Christine replied.

"Where are you now?"

"Not far from your office."

"We cannot meet here." Peter was coming out of his shock and was beginning to gather himself. "Let's meet at the coffee shop at the corner of Washington and 6th in an hour."

"An hour is fine. Please have one of your NAACP pamphlets lying on the table in front of you so that I can recognize you."

After she hung up the phone, Christine let out a deep sigh of relief. That went better than she thought it might. As far as she was aware, she was about to meet her first real Cameroonian. She decided to hold off on calling the other name she recognized until after her meeting with Peter Brown.

Christine arrived early and found a booth in the corner from where she could watch the entire restaurant. She watched as several black men entered and found a table or stood at the coffee bar, but as soon as Peter Brown entered, she recognized him.

He was an ordinary man in his late fifties or early sixties, but he dressed and carried himself with pride, a pride that was almost cocky. He was carrying a briefcase and Christine watched him sit at an empty table, open his briefcase and take out several brochures.

Christine walked up to his table and in a voice only loud enough for him to hear asked. "May I sit down, Mr. Makuna?"

Peter quickly offered her a chair as he checked the room to see if anyone had overheard Christine. "Please don't call me that," Peter said. "My name now is Peter Brown."

"Okay Peter, I'm not here to cause anyone any trouble. I just recently became aware of my real identity and am only trying to find out a few things about my family and my country." Christine told him.

"I don't know how I can help you. How do I even know you are who you say you are? All of the Boinyas were supposed to be wiped out when the Bellos took control of Cameroon thirty years ago."

Christine was prepared for this possibility. She reached into her gym bag and pulled out several photos of artifacts. "These are all in my possession," she told Peter. "They were given to my uncle, President Boinya, by his father and grandfather. Some of these you'll recognize as Cameroonian national treasures. My father and uncle left these for me, knowing that one-day I would have to prove my lineage. Within thirty minutes of here I have the statue of King Amuela and the royal elephant mask given to King Amuela by the Tikaar."

"Even if you are who you say you are, I left Cameroon over thirty years ago, how could I possibly help you?"

"I'm only looking for someone to help me understand what was going on in Cameroon thirty years ago and what's going on there today."

"The best I can do is give you the names of two people here in the states who understand Cameroon the best. I really don't know much about it anymore. The United States is my home now."

"Mr. Brown, after you give me those two names, I'll be out of your life forever," Christine promised.

Peter Brown checked his electronic organizer and then gave Christine two names and telephone numbers—one a professor of African Studies at the University of Texas, the other a seventy-four year old retired businessman living in New York.

"Pierre LeQuoix left Cameroon in the early seventies and set up his business in France. He made millions in shipping and import export. In the late eighties he retired and moved to New York. He has funded the opposition party in the last three Cameroonian elections. He would probably be your best bet," Peter told Christine

"How do you know him?" Christine asked.

"He's a big contributor to the NAACP every year."

"I'm only going to ask you to do me one more favor and then I'll be gone." Christine promised.

"What is it?" Peter asked hesitantly

"Would you call Mr. LeQuoix and tell him that you have someone he needs to meet with right away?"

Peter agreed and dialed Pierre LeQuoix's number. When he answered, Peter convinced him that he had information important enough for him to catch the next flight to D.C. and meet him in the lobby of the downtown Hyatt.

"He'll be at the Hyatt by 8:30," Peter told Christine.

"How will I recognize him?" Christine asked

"He looks like a seventy-year old pirate, with a patch over his left eye, and speaks with a very heavy accent. He's about five foot eight and travels with two bodyguards at least six feet tall and well over two hundred pounds. Trust me you won't miss him."

"Thank you for your help, and as promised, you will never hear from me again."

"I wish I could help you more, but please understand, I am living a different life now. I have a wife and three children."

"I wish you nothing but the best Mr. Brown." Christine told him.

She was eager to meet with this Frenchman. He was the right age to remember her father and he opposed the current government.

Christine had several hours before he would arrive so she decided to use the time for research. She returned to the public library and got on line. She searched the Web for anything on J. Edgar Hoover, and found more than she wanted. She narrowed the search to Hoover's archives and memorabilia.

She found what she was looking for; Hoover was a Freemason for over fifty years. He received the mason's highest award. He was awarded the Grand Cross-of Honour in 1965. His desk and office furniture were no longer at the FBI or at his home, they were on display at the Mason museum where they had been since 1980.

Christine knew that Hoover's office and home had been searched hundreds of times for his missing tapes and files. As she read about his office furniture being displayed at the Mason museum, she wondered how often, if ever, the museum had been searched? She also speculated that it would be easier to break into the Masonic Museum than into Hoover's old office in the Department of Justice building.

Chapter 31

Tom had called Scott and set up a meeting to meet with him and Director Flynn. He asked Scott to make sure the director didn't bring anyone else, because this was extremely sensitive. When Tom arrived, he was disappointed to find Peter Eagelton in the director's office. He looked at Scott for an explanation but all Scott could do was shrug his shoulders.

The director sensed Tom's discomfort. "Tom, I know you wanted this to be just the three of us, but we're getting into very sensitive areas these days. From here on out, it's politically and legally important that we have an impartial outsider at our meetings. We're going to need him to swear that we did the right things later on when we get hauled in front of congress."

"I understand sir, however I have an agency matter that I would like to discuss before we begin our meeting."

"What is it?" The director asked.

Tom handed the director a request to review the personnel records of Special Agent Christine Peal. All requests to review senior FBI agent's records must be approved by the director of the FBI.

"What the hell is this?" the director demanded.

"Sir, I weighed this decision very carefully before I made this request. This is the last thing I need to verify a theory."

"A theory; you better have a lot more than a theory to make a request like this."

"Unfortunately, I do sir. I have a lot of circumstantial evidence. If I could see that file, I believe I could close the Hoover case."

"I don't like what you're thinking," the director said as he signed the request.

With Scott and Peter Eagelton still standing there wondering what Tom and Director Flynn were talking about, the director called in his assistant.

"Debbie, I want you to go and get this file yourself. Then I want you to bring it directly to me. Understood?" The director handed the signed request to his assistant who looked at it and then gave the director a questioning look before she left the room.

"That was rather mysterious." Peter Eagelton said.

"I'm sorry Peter, Tom was right, it's an internal matter, at least for now," the director replied.

"Where are we on the Brooks assassination?" The director asked.

"Funny you should ask," Peter Eagelton said. "I got a call from that attorney of his who was here this morning. He claims that you guys went back out there and took a safe. He wants it back. I told him I would look into it. You're going to have to give it back; I can't stall him any longer."

Director Flynn looked at Scott and Tom. "Why haven't I heard about the safe?"

Scott and Tom looked at each other and shrugged their shoulders. "I don't know anything about a safe." Tom said

"Francine told me about the safe; I'm trying to get a warrant to look in it right now." Scott told the director.

"Brooks' lawyer said that the female agent took it." Peter Eagelton said.

"You mean Agent Peal?" The director asked.

"I guess so. He said she took the whole thing, the entire safe."

Scott laughed, "That sounds like Christine. Where is she anyway?"

"I don't know, I haven't seen her since I dropped her off at her car this morning," Tom said.

"Somebody go find her. Let's find out where she's got this damn safe," Director Flynn instructed.

"Sir, if my hunch is right we won't find her in this building," Tom told the director.

"What are you talking about?" Scott asked.

"Let's wait until Debbie returns with that file before we get into this,"

Tom said.

"OK, what else did we get from Francine?" Director Flynn was beginning to show his frustration.

"She claims to have had an affair with Walter Brooks that ended about ten years ago. She said that last night was just one of those purely sexual things that started with dinner, a few drinks, reminiscing about old times, and then next thing she knew they were in bed together. As far as that goes, I think I believe her," Scott said.

"What part don't you believe?" Peter Eagelton asked.

"They were lovers for about five years," Scott said. "She claims to never have discussed any FBI matters in that entire time. I find it hard to believe that during five years of pillow talk, her job never came up. She admitted to making introductions to certain congressmen and letting him know who could help him with certain legislation. Which is basically the same job we were paying her for."

"Scott, is there any indication that she's part of this Millenium?" Tom asked.

"No, I don't think she is, nor do I think that she told Brooks anything about our investigation. In fact I believe her when she says she wants to help. She thinks that everything we need to crush this Millenium is in that safe. She said she saw two CD-ROM disks and several files."

"I guess we need to find your agent with that safe." Peter Eagelton said.

"Yes, we need that safe," the director agreed. "What about that mercenary we have locked up? Did you get anymore out of him?"

"We got a name from him as well as a signed statement about what his job and instructions were in California. Christine was right to go in and get Feldman out. These guys were on their way in to kill him," Scott said.

Tom was about to ask Scott what name the mercenary gave them, when the director's assistant returned with the file and handed it to the director.

The director took the file, waited for his assistant to leave and then handed it to Tom. "I hope what ever you're looking for isn't in there."

Tom didn't even have to open the file, what he was looking for was printed on a label across the top. Tom's heart sank to his stomach, his face turned white, and he slumped his head in disbelief and anger as he read "Christine Barber Peal" on the label printed across the top of the file.

The director could tell just from the look on Tom's face, that whatever Tom had seen was enough to confirm his suspicions. "OK Tom, we let you run with this long enough; I think it's time to share what you have."

Tom tossed Christine's folder on the director's desk and said, "I found Hoover."

Scott leaned over picked up the file, looked at it, and handed it to Peter Eagelton. "This can't be—this has to be a mistake."

"It's no mistake." Tom said "I checked and double-checked everything. Christine Peal is Hoover. At first I thought she might have been in collusion with Hoover, but now I'm convinced that she is Hoover."

"Okay Tom lay it out for us," Director Flynn demanded.

"It all started to come together with a telephone call from Andy Greenfield this morning. I was borrowing Christine's phone when Andy called to give her an update on something he was researching for her. The research pertained to a black immigrant family supposedly wiped out by the FBI in the fall of '69."

"What was the family's name?" Scott asked.

"Barber." Tom replied.

"I see," Was all the director said.

Tom continued his analysis. "Christine had gone to Idaho to talk to Andy about five months ago. The other things she was curious about were Hoover's Special Projects files and two FBI agents that worked together in the special projects unit in '69. The agents were Ballard and Canon. She knew Ballard was one of them, but Andy told her that Canon was the other agent. Shortly after that, Canon got killed. I think it took her ten years after Ballard to find Canon and then he dropped a dime on the others."

Tom spent the next hour putting all of it together for them. He explained about the flat tire that wasn't, how Christine had opportunities to kill Cedes, Canfield, and Brooks, and he was prepared to wager that if they checked her whereabouts during the deaths of Canon and Ballard, she wouldn't have an alibi for them either. He told them about the Feldman interrogation and how Christine questioned him about Barber.

Tom also told them about his computerized search of the immigration records and that he found the Barbers emigrated from England in 1960. He told them that there was a massive search for a seven-year-old girl after the parents were killed in sixty-nine but she was never found.

Christine, he said, is now thirty-seven.

"The last thing I needed was some way to positively tie her to the Barbers. I never thought it would be as easy as reading her file name." The room fell totally silent when Tom finished. It was hardest for Director Flynn to accept—after all, he had just promoted her.

"Where is she now?" Peter Eagelton asked.

"I think she knows I'm on to her. She may have gone underground. When I called Andy back, she had already spoken to him and he told her I had talked with him. I'm sure she thought that eventually I would figure it out."

"What about the safe?" Peter asked.

"She obviously went back for it. The fact that we haven't seen the safe or heard from her confirms that she's gone underground," Tom said.

"Christ Tom, as soon as you suspected her, you should have put somebody on her," Director Flynn said.

"Perhaps sir, but I would like to think that I would have given any FBI agent with her service record the benefit of the doubt."

"Okay, we're in this mess, now how do we find her?" Director Flynn asked.

"We put a team on her condo and Tom and I will start with her parents," Scott proposed.

"There's one other thing to consider," Tom said, "she was very interested in Hoover's files and tapes. I think she may try to find them."

"That's ridiculous, people have been looking for them since Hoover died. What makes you think that she'll find them?" Peter asked.

"It's just a gut feeling; I think we should put people in Hoover's old office over in Justice and around his old house."

"Do what you think you need to, just bring her in," Director Flynn demanded.

"Where does this leave us with the Millenium?" Peter asked.

Scott thought about the options before answering. "We know Brian Hunt is in this thing up to his ears; if we can't get the disks and files from Christine in the next thirty-six hours, then we'll have to make a deal with him."

"That's not going to make the president very happy," Director Flynn said.

"No, it won't" Scott said, "so I guess we'd better find Christine and those disks."

Tom couldn't believe that Christine would let the Millenium get away with any of this. "I think we may be misreading this whole situation. We're pretty sure Christine killed the people she did because they killed or ordered the killings of her entire family. She's now killed everyone involved except for Bello. I have no doubt that she'll go after him. I don't think she would want anything to happen to any of the other heads of state coming for the conference.

"I think Christine is going to provide us the CDs and the lists. They may cost us something, but she's not going to let the Millenium off the hook."

"You mean she's going to blackmail us for the list?" Peter asked.

"Not traditional black mail, she won't want money, but she'll probably want safe passage out of the country and our guarantee not to chase after her."

"Jesus, Tom, she killed a former president of the United States, a former ambassador, two FBI agents and one of the country's leading citizens; we can't let her walk on that," Peter Eagelton insisted.

"All I'm saying is that's probably what she's going to ask for. Whether or not we give it to her is probably going to be up to the two of you and the president."

"We still have the name we got from the guy in lockup. Let's run it down before we start giving pardons to presidential assassins," Peter said.

Chapter 32

The tails on Brian Hunt hadn't resulted in any further leads and the director was unable to persuade the president to cancel the African summit. A very real threat to the summit still existed.

The director ordered stepped-up surveillance of the supremacist group that Cedes' people were tied to and all other known supremacist groups on the East Coast. Washington D.C. was sure to become a magnet to these groups between now and the end of the summit.

After getting back to his office, Tom ordered the surveillance on Hoover's old residence as well as his old office. He met Scott in the parking lot and they headed out to meet Christine's parents.

"Now that it's just you and me, old buddy," Scott said. "What would you do if Christine called?"

"If these people are responsible for wiping out her family, and I think they are, and if she has information that could shut down this Millenium and stop a race riot when those nuts try to kill the African leaders, I would let her walk. Provided she left the country, never to return," Tom said.

"I guess deep down, we probably all feel that way, even the director."

"You'd have a tough time convincing me that Peter Eagelton feels that way," Tom said.

"He's the attorney general, he can't let her walk."

As they made their way to Kettering, each was lost in his own thoughts until they pulled up in front of the Peal residence.

"This is a nice place for a retired preacher," Scott said.

"Yeah, let's go see what the preacher knows about his daughter."

As Tom put his hand out to ring the doorbell, the door opened and Virgil invited them in. "You guys must be FBI; Eleanor and I have been expecting you."

Tom and Scott looked at each other and followed Virgil to the living room.

"Christine said you would be here to ask us some questions and she told us to tell you whatever you want to know. So ask away," Virgil said.

"Mr. Peal, my name is Tom West and this is Scott Peterson—we work with Christine. We need to know a little about her background. Who were her real parents?"

"She said to tell you the truth. Until the last forty-eight hours, we thought her natural parents were named Barber. We found out, however, at the same time she did, that she is the natural daughter of Winston and Marita Boinya."

"She's a real live princess." Eleanor interrupted Virgil.

"Yes ma'am; how long has she know her real identity?" Tom asked.

"Like I said, she just found out yesterday."

"How did she find out," Mr. Peal?"

"I'd been holding a letter for her that her father gave me in 1969, and she read it yesterday."

"Why did you wait until yesterday to give it to her?" Scott asked.

"Because her father asked me not to give it to her until she was thirty," Virgil said.

"But she's thirty-seven now." Tom said, a little confused.

"This was the first opportunity since her thirtieth birthday that we had to give her the letter and suitcase." Virgil told them.

"What suitcase?" Tom asked.

"Winston Boinya left his daughter a suitcase of artifacts and statues that would prove her true heritage."

"Mr. Peal, do you know where Christine is?" Tom asked.

"No, but when she stopped by this afternoon to pick up the artifacts, she didn't sound like she was coming back. How bad is the trouble she's in?"

"We don't know yet, Mr. Peal, but if she contacts you would you please call us?" Scott asked

"I can't promise that. If Christine says its okay then we will," Virgil told them.

"Do you have a copy of the letter or a list of the artifacts, Mr. Peal?" Tom asked.

"No sir, Christine took the letter and all of the artifacts."

"Did she ever talk about the night her parents were killed?" Tom asked.

"No, she never would talk about it, except to say that she saw who killed them. When I told her to tell the police or the FBI, she said she couldn't. She said it like they wouldn't care if she did tell them."

"We won't take anymore of your time. Thank you for your help, if Christine does call please ask her to get in touch with me." Tom got up and Scott followed even though he looked like he had more questions.

When they were back in the car and pulling out of the driveway, Scott asked Tom why they left so soon; he had several more questions.

"We found out everything we needed to know. Christine didn't know about her Cameroonian roots until yesterday. That means she probably didn't know about the Millenium either and hadn't planned on doing anything with President Bello, at least not until yesterday. We also found out that the Peals don't know anymore than what they told us. Christine's not going to put them in any danger from us or from anyone else. What else do you want to know?"

"I wanted to know how they ended up with her, and how they got the money for the house and all of those fancy schools for her. Did you read her file? She's been to some of the best schools in this country and in Europe."

"They adopted her; the community probably hid her until the FBI stopped looking and then eventually the Peals adopted her. As far as the schools, you'll notice most of them were paid for by various grants. I'm sure that someone managing the funds for the Boinya estate funded them. The house—I bet Christine bought them that. See, there really wasn't much more we could have gotten from them." Tom smiled at Scott.

"If I don't watch it, you'll make director before I do." Scott said, returning Tom's smile.

"You know Scott, the more I hear about Christine, the more I like her. I'm not condoning what she did, but I understand it and I definitely don't want her mad at me."

"Do you think she's going to try and get back to Cameroon?" Scott asked.

"I don't see how she could—after this breaks, the whole world will be after her. You can't kill a former president and then get out of this country alive."

"You're probably right; I just hope she doesn't try to take the Millenium down by herself," Scott added.

Tom and Scott knew their next couple of days would be busy and headed back to the office to make sure they got a jump on them.

Chapter 33

Christine passed on the opportunity to view the disks on the library's computer; she opted for more privacy. She had to wait however until after her meeting with Pierre LeQuoix.

It was twenty minutes before nine and Christine still hadn't seen anyone matching the description given to her by Peter Brown. She was about to check the front desk when she saw two very large black men walking through the lobby, with a smaller man wearing an eye patch and a very attractive young woman hanging on to his arm walking next to them.

Christine waited for the young woman to go to the front desk to check them in before she approached Pierre LeQuoix's. As she approached, one of the guards stepped in front of her. Christine showed him her FBI badge and told him she was here on behalf of Peter Brown and that she needed to talk to Mr. LeQuoix. Mr. LeQuoix indicated to the guard to let her pass.

Christine put away her badge and told LeQuoix that it would be best if their conversation were held in private.

"I promise I won't hurt you." Christine told him, smiling all the while.

Pierre LeQuoix briefly talked to his guards and then escorted Christine to the hotel's restaurant.

"Okay young lady, you have my attention."

"Mr. LeQuoix, Peter asked you to come to Washington and meet with him as a favor for me. Peter will not actually be joining us; this meeting was arranged for the sole purpose of allowing us to meet."

"Okay, you know who I am; who are you?" Peter LeQuoix asked.

"I would like to hold off on that for just a moment, if you don't mind Mr. LeQuoix. Peter mentioned that you do some work with anti-government forces in Cameroon and that you are one of the leading experts on Cameroon in the United States."

Pierre LeQuoix's mood changed instantly from one of friendly and cooperative to aloof and abrupt. "Look young lady, I don't discuss my political views with the FBI, whether they're my views on French, U.S., or Cameroonian politics. I sure as hell hope this isn't what Peter got me down here for."

"Mr. LeQuoix, I think you misunderstand my interest. First of all, I resigned from the FBI today. I used my badge to make it easier to talk to you. Second, I am Cameroonian and want to know more about my history and perhaps discuss how I might be able to help Cameroon."

"I have to be able to call you something, so let's start there." LeQuoix said.

"The name that I have been going under for a number of years is Christine Peal."

"Okay Christine—why did you leave the FBI and exactly why are we talking right now?"

"I left the FBI because our policies conflicted and because I'm thinking about returning to my home country. We're talking because I was told that you know more about Cameroon than anyone else in this country."

"Okay, let's say I believe all of this; what is it that you want to know?"

"I want to know about the Boinya's as a people and as rulers. I want to know about their public policies and how the Bellos were able to get away with slaughtering them. I also want to know what present public sentiment is in Cameroon; if there is support for new leadership and how the Bellos manage to keep power."

"There are many African studies programs where you can get all of this information. What's your interest?" LeQuoix asked.

"Like I said before, I have an interest in perhaps returning to Cameroon," Christine replied.

Pierre LeQuoix finally agreed to answer Christine's questions with a guarantee that he would receive honest answers to his questions before they were finished.

For the next several hours, Pierre talked to Christine about life in Cameroon during the Boinya regime as well as during the Bello regime. He told her that after the Boinya massacre many of the Boinya supporters in politically powerful positions started to disappear. Each time a Bello appointee would replace them. By the end of 1970, there were no more Boinya supporters left in the government and Bello had complete control of the country.

Americans and Europeans began taking over Cameroon's natural resources and establishing a dual socioeconomic structure. There were the foreigners and the elite Cameroonians on one level and the rest of Cameroon reduced to poverty on the other level.

LeQuoix talked about how, by 1972, many of the property ownership rights were being stripped from the average Cameroonians while at the same time they were being expanded for foreigners. It had long been LeQuoix's belief that the U.S. Government, with the help of their CIA, was involved in the overthrow of the Cameroon government in 1969.

Christine began to ask more personal questions. "Did you know the Boinyas personally?"

"Yes, I knew both Shamba Boinya and Mafani Boinya," LeQuoix told her.

"What kind of people were they?"

"They were basically honest and good people. Their interest was with Cameroon and the people of Cameroon. They were always afraid that if they let the westerners in, before Cameroon was ready for them, that eventually, Cameroon would once again disappear as an independent nation. They were obviously right. Cameroon today is no more than a puppet for western business interests."

"Did you know Winston Boinya?" Christine asked.

"Yes, I met him on several occasions and spent the night with him and his family once in England. He was a good man, but I always thought that he should have stayed and helped his brother fight the political war going on in Cameroon."

"Do you know what happened to him?"

"I understand that he came to America and he and his family were killed here the night of the Boinya massacre," LeQuoix said.

"Peter said that you fund anti-government activities in Cameroon. Is there a large anti-government movement?"

"It's very large. If Bello were to allow free and fair elections, his government would receive less than twenty percent of the vote. It's American businesses and American troops stationed at the port of Douala that keep Bello in power."

"Is there a successor to Bello?" Christine asked.

"Not yet; he's still fairly young; he does have a vice president who could be groomed for the job."

"Is there a strong opposition party leader that the people would support in a fair election?"

"There is one that my organization supports. He was a university professor until he lost his job running against Bello in the last election. Exit polls show that he was the clear winner, but the official election results show him getting less than ten percent of the vote. He has popular support and the ideals that could turn Cameroon around."

"Mr. LeQuoix, what do you think needs to be done to return Cameroon to its people?" Christine asked.

"That's quite a question. I guess the first thing you would have to do is get the U.S. and the other western powers out of its government. Next, Bello would have to be removed, probably by force. I don't think he would go of his own free will. Then, free and fair elections could be held and in time a honest and fair government would emerge."

"Where would the Cameroonian armed forces side in a coup?"

"If Bello was still alive and in power, they would have to side with him. If he was no longer in power, they would side with the people."

"What would happen to Cameroonian politics if it was discovered that a Boinya survived the massacre?"

Pierre LeQuoix sat quietly for a moment just staring at Christine. "Are you telling me that there is a Boinya still alive?"

"Would it be a good thing if there was?" Christine asked.

"Yes it would, it would give the country someone to rally around. It's not possible, though, I personally saw the bodies of Mafani Boinya's family and if Winston Boinya had been alive, he would have come forth long before this."

"That's true, Mr. LeQuoix—but what if Winston had a daughter who was adopted after her natural parents were killed and didn't realize who she really was until recently?"

"Are you trying to tell me that Winston's little girl is still alive?" LeQuoix asked excitedly.

"Think about it, Mr. LeQuoix, her body was never found and she would be about thirty-seven now." Christine sat back and waited for a reaction.

"You want me to believe that you are Etina Boinya?"

"I don't want you to just take my word for it. I would like you to read this letter." Christine handed him the letter from her parents and sat back and watched his reaction as he read it.

LeQuoix's facial expressions showed signs of surprise, disbelief, and finally excitement. When he finished the letter he took a long look at Christine before he said anything. Then the only thing he said was, "Do you have the artifacts mentioned in the letter?"

"Yes, sir I do, I brought pictures of some of the items as well as the Bamoun terracotta pipe. It was the only thing small enough to carry with me. Christine put the photos on the table and opened her bag, allowing LeQuoix see the pipe inside.

Pierre LeQuoix stared at the pictures almost in reverence. "Many of these pieces were symbols of the Boinya dynasty and it was believed that Bello destroyed them during the massacre to symbolize the end of Boinya rule.

"I have a copy of the statue of King Amuela and several of these other pieces." Pierre LeQuoix found it difficult to deny Christine's claim.

"In this letter it says that you would receive this letter on your thirtieth birthday. You just pointed out that you're thirty-seven; why did it take you until now to get this letter? LeQuoix asked.

"It's a long story, but simply put, I was estranged from my adopted family for over ten years and just stopped by to reconcile with them yesterday and that's when they gave me the letter and artifacts."

"Does anyone else know about this?"

"My adoptive parents, Peter Brown, and by now at least three members of the FBI, one of whom is the director."

"Is this why you left the FBI?" LeQuoix asked.

"It's one of the reasons."

"Your life is in immediate danger. There are people in the United States, both in government and in business who don't want African politics disturbed. There are, of course, also Bello's men. Should this news get out you would have a price put on your head by both the American CIA and the Cameroonian government."

"I'm not concerned about my life. I would, however, like to help remove Bello from office and return Cameroon to its people."

"I'm getting to be an old man, I would die happy if I could see Cameroon out from under the Bello regime. I'm worth over three billion U.S. dollars; I would give all of it to see Cameroon have fair and free elections. It would be a bonus to see a Boinya back in the presidential palace," LeQuoix said with pride.

"I would like to do all I can to help on the first part, but I'm not ready to enter politics. I would first like to get to know the home of my ancestors."

"Christine, how can I help?" LeQuoix asked.

"I'm being pursued by the FBI and I'm going to need a way to get myself and the artifacts out of the country. I also need access to a high-end computer system and some burglar tools," Christine said.

"Getting you out of the country is no problem. I own a shipping company with twenty-two ocean-going vessels, I also have three company jets and one small private jet. All are at your disposal. You can use one of my offices in D.C. as your base; they're fully equipped with the latest computer technology. For the burglar tools however, I would have to put you in touch with my security people.

"Exactly what do you have planned for the tools?"

"I'm looking for proof that the FBI and CIA were involved in the overthrow of Cameroon and in my parents' death."

LeQuoix was stunned. "You know this proof exists and where it is?"

"I know it exists, and I know where it might be."

"I can see why the FBI is after you; if this became public, the streets in America would run red with blood. The race riots of the past would be considered mild compared to what this could unleash. The international implications are even more staggering.

"I have a special security team that trains in Yuma, Arizona that I'll call in to help you if you want it." LeQuoix offered.

"Thank you, but this needs to be done quickly, and with the right tools, I can be in and out before anyone even knows."

Pierre LeQuoix called one of his guards over. He whispered something in the guard's ear, who then left. "I sent Roger to get you a special telephone. This is a regular phone with my private number programmed in. It also has a homing device installed. Should you run into any difficulty and need my help, push 'star 1' and we'll find you. I'll plan on staying in town until we get you safely out of the country. Tell me where you're staying and will get you back there?"

Christine told him and he tried to convince her that she should stay at the Hyatt with him but Christine wasn't ready to give up the freedom of movement that her current hideaway provided. Christine got the address and security codes to the offices that she would be using and scheduled to meet the head of LeQuoix's security there.

Before they parted LeQuoix hugged Christine and said, "Young lady, don't you get yourself killed. It took me over thirty years to find another Boinya, I don't want to lose you now."

Christine smiled and said, "I plan on seeing you in Cameroon, Mr. LeQuoix."

As she was leaving, Pierre LeQuoix gave his guard instructions that he wanted twenty-four-hour protection for Christine and that nothing had better happen to her.

Chapter 34

Christine went directly to LeQuoix's office after leaving him at the restaurant. She had no problem gaining access to the building or to the office he told her to use. She was pleased to find that LeQuoix's offices were using Micron computers, in her opinion the best in the industry, and compatible with her laptop.

She hooked the lap-link cable from her laptop to the desktop and inserted the first disk from Brooks' safe into her laptop. She placed a writeable CD into the desktop and pulled the files directly from the laptop CD drive onto the desktop CD drive, effectively making a copy of the CD, without leaving a trail on either computers' hard drive. She completed the same process with both CDs. Once she was comfortable that she had made an effective copy of both discs, she put away the originals and booted the copy of the disc that was labeled Millenium.

Christine had found the proverbial mother lode. The table of contents listed everything from the corporate charter, to corporate officers, to the board of directors. There were even sections for funding, assets, and operations.

She held her breath and clicked on the line marked "Board of Directors." Almost instantaneously a list of about fifty names scrolled past. Christine scrolled back to the top of the page and read the name under the chairman heading. The name was Mathew Mitchell, next to the name column was a column for country. Next to Mitchell's name it said USA, next to the country was a column for job and that column said vice president.

Christine couldn't believe her eyes, the vice president of the United States, Mathew Mitchell, was chairman of the board of the Millenium. As she scanned the list of board names, she began to recognize many of them. Most were Americans but there were a number of Germans, French, Japanese, even Switzerland had two representatives as did South America and Africa. She recognized several heads of states from foreign countries and two powerful senators and a Supreme Court Justice. The businessmen on the list were among the wealthiest in the world.

She realized that even if the FBI had this list, there was no way they could bring everyone to justice, at least not all at once.

She returned to the table of contents and clicked on the line that said executive committee. Here she found ten names, several of which she recognized. Walter Brooks was listed as the chairman of this committee; also listed were Brian Hunt, Paul Cedes, Gunther Herman whose name she recognized from the papers as Germany's central banker and Arles Lourdes, head of the French socialist party. Of the other names, she recognized three but couldn't place them.

Christine went to the asset portion of the disc and found a corporation that was sufficient in size to be included in the Fortune one hundred. Their assets ranged from real estate to cash all over the world. In Washington alone, they owned two thirty-eight floor office towers.

Christine searched the corporate charter and found the origin of Millenium. In April of 1970, John Canfield, Walter Brooks, Paul Cedes, Aaron Horst, and Gunther Herman founded Millenium. The name Aaron Horst was new to Christine and he was not on the current list of directors. She made a note of the name and clicked on operations. The disc instructed her to insert the disc marked operations.

She found a corporation with an operations budget in excess of one billion U.S. dollars. The operations were broken down by country with each country having its own historical database, as well as active and proposed operations. Each operation was spelled out in detail including the manpower assigned.

Christine had stumbled onto the most extensive worldwide organized crime operation in history. Armed with this information, crimes throughout the world that had gone unresolved over the last thirty years could now be solved. This information had the power to crumble governments and destroy political parties.

Christine clicked on active operations for the United States and found three: The assassination of the president, the appointment of Judge Hellerman to the Supreme Court, and the acquisition of NPU (Northern Public Utilities), which controls sixty-five percent of the power supplied to the northeast. There was one operation in the planning stages: the reelection of Mathew Mitchell (he will assume the presidency after the current president is assassinated).

Christine was disappointed that the data on the discs only went back to April 1970. She was hoping to find some proof about the overthrow of Cameroon and the execution of her family.

When she pulled up current operations for Cameroon, she found none, but she did find several references to operations conducted there over the past twenty-nine years. It would take Christine days to review everything on these discs, time she didn't have. She was so caught up in what she was doing that she didn't even hear Pierre LeQuoix's security man enter the room.

She jumped when he tapped her on the shoulder. "I'm sorry, Ms. Peal; my name is Victor. Mr. LeQuoix said you might be needing some equipment and perhaps some help?"

Christine shut off the monitor without shutting down the computer. "Yes, I do need some equipment, but I think I better complete the job myself."

"Ms. Peal, I have two men waiting downstairs, they can get you into any building in town in a matter of seconds, and they can cover you if anything goes wrong. They won't even know your name or what you're looking for."

"Victor, I'll accept your offer only if your men agree to do this without taking any weapons at all. I don't want anyone shot."

"I can guarantee that Ms. Peal."

"Good, I'll meet you down stairs in five minutes."

Christine printed out the plan for the assassination of the president along with the timetables, manpower list, and each board member's vote on the plan. The plan also explained that they should use the assassination of President Sossou as the cover for killing the president of the United States. It should look like a stray bullet that was meant for president Sossou of Congo.

Christine exited the program, removed the disk, and shut down both computers. She took the copies and stuck them behind a ceiling tile in the office.

As promised, two men dressed for a night operation were waiting for her in front of the building in a black Saab 93. She gave them the address of the museum– when they arrived, one of the men got out and scouted the building while Christine and the other man waited in the car. She heard her ear mike keyed twice and the other man told her that that was the signal letting them know they had access to the building. Christine was a little surprised, it couldn't have gone any quicker if they'd had a key.

Christine found the director's desk, which was behind a single laser security system. Christine's partner rerouted the system in less than sixty seconds and they began their search of Hoover's office furniture.

They had been searching for quite a while and her frustration was beginning to show. She wasn't looking for the tapes or files, but for something that told them where the tapes might be. They found nothing.

The guard walked up to the desk, pulled out the center drawer, and told Christine that most people check under and in the drawers, but very seldom check underneath the desktop itself. He reached into the slot where the drawer was and felt the underside of the desktop and pulled his hand back empty. "Well it does work sometimes?" Her new partner said with a grin.

Christine kicked the corner of the desk in frustration and they both heard a "click." They froze neither wanting to move while they scanned the area. Christine's partner turned to Christine and told her that he thought the "click" came from inside the desk. He looked back inside the center drawer space and a big smile crossed his face. I think I found what you're looking for."

Christine ran around the end of the desk, pushed him aside and looked inside the space that would normally be filled by the center drawer. There inside the space she found a small flap had dropped down. The flap was no more than three inches wide, six inches long and an eighth of an inch thick. Tapped to the flap were two keys. Christine couldn't believe her luck, she was sure the secret compartment could only be opened with the center drawer out and a tap on the corner of the desk. A combination that could typically only occur intentionally, she was starting to believe that it was her destiny to find Hoover's tapes.

Christine removed the key's, pressed the flap back in place, replaced the center drawer, and headed to the exit.

Her partner rerouted the security system and keyed his mike twice and they were out of the museum just as the car pulled up front.

As soon as the car pulled away, Christine asked if they could call Victor and ask him to meet them at the office building.

When they arrived, Victor was waiting at the front entrance.

"Everything went as planned, I assume?"

"Yes it went better than expected. Your men are quite impressive."

"Good, now what can we do for you?"

"We found two keys, I need to identify them and then make another trip." Christine told him.

"I think I have just the program you need," Victor said.

"I thought you might."

They went into the building's control room on the main floor and Christine was amazed to find this many people still working. She saw at least ten people working on computers and watching monitors. Victor directed Christine to an empty computer.

"Scan the keys in with the number down and we'll see what they open."

Christine followed Victor's instructions and scanned the keys into the computer. Victor opened the program and the computer started searching; five minutes later it had run through the entire program with no success.

"This is highly unusual, how old are these keys?" Victor asked.

"They go back to the early seventies, maybe the late sixties," Christine told him.

"In that case, we'll have to try another approach." Victor logged on to the Internet and into the FBI computer, bypassing the codes and passwords and going straight into the database. It took him less than two minutes to break into the FBI computer and begin his search.

"I didn't realize the FBI was that easy to break into," Christine said.

"It's not, unless one of your companies built the security software," Victor said, sporting a grin.

The computer searched for three minutes before it finally came up with a match. Victor clicked on the match, hit a couple of key strokes and a map of Washington DC appeared displaying a bright red dot for the last recorded place of the lock that matched one of Christine's key.

Christine looked at the map and couldn't believe her eyes. "Damn, we were just there," She said to no one in particular.

"You were just at the Masonic museum?" Victor asked.

"Yes, I thought your guys would have told you."

"Only if you wanted them to. Did you want to go back tonight?"

"I have to, this may be my last chance. Can you call your guys back?"

"They never left, they're in the break room."

"What about the other key?"

"The computer seems to have trouble finding it. We'll keep trying while your gone." Victor told her.

Before Christine went to meet with the two security agents, Victor helped Christine get into Scott's computer at the FBI so that she could send an internal message from Scott's computer to Tom and Director Flynn. Victor left to get his men before Christine started typing.

To: Director, FBI
From: Christine Peal
Subject: Millenium
Sir,

By now I'm sure you have talked to Tom and realize that I have resigned. I don't know what your plans are, but be assured that I have no intention of harming anyone not involved in the massacre of my family.

I have in my possession documents that reveal a conspiracy the likes of which no one has ever seen. It spans the globe and implicates politicians and businessmen throughout the world. These documents list every Millenium member of consequence, by name, country, and profession.

The Millenium infiltrated the highest levels of government. I will give you an example of the value of the documents in my possession. Then perhaps we can talk about a deal. I know, a deal for someone who has committed multiple murders is not something you want to consider. I strongly urge you to consider the circumstances that brought us to this point, and that ultimately what I have is worth more than my head on your wall.

Please don't try to trace this message; I'll call you later and give you an-other chance. Now for my show of good faith: the Millenium was founded in April of 1970 by Walter Brooks, John Canfield, Paul Cedes, Gunther Herman, and Aaron Horst.

The Millenium's short-term goal is to put Judge Nicholas Hellerman on the U.S. Supreme Court. To do that, one of the current judges is going to have to die.

The files I have give the target judge's name as well as the date and time of the assassination as well as the individuals contracted to do the job. It will look like an accident. You have three weeks on this one.

The documents also show which African president will be assassinated and when. This one alone is worth the price of my freedom, because it's a lot bigger than we originally thought.

Oh yes, don't share any of your plans with the vice president.

I'll be in contact!

Etina Boinya

Christine sent the message, cut the connection to the FBI computer, and logged off.

By two-thirty they were back in the museum. They made their way to the basement and into a storage room with hundreds of boxes. Christine instructed them to ignore anything newer than 1972 and anything that didn't lock. By four they had made their way through about three hundred boxes when they uncovered another small storage area about four feet high from the ground and three feet wide and about ten feet deep. This storage space had an iron gate on it with a heavy security lock. Christine looked at Victor who invited her to try her key. Christine inserted her key; the lock was rusted but after several tries, it popped open. Christine pulled the Iron Gate back, got on her knees, and pulled out the first box. When she lifted the lid she was afraid to look. She did look though and saw a notebook lying on top of about fifty reel-to-reel tapes. Christine was startled for a moment before she realized that in the 'sixties cassettes and CDs weren't the tape of choice yet.

She opened the notebook and was amazed to find an itemized listing of everything on the tapes and the dates and times they were recorded.

Christine turned to Victor "What's the chance of getting all of these boxes out of here?" She asked him.

Victor wasn't too excited about the idea. "We'd have to get a pickup down here. That would be taking a considerable risk. The roads are going to get busy in another couple of hours."

"Victor, believe me when I tell you that what's in here is worth the risk."

Victor nodded to one of his men, who disappeared. Christine started going through all of the boxes while they were waiting until she found the boxes for the last six months of nineteen sixty-nine. Those tapes were in two separate boxes. As she reviewed the inventory list, she found several tapes that might be of value. One was dated September 1, 1969 and marked "VP, Ballard, Brooks"—several others around that same date were labeled with Cedes or VP or just Brooks. One tape dated September 2, 1969, which was the day after Ballard and Canon killed Christine's parents, was just labeled Ballard and Canon. Christine was certain that these tapes would talk about her family's execution.

By the time Victor's man returned with a pickup, Christine had selected six tapes she thought might be able to help her cause. The others she planned to store somewhere until she had time to review them. Luck was still with them; they were able to load twenty-two boxes into the back of the pick-up without being spotted.

Christine thanked Victor and his people for their help and drove the pickup away. Christine had now gone almost two days without sleep. She needed to grab at least a couple of hours if she was going to be effective during the next thirty-six hours. In the morning, she would have to find a place to store the boxes; now though, she desperately needed to lie down for a while. She found a twenty-four hour parking garage pulled in and crawled in the back of the camper to lie down for a quick nap. Her last thoughts as she was falling to sleep were, "Where am I going to get a reel-to-reel tape player?"

Chapter 35

Tom and Scott had set up cots in one of the conference rooms. They were doing everything they could to find a lead on either the Millenium or Christine. From now until this was over, this was a crisis situation.

Scott got over two thousand matches on the name Kessler, that he had gotten from the mercenary in their custody. When he ran the name through again asking for only those matches with a military background, the list was reduced to eight hundred fifty. Scott needed a rested mind before he could continue and went to lay down on a cot.

Tom was researching Christine's itineraries around each assassination to try and develop a pattern when his computer gave him a message alert. He looked at the message header and was surprised to find a message from Scott, especially since Scott was sound asleep in the conference room.

When he opened the message he saw that Christine had sent it and before he even read it, he woke Scott.

"We have contact." Tom told Scott.

When Scott was finally awake enough to read the message, they decided to get the director right away.

By the time the director arrived at FBI headquarters it was still the middle of the night and his mood was none too pleasant.

"So we got a call from Christine. I suppose she wants us to forget about all of those assassinations?"

"Yes sir," Tom said. "I think you should read her letter before deciding not to consider it."

Director Flynn gave Tom a dirty look and proceeded to read the letter. When he was finished he stood up and scratched his head. "You know I haven't even had a shower or a cup of coffee. Damn her, why couldn't we get to that damn safe before she did." The director said to no one in particular.

"Consider this sir, if she hadn't gotten to the safe, we may never have gained access to its contents. That attorney would have kept us in court for years. She probably did us a favor by stealing it," Tom said.

"If I didn't know better I'd say that you were a bit smitten by Christine and what she's trying to pull off here," Director Flynn said.

"Let's just say that I am an admirer of Hoover," Tom replied.

The director returned his attention to the letter. "Does anybody know what she means when she said 'don't share any of your plans with the vice president'? Is she trying to tell us that he's part of the Millenium?" The director asked.

"I don't know if that's what she was referring to or not." Scott said "But after we got Christine's message, I narrowed my search parameters on Kessler to government employees in Washington. We know Boxer called Washington to contact Kessler. We got eighteen hits on the name. One of them is with the Secret Service detail protecting the vice president."

"So what does it all mean? Is the vice president in on it or not? Is this Kessler there to protect the vice president, the Millenium or is he there to kill the vice president?" Director Flynn wanted answers.

"We don't know sir" Tom admitted.

"Have you at least tracked down where this damn letter came from?"

"Yes sir," Scott said. "It came from my computer."

"How the hell did this come from your computer? Was she in the building?"

"No sir, we think she broke into the system from the outside and somehow got around my codes and passwords and sent this message from my terminal."

"I guess we really didn't appreciate what we had when she was on our side." Director Flynn said.

"Sir, I think it's worth talking to the president about, we should at least have an idea of what to tell her when she calls in," Tom recommended.

"Okay, I'll talk to the president, meanwhile you guys find out where she is and figure out what's going on with the vice president."

"Sir I think for now we should follow her advice and keep the VP out of the loop." Scott said.

The director agreed. "That's best. I'm going to shave before I call on the White House—he's going to love being woken up in the middle of the night by the director of the FBI. While I'm getting ready, one of you pull up the background check on Judge Hellerman. Let's see why he would be such a good candidate for the Supreme Court."

Scott pulled up everything the FBI had on Judge Hellerman and neither he nor Tom saw anything unusual in the material. The director returned clean-shaven but not in any better spirits.

"Okay, the president is expecting us," Director Flynn said.

"Us?" Scott protested.

"Yes, us—you don't think I'm going to talk to the president at four in the morning with out my star agents do you?" Director Flynn said as he handcuffed the briefcase with the letter and Hellerman's file on Tom's wrist.

When they arrived at the White House, a secret service agent escorted them to the same library as last time. The president joined them shortly wearing a warm up suit.

"Okay Martin, what's got all of us out of bed so early?" The president asked.

"Sir, we've heard from Hoover," Director Flynn said.

"You mean your rogue agent don't you?" The president countered

"Yes sir. Agent Peal contacted us a little over two hours ago."

"What did she want?"

The director took the briefcase off Tom's wrist and pulled out Christine's letter. He handed it to the president and waited for him to read it.

"What the hell is this about the vice president?" The president asked.

"We're not sure sir, we believe that she's trying to tell us that he is part of the Millenium."

"For Christ's sake, Martin, you stood in this very room less than forty-eight hours ago and told me he wasn't. Now make up your mind—is he or isn't he?"

"Mr. President, we may have been wrong. There's a good possibility that he is," the director said.

"Does that clear Brian Hunt then?"

"Not yet sir; we need some more time."

"This letter says that Gunther Herman and Aaron Horst helped start this Millenium. If that's true, then we have a real problem. With the European single currency a reality, Gunther is probably one of the most powerful people in Europe. How reliable do you think her information is?" The president asked.

"Her information comes directly from Walter Brooks' private files."

"If what she says is true about the level of conspiracy, then I think we'd better give her what she wants. If Horst and Herman are involved, this has tremendous international implications," the president said.

"Excuse my ignorance, Mr. President but I'm not familiar with Aaron Horst," Tom said.

"Aaron Horst died in 1985 at the age of 93. There are only a handful of people who understand his importance to the survival of Russia and other Eastern Bloc nations. For most of his life, he controlled the economies of all of Eastern Europe. He's the man responsible for developing the economic plans for keeping the people fed and the factories pumping.

"During the cold war, we ran several attempts at assassinating him, knowing that economically the East couldn't survive without him. If you take a look at Russia today you know we were right." The president reflected on the past for a moment before continuing.

"If Horst helped create this thing, it can't be good for us. Give that damned woman what she wants."

"Sir, we know that she plans to kill President Bello. We can't give her a pardon for murders she plans to commit. That's not right or ethical," Director Flynn insisted.

"Then tell her we'll forget about the rest but she can't commit any other murders or everything is off the table," the president countered.

"I don't think that will be acceptable to her," Tom said.

"Then work it out by God! We need those files."

"Sir, I have one other concern," Tom said. "In rereading the letter several times on the way over here, I was struck by the incongruity of the whole thing. It's my understanding that if a Supreme Court vacancy occurs, then the president of the United States appoints a new one. Is that not correct?"

"That's right. I see what you're getting at, Agent West. How would the Millenium know who I would select?"

Tom offered the president two scenarios. "Sir, the first scenario is that you are guided by your staff to make the correct decision. In this case, we would assume that Brian Hunt is pushing Judge Hellerman, but a even safer route is to have a president in the White House that's controlled by the Millenium and then Hellerman would be a shoo-in."

"Are you saying they're going to try to buy me?" The president was infuriated.

"No sir, they know that wouldn't work." Tom assured the president. "However, in Christine's letter, when she talks about the African president being assassinated, she said, "It's a lot bigger than we thought." Based on everything else in the letter, I think she's trying to tell us that you're a target as well sir. It would make sense if the vice president were part of the Millenium. He would assume your duties after your death and be able to appoint Hellerman to the court."

"That's reading a lot into the letter," the director said.

"There's only one way to figure all of this out for sure. Let's talk to your agent. Right now she's holding all of the cards," the president said.

"We do have that Secret Service Agent Kessler," Scott said.

"What about Kessler?" the president asked.

"He seemed to be the primary contact giving the instructions to take out that judge in California."

"Kessler's not just any secret service agent, he's the lead agent on the vice president's security detail," the president said.

"That would make sense," Tom said. "If the vice president is involved with the Millenium, he would need someone like Kessler to keep his shirttail clean."

"We need more proof before we can accuse the vice president of anything like this," Director Flynn said.

"Let's pull in Kessler and sweat him?" Tom recommended.

"Let's wait and see if we hear from Christine. If we can get her to lay off of Bello, then maybe we can get her to help us wrap this up. Let's give her until noon to get back to us," Scott suggested. "If we haven't heard from her by then we'll have to move forward with Kessler and probably Hunt."

The President agreed to schedule a staff meeting for six that evening. This would be their last chance to prepare for the economic summit and to detain Hunt and the VP.

Chapter 36

Christine woke up when the alarm in the car next to her started going off and wouldn't stop. She checked her watch and it was already eight-thirty. She slept longer than she wanted to even though she definitely needed it. When she got out of the truck she noticed that the entire parking garage had filled up.

Christine locked up the truck and walked to a phone booth on the street. She checked the yellow pages and found what she was looking for: "Springdale Self Storage Center." It provided twenty four hour access, was fully fenced and air-conditioned and the units rented by the month, quarter or year.

Christine drove the truck to Springdale and rented a unit large enough to store furnishings for a three-bedroom home. She opened the unit, drove the pickup inside and closed the unit back up.

Before Christine had left the parking lot, she pulled several additional tapes and files from the boxes. With those in her bag, she took a cab back downtown to pick up her car. On a hunch, she decide to go into the office building where she had been the night before and see if Pierre LeQuoix was in.

Pierre was in and greeted her with enthusiasm. "Come in, come in Etina. Victor tells me that you had a busy night."

"Yes we did Pierre. Your men were extremely helpful. Would you please call me Christine though; I don't think I'm quite ready for Etina just yet."

"Of course, I understand. Victor tells me you took several boxes from a museum last night. Would you like me to keep them for you until you're ready?"

"Thank you Pierre, but I've already taken care of it." Christine told him.

"What will you do now?" Pierre asked.

"I need another favor."

"All you need to do is ask," Pierre said.

"There were some tapes in those boxes. The problem is they're reel-to-reel and I have no way to listen to them."

"That shouldn't be a problem." Pierre picked up the phone and his secretary came on line.

"Get me the audio lab please," Pierre asked.

When the lab tech came on line, Pierre asked him if they had the ability to listen to or copy a reel to reel tape. The lab tech assured him that they did.

"We can do it for you, Christine, we can copy it over to cassette or you can listen to it in the lab—it's up to you," Pierre told her.

"I would like to listen first and then have them copied,"

"Do these tapes have anything to do with Cameroon?"

"I think so."

"Could an old man with very little joy in his life come with you to listen to them?"

"That's the least I owe you. I must warn you though, I don't know what's on these tapes. It may be a waste of time."

When they entered the lab, Pierre LeQuoix had the technician set up the equipment and then made everyone leave the lab.

The first tape they listened to was dated October 22. Christine wanted to hear it because it was listed as a conversation with Paul Cedes in the logbook. They listened to several unimportant conversations until they heard the director greet Paul Cedes.

"Paul, how are things in Yaounde? John tells me you're ready to coordinate an operation."

"I guess Mr. Brooks is getting impatient. He says he needs that oil field in the next couple of weeks or his company is going under."

"We've tracked down Mr. Boinya, he goes by a different name over here, but we know exactly where to find him and what his schedule is. Do you have a date in mind, Paul?"

"We're going to install an already powerful family, but we're going to make them get their hands dirty. President Boinya and Biya Bello, the guy we're going to install, are good friends. Bello's son Furandi will be staying at the palace the first weekend in September. He and two of his men are going to take care of the entire family in the palace."

"Good, with the time difference, if my men take out the Boinyas in Washington the evening of the first, Furandi can do his job the morning of the first."

"I'll set it up. If there are any changes, let the vice president know."

With that the conversation was over and Christine and Pierre sat in stunned silence. Without saying a word, Christine changed tapes and they listened to one dated September first.

It was obviously J. Edgar Hoover at his office. There was nothing of significance until they got into the second half of the tape. Christine sat at the edge of her chair when she heard the caller identify himself as agent Ballard.

"Sir, the two Klansmen we had set up to take care of the Barbers are in jail. I don't think we'll be able to get them out until tomorrow. Should we postpone until then?"

"No, it has to be done tonight. You and Canon do it. Call me when it's done."

Christine and Pierre couldn't believe what they had just heard. In two consecutive tapes, they heard the director of the FBI plan a murder and give the order to two of his agents to carry it out.

"That son of a bitch! I'd heard stories about Hoover but I would never have believed this," Pierre said.

They listened to the rest of the tape and there was nothing else of interest on it. Christine put on the other tape from the same day that was marked, "VP, Ballard, Brooks."

The first two calls were social, this was obviously a tape from his home. The third call was from a voice they both now recognized.

"Sir, it's Ballard. The situation with the African has been handled."

"Good, I want to see the two of you in my office in the morning."

"Mr. Hoover, sir, there is one minor problem."

"What's that Ballard?"

"The girl, she got away."

"What do you mean she got away? Find her!"

"Yes sir."

Christine knew they were talking about her. She would never forget that night.

"I can't believe I'm listening to this," Christine said.

"They knew you were African. They knew exactly who you were." Pierre said as they listened to the next taped call.

"Sir, the FBI has completed its part of the operation. Have you heard from Cedes?"

"Yes, he just called. The CIA met with success on their end as well. Cedes thinks that we may have bought ourselves more trouble than we wanted in tying our fortune to the Bellos."

"He may be right John, You'll want to be careful, remember in six years they will officially be your headache. I don't think Bello senior will be a problem, but that kid Furandi seems a bit unbalanced. Let's just pray his old man stays around a long time."

"I hope you're right about the six- year part. This should lock up Brooks' support."

"I hope so, because the Boinyas were well-liked in Cameroon. The Bellos regime is going to be much more brutal."

"Maybe so, but they'll be much more receptive to U.S. business. We also got them to agree to give us military access to the port of Duoala. If Ackerman would just get his head out of his butt, he would see how important Cameroon is as a launching point to the rest of Africa."

"I think he knows the strategic importance of Cameroon, John, he just wasn't prepared to pay the price for its cooperation."

"That's why I'm not sure that I should wait six years."

"Even with Brooks' support, unseating a popular incumbent president would be difficult and may leave you extremely bloody. It's best to bide our time. As long as Cameroon is still open, you'll have Brooks' support."

"It's just frustrating watching someone that weak leading our country. What about your people that did the job, are you sure we can count on their discretion?"

"Of course, their loyalty is to me. They're part of an elite group of men that do special assignments for me here at the agency."

"I hope you're right, Edgar, because if Ackerman finds out about this, we're both finished. I don't just mean in politics either."

"Don't worry John, everything is under control."

"OK then, I'll see you for lunch on Wednesday."

"Paul Cedes was the CIA's man in Cameroon—I always knew the CIA was behind this. Now we have proof. Now we can get the international courts to do something about it," Pierre LeQuoix said.

"Let's hear the rest of the tape and then we can figure out what to do." Christine told him as the next voice could be heard.

"Venture Oil, may I help you?"

"I thought this was Walter's private line."

"It is, one moment please."

"This is Walter."

"Walter, it's Hoover. I just talked to John, he says that you should be able to turn on the pumps in Cameroon by the end of the month."

"It's about time, I assume that we're dealing with the Bellos now?"

"As of about a half hour ago."

"What about the brother you were telling me about. What's the chance of him returning to Cameroon and taking over?"

"He won't be returning to Cameroon."

"Good, will I see you at lunch on Wednesday?"

"Of course, I wouldn't miss this one."

The next conversation they heard was Hoover talking to his secretary.

"Marge, please schedule lunch with the vice president and Walter Brooks for this Wednesday at the vice-president's residence."

"My God Christine! You've got a bombshell here! I wish I was twenty years younger; we'd give them the whipping of their lives," Pierre said.

"I wish we had a tape of the Wednesday lunch meeting," Christine said.

"That was not at Hoover's house or at his office so I doubt that a tape even exists," Pierre told her.

"I do have a tape of the following day marked simply "Ballard and Canon".

"Let's hear it," Pierre said.

Christine loaded the tape and they had to listen to several purely administrative calls before they heard Ballard's voice. It took Christine several seconds to realize that they were not on the phone but in the same room.

"You guys did a good job last night, but you lost the girl. I want you back

out there until you find her."

"Sir, we think one of those other Negro families took her in and are hiding her from us."

"Then you do a house-to-house search. Use as many agents as you need. If that little Negro girl gets away and tells what she saw, this country is in big trouble."

"Yes sir."

"I want you both here Wednesday by ten thirty. The vice president and some other people want to meet you and thank you personally for what you did for your country last night."

"Yes sir, ten-thirty Wednesday, we'll be here."

The rest of the tape was filled with meaningless conversations, but Christine and Pierre had heard all they needed to hear.

These tapes, along with the files and the CDs, was proof that the U.S. was responsible for the massacre of one of Africa's last remaining royal families and Cameroon's legally elected president.

"I can get these tapes on TV and in newspapers all over the world by this evening. The United States will be forced to repatriate Cameroon," Pierre said.

"Let's think about this first. I'm sure you didn't become a billionaire by rushing into things. There might be a better way to go," Christine told Pierre.

"You obviously aren't aware of my reputation. In my younger days, they called me the black pirate. For several reasons, I wore a pirate's patch over my eye; I'm black but also because I slash and burn and am known for being ruthless in my business affairs," Pierre told Christine.

"If we release all of this information, Hoover and the U.S. government would be disgraced and Cameroon may even get some compensation for damages from the United States. In a few years, however, it would all be forgotten.

"Let's find a way that we can use this information and the rest of these tapes, to get a deal for Cameroon that will reestablish it as a truly independent nation and help it prosper well into the next century."

"That's an ambitious plan. I'm sure if I were younger, I would feel the same way. But I probably only have a few years left and I would like to return home and see smiles on my fellow countrymen's faces," Pierre said.

"If we put our heads together we can make it happen in less than a year," Christine told him.

"Are all of those boxes that my men helped you acquire last night filled with tapes like these?" Pierre asked.

"Yes, they're all Hoover's private recordings and files," Christine admitted.

"I guess you know what you have in those files could unlock untold mysteries."

"Yes I do Pierre, but I'm more interested in getting Bello out of my grandfather's chair," Christine told him.

For the next hour they worked on possibilities until they arrived at what they thought was their best option.

"I promised some friends at the FBI that I would call them back. I should probably do that. I don't suppose you have a untraceable phone around here?" Christine asked.

Pierre called Victor who took her to a room filled with equipment and technicians. "Place your call and these people will do the rest. They think of it like a game. The object is to keep your signal in the air never letting it land in one place. The fastest computer in the world won't be able to track this call." Victor's voice was filled with pride.

Christine called Director Flynn's office. She was put through immediately.

"Christine—or should I call you Hoover?" The director asked sarcastically.

"Christine will be fine sir. I know there are a lot of questions you would like to ask, but our time is very limited. It's now two o'clock, I would like to meet with you and the president, if possible, before five." Christine spoke in a tone that made it more of a demand than a question.

"I don't know whether or not you know this Christine, but Tom and Scott just left to arrest the head of the vice president's Secret Service detail."

"With all due respect sir, you might want them to hold off until they have a chance to see the discs and read the files."

"What makes you think that if you came in, we'd let you go?" The director asked.

"I've made arrangements with someone that if I don't give him a call at a certain time, certain documents will be released to every major print and television news program in the world," Christine replied.

"Alright, five o'clock at the White House—same gate as last time. I'll set it up with the White House."

"Thank you sir. You won't regret this."

"I already do Christine, I already do," Director Flynn said.

When Christine hung up the phone, all the technicians were giving each other "high fives"—they had kept the signal in the air the entire time. Christine's call could not have been traced.

Director Flynn hung up the phone and called Tom to cancel the arrest of Secret Service Agent Kessler.

"She wants to meet us at the White House, I think we're going to get what we need," Director Flynn told Tom.

"What are we going to give her?" Tom asked.

"If this stuff is as good as we think it is, the president will probably give her a full walk. She's requesting some special equipment, so I want you and Scott there about four-thirty to make sure that it's all set up."

"What kind of special equipment?" Tom asked

"She wants a high-end computer with a CD drive and she wants a reel-to-reel player."

"A reel-to-reel player? They don't even make those anymore, do they?"

"Just make sure it's there by five," Director Flynn told Scott.

Chapter 37

Christine trusted Pierre LeQuoix; he would do what's best for Cameroon. She also knew that if he had an opportunity to embarrass the United States, he would take it. That's why she didn't leave copies of the discs or the tapes with him. She did go to her hotel with one of his drivers and brought the artifacts to his office.

Pierre promised to ship the artifacts to England and have them stored in one of his humidity-controlled warehouses until he received further instructions from Christine. He knew that if all went according to plan, the artifacts would soon be reunited with others stored in England and returned to their rightful place: the Presidential Palace in Cameroon.

When his men brought the items to his office, he was in awe and could barely bring himself to touch them. To him they represented the history of Cameroon. He was eager to see them returned to Cameroon for all of the people to enjoy.

Christine returned to "Springdale Self-Storage." She decided she wanted one more Hoover tape to show the White House that she had all of his files. She wasn't sure what she was after, but she picked up a file that had Martin Luther King's name on the label and found a tape that had several conversations with different people, all referencing Martin Luther King.

Christine drove to the Hyatt, checked in under her own name, went to the hotel's boutique and bought a $3,000 Anne Klein pants suit and a $300 white silk blouse. She spent $5,000 on jewelry to accessorize her outfit and another $200 on shoes. She didn't want to look like someone on the run when she went to the White House. She knew if she was to get everything she and Pierre had discussed, she would have to be in control from the moment she got there.

It was exactly four-thirty when Pierre's limousine picked Christine up in front of her hotel. It was the same hotel that Pierre was staying in, and he was already waiting in the limo for her.

Christine handed Pierre her briefcase and the driver helped her in.

"If I were only thirty or forty years younger." Pierre said as he kissed Christine's hand. "You are truly the jewel of Cameroon."

"Please Pierre, you're going to make me blush." Christine said as she took back her hand and the briefcase from Pierre.

"So in that briefcase rests the hopes and futures of thirteen-and-a-half million Cameroonians," Pierre said.

"Not only in this briefcase, but also in this car. For Cameroon to make it, it's going to need your help and leadership. You're the man who can get our best and brightest people to return to Cameroon and help rebuild it."

"That's very kind of you Christine, but it's your name, the name of Boinya, that will rebuild Cameroon."

"It will take both of us. It will also take the support of the United States," Christine said as they pulled up to the White House.

"Christine, you still have my special number, if there are any problems call." Pierre LeQuoix gave Christine's hand a final squeeze as she got out of the limousine.

She was a little surprised to find Tom at the White House gate waiting for her.

"Christine, I don't know how you do it. You should be a mess like the rest of us. You're on the run from the FBI and you still look like you just walked off the set of a fashion shoot."

"Thank you, Tom. I hope the director feels the same way?"

"Well, I guess he's not quite as impressed with what you've accomplished as Hoover as I am."

"Tom, I'm glad it was you who caught me. You're still the FBI's top investigator."

"I wish it hadn't been you. You had so much going for you."

"I still do Tom. I know more about myself today then I did forty eight-hours ago. I wouldn't change anything I did, except go to Idaho and talk to Greenfield."

Tom smiled, "Yeah, Andy and I go back quite a few years. If he hadn't called while I was using your phone, we may never have caught you. What would you have done then?"

"Hoover would have killed Bello and then disappeared, never to be heard from again."

"I almost wish I had never borrowed your phone," Tom told her.

"Things work out for the best. Let's go see the president," Christine said.

As they entered the library, a guard stopped Christine and searched her, finding nothing. They entered the library. Christine was surprised at the transformation. Gone were the eighteenth-century table and chairs, the gilded wood chandelier, and the Argand lamps. In their place was a desk with a computer projected onto a large fifty-inch screen and a reel-to-reel tape machine build into the top of another table. Everyone was sitting in comfortable, but certainly not antique, chairs. The president rose when Christine entered and attempted to set the tone of the meeting.

"Ms. Peal, before we go any further, Director Flynn or Attorney General Eagelton will read you your rights."

Christine didn't let the president's comments faze her. "Mr. President, please understand that what I have done in normal circumstances would have been considered immoral and illegal. However, what I have done, taken in its true context, was as an act of war and as such does not qualify as murder."

The room erupted in anger with all but Tom on their feet demanding an explanation.

"Gentlemen! Gentlemen! Let's give Christine an opportunity to explain. I'm sure she didn't come here just to spout rhetoric." Tom said.

"Tom's right, Mr. President, I didn't just come here with accusations. I came armed with proof that the United States invaded Cameroon in nineteen-sixty-nine, in effect, declaring war. To the best of my knowledge, a peace treaty has never been signed, thus making my actions acts of war and not murder.

"The same kinds of acts the director committed off of the coast of

Vietnam, during that conflict. Which, by the way, like Cameroon, was never officially declared a war."

"Are you comparing what I did in Vietnam to what you're doing by murdering innocent people?" The director was outraged.

"I think you have that backwards, Director Flynn. In Vietnam, thousands of innocent people were slaughtered. I have only killed those who were part of the American invasion of Cameroon," Christine said holding her ground.

"There was no invasion of Cameroon," the president insisted.

"With all due respect, Mr. President, I beg to differ. Once I release the information I have, thirteen million Cameroonians will agree with me as will probably two hundred million Americans."

"Then let's see what you have," Attorney General Eagelton said.

Christine checked out the reel-to-reel player, figured out how to use it, and put on the first tape.

"What you are about to hear are a series of tapes on which you will hear the vice president of the United States, the director of the FBI, and a high-ranking member of the CIA planning the massacre of the president of Cameroon and his entire family. It also discusses the puppet that the United States would put in place and how they tracked down and killed the president's relatives residing outside of Cameroon.

"I looked it up gentleman; in any international court you care to take this to, slaughtering a foreign president and his family in his own palace is an act of war." Christine pushed the play button and stood watching everyone's expression as they listened to the tapes. She quickly changed tapes not wanting anyone to have a chance to think before they had heard them all.

Christine shut off the recorder after the last tape finished. There was a deafening silence in the room, which was finally broken by the president.

"Is that the original tape?"

"Yes it is," Christine replied.

"I don't suppose it's the only copy, though?" Tom asked.

"Of course not. I made one copy for my own protection."

"The American people would never believe this tape," AG Eagelton said.

"They will when they find out that it's part of Hoover's private collection. Especially when we start playing some of the other tapes out of the twenty-two boxes of tapes and files I found last night."

"I knew it!" Tom said almost jumping out of his chair. "I knew you were going after the tapes. Where did you find them? I had the house and the justice department covered."

Christine gave Tom a smile, "You should have read Hoover's bio; he was a Mason for most of his life. A lot of his office stuff is on loan to the museum at the Supreme Council on 16th street, here in D.C. His files and tapes had been locked up in boxes in the museum's basement all these years."

"You have all of J. Edgar Hoover's private files?" AG Eagelton asked.

"Yes sir I do," Christine said.

"Have you read them?" Eagelton asked.

"Only the ones that I thought might pertain to the invasion of Cameroon."

"Damn it Ms. Peal, you know damned good and well it was no invasion. It was a group of rogue people who happened to be in government jobs," the president said.

"Maybe so, Mr. President, but the people I killed were part of an invading force. Even those who plan an invasion are fair game in a war. As a member of the first family of Cameroon, I had an obligation to fight to protect our country against foreign invaders. That's exactly what I was doing when I killed them."

"But you killed a former president of the United States; I can't just wash my hands of that," the president said.

"How about if I trade you his life for that of the current president of the United States?"

"What are you talking about?" The president asked.

"I have proof that the vice president of the United States is planning to assassinate you." Christine told the president.

"We've already thought of that." Director Flynn said.

"I was hoping you'd put it together and prepare for the possibility. What I'm offering though is everyone involved in the conspiracy to kill the president as well as those assigned to carry it out. I'm also offering you the back-up plan in case the president survives the first attempt."

The president turned to Christine. "Would you give us a moment— I think we need to discuss this among ourselves."

"Of course, Mr. President."

The president pushed a button and a Secret Service Agent entered the room and Christine went into the hall with him.

After about fifteen minutes, they buzzed the agent and he returned Christine to the room and left.

"We have a proposal for you that we can all live with." Director Flynn said.

"I don't think you understand, sir. I didn't come here to get a proposal from you, I came here to provide this president and this country a way out. If any of this becomes public, we'll all be wading in blood up to our knees. You see, Mr. President, I also have the Martin Luther King files and tapes." Christine tossed the file on the table in front of the president. She was now gambling, playing on their fear of the unknown. For all she knew the MLK file said no more than the official reports of the past. But she knew they couldn't take that chance.

"Okay what is it you want?" The president asked.

"I want all troops removed from Cameroon and the bases turned over to the Cameroonian Government.

"I want a statement denouncing your support for the Bellos government and encouraging free elections.

"I want a five hundred-million-dollar fund established to help rebuild Cameroon's economy that Brooks and the Millenium destroyed.

"I want the oil fields returned to Cameroon.

"I want a long-term trade agreement that provides for competitive pricing for Cameroon's oil. Our oil will no longer be given away for fifty percent under market.

"I want all of the Millenium's Cameroonian assets turned over to the government of Cameroon, including their two Cameroon-registered oil tankers.

"I want the Millenium destroyed and those responsible arrested.

"I also want to maintain diplomatic ties between our countries and I want Cameroon to set up a full embassy in the U.S.

"Finally, I expect you to accept me as the ambassador from Cameroon." Christine looked at the president and kept her face blank, not wanting to show the nervousness building up inside her.

"I see you've given this a lot of thought, Ms. Peal. What do we get in return?" The president asked.

"You get everything I have. All of the Hoover tapes except for the copies I have made involving Cameroon. You get all of the Hoover files, including these of Martin Luther King, and you get all of the CDs and files from Walter Brooks' safe. You will also get two dead Klansmen to blame for President Canfield's murder."

The president was about to respond when there was a knock at the door. The president went to the door to find his chief of staff, Brian Hunt, on the other side.

"Mr. President your cabinet is waiting, it's past six-thirty. The meeting was supposed to start at six."

"Tell them to sit tight; the meeting will start at seven-thirty," the President told Hunt.

The president returned to the others. "It appears that we're late for my cabinet meeting. At least that's what Mr. Hunt tells me. Now where were we Ms. Peal?"

"You were about to tell me whether or not my requests were acceptable."

"Ms. Peal, I must confess that your requests are quite reasonable although not what I expected. I expected you would want a pardon and millions of dollars."

"I don't need a pardon, Mr. President. I haven't committed any crimes, and as for the money, I just recently came into $10 million."

Director Flynn gave Christine a nasty look, but decided against asking for his money back in front of the president.

"Even if we overlook, as you put it, your 'acts of war' there are still several issues on your list that are beyond my control. For example, the five hundred million dollars would have to be funded by Congress," the President said.

"Sir, I believe these senators and congressmen will help you push it through." Christine handed the president a list of names that Pierre LeQuoix had put together for her. "Also, you'll find certain names on the Millenium CDs who can help you pass this legislation as their last act before you take them down."

The president looked at the list of names. "Quite impressive, Ms. Peal. There is still the matter of the Millenium assets. I would not be authorized to turn those over to anyone. I'm sure they'll end up in dispute for years to come."

"We've done our research on that. Mr. Brooks maintained the lease for the fields in his own name, since they were assigned to him personally and illegally obtained, I'm sure if you look very closely you'll find a way to return the leases to the people of Cameroon." Christine looked back and forth between the AG and the president.

"I'm sure we'll be able to arrange something," AG Eagelton said.

"The oil tankers will be abandoned in international waters and reclaimed by Cameroonian sailors. By international law that's all that's required for Cameroon to claim the tankers." Christine said with a smile of satisfaction on her face.

The president looked to the attorney general for clarification.

"I'm not a naval lawyer, Mr. President, but it does sound right."

"You seem to have worked out everything, Ms. Peal, but how do you propose to become an ambassador for Cameroon with Furandi Bello as President?" The president asked.

"That, Mr. President, will be my problem." Christine said.

"I cannot and will not condone any violence be done to another head of state on my watch. Despite what you've heard on those tapes, not all American leaders rule by the sword."

"I'm pleased to hear that, Mr. President. You have my personal assurance that no harm will come to Furandi Bello on American soil."

"That's not what I said, Ms. Peal."

"I know that, sir. But that's all I can promise you."

There was a long pause between two very stubborn people before Tom broke it.

"Okay, I think we have an agreement we can all live with—let's see the CDs before the president goes into his meeting."

Christine moved quickly, not waiting for the president to protest. She put the CD with the table of contents in first. She looked up and saw the table of contents scroll by on the fifty-inch screen.

She clicked on the board of directors and displayed the names. Behind her shoulder she could hear the president let out a gasp. "My God, these are some of the most powerful people in the world. I can't believe my own vice president is the chairman of this thing."

"Yes, sir, and Mr. Hunt is on the executive committee." Christine clicked on the executive committee.

"Sir, I think you should see this." Christine clicked on the line that said "operations" and inserted the second disk. She then scrolled down to active U.S. operations. The screen in front of them came to life with the detailed plans to assassinate the president. She showed them the back-up plan, where one of the president's secret service agents was going to shoot him with a small-caliber weapon, as if covering him during the commotion of the original attempt, if it failed. There was even a plan in case the first attempt was never tried.

Christine then scrolled down to the file on Judge Hellerman and the plan to put him onto the Supreme Court.

"Jesus, Martin, what are we going to do about all of this?"

"Might I make a suggestion?" Tom asked.

"I'm ready to listen to anything," the President said.

"Sir, Brian Hunt has seen all of us in here; he knows about Cedes' and Brooks' deaths. He also knows Judge Feldman is missing. We can't afford to let him talk to anybody.

"I recommend that we accompany you to your meeting and arrest Brian Hunt, the vice president, and the two secret service agents. We should then hold them here in the White House until we can coordinate with law enforcement officials throughout the world and conduct a simultaneous arrest of all of the board members, executive committee, and officers of the Millenium."

"That could take days. They'll want proof before they move against people with this much power" the president protested.

"Not necessarily," Christine said. "We could provide them the proof in a matter of seconds electronically. Director Flynn and Attorney General Eagelton will have to make the calls with you, Mr. President, and the secretary of state backing them up. In some cases we would have to use UN troops to assist in the arrests."

"Martin, could we pull this off?" The President asked.

"Maybe—it would take the leaders out and then we can take our time and just work down these lists so generously provided by Christine. If word got out prematurely though, we would lose over half of our initial arrests."

"Only send them the proof they need to arrest the people in their country," Attorney General Eagelton recommended. "After we've made most of the arrests, then we should hold some kind of international law enforcement summit and review the damage the Millenium did."

"What about the media? We can't keep this quiet forever. Premature resignations of political leaders always make the press nervous. Especially this many," Scott said.

"We need to come up with a good cover story," AG Eagelton said.

"No, listen to us. We're as bad as the Millenium. There will be no cover-up. I want to see each one of these people tried for what they did," the president said.

"Mr. President, perhaps you should take a look at the historical data base of this group. Cameroon was not the only country overthrown by the Millenium," Christine said.

"Peter, when we're done here tonight, I want you and Martin to review these disks and find enough current criminal activity involving the vice president and Brian Hunt to send them to jail for the rest of their lives, without starting a war somewhere. Do you think you can do that?" The president's voice was loud and clear and filled with anger.

"Mr. President, from what we've seen so far, we have enough to convict both men of high treason, conspiracy to commit murder, as well as conspiracy to assassinate the president of the United States," AG Eagelton said.

"Ms. Peal, you have your deal. You are welcome to wait here until this is over or leave. Thank you for all of your help. I actually do hope that someday I will be able to receive you as ambassador from Cameroon. You have done this country a great service here tonight."

"Thank you Mr. President; before you step into your cabinet meeting however, I think you should review the list of names on the officers' list. It's quite extensive and although I didn't recognize anyone else you might."

The president, Attorney General Peter Eagelton, FBI Director Flynn, and Special Agent Scott West all watched the computer screen as more and more names scrolled by.

Tom and Christine stood in the corner of the library talking. "I thought the director was coming across the room to strangle you when you mentioned his $10 million," Tom said.

"Tell him I'll return it to him before he has to explain it to anyone. I really don't need it. Tell him not to be too hard on Martinez. His little ruse almost got me caught."

"What are you going to do now?" Tom asked.

"When the president and Director Flynn start calling law enforcement officers from other countries to have Millenium members arrested, I'll be in Cameroon to make sure that the request is carried out in regard to Furandi Bello," Christine said.

"Who's going to arrest him—he runs the army?"

"He'll be arrested by the people's army and held for trial."

"You're going to use a revolutionary government to hang him?" Tom asked.

"No, he'll be arrested and held on one of those tankers in international waters. The army will have no one to lead them, and with the Millenium shut down and the U.S. military gone, there will be no one to pay them. With the president's call for free and fair election and a desire to establish diplomatic relations with the new government, the people should be able to choose a new leader within thirty days.

"There are already good people throughout Cameroon waiting for this moment. There is a professor over there who actually won the last election. He should make a good leader. I've also made some new friends in the last forty-eight hours who'll help.

Once that government is in place, Furandi Bello will be brought back to Cameroon where he'll face a fair trial for crimes against his people before he's executed. At least that's the plan," Christine said.

Tom laughed. "You really have given this a lot of thought, haven't you?"

"Hoover wouldn't have come here without a plan, would he?" Christine asked.

A quick peek at Robert Bitterli's upcoming novel.

"The Merger."

The Merger

Yingen Wu didn't like to think about what he was getting ready to do, but he had no choice—his family's lives depended on him. He took one last look at the photograph on the passenger seat of his car. When he saw the man in the picture begin to cross the street, Yingen Wu accelerated and ran the man down.

Wu got out of his car and made his way back through the gathering crowd, in time to see a man kneeling over the body shaking his head. Wu was getting sick and beginning to tremble when he heard several voices turn on him.

"That's him!" An old woman said pointing at Wu.

"That's the one! He just ran that man down!" A young boy yelled.

Somehow Wu managed to get back to his car. He sat in the driver's seat, took a pistol from under the photo, pointed it to his right temple, and pulled the trigger.

The people chasing Wu stopped in horror when the driver's side window exploded with blood.

Three hundred miles south and six miles off the coast of Long Beach, Frank Hauser and four of his friends were on their way to Catalina Island on Frank's 40-foot Bayliner Motoryacht, "Bankers' Hours." Carl Duncan and Chris Woodard were laying out the fishing gear when Frank spotted an overturned sailboat in danger of sinking. Carl got his binoculars and saw two bikini-clad women fighting to flip the boat upright.

Frank pointed "Bankers' Hours" toward the sailboat and increased his speed. When they arrived, the women pleaded with the men to help them save their boat. Frank's friends, all in their mid-fifties and usually desk bound, found it hard to resist two young, gorgeous women in distress. All except Frank, who stayed on his boat, stripped down to their underwear, and jumped into the ocean.

As they swam closer to the distressed boat, they noticed dark shapes just below the surface of the water. Before the shapes registered with the men, three scuba divers in black suits grabbed three of the men and pulled them under the water. While the men tried to break loose, the divers continued to descend towing their struggling prey.

Carl Duncan, watching his friends being pulled under, realized what was happening too late. As he reached for Chris Woodard's flailing arms, the two women jumped him and held him under. He gasped as he was being forced under and instead of a breath of air, he swallowed the salty ocean water. Panic set in as he attempted to cough and breathe at the same time. Each breath, though, only brought in more salt water, sealing his fate. Chris Woodard's final memory before he felt himself being pulled to the bottom, was of a topless young woman with a yellow polka-dotted bikini bottom.

Frank Hauser saw the women jump his friend and hold him down. He rushed to the railing of his boat yelling at the women, when out of nowhere, someone grabbed him from behind. A large pair of arms wrapped around his chest squeezing his breath out of him. With his chest being crushed, Frank could feel himself fall over the railing into the ocean, all the while being held tightly in a bear hug. He hit the water and temporarily bobbed to the top before he and his assailant began drifting deeper and deeper into the ocean's darkness.